HIGHLAND DESIRE

Edana looked into the eyes of the man who had saved her. "I asked before and you refused. Grant me my wish now. I want to see you. I want to know who you really are."

"My answer is the same as before," the Phoenix whispered. "You must promise me you will stay away from your adopted brother. I want no one taking liberties with you."

With those words he bent and kissed her on the lips. She felt that wonderful sensation she so well remembered from their last encounter. But how could she feel this way in the arms of a man she did not know, who would not even show her his face? She felt strongly toward him—there was no denying it. She put her arms around him and kissed him back hungrily as he kissed her on the throat, ears, and lips.

"You are a dream, a temptation," he whispered in her ear, even as he brushed her neck with his lips again. "One day soon we will be together."

He held her tightly and she shivered as he pressed to her. But he withdrew suddenly and looked at her. "If we begin," he said, looking into her eyes, "we will never stop."

Edana couldn't speak. She couldn't find the words to tell him what she desired: She wanted him.

Books by Joyce Carlow

TIMESWEPT
A TIMELESS TREASURE
TIMESWEPT PASSION
SO SPEAKS THE HEART
DEFIANT CAPTIVE
HIGHLAND DESIRE
HIGHLAND FIRE

Published by Zebra Books

HIGHLAND FIRE

Joyce Carlow

Zebra Books
Kensington Publishing Corp.

http://www.zebrabooks.com

ZEBRA BOOKS are published by

Kensington Publishing Corp.
850 Third Avenue
New York, NY 10022

First Printing: June, 1999
10 9 8 7 6 5 4 3 2 1

Printed in the United States of America

Prologue

Scotland
November 1689

The cold, hard rain fell in sheets of water. It was a curse from the dark skies, a harbinger of winter. This wretched downpour was colder than mere rain, yet not quite sleet.

Mary Louden pulled her black wool cloak tightly about her, though it was nearly soaked through and no longer offered protection from the elements. She was cold, and shivered even as she wiped strands of her fiery red hair from her forehead. Her skin was as pale as fine porcelain, her green eyes were filled with sadness, and her lips were pursed together as she made her way through the brittle brush that covered the hillside.

She glanced upward. Above the treetops, enormous dark clouds were being propelled through the sky by high winds. It was obvious to her that the storm would continue long into the night and perhaps into tomorrow.

"I must find shelter," she said aloud. It didn't matter that she was talking to herself. There was no one around to say she was daft; in fact, there was no one in her life at all. William was gone, probably dead. There was no one who cared about her, no one who cared enough to call her insane. Not for the first time, the reality of her aloneness filled her, and she fought to hold back more tears. Yes, they were tears of self-pity, but who in her position would not feel sorry for herself?

Mary looked to one side of the rutted path. Through the dense brush she spied a cluster of rocks, and noted the wide overhang. It was a cave; it could be a wolf den. She weighed the possibilities, and decided to chance it even though she knew full well that packs of wolves roamed the Grampian Mountains, and that while they seldom attacked humans, such attacks were not unknown, either.

She fought her way up the incline and crawled under the ledge. It was a dry sanctuary from the wind and did not appear to be inhabited by wolves. There, sheltered by the ledge, she sat down close to the cave entrance and closed her eyes to dream of a warm fire, a hand extended in help, the comfort of love.

Inevitably her thoughts again settled on her beloved, William Mamore, and the short springtime of their passion. He had been the first and, she presumed, last love of her life.

For all of her seventeen years, she had been alone. Her mother had died when she was a small child, her father never remarried, and as a result she had no siblings. Her father was an important man, a close relative of the clan chieftain Angus Campbell. Angus Campbell trusted her father; indeed, he had made her father his tacksman—the person responsible for collecting all the rents in the district. Her father's position meant that while she had enjoyed the material benefits of his position, she also had suffered from it. The mothers of children her own age did not wish to have her in their houses. They believed she would report back on their possessions, or tell her father about their general state of well-being. They feared their rents would be raised if they were thought to be too well-off. As a consequence, she had been shunned by the other children. She would be bitter, but the sad truth was, their fears were not unrealistic. Those thought to be prospering did have their rents raised and often found themselves having to give over some of their livestock as well. Unhappily, knowing the reasons for her forlorn state did not make it any easier to bear.

Her father was not only a feared man, but also a cold and somewhat grumpy man. Certainly he was not a man she could confide in, not a man who would understand her current plight. No, her father would not help her. In fact, had he known of her condition, he would have turned her out if she had not already run away. He was a strict man and she was most assuredly a sinner in his eyes. Not that she had intended to sin. She had fallen victim to warmth and kindness, to affection, and finally, to an overwhelming passion. Yes, her love for William and his for her, indeed, had been the springtime of her life. She had been alone before and she was alone now, but for a short time she had known love, and only the memory of that time sustained her.

William Mamore had come into her life suddenly and filled it completely. They were not related to one another except in the remotest possible way. They both belonged to Clan Diarmid, which traced its origins to a great hero of Celtic mythology, Diarmid the Boar. Fanciful though this tale of family origin was, it was a source of pride and served to unite those who could trace their ancestry back to the ancient inhabitants of Strathclyde.

William was related to the Campbells of Cawdor while she traced her origins to the Campbells of Argyll. William had come to Argyll to meet with others of the far-flung clan. The purpose of the meeting was of no concern to her, and until she met William, she had known little about the ever-shifting loyalties of various families or of the jealousy, rivalry, and brutal warfare that was the hallmark of the Highlands.

She had first seen William the day he arrived. She had gone with her father to deliver the rents to the laird. William had been there with the laird.

William had been a tall, muscular, good-looking man, with hair as red as her own and soft, brown eyes that had attracted her. His eyes had caressed her the first time he looked at her, and she felt captivated by his charm. She later learned William was visiting and would remain with the laird for some months.

During those months, William had come to call on her more than once and her father had said nothing. After a time, they began to meet near the stream and William delayed his return

home to be with her. They talked for hours and then their talk
turned to sweet kisses and increasingly amorous caresses.

William had not returned home. He had asked her to marry
him and promised to speak to her father. He had kissed her,
and his hands had moved across her body in a way she could
still remember, indeed could still feel: His velvet-brown eyes
soothed her, his lips silenced her, his fingers danced on her
flesh till neither protest nor withdrawal was thinkable—not that
she had protested or even tried to push him away. There had
been too much heat in their bodies; they quickly became lost
in fiery lovemaking.

As suddenly as he had come into her life, William had been
compelled by others to leave it. He had been summoned to
fight—and fight he did. "I saw him cut down," one of the
laird's men had told her. His words were spoken casually, but
she had only asked after William—she had not revealed her
feelings—so how could he have guessed that his words took
her breath way and cut through her heart as if she had been
stabbed?

Mary again shivered and abstractedly felt her swelling womb.
She was with child and she was alone, dispossessed and friend-
less. There was no one she could turn to: no mother to help
her, no brothers or sisters to extend their hand, no father to
take pity on her . . . Her grief consumed her and she felt herself
dying as surely as she felt life growing inside her.

But what was she to do? Who would see her through the
birth of an infant? How could she care for a child? She felt
overwhelmed, yet a longing to hold her child kept her from
taking her own life.

"I want to see the face of the child you fathered," she
had said, speaking to William's ghost, as she often did now.
"Somehow, some way, I will hold our baby and give it the
love I never knew." With that vow her only goal, she had
gathered up a few of her meager belongings and set out in
search of a strange medicine woman named Meara who lived
in these mountains. She had cause to believe Meara might help
her.

The village girls said Meara was a witch, others said she

was mindless, while still others swore by her remedies and gave testimony to her competence.

"I must find you," Mary whispered. "I must find you."

The sun rose, but it did not break through the heavy clouds. Instead, it illuminated their edges, making them look not only ominous, but also otherworldly.

Mary awoke and coughed violently; she was a frail woman and the ordeal of the cold, wet night had aggravated her already fragile condition. She pulled herself up and forced herself outside into the wind, which whistled through the trees, shaking their leaves and sending them into wild flight. Her body ached, and was so filled with cold that she was certain she would never feel warm again. With strength born of necessity, she pushed on.

After a time, Mary came to a fork in the path and for a long moment studied it. After a few moments, she chose the left fork and stumbled down it. It was said that Meara lived near a fork in the path. She was reminded how many times she had taken the wrong path. She asked herself if it had been wrong to have loved William. But her questions had no answers.

"Meara!" Mary called out. "Help me! Someone please help me!"

She felt a moment of dizziness, another violent chill, and then the descending gloom. She crumpled to the ground, holding her hands out.

Was it a death vision, or had she seen an old woman step into the center of the path? The world went dark and Mary floated off into unconsciousness, her hand on her stomach.

When she opened her eyes, Mary found herself in a cottage, lying on some sheepskins in a dimly lit but warm room. The dwelling was a little larger than a common crofter's cottage. A fire burned in the hearth, and from every rafter, plants of great variety hung, drying slowly in the heat. As her vision cleared, Mary saw shelves of dried herbs and containers full of odd concoctions. Even before she could focus her eyes, Mary smelled the aroma of medications that were Meara's trade. It was an odd combination: the smell of smoke mixed with herbs, and the alcohol needed for the many tinctures mingled with the aroma of food and the odor of the earthen floor. The whole place filled her nostrils, making her olfactory sense of the place far sharper than her visual impression. The room was so badly lit that the old woman who tended the fire almost blended into the dark walls.

"Are you Meara?" Mary ventured.

The woman turned, revealing a face with deep lines and small dark eyes. "What brings you?" she asked in a raspy voice. "What brings you to Meara the Witch?"

Mary was too weak to run away, too tired to be frightened, too desperate to be put off. "Are you a witch?"

"Some say I am," the old woman replied.

"I've heard you are a medicine woman. I've heard you could help me."

Meara stepped closer; Mary could smell her decaying teeth. She forced herself not to flinch, though Meara peered into her face with an emotionless expression. What had she expected?

Meara leaned over and ran her hand across Mary's stomach. "You are six months with child," she declared.

"I'm Mary Louden. My husband is dead."

The woman scowled at her, "Do not make up fanciful stories for me. You are Mary Louden, the tacksman's daughter. You have no husband. It is your lover who is dead."

"I did not mean to lie."

"It is useless to lie to me. Why have you come here?"

"I had nowhere else to go," Mary answered. "I heard the village girls talk. They say you help people like me."

"Once," the old woman said slowly.

Mary sensed a tone of regret in the old woman's voice. Meara was looking away, as if focusing on some distant object.

"Please, you must help me," Mary pleaded. She held out her hands to the old woman.

"Do you want the child?" Meara questioned gruffly.

"Yes. It was conceived in love. Yes, I want it. But how can I care for a child? I am alone."

"Once I took such children and found homes for them. But

I am too old to see you through birth, to do all the work of finding a suitable home.''

"You must help me. . . .'' Mary looked up, eyes filled with tears. There really was nowhere else to turn.

Meara looked away. "I knew your mother,'' she said slowly.

"My mother? Did she come to you for—?''

"Oh, no. But sometimes she helped me find homes. She was a gentle woman. You have her hair.'' Meara gently touched Mary's hair. "But then, such fiery hair is only found among the members of your clan.''

Mary frowned; the woman's mind seemed to be wandering. Again Mary formed the word "Please,'' but she could beg no more.

"Such things are not without cost. What could you give me?'' the old woman asked suddenly.

Mary briefly touched the two gold chains that hung around her neck. They had belonged to her mother and they were all she had in the world.

The unconscious reflex of Mary's hands did not go undetected. "Let me see them,'' Meara demanded.

"They were my mother's.''

"Hand them to me!''

Mary slipped the chains off her neck as she unsteadily rose to her feet.

Meara held them up to the light of the lamp. Then, one at a time, she took a section of each between her rotting teeth and bit down to make sure they were really gold.

"I'll take these,'' she said finally. "But you'll be the last pregnant girl I'll tend. I'm too old.''

Mary let out her breath. She need not go back into the cold rain. She need not fear for how her child would be born. It did not matter that Meara's breath smelled, or that her face was like old leather, or that she was peculiar and crotchety. She was known to be caring and her own mother had helped Meara help others.

"Thank you,'' Mary whispered, reaching out her hand in friendship.

Meara withdrew from the touch and nodded. "Lie back

down, rest well. You are a frail girl and you're ill. It will be hard for you; you need to rest. Are you afraid?''

''Not for myself.''

Meara nodded again and then turned away. ''I will give you a sleeping potion and some dry clothing. You will have to sleep on the pallet in the corner.'' She waved a scrawny finger toward the dark portion of the room.

Mary watched as Meara turned away and shuffled off to prepare the potion. *Yes, sleep.* She wanted to sleep. She wanted to forget the agony, and escape into dreams of the recent past. She wanted to forget the reports of William's death and dream only of their moments of happiness together.

The Grampian Mountains were heavily forested, and punished by both wind and water so that over time, deep glens and lochs had been carved through them. In the higher altitudes the trees disappeared, and only huge boulders dotted the landscape. It was as if demons beneath the surface of the earth had pushed them to the surface in a fit of anger. Meara called them the devil's fingers and she spoke of the demons that lived beneath the earth's now snow-covered crust.

It was the first of March and outside, the wind howled and snow still covered the usually sodden ground. The weight of the snow and ice bent the branches of the trees until those closest to the ground kissed the earth.

Wrapped in heavy clothing and now huge with child, Mary could only venture a few steps from Meara's house, the snow was so deep. It was unusual to have such deep drifts and sometimes it seemed as if the weather conspired to keep her inside.

She was only a few feet from the overhang of the cottage when she felt the first sharp pain. Mary doubled over and let out a cry as she dragged herself back toward the door.

''Meara!'' She screamed out the old woman's name, and then she called out again as the pain dissipated.

Meara came and silently helped her to lie down.

''I think it's time,'' Mary gasped, just as another pain seized her whole body. She had expected pain, but this was far stronger than expected; it shot through her, and it lasted for what seemed an eternal moment.

Meara had already undone Mary's clothing and was roughly pushing her into position. "Yes," she muttered. "Your time has come, Mary Louden."

Mary closed her eyes and gave herself over to the agony of the next pain. It was longer and sharper. "How long will it take?"

Meara shrugged. "You're past due, not long."

But Mary hardly heard the old woman's answer because the next pain was so much worse than the previous ones. She let out a scream that filled the small cottage.

Meara examined her and then began to knead her womb as if it were a loaf of bread. "Scream all you want," Meara said. "It seems to help most women. There's no point holding it in. There's no one to hear you up here."

The pain subsided and Mary drew in her breath.

Meara finished her kneading and wiped Mary's brow with a cloth.

"When it comes next time, if you're not screaming, pant like a dog and push when I tell you. The pushing's important."

Mary felt the pain coming again and she tried to do as Meara instructed. The pain was longer than all the rest combined and she panted, but she could not hold in her shriek even though she pushed.

"Dear heaven," she heard Meara say.

"What is it?" Mary cried.

The old woman's voice was filled with amazement, and in spite of the pain Mary heard her exclamation of surprise. "There's more than one!"

Mary clenched her fists as another pain wracked her body. . . . More than one? Was she having twins?

"I can see the first one," Meara said loudly. "Push, my girl. . . . Push!"

Mary pushed and screamed. Her fingers scratched at the sides of the bed and dug deep into the skins that covered it.

It seemed to Mary as if the pains would never stop. She lost track of how many, or how long they lasted. She concentrated only on pushing, on giving birth, on making the pains end.

* * *

The fire flickered in the hearth and Meara stared down at the two little girls. They were identical, and both had the bright red hair that marked them as descendents of Clan Diarmid.

"Poor little orphans," Meara intoned. She glanced at the birthing bed.

Mary Louden had died just after the birth of the second of the two little girls. Meara had cleaned up the blood-soaked bed, wrapped Mary in cloth, and taken her outside to the shed. Tomorrow Meara would ask one of the boys who lived in the hollow to deliver the body of Mary Louden to her father the tacksman. But she knew he would not want the children, or even anything to do with them. He was a hard and, some said, a cruel man—a man who had driven out his wife and caused her death. Now he had caused his only daughter to run away in fear of his reaction to her plight. This was a wretched tragedy and Meara shook her head.

I'll let it go no farther, she said to herself. *He will not know about the babies. He will not ruin their lives as well.* At that moment Meara, whose mind was not what it had once been, made the decision to take the baby girls and leave the mountains. *I will take them far, far from here,* she vowed silently.

"But first the naming," she said, leaning over the sleeping infants. She touched her wrinkled finger to the forehead of the infant on the right. "You shall be called Edana, 'fire' in our Gaelic tongue. And you"—she touched the forehead of the other—"shall be called Aileena, 'flame' in our tongue. For your hair, your flaming, fiery-red hair, my little ones."

Meara set about packing her wagon and hitching up the she-goat, which, fortunately, was in lactation. Meara's mind was a muddle of thoughts and fears. Deep inside she feared for the babies, though she was less than pleased to have two infants instead of one to look after.

Her thoughts wandered to Mary Louden's mother, a woman of great kindness, whose husband had beaten her when he drank and who had made her life an agony of work and fear. Meara thought, too, of the rivalry among the Campbells, and of the invading MacDonalds. These infants were marked by their red hair, and sooner or later they would be killed, as the war raged on between the Campbells and the MacDonalds for control of the land. It was best to leave this place, never to let the tacksman know of his daughter's children, and to find peace elsewhere. After all, a master of herbs and medicines could always make a living. And what was there to keep her here? It was a land of great beauty torn apart by fighting. It was no place for her, and no place for these small innocents who had been delivered into her care.

The summer sun shone brightly, and thin, almost transparent white clouds drifted across the blue sky on high winds. All along the shore of Loch Linnhe, golden flowers bloomed on spiny, brushlike plants. Across the deep-blue waters of the loch, forested mountains rose in the distance. There was still a dusting of snow in their high valleys and along their rocky yet flat-looking tops. Below the mountains was the village that surrounded the British fort.

Meara sank to the ground. Edana and Aileena slept, but during the days they slept less and less and demanded more and more of her attention. "Six months," Meara muttered. She was tired and could remember little of the immediate past, though memories of events long ago surfaced with a brilliant clarity. She talked all the time to herself or to the two children who, while they did not answer, often seemed comforted by the sound of her croaking old voice.

"My body has betrayed me," she croaked. She held out her hand. It quivered uncontrollably now; it seemed she had little or no control over her own movements. She knew her eyes were dim, too, as they were clouded by white cataracts.

Meara shook her head in dismay. As a medicine woman, she had seen many others with the symptoms she now displayed, and she knew with a fatalistic certainty that her time was coming, that soon she would die. And once again, she asked the question she had asked herself for weeks: *What will become of the babies?*

She lifted her old eyes heavenward, and then gazed downward at the peaceful, gentle flow of Loch Linnhe as it made its way to the sea.

"Moses," she said. Yes, he had been placed on a raft among the reeds. He had been found and reared by the daughter of the King of Egypt. Eventually Moses had grown powerful enough to set his people free. There were other similar tales, powerful stories of children set adrift who were recovered and brought up by good folk. The more she thought about it, the more it seemed like a solution to her.

Fate, yes—let chance decide what would become of these children. Let God take them into His hands and let Him find a home for each of them. She bit her lip and looked into their angelic little faces. Yes, that was what she had to do. She could no longer care for them; even the she-goat had gone dry. She could hardly care for herself—not that it mattered much, because she knew she would soon be gone. *Yes, my darlings, you will be in God's hands.* Surely no child put on a raft had ever been harmed; surely, like Moses, they had all been found.

With a singular purpose, now that she had thought it all through, Meara set about making the two rafts. To each, she would attach a small bit of parchment with the child's name and date of birth. She took the gold chains that had belonged to their mother, Mary Louden, and put one around each of their necks. Then she bound each protesting infant to her own raft. Even though they shrieked and Meara herself cried, she set them adrift, and watched as the current, which seemed swifter now than it had first appeared, carried them away—until she could neither see their rafts nor hear their plaintive cries.

"Godspeed, my little ones," she whispered. Again she looked heavenward, and said a little prayer.

For as long as he had been a seaman, Dennis Forbes had sailed for Donald MacLean, whose lands composed most of the Isle of Mull and a large area of the adjacent mainland. The vessel Forbes sailed traveled to Lowland ports once a year to sell wool, while the rest of the year it was used to fish from the coastal waters. Donald MacLean was a wealthy man, as well as a man known for his kindness. He was a good employer, who rewarded hard work and sent slackers packing. Forbes felt pleasure being employed by one so well liked.

On this summer morning Forbes was contemplating his good fortune when he heard a cry of dismay from the deck. He jumped to his feet and went running toward the sound. At least, he ran as fast as a portly man was able to do.

"What is this?" he queried. A bushy eyebrow shot upward and his mouth opened in surprise.

"By heaven!" his first mate swore. "It's a wee baby was floating in the loch. A wee, redheaded baby!"

Dennis Forbes looked down at the raft that had been retrieved from the cold, clear waters of the loch. It was a crude thing, and he was surprised it had survived the swift current.

The child, who was certainly less than a year of age, stared up at him with clear green eyes. He bent over and undid the swaddling clothes in which the infant was wrapped. The child did not cry, and that alone surprised him.

"It's a girl baby," he announced without surprise, as he quickly did the clothes back up.

"She's a little beauty," one of the crew commented.

And that she was, Dennis agreed silently. Her skin was like porcelain, her eyes large and green and ringed with gold around the pupils. Her red curls were a fiery color and they caressed her little round face. He lifted the parchment and read it.

Written in a hand that clearly showed the author to be palsied, it gave the child's name as Edana and her birth date as March 1, 1690.

"Shall we leave her at the monastery in Iona?" one of his men asked.

Forbes rubbed his stubbly chin. Edana—it meant *fire*. She would most certainly be a fiery beauty when she grew to womanhood. It did not seem to him that a refuge in the church was quite the place for such a child, angelic as she appeared, her green eyes studying everything, her tears and plaintive cries held in almost defiantly. Yes, it seemed to him that this was a most unusual child, a child of great interest even if her origins were a complete mystery.

"I think not," he replied. "I think we shall take this child

to the laird and consult with him. This is someone's life, and
we would not wish to make the wrong decision.''

Donald MacLean was a large man of over six feet. His wife,
Carolyn, who had borne him two strapping sons, was a tiny
woman, with brown hair and dancing brown eyes. Together
they looked at the little girl.

"I had the ship's carpenter build her this cradle," Forbes
explained. "And we kept one she-goat, so the child had plenty
of milk."

"She's old enough to have more than milk," Carolyn said,
lifting the little girl into her arms.

Donald MacLean smiled. Carolyn had always wanted a
daughter; indeed, she had pined for one. She had two sons, but
now she could have no other children.

"It was suggested we take her to the monastery so a home
might be found for her." Forbes spoke the words without
conviction. He knew about Carolyn MacLean; he had heard
how much she wanted a daughter and that she was now barren.
It seemed obvious to him that she already loved this child and
that this child would be going nowhere. He smiled to himself.
Destiny was a strange thing. He, who had thought he might
never have an effect on anyone, had made a wise choice. He
knew as he looked at them that this child would make a difference, and that he had changed the destiny of three people.

For her part, Carolyn looked at her husband and said nothing.
She did not have to speak because he knew what she wanted.
Their love was legendary on Mull. Donald MacLean adored
his wife with an oft-spoken passion, and she returned his adora-
tion. This was no ordinary arranged marriage; this was a marriage of two lovers, and their happiness was contagious. It
would envelop this little girl. Donald MacLean smiled at his
wife and nodded. "Rear her as you would rear your own. God
works in mysterious ways and this child has been brought to
us. Here she will stay."

Chapter One

The Isle of Mull
February 28, 1707

February was a cruel month in the Highlands. It most often brought high winds and snow, or sometimes a hard-driving rain if it was not cold enough for snow. This February, Edana observed, was unusually mild. Still, persistent rains caused rivers of mud, and many days had to be spent inside. On this particular rainy day, Edana was waiting for her friend Moira.

Edana was the daughter of Donald and Carolyn MacLean, and Moira Lachlan was the daughter of Donald MacLean's fourth cousin, Flora MacLean, and her husband Murray Lachlan.

The two girls were both nearly seventeen years old and the closest of friends, as they had been tutored and reared together. They visited often, spending quiet afternoons sewing and gossiping. Now that they were both older, they often talked about the various eligible young men in the area; indeed, young men were Moira's favorite subject.

Edana turned away from the window as she heard Moira bounding up the stairs. In a second Moira threw open the door of the sewing room and came in, breathless from her climb, and clearly excited.

Moira's round face was framed with light-brown curly hair. She was several inches shorter than Edana and given to plumpness. When she was still, she seemed quite plain, but when she was animated, as she was now, she projected a liveliness that seemed to change her appearance.

"Oh, good, you're alone," Moira said, in a conspiratorial whisper. Her round cheeks were chafed a rosy red from the wind.

Edana laughed gently. "Did you expect my brothers to be here?" John and George were considered to be among the district's most eligible men, but Edana knew full well that Moira did not like either of them, which made teasing her about them all the more enjoyable.

"I should leave straightway if they were here," Moira said, flouncing down on the chair. The sewing room was a comfortable room with good light, so that those who utilized it could see well enough to work. On a huge wooden frame, a half-done quilt was stretched out, while piles of cloth were neatly covered on long wooden shelves. In the middle of the room, a large table was used to cut the material into the needed pattern-pieces. In addition, there were several comfortable chairs in which to sit.

"Why are you so breathless?" Edana asked.

Moira clenched her fists and whispered loudly, "Because I heard he is in the district! Can you imagine? He's right here, lurking somewhere nearby. I'll wager he's planning his next crime."

There was no need for Moira to explain who "he" was— "he" was the Phoenix, and the Phoenix was a legend all over the Highlands.

"Weren't you afraid to come alone?" Edana asked, leaning toward Moira. "They say he is quite dangerous."

"I'm no beauty as you are! Besides, my father is not an important man. It is you who must beware when you go out. He's taken many a daughter of influential men and held them for ransom. But they say he always chooses the best-looking ones."

Edana smiled. "I'm not afraid." Her green eyes sparkled. "Actually, I think I should like to see this rogue."

"That's wicked. There's no telling what he might do to you."

"I'm sure he would do nothing at all. Why would he?"

"Because you are the daughter of the laird and because you are a beauty. He fights the large landowners and some say he ravishes their daughters. Maybe he would kidnap you and hold you for ransom. Maybe he would . . . well, you know—make love to you." She sighed and shook her head. "No, I'm sure he wouldn't bother me."

Edana smiled. The truth was, Moira sounded quite disappointed that she might not be kidnapped and ravished.

"Moira, making love and being ravished are not the same thing. And don't say you aren't pretty—you are pretty."

"Not like you. Anyway, I didn't mean I wanted to be. . . . I just meant . . . Well, he sounds so exciting. In any case, you ought to be careful."

"Father always sends me with a guard. If he knows this rogue, this man who calls himself the Phoenix, is about, he'll probably double the guard."

"I'm sure he will." Moira paused thoughtfully, then added, "You know, they say he is very handsome. They say he has flashing eyes and that he is tall and strong and loves the ladies."

"I really do think you want to be kidnapped by him, Moira. You sound quite in awe."

Moira's face turned crimson. "Well, life here is dull. I think it would be thrilling just to spend a little time with him. I mean, I don't think he's ever really forced himself on any woman, or anything like that. I've heard he doesn't have to—that women just fall into his arms."

"He's a thief who has made himself a reputation. I rather imagine that if he's caught, he'll be hanged."

"But that's why he is called the Phoenix. There are those who claim to have killed him but he appears again, as if he were immortal. And once, he was said to be in jail, but he turned up in another district almost immediately."

"Then he is a cunning thief, but a thief nonetheless."

"And probably a very good lover," Moira sighed. "I've

heard that when he makes love to a woman he's kidnapped, she never complains. Think what it would be like to be held by such a man, to be . . . well, to be set aflame with forbidden passion." Moira clasped her hands together and rolled her eyes melodramatically.

"I think you long for this Phoenix, Moira." Edana could no longer suppress a slight laugh. At the same time, she could hardly blame Moira for feeling bored.

Moira pursed her full lips together and her eyes glimmered. "Maybe," she said. "I want to know more about this man."

"I want to understand his political aims," Edana said thoughtfully.

"Yes, I, too, would like to know more about that. Ask your mother about him," Moira prodded. "She knows about these things. You're so fortunate, your mother is highly educated, she knows about politics and all the things that occupy men."

"I'll speak to her about this rogue. But you should remember that it's unwise to give one's heart to a man who will be hanged one day."

"I should like to see how you would react to him. I don't think you would be unlike the others. I think you would like to meet him and just won't admit it."

"I admit to romantic daydreams, but they're not about being ravished by a masked stranger who commits all manner of crimes."

"I'm sure he's better than your brothers."

Loyalty kept Edana from agreeing, though silently she did agree. Her brothers were less-than-admirable in their relations with women, and they were to boot selfish and conceited. Their father had rebuked them on many occasions, and yet they persisted in drinking too much, in womanizing, and in not fulfilling any of their duties. Moira's low opinion of them was sadly true. There was not much to be said for either of them.

"We should finish our quilt," Edana suggested, as she looked for her needle and thread.

"Yes, I know." Moira paused and looked down. "May I ask you a favor?"

"Of course you can—you can ask me for anything."

"Will you come and visit me next time? I love being here with you, but I always run into John and he pesters me."

Edana nodded. "Of course I'll come to your house."

"I know it's not as luxurious."

"You know I don't care about luxury. Moira, is there something you're not telling me? Something about John? Has he really been bothering you?"

For a moment there was silence, then Moira bit her lip. "No. It's my father. I fear he might try to arrange something with your father, between George and me."

"Are you talking about marriage?"

"Yes. My father would like to strengthen his position. Such a marriage would accomplish that. I dread it, Edana. I love you like a sister, but I don't want to marry your brother George."

Edana put her arms around Moira. "I'll see what I can find out. Don't be upset—I'm sure your father would not try to arrange a marriage between you and George. Surely he knows George's reputation."

"Men don't care about such things, Edana. Your father believes that all George needs is a wife to calm him down, and my father thinks the same. 'Responsibility makes the man'— that's all he can say when I protest. He insists that George is wealthy, influential, and will one day be laird. He even tells me George is good-looking. But looks are not everything. I'm not pretty; even if we were married, George would keep a mistress. He doesn't want me and I don't want him."

Edana nodded. Moira was right about George, and doubtless she was right about her father as well. She had seen Moira's father and MacLean together in earnest conversation, conversations that might well have been about marriage. But she decided not to mention that to Moira. It would only make her more miserable. *I'll find out what's going on,* Edana thought. *And then I shall try to see if I can help Moira in some way.*

"Can you come to my house on March fourth?" Moira asked.

Edana again gave her friend a hug. "The fourth will be fine."

* * *

Donald MacLean looked out the window of his study high on the fourth level of his stone tower house. It was not a castle in the grand style of Glamis, Stirling, or Falkland Castles, nor was it as sprawling as Linlithgow, the birthplace of Mary, Queen of Scots; rather, it was a stone edifice of four stories, a large, square tower. Indeed, such a design, which usually had one or more chimneys, was the most common in Scotland. Its stone outer walls had been constructed several hundred years ago. The Highlands were forested but the timber was unsuitable for the construction of houses, thus the wood for the great beamed ceilings had to be imported from the Baltics. This made building proper wooden houses highly expensive, so the tower house became a matter of practicality since it used fewer beams. One room atop another meant that the ceiling of one was the floor of another. At one time, his tower house had consisted simply of four huge rooms and a great cellar. When Donald had brought his wife, Carolyn, home to live here many years ago, he had built a new internal facade. Each floor was divided into four rooms, served by a center hall with a flight of stairs at either end. He had chosen this room on the fourth floor, which overlooked the rolling hills, for his study.

The sound of footsteps on the far staircase caused Donald to turn about. It was Edana. He had asked her to come, and now he steeled himself for their conversation. He had already confided parts of what he would say to his two sons already, primarily because both of them had planned to be away. Still, he had not told them everything, and he knew what he had not told them would be far more difficult for Edana than for them. He felt uneasy, and he knew Carolyn was extremely apprehensive.

He waited for a long moment, and then he heard the light tap on the door.

"Come in," he called out.

Edana came in and smiled warmly. She was a beautiful young woman, her father thought, as he looked at her—her waist-length hair fiery-red, her skin white and clear, her eyes as green as emeralds. Her figure, hidden beneath modest clothing, was all any man could ask for. His fondest wish was to protect her, and yet he knew that in reality, she had to protect herself, and no doubt would be able to, as she grew older. She was quick-witted, highly intelligent, and, truthfully, far more intellectually ambitious and talented than his sons.

"You summoned me, Father?" she asked, in a soft, lilting voice.

"Yes, it's time we had a talk, Edana. Time I told you the things you ought to know, past time I told you what is on my mind and in my heart."

She smiled, and he felt her smile warm the whole room. "You sound so serious, Father."

"I am serious because we have to discuss a serious matter."

Her brow knit into a slight frown. "Have I displeased you in some way?"

"Good heavens! Not at all. Please, sit down, my dear."

Edana sat down opposite him.

"Now that you're here, I hardly know where to begin."

Her eyes searched his face, and for a moment, he felt tongue-tied. Perhaps he should have told her years ago, perhaps she should have known everything there was to know from the beginning. But his wife had not wanted it that way and he had acquiesced to her wishes.

"Begin at the beginning," Edana said. "You're so very serious, you worry me."

"The beginning. . . . Well, it began with your mother. Carolyn gave me two sons and desperately wanted a daughter. Then she was told she could have no more children." He paused and watched as a look of puzzlement covered Edana's face. He raised his hand to silence her unasked question.

"One of my vessels was headed home from the Lowlands when it lay anchor in Loch Linnhe. A bright-eyed seaman in my employ spied a bundle floating in the water. It was a tiny raft, and on that raft was a baby girl with bright green eyes and fiery-red hair."

Edana's mouth opened in surprise. "I—I was a waif?"

"Yes, washed up by the sea."

"You took me in?"

"Yes, my daughter. The captain of the vessel brought you

to Carolyn and me." He leaned forward. "We adopted you and reared you as our own. We've not had one single day of regret, Edana. You have brought nothing but joy into our lives, and when I die you will share in the inheritance just as if you were born of my own seed. In my heart, and with considerable pain, I admit that I suspect that portion of my estate which is left to you will be in the most competent hands. Your brothers are a disappointment to me." He shook his head. "Your mother and I are most concerned with just how you will accept the truth of your origin—but let me say again, you could not be more my daughter . . ."

Tears filled Edana's eyes and she reached across the distance between them to take his hands in hers. He was stumbling over his words and it was obvious he was filled with emotion. Edana felt herself overcome as well. "You are my father and Carolyn is my mother. I know no other. It's hard for me to believe what you have told me, but I know it's true."

Edana paused and thought for a long moment. Then she looked again into her father's eyes. "I have told no one, but if I might tell you now, I have something I must confess."

"I'm sure you have nothing serious to confess to me or anyone else."

"I have dreams, strange dreams."

"One cannot be responsible for his dreams," he smiled indulgently.

"They are not dreams of wrongdoing. I dream of someone—someone I don't know. I have—only now and again—odd feelings during my waking hours, too. It is as if sometimes I feel that I am a part of someone else, a person I don't know."

"Do these dreams frighten you?" he asked with concern.

"No, though sometimes I feel danger or apprehension and I don't know why. I have these odd feelings when I am in no danger and have no reason to feel anxious."

"I'm sure it's just your age. I feel certain that these feelings and these dreams will pass."

Edana looked down. He did not understand the power of her dreams and of the fleeting feelings she had described to him. Perhaps he could not understand; perhaps he was simply too preoccupied with the difficulty of what he had just told her.

"Your seventeenth birthday is tomorrow. That is what prompted me to tell you about your origins—or more accurately, how you came to us. I wish I could tell you about your origins, but I cannot. We considered you a gift from God, Edana."

"I think it is I who received the gift." She decided not to speak further of her strange feelings of "otherness," or of her dreams. She did not understand them herself. How could she expect others to understand? But now she wondered if her feelings and her dreams had anything to do with her being a waif, if in fact they might be related to some dormant memory. Were such things possible? She was unsure, but decided to speak of it no more.

"I have one other matter to discuss with you," Donald said with hesitation. "I'm going to take your mother on a journey to Inverness. George will be back next week and John will be home in three days' time. When George arrives home, he is to collect the rents from our tenants on Mull. Moira's father will collect them on the mainland. Please remind George to do so."

"I shall. Father, are you taking Mother to the doctor in Inverness? I know she's not been feeling well lately."

He nodded and did not look up into her clear green eyes, which always demanded the truth. He did not want her to know the depth of his concern. "It would be good if you went to her. She is worried about what I've told you, worried about how you will feel about her when you learn the truth."

Edana wiped a tear off her cheek. "As I have always felt. I love her—she is my mother. I'll go to her right away."

Donald MacLean stood up and so did Edana. He pulled her into his arms and hugged her roughly and planted a fatherly kiss on her cheek. It was hard for him to express his feelings. He was a stoic man who seldom displayed any emotion.

Edana kissed him in return. "I'll go talk with Mother."

Donald MacLean raised his hand. "Please, I almost forgot something."

Edana watched as he withdrew a long gold chain from his pocket. "When you were found, this chain was found with you. I assume it is from your real mother, and I think it's time you had it."

Edana took the chain and turned it in her hand. Then she slipped it round her neck. It felt right—it was as if, when she put it on, she had made some kind of connection with her lost family.

"Thank you," she whispered.

Donald MacLean nodded. "Away with you now," he murmured.

As she hurried down the stairs, Edana stopped to pause on the landing before she descended into the kitchen area. A strange feeling overcame her and she stood stock-still. It was one of those moments of "otherness." She felt as if she were another person, as if she were somewhere else. *I'm just reacting to finding out I'm adopted,* she told herself. But the truth was, she felt little reaction to the story of her adoption. If her real family had loved her, they would not have cast her out. Donald and Carolyn MacLean were her parents in every sense of the word. She loved them and she felt secure in the fact that they loved her. That was not to say that this morning's revelations had not made her curious—they had. But in all honesty, she had always felt just as much estranged from her brothers as she felt close to her parents. Deep inside, she had always believed she could not be related to either John or George. Both of them were lecherous and lazy, both of them cared little for anyone but themselves.

She felt a little amused. "Now I'm a mysterious person," she said aloud and somehow the thought that she was adopted seemed more exciting than upsetting.

As her carriage jolted along toward home, Edana thought about her conversation with Moira.

"Adopted!"

Moira had been completely taken aback when Edana told her.

"It's so exciting! You might be anyone! You might be a queen!"

"Or I might be the child of a beggar," she had replied. "I'm happy to be who I am and where I am."

That had not ended their long conversation. They had talked

for hours and finally they had gone to bed and talked until they both fell asleep. Then Edana had risen early and summoned the guard who had been sent with her to escort her home. It was important she arrive by afternoon because her father and mother were leaving for Inverness and they would be gone for many days. The journey from Mull to the capital of the Highlands was long and arduous, especially at this time of year.

Edana was completely lost in thought, and was jolted out of it unexpectedly when she heard shouting.

"What, ho!" the guard shouted loudly, and Edana felt the carriage pull up abruptly. Outside there was much shouting and she heard a deep voice order the guard and the driver down. Again there was more noise, and then an eerie silence.

Highwaymen? Here? Edana sat straight up as if glued to the leather seat of the carriage. The door of the carriage was flung open and she found herself face-to-face with a tall man wearing a hood that completely covered his face.

"Ah, what have we here?" he asked, peering into the carriage.

Edana glared at him angrily. "You have me, Edana MacLean, daughter of the laird. You have unwisely chosen the wrong carriage to attack, sir."

The hooded man stared at her with smoldering brown eyes. "Have I indeed?" he replied. She could not see his mouth beneath his hood, but from his tone she was sure he was smiling, no doubt laughing at her. It was most annoying.

Edana could also tell he was disguising his voice. "You will be severely punished for stopping me when my father catches up with you."

"Ah, then you are the daughter of Donald MacLean, lass?"

"I am."

"Come out of that carriage and let me see what I've caught."

He said no more, but reached in and seized her wrist, pulling her toward him so that she was obliged to stumble from the carriage ungracefully.

"Let go of me! You made me trip!" Edana snapped. She kicked him in the shins as hard as she could and he winced in pain, swore an oath, and stepped back, releasing her wrist.

"What have you done to them!" Edana ran to the guard and driver, both of whom lay on the ground.

"Enabled them to take a short nap," her captor replied, studying her from the short distance between them. Considering the pain in his leg, he was rather glad there was distance between them. If this beauty was afraid of him, she did not show it, and she didn't seem too stupid to be afraid.

"You've tied them up! I demand you let them go, and let me go as well!"

"And who are you to demand anything, my fiery little hellion? Why, you're not even a woman, just a slip of a girl!"

But a ravishing slip of a girl, he thought to himself. Her red-gold hair was magnificent, and her tiny waist made her round hips seem all the more delectable. She was young, beautiful, and well-developed. He felt drawn to her green eyes and fighting spirit. This was no ordinary girl, no pampered daughter of privilege. And yet he knew of the family. The brothers were young rotters and the father too old and too lenient to control them. But could the young rotters have a sister such as this?

"I am not a girl, I'm seventeen."

"Ah, does that mean you're woman enough that I can make love to you?" He noted that she didn't flinch but rather held her ground and glared at him.

"It would not be love. If that is what you choose to do, it would be a cowardly act. But then, I suppose you must be a coward or you would not be hiding behind that hood."

"There are other reasons for concealing one's identity, my dear young woman. And the truth is, I have no need to force myself on you or on any other woman."

"You're conceited," she spat back. "And I demand you let me go and release my driver and guard."

In one swift step, he was in front of her and his strong arm circled her waist as he drew her closer. "You can release them when they regain consciousness, my girl. But first I shall relieve you of that quite lovely gold chain."

He held her tightly against him with one hand though she struggled to free herself from his grip. He pulled the chain over her head and dropped it into his pocket.

"That's mine! You're a common thief!"

"Ah, you seem to know who I am." He held her tightly and looked into her lovely face. Her body was warm against his, and he could feel the tips of her breasts pressing against his chest. The sensation was most enjoyable.

"I suppose you must be the man they call the Phoenix."

He did not release her; in fact he held her even closer and she struggled until she seemed to realize he was enjoying her fruitless movements. But she did not kick him again, though she could have.

For a single moment, Edana was mesmerized by the sensations that surged through her. She could feel the heat of this stranger's body against hers, feel his strength. What was this feeling? *For heaven's sake,* she thought, silently reprimanding herself, *this man might be a hero to some people but he took your gold chain.* In her eyes he was no more than a common highway robber.

"You should be ashamed of yourself," she admonished. "I have heard the Phoenix stands for high political aims and he stands up for the rights of the people. My father gave me that chain." She did not tell him the rest of the story, though she badly wanted her chain.

"I do indeed have political aims."

"And what have they to do with taking gold necklaces from women?"

"I'll sell it and give the money to the poor. Your father is no ordinary man. He's wealthy and privileged. He can buy you another trinket."

"My father is a good man who cares for his tenants."

"Then your brothers are not cut from the same cloth."

Edana glared at him. "You're a criminal and you'll hang for your deeds."

"Then I should have some pleasure before my death." With that, he again held her fast, then bent and kissed her lips. She hit him with all her might, but it was to no avail. He held her tightly with both hands now, and the harder she fought, the closer he held her. The movement of his lips on hers was not unpleasant, nor, indeed, were the sensations she felt. For a moment, she forgot to struggle, and then he released her and laughed.

Edana stood stock-still as he walked away from her. His dark cloak billowed in the wind and his heavy boots left footprints in the light snow that had fallen the night before. He mounted his horse and waved to her, calling out, "We'll meet again, my young beauty."

Edana felt her face flush hot in spite of the cold wind. "At your hanging!" she shouted after him.

She stood still for a long while until he disappeared, then she turned about and began untying her guard and driver. The guard had begun to move and she put cold snow on his face to revive him. Soon both of them were conscious and nursing their heads. Both begged her not to tell her father what had happened to them. But how could she tell him? She had not seen what happened initially so she could not truly testify as to how hard they had fought to defend her. Nor had this Phoenix, as they called him, hurt her. But he had taken her chain, and silently she vowed she would get it back. It was, after all, no ordinary bit of jewelry. It was the only key to her origins and it was worth more to her than its value in gold.

Bram rode into the wind and soon reached the rocky terrain that so well hid his horse's hoofprints. Donald MacLean would send forth no riders to look for him today because MacLean was leaving for Inverness.

He thought for some time about Donald MacLean and his wife Carolyn. As landowners went, they were probably the best of the lot. It was not MacLean per se that he objected to; rather, it was what the man stood for—a kind of feudalism that gripped all of Scotland. He might be a kindly, responsible laird, but he was a laird nonetheless. He had land, and those who worked it and tended his sheep were no less than serfs. Disguised as the Phoenix, Bram personally fought for an end to the power of the landowners who held the life of their tenants in their hands. He also fought to end British power because it threatened his country. There were other men who fought with him, but far more of the populace were complacent, willing to give up freedom, willing to continue a system that should have ended a hundred years before. Still, he knew that Donald MacLean was far from the worst of his breed. The trouble was, his sons would inherit eventually, and they would be worse than Donald, worse even than many of the others.

He slowed his pace and let his horse meander a bit. He felt into his pocket and put his fingers around the cold gold of the girl's chain. Thoughtfully he took it out and held it between his fingers.

"Such a lovely white throat you caressed," he said to the chain, before slipping it back into his pocket.

He beamed as he thought about Edana. She was quite stunning. But it was more than perfect looks that caused her to linger in his thoughts; it was her obvious intelligence and the spirit she had demonstrated that drew him to her. She also had a fierce loyalty to her father that he could only admire. She was concerned for her guard and driver, and outraged by Bram and what she perceived as his arrogance. Of course, her anger had only served to encourage him, to make him want to tease her more. Besides, he thought, grinning, he had a reputation to uphold. He always kissed the ladies, and even though this one was younger than most, she was on the edge of womanhood and would no doubt tell everyone about their encounter.

He once again took the chain out of his pocket, and this time he tossed it once into the air. At that moment he decided to send it back to her. He also vowed he would see her again. Young though she was, she intrigued him. And how in heaven's name could such a divine young woman be related to George and John MacLean? That really was a puzzle.

"I'm like a moth drawn to a flame," he said aloud, as once again he thought of her cascading red hair.

Katherine MacQuarrie lived outside a tiny village on the tip of the Isle of Mull, the second-largest island of the Inner Hebrides. It was separated from the mainland only by the narrow Sound of Mull and the Firth of Lorn. More than two-thirds of the island belonged to the MacLeans, while the rest belonged to the MacQuarries. More specifically, it had belonged to Katherine's late husband and was now, in the absence of a male heir, overseen by her, pending claims by male relatives. The British government would settle any claim, though they currently showed no interest in changing Katherine's status or limiting her power. As a result, Katherine collected the rents and benefited from her deceased husband's money. But regardless of what male was ultimately chosen, old MacQuarrie's will was clear. Katherine was to be supported by the rents collected as long as she remained on Mull.

Katherine MacQuarrie's maiden name was Duncan and she came from Edinburgh where for many years she had worked as a nurse. In 1700, while George and John MacLean were in university in Edinburgh, old Kenneth MacQuarrie had gone to visit the Lowland capital where he met Katherine, who was caring for his elderly relative.

Much to the shock of his friends and neighbors, Kenneth MacQuarrie returned with a young and beautiful wife, a mysterious woman who was forty-five years younger than he.

Katherine Duncan MacQuarrie was known for her ravishing, curvaceous figure and thick black hair, which fell to her waist. She was, however, unfriendly. As a result, even while her husband was alive, neighbors and tenants alike looked at her suspiciously. Six months after their marriage, old Kenneth died suddenly at the age of seventy, though his good health was legendary and most in his family lived to be eighty or more.

George MacLean had not known Katherine in Edinburgh, but he had heard of her soon after she returned to Mull with her husband. He had visited the two of them several times, and when Kenneth died, he wrote to Katherine offering his deepest condolences. After that, he began to visit more often.

Katherine was the subject of much gossip. It was said that she was distant, and some even said she was cruel. She treated her tenants with derision and her household help were made to work overtime to please her. Moreover, many believed she had contributed to her husband's sudden demise.

Katherine, as pleased as she was with her newfound fortune, was not so happy living on Mull. Thus, when George MacLean, a handsome young man several years younger than she, began to visit regularly, she was both pleased and intrigued.

On this particular afternoon Katherine was expecting George, and in order to prevent more unwanted gossip, she sent her

servants away so that they could spend a productive and unob-
served visit together. George, she decided, not only prevented
the boredom that made life unbearable, but held forth the promise of becoming useful to her future. *Yes,* she thought as she
readied herself for his arrival, *if properly manipulated, George
could change everything.* He was the eldest of the two sons of
Donald MacLean, the wealthiest man on Mull, and one of
the wealthiest in all of the Highlands. To Katherine's way of
thinking, money solved most of life's problems.

On this particular March afternoon, Katherine chose to wear
a long, full, red-and-black woolen plaid skirt fashioned from
the tartan of Clan Robertson, the clan with which the Duncans
were associated. Around her tiny waist, she wore a two-inch-
wide leather belt and on top, a dark woolen knit which clung
to her full breasts. Over the knit, she wore a proper, prim jacket
with gold buttons and long sleeves. Her hair was pulled loosely
back with shorter strands framing her face in soft, wavy curls.

This was the day Katherine had decided to seduce George—
not that much seduction would be necessary. George had been
willing to couple with her almost from the first moment they
had met, but Katherine knew her prey well. Time made such
a liaison more desirable for a man like George. Moreover, it
would have been unwise to begin an affair with George
MacLean while her husband was still alive. But now she was
free.

George MacLean rode toward the MacQuarrie residence. It was
not a tower house such as the one he lived in, but rather a
spacious stone house of the sort a wealthy merchant might
build. George felt obsessed with Katherine and willingly would
have met her almost anywhere. She was an incredibly desirable
woman and while he had many women, she seemed the most
pleasing. Each time they met, he thought she would sleep with
him, but she did not. Instead, she ended each and every evening
with a passionate kiss and the unspoken promise of more intimacy on the next occasion.

Perhaps tonight after a long afternoon together, he thought
as he rode along. Vaguely he wondered if recent events would

prevent him from performing satisfactorily. But he quickly cast the thought aside. He was quite certain Katherine could make him forget the lecture his father had given him last week, just before he had left. "You're a ne'er-do-well," his father had proclaimed, "and the greatest disappointment of my life. The tragedy is, your brother is little better."

George had looked down rather than back into his father's eyes. That he had not fulfilled his father's expectations came as no surprise. But to his way of thinking, his father was a sullen old man who did not know how to enjoy life.

"Seventeen years ago, I adopted a baby girl. It would seem that she is more intelligent, more loving, and more ambitious than my own flesh and blood!"

George's mouth dropped open. He had been so stunned by his father's statement that he ignored the rebuke and stammered, "Edana's adopted?"

"Yes. At the time she came to us, you were young. I told you and your brother she had been away because she was ill. Neither of you ever questioned that statement. But the truth is, she was adopted and, as I will tell her today, it is only fair that I tell you and your brother as well."

"Edana is adopted." He had said it over and over, since the day he learned the truth. He had to repeat it in order to believe it.

Edana was the most beautiful woman in the district. She was without question the most beautiful woman he had ever seen. Katherine might be a close second, but Edana was stunning. Her red hair was enticing, her body flawless, and her eyes sea-green pools. He had always thought her different from himself and John; now he knew she was different. They were not related at all!

Amazement was hardly the only emotion he felt. He felt anger, and he felt deceived. His father had made it quite clear that the inheritance would be shared. It would not, as was the tradition, all go to the sons. Instead, it would be divided. Not just between himself and his brother, but also with Edana. He was comforted only by the knowledge that she could not become head of the clan. That mantle would be passed to him, in spite of his father's feeling toward him. Perhaps, in time, he would figure out how to get Edana's inheritance; if his father died before she was married, that might present a way.

"Forget it," he said aloud. He was going to have a fine time with Katherine. He turned down the lane that led to the house just as a light snow began to fall.

George drew in his horse and quickly dismounted. The house was dark save for the small, intimate parlor. He smiled to himself; Katherine had sent the servants away. Happily, all thoughts of his father, his adopted sister, and his brother fled his mind. He could think only of Katherine.

In response to his knock, Katherine herself opened the door, thus confirming his suspicions that the servants were gone.

She crooked her finger, beckoning him to follow as she silently led him into the parlor. The room was festooned with flower-scented candles. He looked around with pleasure. There were two lounges, both covered with a sensuous, soft material, and a fire flickered in the hearth. Katherine's red-and-black dress made her dark hair seem even darker. She looked breathtaking, and when he bent to kiss her, he inhaled the rich, musky aroma of her perfume. It was an aroma that made him thirst for her almost instantly.

"Is it snowing?" she asked.

He nodded. "Yes, and it's getting colder."

"Not in here," she replied, as she slowly discarded her prim jacket and revealed the knit top that clung to her full breasts. He drew in his breath. Through the knit material, he could see her hard nipples, and again he felt overcome by her sensuality.

He stepped toward Katherine and felt his face grow hot with a flush that seemed to surge through his whole body. He desperately wanted to touch her, to feel her hard nipples through the material that covered them. The promise of her was driving him insane. He lifted his hand to touch her, and she grasped his wrist with her own hand. "You are much too anxious," she whispered.

In his mind, he could imagine her firm breast with its dark nipple. And beneath her full skirts, he was quite certain she had a forest of dark hair and long white limbs that would hold him. "How can I not be anxious?" he asked.

"You must wait. We have the whole day, perhaps longer.

We have supper to eat and wine to drink. Waiting will make it all the better, my love.''

Did that mean she would sleep with him tonight? He did not want to wait. He wanted to lift his kilt and take her now.

"Then let me kiss you, at the very least," he bargained.

She lifted her face and he kissed her lips, forcing her mouth open and sucking on her lower lip. Then he felt her hand beneath his kilt and much to his surprised pleasure, he felt her hand encircle his member.

"It's like a volcano," she whispered. "The pressure must be released."

His mouth fell open in sheer amazement as she dropped to her knees before him. He grasped the side of the table to steady himself. Katherine MacQuarrie was the devil's mistress! Only such a woman could perform this most delightful act.

"Edana! I was afraid you would not return home till after we left."

Outside, the carriage was waiting to take her father and mother to the docks where they would take a vessel to the mainland. By the door, two bags were waiting to be taken to the carriage.

Edana ran to her mother and embraced her. Carolyn leaned against her and trembled slightly. Her mother's face was ashen and her long hair had grown thinner in recent weeks, just as her body had grown more frail.

"We were waylaid," Edana said softly. "I did not mean to be late. I left Moira's early."

"Waylaid? Was there trouble with the carriage?" her father asked with concern.

Edana glanced at the guard and driver, both of whom hovered by the door. "Just a little," she replied. "Our wheel jammed in a rut."

Neither of the two men said anything. Neither would want to admit to being taken prisoner and thus endangering the life of the laird's daughter.

"Ah," her father said knowingly.

"Well, the important thing is that you're safe and arrived in time to say good-bye."

Edana nodded and again embraced her mother. "I pray you'll feel better soon," she whispered.

Her mother said nothing but Edana could feel her mother's sadness, and in her heart Edana knew her mother regarded this trip to Inverness as a waste of precious time.

As if to confirm her thoughts, her mother whispered, "I really don't want to go, but your father insists."

"Please get well," Edana said softly. "I need you."

Her mother shook her head. "That was once true, but now it is myself who needs you."

"We have to leave now or we'll miss the high tide," MacLean said.

Carolyn MacLean turned and took her husband's arm. "Then let's get on with it."

Edana watched as they walked down the path and disappeared into the carriage. In less than two hours they would be at sea and headed for the mainland. *Please let her be better,* Edana prayed silently.

George MacLean lay in the middle of Katherine MacQuarrie's huge bed. Beneath the sheepskin that covered him, he was quite naked. His kilt, his long hose, his shoes, and his sporran lay scattered about messily where Katherine, in a fit of passion, had flung them as she undressed him.

He smirked as he thought of the night before. Her clothes also were scattered about, half of them in the parlor, a few on the stairs, and the rest near his on the floor.

He had bedded younger women; indeed he had bedded virgins. But he had never had any woman more attractive and never any woman who made him feel as Katherine did. She had done exciting things he never dreamt any woman would do to him: she had teased him and taunted him and drained him dry not once, not twice, but thrice in the course of one night. He grew ready again as he imagined her silky limbs entwining him, her hands running over him, her hot breath on his neck. Where had she learned such acts? Had old MacQuarrie been such a lover?

George almost laughed aloud. No wonder he had died so suddenly after taking Katherine for his wife. She had probably worn the man out, draining him of his last seed and leaving him panting and crying for more. He tried to imagine them together, but he could not. She was so young, beautiful, and anxious, while MacQuarrie had been so old, doddering, and empty-headed. Still, one man's loss was another's gain. Had old MacQuarrie not brought her to Mull, George might never have known the sublime pleasure of last night.

At that moment, Katherine swept into the room. She was only half-dressed in a thin lacy chemise that could only have been imported from France. Her full breasts looked as if they might burst through the material which clung to every part of her as if it were wet.

"You're awake, my sweet."

His mouth felt dry. Was it possible that he might be aroused again so soon? Perhaps he would soon get over this—perhaps he would soon gain control of the situation. Certainly he did not have control now, and that troubled him. For the moment, Katherine was very much in charge. He knew he could deny her nothing for fear of never having another night like the one he had just experienced.

"Come, sit beside me," he said, beckoning her toward him.

She came and sat beside him. "You're insatiable," she said in a husky voice. "Were you unloved as a child?"

It struck him as a strange question, but sometimes she said odd things. "What has that to do with wanting you?"

She shrugged. "Nothing, I suppose. I meant to ask about your parents. Darling, I know so little about you, really. . . . I only know what I've heard from my servants; you know the neighbors can't bear me, nor I them."

George twisted his face. "My father's not given to emotions and my mother is ill. My brother wants everything for himself, and in a fit of madness, my father has decided to include my adopted sister in his will."

"But that's terrible. You should not have to share your estate with a woman who is not even of your own flesh and blood."

"She is their favorite. They like her better than either my brother or me."

"And what is this adopted sister like?"

"She's very beautiful."

"Ah, that's it. She has bewitched your father with her beauty."

George quickly shook his head. "No, my father loves my mother. If anyone is bewitched with Edana, it is my mother."

Katherine nodded and digested the information. "How ill is your mother?" she inquired.

George shrugged. "My father is taking her to Inverness to see the doctor."

"She must be very ill."

Again George shrugged. "We'll see."

"Yes, it is better to wait and see what happens." With those abstract words, Katherine slipped her hand beneath the cover and George felt himself go weak with desire for her. Her fingers played on his flesh and he could not control his desire.

"I want you to introduce me to your parents. You're not ashamed of me, are you?"

In spite of his state of wantonness, a flash of misgiving surged through him. His father and mother would not approve of Katherine—he was sure of that. But what was he to say to her? If he did not introduce her she would be angry and then perhaps she would not see him again. There was nothing to do but to say yes.

"Of course you can meet them. I'm certainly not ashamed of you."

She leaned closer and once again he was overcome with the smell of her perfume and her soft touch. "We'll wait, though—perhaps till my mother feels better."

She slipped into the bed beside him. "As long as it is not too long."

Chapter Two

March 1707

Edana stood at the edge of the clearing that surrounded the tower house and peered into the forested area beyond. A rutted path gradually wound its way through the trees and then upward for several miles. After a time, the taller trees disappeared and gave way to heavy brush and giant granite stones. Eventually the ardent climber would reach the highest point on the island, the craggy peak of Ben More. A hiker who reached the summit was rewarded with a panoramic view of Loch Seridain, much of her father's land, their tower house, and the wild, rock-strewn shoreline. Climbing Ben More was a long and arduous hike which Edana enjoyed taking. It was not an adventure that could be taken alone, nor was it at all advisable during the winter months of winter and early spring, when the ground and the rocks were often icy and thus treacherous to the climber. Moreover, the packs of wolves that roamed the higher elevations were hungrier in winter, and some said this made them more likely to attack humans. Edana had only heard stories of such attacks and she suspected that if they occurred at all, they were rare indeed.

Edana had no intention of taking the path this day, though she thought that it would be calming to climb to the summit and survey her world. The stillness of the summit, the view, and the isolation would have made it an ideal place to contemplate all that had happened to her in the last few weeks.

Yes, she had much to think about. First, there was the matter of her adoption. Apart from wondering why the woman who gave birth to her had set her adrift, she felt unaffected by what her father had told her. She was in fact more stirred by her dreams: dreams she had experienced for many years now, dreams which were vivid and left her with sensations she was unable to adequately put into words. Her father was only trying to be comforting when he had told her she would outgrow her dreams. He had not understood. The fact of the matter was that, far from diminishing, they were becoming stronger and more frequent. Her dreams did not trouble her, however. She was interested in them, in the reason why she had them, and in how real they often seemed.

So, Edana concluded, *I have this new knowledge about myself. I feel curious, and I still have my dreams.*

She shook her head and silently admitted that her most distressing experience had been with the Phoenix. She closed her eyes and trembled; she could still feel his arms around her and the burning sensation of his lips on hers. Why couldn't she forget him? And why had she not told her father about the incident? It was certainly not to protect the guard or the driver, though both were suitably grateful to her for not revealing their inadequacy.

The truth was, she had not told her father because she did not want him to send out his men in search of this devilish rogue. She touched her lips. *You gave me the first romantic kiss I've ever experienced. It really wouldn't do if you were hanged.*

She pursed her lips together and thought about her gold chain. No matter what she thought about the Phoenix or her reaction to him, she wanted the chain back. When she wore it, the "other" of her dreams felt closer. She promised herself she would find this man on her own and retrieve what was hers.

Again she glanced at the sky. Moira would come soon, and they would spend the afternoon together. Should she tell Moira about the Phoenix? No. She decided not to discuss her encounter. Moira was a good friend but she was given to romantic daydreams. This was just not the kind of information Moira could keep secret.

"Edana!"

Edana turned slowly to see Moira heading across the clearing. Her plaid-trimmed cloak billowed in the wind. She waved her arm and ran across the thin covering of wet snow.

"My goodness, you aren't considering a hike today, are you?" Moira's breath curled like white smoke in the cold March air.

"No, it's far too cold. I just came out for a little air. You know, sometimes deer come down to feed off the tender shoots of the trees closer to the house. I love to watch them—they're such graceful creatures."

"You have a faraway look in your eyes, Edana. What are you thinking about?"

"Many things. My mind seems to wander from thought to thought these days."

"Well, think about this: I hear the Phoenix is still in the district."

"I can hardly imagine why," Edana responded, trying to sound nonchalant so as not to make Moira suspicious.

"They say he's working against the British and the landowners. They say he's trying to get people to take power into their own hands. It's very exciting," Moira continued enthusiastically. "I think he must be a very intriguing man."

"But why is he here specifically? Surely if that is his true purpose, he could do more on the mainland. Mull is a quiet place and there are few landowners here."

"Except for your father and that woman—the one who married old MacQuarrie just before he died." Moira giggled. "They say she killed him with lovemaking."

"You're terrible!"

"I know, but he was an odd old bird and she is, well, this amorous creature, eons younger than himself."

Moira's eyes were filled with enthusiasm. She adored gossip. "Where is everyone, by the way?"

"I should have told you the other day. My father took my mother to Inverness to see the doctor. She's very ill."

Moira frowned. "I didn't know, though I know she hasn't looked well for some time. You must be very worried about her."

"I am. She seems to grow weaker by the day and no matter what we feed her, she just grows thinner."

"I hope it isn't wasting disease," Moira said softly. "I'm so sorry."

"She was troubled about me, too," Edana said.

"Why on earth would she be troubled about you? It's your brothers who should trouble her."

"They do. She was worried about me for a different reason. I think she feared that when I learned she was not my real mother, I would care less for her."

"How do you feel?" Moira asked.

"As I have always felt. Carolyn is my mother—no other could ever take her place. She is more than my mother: she is my friend. She's different from other women; she cares about what is going on in the world."

"How fortunate you are to be so close to your mother. I have only my father, and as you well know, he's a distant man."

"I know I'm fortunate," Edana said. She remembered her first conversation with Moira about the Phoenix. Moira had suggested she ask her mother, and now Edana decided to do just that, without revealing the fact that she had encountered him.

Bram Chisholm held up the gold chain and slowly turned it in his fingers, watching as the light caught its flat surfaces. Abstractedly he raked his hand through his dark hair and thought again about the girl. She had told him her name was Edana— *fire* in Gaelic. It was a truly appropriate name for a young woman of such spirit and such wild beauty. He thought again of her long white throat. It cried out to be kissed, just as her wonderfully shaped, upturned breasts cried out to be caressed. He suspected she would be wildly passionate once awakened, and fortunate would be the man who had the opportunity to awaken her. He suspected that simply to view her unclothed would be an experience to remember. With skin as white as snow, her breasts were most certainly rose-tipped. For a moment he imagined her unclothed, with her yards of red-gold hair splayed out on a snow-white pillow.

The mental vision filled his mind, and he recalled a trip he had taken to Italy some two years ago. There, in Florence, he had seen a painting by the artist Sandro Botticelli called *The Birth of Venus*. Yes, Edana MacLean reminded him of Venus. She looked amazingly like Botticelli's model; although, on reflection he did not think the painting depicted a woman with green eyes—but the skin, the fine figure, and the hair were similar. Edana's eyes were unique, however. Many with her fiery coloring had blue eyes, but Edana's eyes were deep-green pools. They were eyes that compelled one to look at her and indeed, to listen.

Again he let the chain slip through his fingers and onto the table. His left hand rested on his knee and he tapped his foot while he considered matters. After a time, he decided to continue his work here on Mull and then return to the mainland. He also decided he would return the gold chain. Such a magnificent throat deserved adornment and, after all, Edana was not his enemy. He smiled again to himself; she might, however, be the enemy of his concentration. He could not stop thinking about her.

Katherine Duncan MacQuarrie ran the silver brush through her long dark hair and studied her image in the mirror. George MacLean had left for home and was, on his departure, a happy man indeed. "Insufferable, but easily manipulated," Katherine said to her image.

"I'm terribly glad to hear that, my dear."

Katherine turned to see Superintendent Holden Crane standing in her bedroom doorway. "Make yourself at home," she said sarcastically.

Far from being put off by her tone, he simply laughed. "What's the matter? Did your young swain wear you out?"

"He is not my swain, as you so colorfully put it. You of all people know that George is more of a business endeavor. He is certainly not a pleasure."

He laughed again, a little louder this time. "My dear, you forget with whom you are speaking. The British government is pleased to make use of your—shall I say, skills? But I am quite aware that you have your own agenda and that agenda has little to do with us. The pursuit of George MacLean for what he can give you is strictly your own endeavor."

"You know full well that if I succeed I will ultimately deliver the support of one of the largest landowners to your government. That is what you want, is it not?"

He walked up to her and stood behind her. Katherine did not turn to look at him; rather she spoke to his image, which appeared in the mirror together with her own. "What's the difference if we both achieve our ends?"

He touched her shoulder with his hand, left it still for a moment, and then ran his hands over her shoulders and down her back. "You have incredibly smooth skin," he said, staring hard at her.

His hand was not at rest for long. He ran it across her throat and then plunged it down into her chemise.

Katherine closed her eyes as he pinched her nipple lightly and then withdrew his hand.

"What makes you so confident that you will be able to exert sufficient influence over the MacLean family to achieve our goals?"

"I rather imagine things will go as planned. Dear Crane, I almost always get my way. Mind you, it will take time."

She was a magnificent woman. Her thoughts were on power and yet she was flushed, excited by his abstract probings. She was used to being in charge and she did not know quite how to handle him. But, nonetheless, she allowed him to do as he wished and he did, coming and going from her home as he pleased, and always careful not to treat her too well. She only really liked men who remained a challenge for her and he had no intention of becoming one of her minions. No, he had work to do here, and while she was a vital part of that work, he could not allow his personal pleasure to interfere with his job.

Edana returned to the window again and again, as she paced back and forth, waiting anxiously for her parents to return. Now that both George and John were back, she spent much time in her room, or in the sewing room in order to avoid them. But when her parents returned, it would be different. Things would return to normal—at least she hoped so. But she did worry; she worried that the situation might grow worse instead of better. Her brothers had always been difficult but now that they knew she was adopted and not their real sister, they had become annoying in a new way. Moreover, it seemed quite apparent that they were both bitter because their father had made it clear that a portion of the estate would go to her unless she married. If she married, it would provide her dowry.

In the past month, she had noticed a marked change in her brothers' attitudes toward her. George was sullen and contemptuous, and John pestered her, coming dangerously close to making inappropriate advances. He kept saying, "Everything has changed." Last night, he had told her forthrightly, "To me you are now just another woman. We're no relation, so there's no reason why we couldn't have fun together." By "fun" he meant intimacy, and though she had been shocked at first, she had come to understand that John was quite able to rationalize treating her as he treated others.

He had tried to corner her and touch her in improper ways. Her reaction to him had been cold withdrawal and twice she had warned him off. Edana felt quite certain that he would not do anything too rash; he *was* afraid of his father's wrath. Still, she vowed to be vigilant and to avoid him in general since she found his advances troubling and knew if he persisted she would have to react strongly. This she wished to avoid because dissention hurt her mother deeply.

Edana turned sharply when she heard the dogs barking and the clattering of the carriage. They were home! She rushed from the sewing room and down the stairs. She flung open the door and stood in the doorway as she watched her father lift her mother down from the carriage.

One look at her father's expression told the story. Her mother was indeed seriously ill, and her trip to Inverness had been for naught.

The room Carolyn MacLean shared with her husband reflected her taste and interests. She was an unusual woman who had, before falling ill, managed a large household and still found the time to read and help the less fortunate among the crofters who worked the land and tended the livestock. There was no one on the estate who did not like and respect her.

The drapes that hung over the window were a golden color, as was the covering on the large bed. The furniture in the room was simple and had been made by one of the local craftsmen and upholstered by another. It was a neat, clean room without frills and, in spite of her husband's worth, it was without imported luxuries save for the books that lined one wall.

But Carolyn no longer read. Nor did Donald MacLean sleep in the room anymore. He feared he would disturb her and so had taken to sleeping in the room next to their room.

Edana paused in the doorway for a moment. Her mother was lying in the center of the great bed and she looked tiny and exhausted after the long journey by land and sea.

"Are you awake?" Edana asked softly.

Carolyn opened her eyes and lifted her hand to motion Edana into the room.

Edana sat on the side of her mother's bed and gave her a tender kiss on her cheek, thinking how very soft her mother's skin was. "I missed you so," she whispered. "What did the doctors say?"

"They were honest. I asked them to tell me the truth. Edana, it was my fondest wish to see you married to a good man, but I fear I will not live to see my wish fulfilled."

"Mother—" Edana felt her eyes filling again with tears.

"Edana, you have given me great pleasure, and when you learned the truth and still thought of me as your mother, it was the most gratifying moment of my life. I feared for how you might react when you learned the truth—I feared you would no longer love me.''

''I could never stop loving you.''

''Nor I you, my child. I loved you from the moment I laid eyes on you. I loved you as if you were my own child.''

''Please don't leave me,'' Edana whispered.

''I will not leave you willingly, my daughter. It would seem God is calling me—it is a call none of us can refuse.''

''What is this awful illness? Is there no hope?''

''I think not. It is, as we all thought, wasting disease. My body is eating itself and growing large tumors. The pain is very great and soon I shall have to take opium which the doctor has given us.''

''Oh, Mother.'' Edana could not stop the tears from running down her cheeks. She could only bend over and hold her mother tightly. ''I won't let you go! I won't!'' she sobbed.

''I'll take you with me in my heart, and you will keep my memory forever in your heart. We cannot really be separated.''

Her mother's voice was almost inaudible and Edana had to strain to hear her.

''You must beware of your brothers,'' Carolyn whispered. ''They are my own sons, but they've got bad blood. They are not good boys. May God forgive me for saying this, but I do not trust them. I will talk to your father about a husband for you. You must be allowed to choose for yourself. I love Donald dearly, but he's a traditionalist, and worse, growing forgetful himself. He will not choose a suitable husband. This, as I said, is my greatest regret—I wanted to live to see you married. I wanted so to hold your children.''

The last of her mother's sentence was spoken only in a whisper. Edana continued to hold her mother's hand and after a few moments, her mother closed her eyes and drifted off into a drugged sleep. Edana continued to sit by her mother's side. She told the cook to bring her supper and she decided to make a bedroll in the corner. She shook her head. Why were her brothers not concerned? They had not even come to welcome their own mother home.

She considered briefly what she wanted to discuss with her

mother, but Carolyn was simply too ill. The Phoenix would have to wait for another day.

John MacLean was taller than his brother George by several inches. He stood six foot two, had brown hair, small, dark eyes, and a full beard. George was the firstborn, and twenty-four years old. John was twenty-two. Of the two brothers, George was more quick-witted, while John was slower but more belli- cose. Neither, it seemed, had their father's sense of honor nor his attitude toward hard work. John had been in and out of trouble for fighting, drinking, and threatening young women since he was fifteen. George had been accused on more than one occasion of cheating at cards. As a result of their attitudes and partial estrangement from their parents, both of them spent much time on the MacLean estate on the mainland. They made no secret of the fact that they intended on moving the family seat of power from Mull back to the mainland as soon as they were able to do so. But tonight, they were both at home on Mull and met in their father's study. They were quite alone, since their father and sister were with their mother.

George poured himself a scotch from the decanter and, hold- ing it up, silently offered John a drink as well.

"Yes, pour me a double. One must do something to break the monotony of being on this dreary isle."

"Personally, I don't find this island as dreary as I used to," George said, smirking.

"Ah, yes. I've heard you have a new lady friend, if indeed one might call Katherine MacQuarrie a lady."

"Fortunately, Katherine MacQuarrie is more than a friend and something less than a lady." George smiled wickedly and winked.

"You always were a braggart. Don't tell me you have seduced her already—her husband is hardly cold in his grave and you've only known her a short time."

"Seduction wasn't even necessary, my young brother. She seduced me. She was more than willing; indeed, I would say she was positively anxious."

"I thought you returned home in a better-than-average mood."

"She's unique and performs ... well, does things other women do not. I can't think I've ever known a woman quite like her."

John nodded and said nothing. Katherine MacQuarrie was an exotic female whom the entire population of Mull talked of endlessly—not that there were many women in the vicinity. Nonetheless, Katherine was the type who would no doubt be talked about no matter what the locale. She had lovers, and she flaunted them before the all-too-conservative populace. "You'll set tongues wagging and Father will become irritated with you," John warned.

"Our father is always irritated with the both of us. The only one he cares for is Edana and she is not even his own flesh and blood. And we have to share with her—it's quite unbearable." George made a face as he spoke, then added, "I for one have no intention of sharing anything with her. When the time comes, I think we can find a way to—shall I say, *modify* our father's will."

John shook his head at George's comment. "You're more optimistic than I, my brother. He is quite set on seeing to it that Edana inherits enough money to be independent."

"Situations change," George said, sipping his scotch.

"Well, you have your enjoyment with Katherine and I'll pursue Edana. She's a beauty, much more attractive than your Katherine MacQuarrie."

"And just what do you have in mind? Are you planning to marry your adopted sister in order to get more money from the estate?"

John stared into the amber liquid. "Marriage is not what I had in mind. But it's a thought."

George studied his brother thoughtfully. He wouldn't put it past John to try such an underhanded move. In all likelihood, Edana's adoption was not legalized in any way—there was probably no impediment to one of them marrying her—no impediment save her will and their father's wrath. "I hardly think our father would approve," George ventured.

John drained his glass and scowled. "All our lives we've

had to share everything with Edana. Our mother doted on her and our father admires and even consults her. Now we discover she is not even our real sister. I don't want the approval of our father, and I don't give a damn what Edana wants. When the time comes, I imagine she can be convinced, one way or another, to do as we tell her."

George did not reply but he noted his brother's words and reminded himself that John would bear watching. Not because he cared what John did to Edana, but because John had just shown himself to be too ambitious. He had no intention of sharing his inheritance with either George or Edana. He intended to find a way to have it all.

The MacLean lands needed tough management, not near enough was collected in rents. His father was far too lenient, far too generous with those who lived on his land, both here on Mull and on the mainland. George intended to end all of that. There would be no more leniency and he would change other policies as well. The British government and their hand-picked Scottish Parliament had passed the Act of Union, and Scotland had become part of England.

Those who supported the union and the British had many opportunities, or so Katherine had told him: "If you were a supporter of the Crown, your claim to the land would be protected, you might well become a Lord of the Realm, and your power and wealth would be increased." Katherine was more than beautiful; she was intelligent and she understood politics as he had not. Now he understood and he saw quite clearly what had to be done.

George paced the living room. This evening was not turning out as planned, and Katherine was not even here yet. He recalled his recent conversation with Edana.

"I'm having a guest. I want you to eat with us."

"I can't," Edana had responded crisply. "I won't leave our mother's side. She's lucid tonight and wants me to read to her. I'm sure your guest will understand."

"She won't understand!" He recalled demanding Edana eat with them.

Edana had only narrowed her eyes and replied, "You're despicable! I keep the accounts, I care for Mother, I cover up your mistakes! Don't you order me about like a servant, George."

With that, Edana had left.

Worse yet, John was away and would not be back in time for dinner. George thought about it; he really didn't want John about, anyway. He was too handsome and surely would have flirted with Katherine and ruined everything.

Truly it was his father with whom he was annoyed. He had told his father well over a week ago that he would be having a guest and now his father did not even seem to recall the conversation. His father, George thought with irritation, was growing worse by the day. He was sometimes strong and sharp-tongued; at other times he could hardly remember his own name.

"Who is this woman?" his father asked again. Donald MacLean was standing by the window looking out, his back turned to George, and George felt grateful. He was sure he looked as put-out as he felt.

"Katherine MacQuarrie. Old MacQuarrie's widow. You remember, he died months ago. Katherine is quite alone. I felt we should invite her, get to know her."

"I wish you had waited till your mother was better."

George suppressed the desire to shout, *She's not going to get any better!* His father was absurd, holding out hope against hope that Carolyn would recover.

"When did you say old MacQuarrie died?" his father suddenly asked.

"Months ago. I don't remember the exact date."

Donald MacLean shook his head as if dispelling cobwebs from his mind. He hated it when he was confused. "I haven't seen old MacQuarrie in over—two years, I think. Funny, we share this island and haven't seen each other for so long."

"He's dead," George repeated impatiently.

"Yes, you said that. And this woman is his widow?"

"Yes, Katherine." *My God,* George thought, *what is tonight going to be like?* Katherine would be so appalled she would probably never want to see him again. His father was so forgetful! At this point he actually wished Edana was not so angry. At least she was capable of having a conversation. This evening was almost certainly going to be the embarrassment of his life.

"I don't recall that you ever had a woman for dinner before," his father said.

"It's true, I haven't. But this is a neighbor. We should be more friendly."

His father frowned. "I remember. Old MacQuarrie went to Edinburgh and came back with that young girl. Is that who's coming?"

George drew in his breath. He almost wished his father had not remembered. "Yes. She's not a girl, she's a woman. She's lonely."

His father turned toward him. "People talk about her. How did you meet her?"

"At the funeral," George said.

"Whose funeral?" his father asked.

"Old MacQuarrie's funeral"—George wanted to scream— "two, maybe three months ago."

"It's bad to die in the winter. Then you can't be buried till spring."

"She's coming. I hear the carriage." George felt ill, truly ill. He turned away from his father and sincerely hoped they would not be forced to discuss the difficulty of dying in winter during dinner.

George hurried out of the living room and to the front door, where their manservant was just admitting Katherine.

She looked breathtaking! She discarded her heavy cloak and he could see that she wore a long black gown trimmed in white. It fit the contours of her body perfectly, but at the same time it was modest and in keeping with the fact that officially, at least, she was still in mourning.

"Welcome to my home," he said, taking her arm.

"It's quite enchanting," she purred. "I've always loved tower houses; they're so in keeping with our traditions."

George ignored her. He personally hated this house. "Our mainland castle is much more to my liking," he said, hoping she would be impressed with the knowledge that they had more than one residence. "Come, meet my father," he said, leading her toward the living room.

"I shall be delighted."

"Perhaps not," George whispered urgently. "He's not himself lately. He's getting more and more forgetful by the day. Lord, tonight he did not even realize your husband had died."

"I see. Don't be so concerned, darling. I've seen dementia before. Your father is old and no doubt worried about your mother."

"Yes. Thank heavens you're so tolerant. He drives me crazy."

George paused outside the double doors that led to the living room. "I'm also sorry to tell you that John is away and Edana is by my mother's bedside."

"Don't apologize. I'm sure the three of us will have a splendid time."

George felt relief spread over him. Katherine was so understanding. "I do hope so. I planned every course of our meal. I did want it to be memorable."

Katherine smiled coyly. "Will you be able to steal into my room in the dark of night?" she whispered.

"Of course."

"Then I know the evening will be memorable."

He felt flustered all over and wondered if his father would notice. He opened the doors and ushered Katherine in.

"Father, may I present the Lady MacQuarrie."

They were greeted with a loud *snarf*. George stared at his father. He was sound asleep in his chair.

"Good heavens," George muttered.

Katherine squeezed his arm. "Wake him gently."

George did so and his father's eyes opened wide. He blinked at Katherine. "An apparition," he mumbled.

"This is Lady Katherine MacQuarrie," George repeated.

Donald MacLean stood up and walked to Katherine. He kissed her hand. "Isn't your husband coming?"

Katherine took his arm. "Come along. I shall tell you all about that at dinner," she said, leading him into the dining room.

George followed in their wake. Katherine was positively wonderful!

It was late April before the first signs of spring came to Mull, and even then it was tentative. The buds on the trees appeared but seemed reluctant to open, and the cold wind persisted, ensuring that in the early mornings, a thin crust of ice covered the puddles.

But spring is coming! Edana thought as she once again walked the perimeter of the cleared land around the house. As she did so often, she peered into the woods and then decided to follow the path for half a mile up the hill. She halted suddenly when she saw a fawn and its mother drinking from the stream that paralleled the path.

It was a lovely sight. The little fawn with the spindly legs, and the proud mother, protecting her young. It was the way her mother had always protected her. She glanced back at the house uneasily. She seldom left her mother's side these days, but early in the morning when her mother slept, she tried to go out and get some fresh air. And oh, she did love the spring! Even when it was colder than usual, even when the buds were late. The earth had a certain distinctive smell, a rich, heady odor that was always the precursor of warmer weather.

The path was rutted and uneven so her eyes were cast down as she walked. One could easily trip on an exposed root or stumble into a hole.

She started as a shadow appeared. When she looked up, she saw the hooded man with the billowing cloak in the middle of the path, blocking her way. Edana came to a sudden halt with a silent scream on her lips. Not that she was afraid, but because he had startled her.

"Shh!" he said commandingly, and the scream died on her lips. "Good morning, beauty."

"It's you," she whispered, looking at the Phoenix.

"I thought you might miss me."

Edana frowned. "You are arrogant."

"You obviously did not tell your father about our previous

encounter. I should like to thank you. Your silence saved me considerable discomfort.''

''And just how do you know I didn't tell him?''

''Had you told him, troops would have been out looking for me. There were none, so I suspected you told no one. Then, too, I know he left for Inverness that day.''

''I told no one so the guard and driver wouldn't get in trouble, not because of you! I really don't care what happens to you.''

''I wish you did.''

His soft tone took her aback. She could spar with him when he was being arrogant, but for a moment he sounded almost vulnerable, and she was unsure how to respond.

''Of course, I realize I behaved badly. I really couldn't expect you to be enamored with a man who took your jewelry.''

''To say the least,'' she replied. What game was this man playing? He perplexed her.

''I've come to return your gold chain, and to say I'm sorry that your mother is so ill.''

He held out her gold chain and Edana took it. This was a surprising turn of events; she hardly knew what to say. She reached for the chain and he let it drop into her hand.

''I'm surprised you didn't sell it immediately. And how did you get in here? My father has men posted.''

''Your father's men all seem to lack a certain talent for their jobs. But you need not tell him that.''

She almost let down her guard and smiled. ''How did you know my mother is ill?''

He shrugged. ''This is a small community. I heard she was very ill, and I've come to wish her the best.''

''Good wishes don't usually come from a man wearing a disguise.''

''Perhaps not, but I wish her well in any case.''

''Who are you?'' Edana asked, still frowning at him.

He stepped closer to her. ''The Phoenix. I have no objection to the name I have been given.''

Suddenly he slipped his arm around her waist and pulled her roughly toward him. Again, he kissed her, but this time it was a longer, more exciting kiss than the first one had been—a kiss that sent a chill through her whole body; a kiss from which she did not try to withdraw. When he released her, she felt her face burning red with embarrassment. She knew she should have struggled. She should have objected. But she had done neither! She had stood motionless and let him kiss her!

"You do like me," he said, looking into her eyes.

Edana struggled free and stepped away from him. "You take surprise for acquiescence. They are not the same."

"I know one from the other. I also know pleasure when I feel it on a woman's lips. You wanted me to kiss you."

"I wanted no such thing!"

He laughed. "But you did want your chain back?"

"Yes, of course I did. It is not just a bit of jewelry, but something quite special to me."

"Then I am glad I've returned it."

She wanted to see beyond his hood and the rest of his disguise. But all she could see were his hooded eyes.

He looked at her for a long moment. Then he turned and disappeared into the brush.

Edana stood rooted to the spot. Where had he come from? And where did he go? She touched the gold chain and smiled to herself. She would never admit it to anyone, but his kiss *had* pleased her. There was something exciting about this man, and clearly he found her intriguing as well. He had come back after all, and she knew that she must learn more about him—at least as much as he seemed to have learned about her.

It was close to midnight and the full moon shone through the window and cast eerie shadows on the floor. Edana lay in her bed and stared at the ceiling, unable to sleep.

For a long time, she had slept in her mother's room, but now her mother had to take opium powder, and she slept more soundly and for far longer periods than she had slept before. Knowing she would not be needed during the night, Edana had given up her bedroll in the corner and returned to her own room. She left orders with the nurse to summon her if there was any change in her mother's condition. This disease knew no night or day. The sufferer was in pain all the time, except when rendered unconscious by the powders which themselves destroyed the user.

Edana turned her thoughts away from her mother and let her mind carry her back to that morning. She touched her finger to her lips and was well aware of the lingering feel of the kiss taken by the stranger. Why had she felt so vulnerable in his arms? She had felt—weak, almost unable to stand. She had found him exciting, his touch warm on her skin. But what did he look like beneath his dark hood and flowing cloak? All she knew of him was the general shape of his body—tall, muscular, and lean. And she knew the color of his eyes, a soft, warm brown. His hair, hidden beneath a hood; his face, his smile— everything else about him was a mystery to her. And vaguely she wondered about his age, though she felt he was in his early twenties. Was his skin smooth or bearded beneath his hood? Was his complexion clear or pockmarked? Was his hair blond, brown, or red-gold like her own?

Ponder as she might, she could put no details to her picture. Still, she could not forget the feelings that had swelled within her. He had hardly touched her save for her lips, but she had found the closeness of him both enjoyable and troubling. She wanted . . . But what did she want? After a while, Edana decided she would speak with Moira who knew more about such matters. In fact, Moira seemed to know a great deal about coupling. Then Edana shook her head to dispel her thoughts. It was wrong to think of pleasure at a time when her mother was dying. She turned on her side and closed her eyes.

George MacLean stood before his father in stony silence. It was as if he were again twelve years old, and not a full-grown man. This command appearance was more humiliating than usual because his father was growing more forgetful by the day. Katherine was right: his father was suffering from dementia. Yet his father had days when he was perfectly lucid and could still be commanding. Today seemed to be one of those days.

His father sat behind the great oak desk, the neatness of which revealed his orderly personality. In one corner, his quill pen was submerged in the inkwell. In front of him was a pile of parchment paper and behind him was a drawer that held all the accounts—accounts now kept by Edana.

But it was not business that his father wished to discuss. It was something rather more personal, a subject that surprised George, and somehow angered him. Not that arguing would do the slightest bit of good. Once his father had made up his mind, it stayed made up, regardless of his senility.

"I've made no secret of the fact that you've not pleased me," he said evenly, as he looked into his son's eyes.

"Yes, sir," George replied. His father was not a man with whom you disagreed, even these days. Things were quite bad enough without having a fight with his father. He was sure that if he was not careful, he could end up being completely disinherited. And so he stood respectfully at semi-attention, trying to take his mind off his own anger.

"Being an undisciplined young boy is one thing; being an undisciplined man is quite another."

It ran through George's mind that perhaps his father had not liked Katherine, or had heard gossip about George's liaison with her and disapproved. It went without saying that he would disapprove if he understood it. He wondered if John had told him. It was just the kind of thing John would do. But he was afraid to ask if that was in fact the reason he was standing here like a child. It might well be something else.

"I've been giving some thought to your future, such as it is." His father sighed. "I've decided that part of your problem is that you haven't taken a wife."

George's blood ran cold. A wife? What was his father talking about?

"I have decided that if you expect so much as a tuppence, you had better get married. Do you have a woman in mind?"

George felt stunned. He certainly could not answer with Katherine's name. His father would not allow such a thing. In any case, MacLean still did not seem to understand that MacQuarrie was dead.

"No," George stammered.

"That being the case, you will marry that girl . . . ah, you know, that girl who is here all the time. Her father has been loyal and she is in need of a husband."

"Moira?" His father could not even remember her name and he wanted George to marry her? He made a slight face at the thought of Moira. She was Edana's friend, a plump little girl who was not without appeal, but he certainly did not want to take her for a wife.

"Yes, Moira—that's her name. She comes from the right family and she will bear you children aplenty. She's a good seamstress, a good cook, and a fine young woman. I hardly think you could do better."

MacLean sounded as if he were repeating whatever Moira's father had told him. George felt as if he might shriek. He didn't want to marry Moira; he wanted to be with Katherine. Of all the women he had known, she was the most intriguing, and he thought of her constantly.

"It's all arranged. All you have to do is present yourself to Moira's father formally. I think a summer wedding will be the right thing."

George felt as if his head were spinning. He had to return to Katherine immediately. He had to tell her what his father had planned for him. But what would she think? He would most certainly be diminished in her eyes, seen only as a boy whose demented father made all his decisions for him.

"When do you wish to go?" his father prodded.

"I have to go away—I can't do it for at least a week. I have to go away. I need some time to think."

"A settled man is more able to fulfill himself," his father intoned. As he spoke, Donald MacLean shoved a piece of paper across the table.

George stared at it. It was a marriage contract.

"Yes, go away. Think. But sign this now," his father said.

Trembling with confusion and anger, George scrawled his name in the appropriate place.

All he could think of was Moira. She had a kind of plump sexuality, but she really did not appeal to him at all. And no matter what he did, he felt certain she would not make love as Katherine did. No, he did not want to marry her. What could he say or do to change his father's mind? The truth was, he probably could not say or do anything. This was a decision

taken by the two fathers and neither the son nor daughter would
have anything to say about it.

No doubt Moira was enthralled. He knew he was considered
handsome and quite eligible. Naturally, he would be able to
have other women—though he was not sure he could have
Katherine. Moira's sole task would be to have children, and
he supposed he would be able to keep her pregnant, thus satis-
fying his father and hers. What more was there to think about
now? He had already signed the contract. *Katherine, Katherine,*
he thought. If only he could find a way to keep her in spite of
having to marry Moira.

Moira's father, Murray Lachlan, had long been Donald Mac-
Lean's confidant and *ceann-cath,* a term which historically
applied to a war leader or commander, but which had come to
mean the person on whom the leader most depended; it was a
kind of commission which provided improved income and status. If a clan was leaderless, as might be the case if a woman
inherited, or if the eldest son had not attained a certain age,
the *ceann-cath* was important indeed. This was not the case
with the MacLeans. Moira's father owed his position more
to the fact that Donald MacLean knew his own sons were
incompetent and thus had come to depend on his friend, the
husband of his fourth cousin, Flora. It was as a result of her
father's position that Moira had grown up with Edana. Now
she sat in Edana's bedroom with her eyes swollen and tears
running down her round face.

"What am I to do? I love you like a sister, and there is no
one I would rather have as a sister-in-law, but I despise George!
Marry him! I wish I were dead!"

Edana put her arms around her friend. "I don't know what
to say to you," she admitted.

"There is nothing you can say or do. My father's mind is
made up."

"I could speak to my father."

Moira shook her head. "I objected enough already. It will
just make more trouble. In any case, I know they won't change
their minds. Your father believes that George will grow more

responsible if he marries me, and my father wants to solidify the family ties.'' She sobbed again and buried her face in the pillow. ''It is my destiny.''

''Maybe George *will* change after he's married,'' Edana suggested, although in truth she did not believe such a thing could happen.

''I knew my father would arrange my marriage and I always feared it would be to your brother.'' She shook her head in disbelief. ''My father doesn't even like George.''

''It's very bad,'' Edana said. ''As much as I honor my father, if he wanted me to marry someone like George, I could not do it.''

''What would you do?''

''I suppose I would run away.''

''I have nowhere to run,'' Moira said dejectedly. ''I have no choice. How will I ever bear coupling with George?'' No sooner had she said the words than tears again began to run down her face.

''Tell me what you know about coupling,'' Edana asked. She was anxious to talk about this, and it occurred to her that perhaps it would help Moira to think through her dilemma.

''Hasn't your mother spoken to you?'' Moira asked in disbelief.

''She's been so ill. All she has ever said is that she would speak to my father about allowing me to have some say in the matter of my marriage.''

''I wish my mother had asked for such a promise!''

Edana nodded. ''Please, you must tell me what you know. My mother is far too ill now to talk to me about such things.''

Moira stared at her friend and then tilted her head slightly. ''Has something happened? Is there someone to whom you are attracted?''

Seeing that this bit of gossip took Moira's mind away from her pending marriage, Edana smiled slightly. ''There might be,'' she hedged.

''Who? There is no one around here! I know that.''

''Well, perhaps he is from away.''

Moira's eyes grew large with curiosity. ''Tell me,'' she demanded.

"You must tell no one. Really, you must promise."

"I promise."

Edana still felt uneasy about confiding in anyone. "I really shouldn't say anything."

Moira's mouth suddenly opened in silent surprise and she whispered, "It's him! It's the Phoenix, isn't it? That's who you've met! That's who it is!"

Edana nodded. "You must tell no one."

Moira seemed to have completely forgotten George. She leaned toward Edana. "Tell me what happened. Did he ravish you? Was he as dashing and handsome as they say? Are you in love?"

Edana felt her face grow hot as she blushed. "I don't know what love is," she said. "At least not that kind of love."

"I haven't experienced it, but the older girls in the village say it fills one with desire. Start at the beginning—tell me everything."

"I was waylaid on the way home from your house some time ago. He easily overcame the guard and driver."

"What does he look like?"

"He's very tall, taller than either of my brothers. And he's very strong. He's lean, but with broad shoulders and fine muscles. I couldn't see his face or hair because he wore a hood and a voluminous cloak."

"What did he do to you?"

"He stole my gold chain and then he kissed me."

"Did you faint?"

"Of course not. I fought him—but I liked it, Moira. I think I wanted him to kiss me again."

"I don't understand. You're wearing your chain."

"He returned it to me. He came here and returned it to me."

"Heavens above! Returned it to you? I've never heard of the Phoenix returning anything."

"And, of course, he took a terrible chance coming here," Edana said.

"I'm sure he is quite fearless."

"It would seem so."

"What happened the second time? When he returned your chain?"

"He kissed me again, this time more intimately. Moira, I *wanted* him to kiss me—I wanted him to ... I don't know what I wanted. On the one hand he angered me greatly; on the other, I felt this kind of longing."

"Desire," Moira whispered. "You felt desire for him. I will never feel desire for George. I would rather go to a convent than marry him, but my father won't even let me do that."

"Please tell me more about coupling."

Moira nodded. "I'll tell you what my mother told me. But then I'll tell you what I heard from the girls in the village. It was rather more interesting."

"Please," Edana said intently. "I must know everything."

Chapter Three

July 1707

Donald MacLean felt he was at least a hundred years old. His marriage to Carolyn had been arranged, but they loved each other deeply. Now, as she lay dying, he could hardly bear to look at her wasted, tiny body. And yet he loved her still; her spirit filled the room and her goodness covered him with warmth. What would he do when she was gone? He could not begin to imagine life alone. He knew his own condition was daily growing worse. Carolyn had been his mind, directing him gently, hiding his frailties from the world. There were matters on which he could still be strong—such as insisting his son marry Moira. Beneath the surface, however, he knew he was weaker than he appeared. He was now only a shell of the man he was a year ago and the feelings that sometimes came over him were terrifying. The thought that his mind was failing him was more frightening than the stiffness he so often felt in his joints. He remembered his own father—he remembered his senility—and he knew he was slipping into a similar state. It was a terrible trip back into infancy: he would drool and become incontinent; he wouldn't know anything about what was going on around him. He knew the signs, all right, and it made his condition all the more frightening.

Carolyn looked up at him with eyes made larger by her shrunken face. She was naught but a bundle of bones beneath the covers of her bed, he thought.

"You must promise me something," she said evenly.

That she was even lucid amazed him. Had he been as sick as she, he was certain he would not be able to speak so clearly; her thoughts seemed quite in order while his own were muddled. The miracle was, she often spoke logically in spite of the opium she was obliged to take for her pain.

"I would promise you anything," he managed.

"You must not marry Edana to a man she does not accept of her own free will."

"It is my duty to find her a husband."

"Yes, but I would have you seek her approval. She must want to marry this man you find for her. You must promise me this one thing."

Donald MacLean nodded. "I promise." In truth, he could not imagine trying to force a marriage on Edana. She had a will of iron, and custom or no custom, she would fight if she were truly displeased. At the same time, he knew she respected his authority. If his sons had half her spirit and only a fraction of her respect, he knew he would be a happier man.

"I shall die very soon now," Carolyn said, as he pressed her hand. "Ask Edana to stay with me."

Again he nodded, as if he would have to ask. Edana rarely left the house now, and she was always with her mother.

He looked up and saw her framed in the doorway. Her hair was loose and flowing over her shoulders. She was pale and looked tired. With his free hand, he beckoned her into the room. He knew she had only left to give them some time alone together.

Edana came to the bed and put her hand on his shoulder, then she quietly sat down on the side of the bed.

"I have to sleep now," Carolyn managed. Edana nodded and watched as her father stood up. She knew he would not cry in front of her, but his emotions were raw and close to the surface. Sometimes she found him in his chair, tears running down his face.

He bit his lip and hurried away before she could see the moisture in his eyes. She held her mother's hand tightly.

An hour went by and Edana felt her mother's hand grow cold. She leaned over. "Do you want another cover?" she asked softly.

But no answer came from her mother save a nearly inaudible gurgle. Edana smelled a strange, fetid odor, which seemed to arise from her mother's throat. Then her mother partially lifted her head and fell back against the pillows with another, deeper gurgle. Carolyn MacLean's hand fell limp and Edana knew her mother was dead.

She stared for a long moment and then cried out. Her father and the nurse both came running. Edana stepped back from the bed, too drained to cry anymore.

"She's passed on," the nurse said, crossing herself.

"What is that odor?" Donald MacLean asked.

"The foul breath of death. It is always so," the nurse intoned solemnly.

Donald MacLean stood for a long moment and then he began to shake all over and sob. Edana held him tightly. This was unlike her father, completely unlike him; and reluctantly she admitted he had changed during the long months of her mother's illness. He kept to himself far too much. He was a broken man. "Let me help you to a chair," she whispered.

Neither George nor John was home. She cursed them silently for their lack of concern as she led her weeping father to his chair.

Edana took his trembling hand and held it tightly. She could only pray that her father would return to normal. But she knew how ferociously her parents had loved one another; she was afraid now for her father. It was as if Carolyn had truly been his heart, and now his heart had been ripped from him. She had watched him change slowly as her mother died, but now she saw a new vacancy in his eyes, a new frailty in his being.

* * *

Katherine stood in the doorway that separated the parlor from the reception room. She was a tall woman, though George thought she looked even more statuesque than usual tonight. She was dressed from head to toe in a full-length black velvet dressing gown, with a high neck and long sleeves. Around the middle of the slinky garment, she wore a heavy gold chain. The soft material clung to her elegantly shaped body so that nothing was left to the imagination. George felt positively possessed with longing when he looked at her.

"I wasn't expecting you," she said coolly.

George shifted uneasily from one foot to the other. They were intimates! Surely she did not mind his sudden appearance. "I could stay away from you no longer."

She did not smile. "Is longing what brought you here?"

"Longing and deep distress, my darling Katherine."

She smiled without showing her teeth; her eyes seemed to bore through him. He somehow felt uncomfortable, as if he were a butterfly pinned to a collection board.

"Tell me first about your distress." She walked slowly toward him, and little beads of perspiration broke out on his forehead as he remembered the last time they had been together. When he had made love to her it had been easy to imagine himself entangled with a snake, though she was a most sensuous snake, to be sure.

"I don't know how to begin—I am so filled with longing." It was quite true. At this moment all he could think of was the feel of her mouth on his body and the way she wrapped herself around him. All thoughts of his coming marriage to Moira had been chased away by the reality of Katherine. All he wanted was to take her in his arms and feel her against him.

"Tell me what troubles you," she said again. "Then we shall see about your needs."

She came closer to him and took his hand, leading him into the parlor. She smiled and pointed to a comfortable chair. "I'll get you a scotch."

He watched her as she poured his drink. Her fingers were long and slender; her ravishing dark hair fell loose to her waist. The gold chain was all that held her robe together. He could only think of loosening it, of brushing her robe aside, of revealing her.

"Tell me," she said more authoritatively, as she handed him his drink.

He gulped a few mouthfuls and then wiped his mouth.

Katherine arched her brow. "That's no way to drink aged scotch."

George felt like a chastened child. "Sorry," he mumbled.

"Just tell me what has happened."

"It's my father. He insists I marry this girl—I don't even like her."

"And? Is it so unusual for one's father to arrange a marriage?"

"Of course not. It is most usual. But I want you. I don't want to be married to some plump young girl."

"A plump young girl, is she? I should think you would like that."

"I want only you."

"Has it occurred to you that it might be better if you married someone else, at least for now?"

George frowned. "I don't understand. What do you mean, 'for now'?"

"I mean what I said. Certainly your marriage would have nothing to do with us. We would still see each other."

"You wouldn't mind?"

"Of course not. Dear, sweet George, you must be logical. It would benefit both of us if you did as your father wishes, and if indeed we can find a way for me to get closer to your father."

"You want to get closer to my father? I don't understand." He momentarily forgot her luscious breasts and sinuous legs. Her words intrigued him. What on earth did she have in mind?

"Darling George, did you not tell me that you had to share your inheritance with your brother and adopted sister even if you become laird?"

"Yes, unfortunately, that is the case. And if I do not marry Moira I shall not even get my third."

"Then marry her. Ultimately we will manage to have everything."

"How can that be done?" George felt perplexed, unsure of what she was thinking.

"I will devise a plan."

George wondered if Katherine understood that his father was not given to the same weaknesses of the flesh that he gave in to with abandon. No, his father was a most conservative man. He could not even imagine his father having a sexual liaison, though he supposed he must have done so or neither he nor John would be here. Still, his father did love his mother, and if Katherine imagined she could somehow make his father love her, she was mistaken.

"I don't think you can influence him so easily—you're the most sensuous woman I've ever known, but my father will not fall in love with you."

"Love!" Katherine laughed, raising her right arm in a sweeping gesture. Her laughter filled the empty rooms. "I do not speak of love. You must leave the details to me, dear George. I will reveal everything to you when the time comes."

"Are you sure you can manage to do something?" George supposed that Katherine might have some magical effect on doddering old men.

"Don't dwell on the details. Just think of the possibilities, darling," Katherine was whispering. "I promise you we will have it all." Katherine smiled wickedly and leaned toward him so that her robe fell open, partially revealing the curve of her upturned breast.

George could stand it no longer. He plunged his hand into the folds of her robe and fondled her clumsily.

"I await your lips," she said throatily.

He bent his head and she ran her fingers through his hair. "I shall see to everything," she promised. "Then there will be only the two of us."

It was a rare day in summer. The trees were covered with lacy new leaves, the sky was blue, and it was unusually warm. Edana followed the path into the woods but instead of heading up the mountain, she followed the stream till she came to a waterfall and a clear, cold pool. Above her, the stream ran down the mountain, tumbled over the edge of a cliff, and fell over piles of giant boulders. The pool into which the water splashed was no ordinary pool. It had been created by a once active granite quarry, and as a result its waters were a clear turquoise blue. The sun shone brightly on the water and gave it the appearance of a shimmering jewel. This was Edana's special place, and on the warm days of summer, she and Moira came here often to swim.

Slowly she disrobed and then plunged into the still, cold waters of the pool.

Initially Bram Chisholm had lingered on Mull, remaining long after his work was done. Filled with regrets, he had finally returned to his home on the mainland. But now he had returned, drawn by the memory of Edana. He wanted to speak with Edana today, and so he had followed her into the forest.

"You have complicated my life," he said aloud. He had been unable to forget Edana MacLean. He told himself a thousand times that a liaison with her would be too dangerous and completely futile. In the end, he could not fight his longing to see her again.

He had arrived on Mull only yesterday and it was then he had learned that Edana's mother, Carolyn MacLean, had died.

He shook his head sadly. By all reports, she had been a kind, intelligent woman with a strong social conscience. She was well-educated and politically astute. Above all, she loved Scotland, and abhorred the idea of union with Britain. Edana had surely learned from her mother even if her brothers had not.

He rounded the corner of the path he followed. It more or less paralleled the main path Edana had taken, though it was not as wide. Obviously it was not a footpath, but a deer trail. He stopped short by a large tree. Edana had stopped walking and she was now disrobing, clearly intending to swim.

He stood mesmerized as she dropped her last garment and then gracefully plunged into the icy pool. She was a vision of loveliness—a creature of such beauty he could hardly believe his daydreams had materialized. Since the first moment he had seen her, he had thought her a rare beauty, but now all his imaginings were confirmed.

Her perfectly shaped breasts were tipped with roses, her legs were long and shapely, her waist tiny, and her hips rounded and tempting. Her hair was loose and splayed out over alabaster shoulders. It fell below her waist.

She swam for a few minutes, then she climbed from the water.

Suddenly she stared toward him. He realized that he had been so enamored of his vision that he had stepped out from behind the shelter of the trees into the clearing and she could quite easily see him.

Her mouth opened in surprise and she reached for her clothing to cover herself even as her face flushed with embarrassment.

"You!" she said, lifting her well-shaped brows. "How dare you spy on me!"

"I wanted to see you . . ." he stumbled, saying what he had not intended.

"Well, you have," she replied sharply. "And you've seen more than you deserved to see!"

"I—"

"Turn around immediately and let me dress! How dare you watch me swim! How dare you!" She stomped her foot so hard she almost dropped her dress. He smiled and turned around, the vision of her nakedness still vivid in his mind.

After what seemed an eternity, he heard her say, "You may turn around now."

He did so and strode closer to her. "I didn't mean to see you so—so close to your natural state."

Her face was truly pink. "I'd say you have the advantage. I have never even seen your face."

"And for your own safety I cannot reveal myself to you, my woman."

"I am not your woman! I did not intend to reveal myself to you, either."

"You're a stunning woman," he said, stepping still closer to her. She did not step away, and though he could well believe she was angry, it was nevertheless clear that she was attracted to him just as he was drawn to her.

"And just what is today's excuse for following and watching me?"

"I followed you to express my sympathy for your mother's death and to tell you that my work on Mull is done and I am leaving for the mainland and will not return for some time."

She lifted her chin. "And what concern is that of mine?"

His arm was once again around her waist and he drew her close and looked into her green eyes. She neither fought nor pulled away. He pressed against her and then bent and kissed her lips and then her throat. She moaned slightly and when he withdrew his lips from hers, he looked down on her.

"I believe my leaving is of concern to you." He shook his head. "You are not a woman for the taking," he said, all too aware of his own desires and her response to him. "I will see you again. Somehow, we will be together."

Edana felt dumbfounded, not just by the sensations she felt, but by her own reaction to this stranger. As before, she had not fought him nor had she objected to his kiss. She wanted him! She could only step away and nod her head. She knew as surely as she knew herself that he would be back, because he was as intrigued with her as she was with him.

What was this desire? What made her weaken when he held her, and why did she respond so to his lips when he kissed her? Why did she care if she ever saw him again? All she really knew was that she did care, in spite of the fact that she had not even seen his face.

"I cannot bear not knowing what you look like. And can't you speak in a normal voice? I know you disguise your voice."

He stepped away from her and shook his head. "You know my reasons."

Edana nodded. "When will you come back?"

"I cannot say for certain." He looked at her steadily. She was so unlike any woman he had ever known before—she was utterly without guile. She knew she could no longer pretend not to want him. Young though she was, he knew she was the woman he had waited to find. There simply could be no other.

She looked back into his eyes. "I must judge you by your eyes alone," she said softly. "Please do come back. Come back soon."

He once again stepped closer to her. He bent and kissed her again. But this was a different kiss—a kiss filled with tenderness; a kiss that would linger; a kiss that was a promise.

The stone chapel was the oldest on Mull. It had been built many summers ago in the center of a field of wildflowers, which on this August day surrounded it in colorful splendor. It was not an elaborate place of worship, but it suited those who lived on the island. They were, for the most part, simple folk who eschewed grander churches.

Moira was dressed in the black-and-red tartan of her father's clan, a branch of the MacLaughlans of Argyll.

Edana wore the tartan of the MacLean clan, as did most of the MacLean women present. George and his father wore their dress kilts. Neither the bride nor the groom looked happy, and as she sat in the front pew of the chapel Edana's heart ached for Moira, whose large, round eyes were filled with sadness.

The priest, who seemed to have been on Mull for as long as the ancient stone chapel, was small and shrunken. He recited the ceremony from memory rather than reading it, and his hand trembled when he lifted it to give the blessing. The ceremony was followed by Mass, and when it was over, the pipes wailed and George and Moira hurried down the aisle. Once outside, they climbed into the carriage to ride to the docks. They were going south to Edinburgh. In four weeks' time, they would return to the MacLeans' tower house, where Moira would live.

Edana stood and waved as the carriage grew smaller and smaller in the distance. She silently prayed that Moira would be happier than she believed, and that George, now that he had a wife, would change. She shook her head. She prayed for it, but she did not believe it would happen.

"It is as it should be," Moira's father declared.

"As it should be," Donald MacLean agreed.

Edana watched her father carefully. He was disheartened and troubled, far from the man he used to be. He appeared older, more distant, and always confused. Since the day of Mother's death, he had changed profoundly. Now and again he was himself, but he was deeply depressed, and though she had noticed his forgetfulness before, it seemed much more pronounced of late, as if he were spiraling down a black hole. She had hoped he would return to normal, but he had not.

"It's time to go," he said to her. "Time to go home and have dinner."

"There are others coming," Edana reminded him.

"Others?" he turned to her with a somewhat blank expression.

"The Lachlans, Father. They're coming to celebrate the wedding."

"Oh, yes. Of course." He shook his head. "I seem to have cobwebs in my brain."

"Is your father all right?" one of the Lachlan women asked.

"He's just tired," Edana answered. "He's still in mourning."

She nodded knowingly. "Everyone always said that they were closer than most married couples."

Edana suppressed the desire to say, *Yes, certainly closer than Moira and George will be.* But she didn't say it—perhaps because many of the women had made a case against the marriage. They already knew that Moira would be unhappy. Edana knew that Moira's father and her own had been the prime instigators of this wedding. But, she had told herself over and over, matters could be worse. Moira would at least have money and status. She would live well, and they would be under the same roof, so she would have someone in whom to confide.

Edana promised herself that she would try in every way to make her new sister-in-law happy, in spite of everything.

After they landed on the mainland, Moira and George traveled south by coach. They stopped at a small stone inn on the windblown moors of Argyll to spend their first night as man and wife. Like all Highland inns, it consisted of a tavern on the main floor and a winding staircase that led to three or four bedrooms on the second floor. The one they were given was under the eaves and had a sloping roof so that it was high-ceilinged on one end and low on the other. It was a small room,

meant only to offer the overnight traveler a place to sleep.
There were no luxuries here, just a bed and a quite ordinary
room. The bed was actually under the sloping eave so that if
you sat up suddenly, your head would hit the low ceiling.

Moira stood before her new husband and trembled violently.
She wore a white chemise with dainty blue ribbons, and her
brown hair was loose and fell over her shoulders. George lay
on the bed and stared at her. He sighed, her breasts were large,
but then, she was plump all over. She was round and soft like
a big baby.

"Are you a virgin?" he asked, lifting his brow.

Moira nodded and wondered why she had bothered to resist
the young men of the village. George certainly was not the
person for whom she had been saving herself.

"Are you?" she asked back, proud that she had spoken up.
Naturally she knew the answer before it came.

"Of course not!" George replied irritably. This cow-eyed
girl who was his sister's best friend was not the woman he
wanted. He desired Katherine and he felt nothing but disdain
for Moira.

"I suppose you want children," he said flatly.

In point of fact, Moira had never really thought about "wanting" children. It was more or less something she took for
granted. Vaguely she wondered if George knew how much she
had fought this marriage, how much she hated being here with
him.

"I suppose it depends on who the father is," she answered
sarcastically.

Was it possible that this plump little calf did not want him?
He studied her. He had never even noticed her much before
his father had ordered him to marry her. She was truly beneath
him, not a woman with rich hair and a good figure, but a plain,
plump girl with huge eyes. Moira was not like his adopted
sister who was, he acknowledged, a real beauty. Small wonder
that John desired Edana. But George did not desire Edana
because, though he couldn't really admit it to himself, she was
of much quicker wit than he. He turned his thoughts back to
Moira.

George raised his brow and again assessed her. It rather

stunned him that she did not seem any more interested in him than he was in her. He felt she should be anxious for him. After all, how could she have done better?

"Get into bed," he ordered, as he rolled out the other side and began to pull on his boots.

"Where are you going?"

"Downstairs to drink. I'll have you later, when I'm drunk."

Moira turned away from him. He was a hateful person. He was trying to hurt her, and if she had cared for him, he would have succeeded. As it was, she hardly cared if he was drunk or sober. The thought of coupling with him was nauseating, and she only wished that getting drunk was an option for her, as well.

Moira said nothing as George pulled on his clothes and then headed downstairs. She wearily closed the door after him and went to bed.

Moira climbed from the bed at the first light of day and scrambled, as silently as possible, into her clothes. She would have liked to plunge her entire body into the cold water of the granite quarry where she and Edana usually swam. But here in this tiny inn, there were no facilities for a bath.

As soon as she was dressed, she turned to look at the bed. Enough light filtered through the heavy drapes, that she could see George clearly. He lay on his back, his mouth open, and he snored loudly while a trickle of spittle ran down from his lips.

"What an attractive sight!" she said under her breath. She sincerely hoped that no one would ask her about her wedding night. It had been horrible, though not in quite the way she had anticipated.

George had returned hours after he had left. He had groped for her and roughly fondled her. She had lain absolutely still, imagining herself to be a dead body. He had pushed her legs apart and tried to enter her, but his member was like rubber and he cursed and reared up, hitting his head hard on the ceiling above. He had not even let out a cry, but rather slumped to the bed and promptly passed out. She had turned over and slept quite soundly on the edge of the bed, smiling ever so slightly at the thought of the bump he would have in the morning.

Not that the evening had solved her problem. He would couple with her eventually and she would have to endure it. But for now, she felt as if she had escaped, and she was quite certain that once he woke up, he would remember very little. Although, she thought, he might well wonder where the lump on his head had come from.

Outside, the gray skies of November made it seem like late evening, though in fact it was midmorning.

"Father?" Edana walked softly to his chair. Her father had fallen asleep at his books. It was not a normal sleep, but a distressed sleep. She watched him for a long while. He twitched slightly and moved about restlessly, as if trying to attain a more comfortable position. She shook her head sadly. He continued in his deep depression, sleeping far too long and too often, giving up his walks, and seldom finishing his work. It had been three months since George and Moira had wed, and over those three months her father had deteriorated still further.

As if he sensed her presence, he snapped open his eyes and then a smile crossed his lips. "Is it time to go to work, Carolyn?"

Edana touched him gently. "It's Edana, your daughter," she said.

"Edana, yes. Where is Carolyn?"

He trembled slightly and Edana noticed he had difficulty moving his left arm. How should she answer him? She bit her lip, not wanting to make him remember, but knowing in her heart that it was necessary.

"Mother died months ago. Don't you remember?" She said it softly and as kindly as she could.

Tears suddenly filled her father's eyes and then ran down his cheeks. "Yes . . . I remember."

"I'm sure he doesn't," George said, as he strode into the room.

In the months since George and Moira had returned, Edana had become aware that George was taking over the decision-making from their father. He sensed their father's weakness and he had wasted no time at all pressing his advantage. He became more authoritative by the day.

"I'm sending for a nurse," George announced calmly. "You don't have time to look after him alone."

It was true that since her mother died she had kept the records and looked after all the details of running the estates here and on the mainland. It was nearly time to collect the rents from all the tenants and that was a long and arduous task, which meant many weeks of traveling. The tacksman would take care of that, but she would have to do the records when he returned. She was tired—caring for her father drained her—but she did not trust George. Her every instinct told her George was up to something. "What's wrong with the nurse who looked after Mother?" Edana asked. "She's close at hand."

"I have someone else in mind."

Edana glanced at her father. He had slipped back into sleep in spite of their discussion. "Perhaps we should step out of the room," she suggested.

George nodded and they walked out of the study and into the corridor.

"I am the eldest; it is I who must make the decisions since Father seems no longer able to do so."

Edana knew she could only agree that their father could no longer make decisions—but that George should make them was something with which she did not agree; not that she could stop him. Unhappily, the law was the law. If their father was unable to carry on, it was the eldest son who would take over regardless of his competency.

"Who do you have in mind?"

"I'm sending for Katherine MacQuarrie. She's highly qualified."

"As what?" Edana asked, in a shocked tone.

"As a nurse. She studied and worked in Edinburgh."

Edana could hardly believe her ears. "She has a terrible reputation. Everyone says—"

"I do not care a fig for what 'everyone' says," George snapped. "It is for me to decide, and I have done so. I'm sending for her and she shall care for Father."

Edana felt she might explode. She stormed past George, doubled her fists, and cursed under her breath. She certainly could not depend on John for support and there simply was no one else. She felt trapped and frustrated, but most of all, she felt a deep concern for her father. In her heart, she knew George was up to no good.

"One other thing," George said, as he pursued her down the hall.

Edana looked at him stonily. "And what would that be?"

"When the time comes, you and John are to go out together and collect the rents."

"What about Moira's father? He is quite capable of collecting the rents."

"The hell with Moira's father. I have absolutely no intention of furthering her father's ambitions. As you well know, I was forced to marry her."

Edana was about to argue with him, but George turned around and walked away. He was exerting himself, and his resolve surprised her. Never before had he exhibited much will, nor had he appeared to have a sense of direction. Now it was as if he had found some new power within himself and she could not help wondering if Katherine MacQuarrie had something to do with George's newfound strength.

She watched George till he disappeared down the back staircase. If only there were someone she could confide in; if only there were someone who could offer her sound advice. Moira was her friend, but she knew nothing of legal matters.

Edana closed her eyes and thought of the Phoenix. Why had he not yet returned to her?

"I need you," she whispered.

Edana tapped lightly on the door of Moira's top-floor room. This tiny room overlooked the grounds behind the house and was a place of Moira's own choosing. George, who slept two floors below, had not objected in the slightest. Not that George had failed to claim his wife, but he slept with her infrequently, and as far as Moira was concerned, infrequently was far too often.

Moira opened the door hesitantly, but when she saw it was Edana she flung it open. "I was afraid it was George," she said, admitting her sister-in-law.

"He's gone off to fetch Katherine MacQuarrie," Edana blurted out.

Moira's brows shot up. "Katherine MacQuarrie! What on earth for?"

"To serve as my father's nurse."

"You couldn't stop him?"

"No, I don't know what to do. Father can no longer make decisions. George is the eldest." Edana closed the door behind her. There were no chairs in the little room, so she sat on a corner of the bed. "Is it true Katherine is a nurse? George says she is a nurse."

In spite of everything, Moira still seemed to know what was going on. She talked to people all the time, and because she was the kind of person she was, people confided in her. She heard gossip that Edana never heard because she was Donald MacLean's daughter. The immediate members of the MacLean family had stature, but they also represented power, and the common people did not gossip with those in power. But Moira was different. It was common knowledge that she had been married to George MacLean against her will. She was seen as a victim of power and thus not a real MacLean. Even before Moira had been forced to marry George, she had heard and known more of people's true views than had Edana. Edana had always depended on Moira for information, and she depended on her now. The only problem was that Moira did not always understand what she heard because she did not understand the larger context.

"I do believe she is a nurse," Moira admitted. "But Katherine MacQuarrie? What will people say? There are all sorts of rumors about how she killed old MacQuarrie, and I've also heard she supports the British and is very close to the British representative, Superintendent Crane. She's supposed to be close to the Campbells. I don't understand it all, but I know no one likes her." Even though she knew who was on the outs with whom, Moira was not familiar with the history that had created the situation in Scotland.

"Our country is torn apart by many forces," Edana said, hoping she could help Moira understand. "A few clan chieftains accept the Act of Union with England, but most object to it. At the same time, most of the common people want to limit the powers of the big landowners. People want a say in their own destinies."

"You're so smart, Edana."

"My mother discussed politics with me. We had a long talk before she got so sick she couldn't talk. I asked her about the Act of Union."

"It's the power of the landowners that the Phoenix fights. That must mean Katherine MacQuarrie is his enemy. Did you ask your mother about the Phoenix?"

"I didn't ask her directly about him," Edana said, shaking her head. "I wish I had. She did say that many were afraid that the Act of Union would eventually result in the elimination of most of the clan chieftains and put all the power in the hands of a few like Colin Campbell of Argyll. She told me the British would give those chieftains who supported them even more power, and the people would suffer."

Moira looked puzzled. "I know your father was opposed to the Act of Union, but George seems to favor it."

Edana considered Moira's statement carefully. "I imagine he thinks if he supports the British he will be given special favors. I think it must be Katherine who put these ideas in his head."

"My father told me that the Campbells were greatly rewarded for their support. They were given new and larger tracts of land—land taken from others," Moira said.

"Yes, the MacDonalds."

"I think you're right, Edana. I think Katherine MacQuarrie must have influenced George." Moira took Edana's hand. "Be careful, my sister. Sinister forces are gathering. I do not know as much about politics as you do, but I know Katherine Mac-Quarrie has a reputation—she is a devil, that one."

Edana nodded. "I know how much you hate being married to my brother, but I'm glad you're here. I need an ally."

Moira smiled. "I shall always be your ally."

* * *

Edana turned restlessly in her bed and then, eyes wide open, she stared into the darkness. She thought of the Phoenix. "I want you to come back," she whispered into the darkness. "I know you will come again, but I wish you would come soon."

She thought for a moment that she would ask him more about politics, but it was not politics she really thought about. It was the feel of this man, the sensations she felt when he touched her, the mystery of him. "I'm nothing but a silly romantic girl," she said, chastising herself aloud. But it was no use; she could not forget her encounters with him. On all three occasions he had simply appeared—as if he had been watching her from afar for some time.

How did he know of her comings and goings? How did he know of her secret places on the estate? On all three occasions he had kissed her and she had responded, wanting him to hold her tightly, wanting him to make love to her even though she had not the slightest idea what he looked like. What made her thrill to his touch and respond to his stolen kisses? What made her think of him so often? Deep inside she felt a terrible longing to be with him again and to confide in him. "I'm being absurd," she told herself. How could she be sure of what he was really like? Perhaps he was a womanizer, a man who took advantage of his reputation to have romantic interludes.

Edana forced herself to close her eyes. *I must sleep; I must keep my wits about me. Tomorrow Katherine MacQuarrie is coming and I must keep an open mind, but watch her nonetheless.*

Edana thought that Katherine MacQuarrie was an elegant-looking woman, well-dressed and well-groomed. She arrived with several cases and a box of personal belongings. Edana frowned as she watched the servants unload the carriage. She appeared to be moving in.

Edana noted that George watched, too, his face glowing. It was obvious that George had some kind of relationship with this woman. Perhaps she was his mistress.

Moira watched as well, and Edana thought, had she cared at all for George, she might well have been jealous. But she did not care for him, and she apparently was not even concerned. Indeed, Edana thought, Moira might even be relieved to have George's mistress in the same house. Such an arrangement no doubt meant that she would be left alone entirely by her husband, and that, Edana realized, was most assuredly Moira's most fervent wish.

"This is my adopted sister, Edana," George said stiffly.

"Edana—I've heard so much about you."

Katherine held out her hands but she was stiff, and Edana felt she was disingenuous. Edana had an immediate sense of discomfort in Katherine's presence—not because of the woman's reputation, but because of her demeanor. She had an air of superiority and disdain. Her smile was not warm, but cold. Indeed, everything about her was cold.

Edana thought of the conversation she and Moira had had yesterday. They had guessed correctly; there could be no doubt that George had a relationship with Katherine. As both she and Moira watched, George all but fell over himself to serve and impress Katherine.

"This is my wife," George said, indicating Moira, who stood back, behind Edana.

"I'm so pleased to meet you," Katherine said.

Moira only nodded.

"And John, my brother."

Katherine took both of John's hands and looked boldly into his eyes. "George has told me a great deal about you, too."

John did not flinch. He also did not drop her hands. "George is very talkative, it would seem." He smiled at her and it was a smile that betrayed little else but lechery.

Katherine discarded her lightweight summer cloak into the hands of a silent, waiting servant. "I should like to see my patient right away," she announced.

"Of course, follow me," George said, leading her away.

John followed, but Edana and Moira remained behind.

"You're very distressed, aren't you?" Moira observed.

Edana nodded. "You're right, that woman bears watching."

"George will be in her bed tonight and no doubt every night."

"Only if John does not interrupt them."

Moira half smiled. "I confess, I'm relieved."

"I only wish I were," Edana replied. "I do not trust her, nor do I trust George. I wish I knew what they were up to."

Moira sighed. "You won't have long to wait."

Chapter Four

November 1707

The curtains in Donald MacLean's study were drawn. He had slept there, during his wife's prolonged illness, and he continued to sleep there, as if he were afraid to return to the room they had shared for so many years.

Most of the time he sat silently in his chair and stared into space, taking food only when fed.

"Father," George said, as if his father were quite himself. His words, however, had no effect. His father did not even look up; his mind was obviously elsewhere, as he seemed to look right through his eldest son.

"This is Katherine; she's come to care for you." George jostled his father's shoulder ever so slightly.

Donald MacLean turned slowly; his eyes came to rest on Katherine. "Carolyn?" he questioned. He stared at the young woman with the long dark hair. Yes, when she was younger, Carolyn had had such hair.

He blinked. But how could this be? He was quite unable to express himself since he could not seem to put words together in the right order. He was no longer certain who people were or what they were saying. He wept unexplainably and he felt lighter than air, though he could not move. He felt dead, though in fact he knew he was alive. He was a disembodied spirit around whom strangers moved in inexplicable circles.

A cool, soft hand covered his. "Yes," the voice answered in a soft whisper. "I've come back to you and I've brought you some medicine."

His lips moved and his quivering hand reached up to touch the hand of his vision.

Katherine dissolved a white powder in a glass of water. She held it to his lips. "Drink this. It will make you feel better."

Donald MacLean did not take his eyes off her, but his trembling hands encircled the glass and he gulped down the foggy liquid.

George watched. "We must talk," he said urgently. "I've not much time to tell you all you must know."

She turned sweetly and spoke softly. "We'll talk later. Now I must see to my patient."

"Aren't you taking this a bit seriously? I wanted you here so that we can be together," he whispered.

Katherine shot him a nasty look and hissed, "You really don't understand at all, do you?"

"Understand what?"

Katherine took his sleeve and pulled him away. She spoke to him in a whisper. "I told you we would talk later. You must not underestimate the ill. Sometimes they understand quite well and often they manage to repeat what they've heard."

"But Katherine, I've longed for you—"

"Later, George. Perhaps tonight."

George felt as if she had hit him. He nodded dumbly and turned around to leave. In his wildest dreams, he had not expected her to really care for his father. He had expected her to give George her undivided attention.

Katherine listened as George closed the door. "Such a toad," she murmured. George was so in need of direction. First of all, he should have gotten rid of his adopted sister long ago. She was far too bright. "But this is not the time," Katherine said to herself. After Donald MacLean, his son John was the more important priority. Charming though he was, he did not appear as easy to control as George. He thought more of himself, he was volatile, and he had ambitions of his own. She conceded that John might have some entertainment value in the meantime.

Katherine turned again toward her patient. "I must act quickly," she said aloud. She knew he would not last long. In addition to his dementia, he apparently had had a stroke and now suffered from apoplexy. The powders she gave him would cause him to deteriorate far more quickly. A weak heart plus his daily dose of powders preordained his fate. She sighed; it was truly amazing how long the ill could survive. "But not you," she said, turning to the dozing Donald. "You will have help. I haven't a lifetime to wait for the riches I deserve. What's important is that when you die, I be something more than your nurse. Then, John and Edana will be next."

A single candle burned in George's room as he lay awake anxiously awaiting Katherine. She came suddenly, not even bothering to knock.

She was dressed entirely in a flowing white nightgown and her hair was pulled back. How delectable she appeared. His whole body was rigid with desire.

"I've waited so long," he muttered.

"And you shall wait longer. We must talk."

"But dear Katherine, I've been lying here thinking of no one but you. I crave you as a starving man craves food. I beg you, make me wait no longer!"

"Stop being childish, George. We have matters of import to discuss."

His face reddened and took on a pouty expression and he nodded.

"If you are to inherit everything and cut your sister and brother out of your father's will, then I shall have to marry your father," she said calmly.

"Marry my father? But he's senile," George protested.

"Yes, precisely. We'll assist him into the hereafter and then I will become the overseer of his estates until you are made chieftain. You and I, darling, will have everything."

"But how can you get him to marry you?"

She laughed. "He already thinks I am his wife. He is quite demented and his heart is weak. We must do this quickly; there is no time to waste."

"But what will people say? What will John and Edana do? They will protest."

"To whom?"

"The authorities, I suppose."

Again she laughed. "You, George darling, are so naive. The authorities do not like your father—he is one of the chieftains opposed to the Act of Union. They would be only too happy to have the MacLean estates fall the into hands of someone who will support the union, as we do."

George digested the information. "But what will we do with John and Edana?" he persisted.

"John and Edana will be sent to collect the rents. That will take them nearly a month. When they return, I will already have married your father. After the marriage, I'll arrange a marriage for Edana, thus ridding us of her. As for John, I'll give him some thought."

George looked into her eyes and was about to ask a question when she touched his lips with her finger. "After a decent period, dear George, you and I will be married."

"But I am married! What about my wife?"

Katherine laughed. "You will convert to Protestantism. Then you will simply divorce her and send her away."

"You're a brilliant woman," George breathed in admiration.

Marry Katherine—yes, he would marry her and she would be his forever. He could already imagine himself living on the larger MacLean estate on the mainland, having the money to refurbish it. He had never understood why his father insisted on remaining on Mull. It was so isolated! But perhaps he should put that to Katherine immediately. Was there a need to wait?

"I think we should move to the mainland," he said quickly.

Katherine ran her finger over George's chest. "After I marry your father. I cannot leave Mull under the terms of MacQuarrie's will, so naturally I must have the security of another marriage first."

"Of course," George mumbled, as Katherine continued to

stroke him. He felt he would go mad with the heat of her hand on him.

"You will send John and Edana away tomorrow," she said evenly. "They can begin collecting the rents on the mainland first and then return to the island to collect rents here. By the time they return, we'll be fully in charge," Katherine said.

"Come to me," he begged.

Katherine stared into his eyes and continued to run her hands over him. "With pleasure," she breathed.

Edana tossed restlessly in her sleep. She seemed to be walking through a thick mist, and then, out of the fog, a great, rambling wooden house emerged. It was not a castle, but a sprawling edifice with two stories. It was unlike any house she had ever seen, and in an unfamiliar locale. It was on the crest of a knoll, set among the rolling hills, surrounded by barren rocky ground. It was not the first time she had dreamt of this house, and as before, she felt she had some connection to it. Then, as was so often the case, she saw herself, or someone she took to be herself, on the moor. This other self was running through the heather toward the house. A great feeling of sadness came over her, and as the mists dissipated, Edana was aware of the fact that it was a dream, and she blinked open her eyes.

Again and again she asked herself about the girl in her dreams. It was odd. She had dreams about herself where she was herself, but in this recurring dream the person who appeared to be her, was not her.

Edana sat up and poufed her pillow. Then she forced herself into an upright position and sat fully awake, in spite of the hour. She knew in her heart she was deeply troubled, and that she often had these dreams when she was upset, though in fact the dreams seemed to have nothing to do with her problems.

She stared into the darkness and, turning from her dreams, she thought again of her frequent feelings of "otherness." She was often consumed with the idea that she had seen a certain place before, or had had a certain conversation in the past. She had told her mother, father, and Moira about her dreams, but she rarely spoke of the feelings of "otherness" that came during her waking hours. She decided that it was better not to discuss certain matters, even with family and friends.

Edana turned her thoughts to her dilemma. She felt as if they were all plummeting toward disaster and that she was powerless to prevent what was happening.

No doctor, regardless how sympathetic, would say that her father was competent. If her father were incompetent, as he certainly seemed to be, then legally George, his eldest son, had the right to make the kind of decisions he had already made.

But George, she well knew, could not be trusted. Again and again she wondered what George and Katherine were planning. She worried about her father and about Moira, but what could she do? George had isolated her father and only Katherine was allowed to spend much time with him.

Edana sunk back against her pillows and pulled the sheepskin close around her. She was allowed to see her father only a few minutes a day and during that time, she had to admit, Katherine seemed indulgent, seeing to his every need. But what if she did not insist on seeing him daily? Indeed, what happened during the hours when she wasn't present? Her father seemed weaker by the day and she strongly felt that he was dying.

Tears of frustration filled her eyes and she tightly clenched her fists together. She and John would leave for the mainland tomorrow and would be gone for nearly four weeks. It wasn't just a matter of collecting the rents; they had to visit with each family and it was a time-consuming process. While she was gone, Moira would be alone. She could do nothing to prevent Katherine and George from doing whatever they liked.

Let me be wrong about them, Edana prayed. *Please, let me be wrong about them.*

The rents were always collected at the end of the harvest, usually in November. It was the custom to start at the point farthest away, and work back to Mull.

Dressed warmly in plain woolen travel clothes, Edana accompanied John MacLean, who wore his kilt and carried an array of weapons. He took his pistol, his broadsword, and his hunting knife. She carried the record books in which to record the necessary information. She was to record the tenant's name, the number in the family, who had died during the previous year, and who had been born. She would credit the amount of the rent paid, and make notes concerning any amount owed and why. It was also her duty to write down the details of any disputes or matters which required the judgment of the chieftain. Normally such matters would be brought to her father's attention and he, in turn, would summon the necessary parties and settle the matter fairly. Such fair judgment, Edana feared, might well come to an end when George took over. The Phoenix had warned her of this, and she thought of him now as she and John set forth. *How I need to talk with you,* she thought. She felt mystified. He had promised to return, but he had not done so. Still, she waited; if he did return, she had much to ask him.

"You're very quiet," John said, as they boarded the vessel that would take them to the mainland.

"I was just thinking of all that has to be done."

"You never think of enjoyment, you only think of work."

She did not answer him. John knew only one kind of enjoyment, and she wanted no part of it.

She drew in her breath. She felt invigorated by the morning air, which was cool and crisp. The carriage had been stuffy and she had hardly been awake when they left.

Once set ashore, they would travel for nearly a day by wagon to the most distant of the MacLean lands. They did not travel alone; an armed guard of four accompanied them since, as they worked their way home, the amount of money they carried would be sizable.

They had to cross the Firth of Lorn, which was always choppy. John kept to himself so that no one would know he was seasick. He was always seasick and had suffered from the malady for as long as she could remember.

"I'm going below to plan our journey," he announced.

It was already planned, but she said nothing. Edana was pleased; she did not have to worry about John now. "I'll stay here," she told him, as she sat down on a bench that ran along the deck.

John disappeared and Edana knew that for several hours she

would be alone with her thoughts. When they landed, they would head for Taynuilt.

John and Edana were half finished collecting the rents, and as they rode along, Edana thought about their journey thus far.

At first, when they had set off toward Taynuilt, John had remained silent and sullen. But the farther they had traveled, the more he had seemed to forget what was troubling him, and after a time, he began to talk to her.

Sometimes, Edana acknowledged, John could be good company. The main problem she had with him was his lecherous nature. Ever since he had learned that they were not blood relations, he had made advances toward her. It was for this reason that she had dreaded traveling with him. Still, the guard was with them and she felt certain John would not become bold under the circumstances.

A week passed, then two. Wherever they went, they received reports on how things were going. It had always been her father's custom to listen to the difficulties of his tenants and to levy the rents accordingly. If a family had sickness, or a new child had been born, or if the weather had caused a problem, the rents paid were lower. If all was well, the rents were higher. Edana knew her father to be a generous and just man. Yet in her heart, she knew the Phoenix was right. Regardless of how just a chieftain was, he still held the power of life and death over those who lived on his land. In that sense, Donald MacLean was a feudal lord just as the Phoenix said he was.

Because her father seldom used his power, but instead ruled by consent, his tenants and his clan were a happy lot. Or, at least they had been happy. John was not inclined, as his father had been, to listen to complaints or to consider the individual circumstances of the tenants. He was short-tempered with them, demanded the rent, and daily complained to Edana that he had no time to listen to the "bellyaching" of so many people. For her part, Edana hoped that her father would be better when they returned. She recorded everything, and tried to give comfort to the tenants where she could.

They were nearly finished collecting on the mainland, and

Edana felt anxious to return to Mull. Of late, her dreams had been supplanted with nightmares about her father, George and Katherine. She was distraught with the way John treated people, and weary with traveling.

"We'll reach the firth soon," she said, arranging her skirt about her. "I feel uneasy carrying this much money."

"It should be more; it always should have been more. Father was too easy on these people. You can bet that Colin Campbell doesn't treat his tenants this way. They either pay or they're cleared out."

"Father's tenants are loyal. Loyalty is worth a great deal."

"Hogwash," John muttered. "I'm tired." He pulled out his pocket watch. "Let's stop early and picnic by the river."

"If you think it's safe. I thought perhaps we should travel a little faster and try to make the firth by nightfall."

"What's the hurry?"

"We're carrying a large sum of money. There are high-waymen, and . . . well, you've heard of the Phoenix." She threw his name out. In truth she wished he would appear.

"We've a good guard. As for the Phoenix—well, I'm not worried about some hooded fool who's been turned into a hero by the ignorant masses."

Edana said nothing. No one save Moira, whom she had confided in long after the fact, knew of her brief encounters with the Phoenix, no one knew they had spoken, and not even Moira guessed that she daydreamed of the Phoenix, and longed to see him again. There was no way she could contradict John without giving too much away.

"What did you bring to eat today?" he asked.

Wherever they were, it was her custom to pack a basket in the morning so that they could eat while traveling. Their nights were usually spent with the tenants, and the accommodation depended on the well-being of the particular tenant. Some were far better off than were others. They had spent last night with one of the more affluent tenants. They had had wine with dinner and dined on roast pork, bread, and assorted greens from the root cellar.

"I brought bread, meat, cheese, and some wine," she answered.

He smiled at her. "Good. I'm quite hungry."

She wondered how he could possibly be hungry; only a few hours ago he had devoured a huge breakfast consisting of poached fish, bread, porridge, milk, and berries.

He gave no warning as he suddenly turned the wagon off the road and headed down a rutted path toward the river that sprung from Loch Nell. He turned back to the guard and shouted, "Stay by the main road."

"I think they should be with us," Edana protested.

"I think we deserve some privacy," he retorted. "I'm tired of being in the company of those wretched louts twenty-four hours a day."

"They are with us to guard the rents."

"I can take care of myself."

John brought the clattering wagon to a halt by the river. It was a rapid stream with huge boulders on either side of it. The glen was grassy, and above, the sun was unusually warm for late fall.

John scrambled down from the wagon and Edana took the basket and started to climb down. John put his hands firmly on her waist and lifted her to the ground.

"Thank you," she stammered.

"I wanted to span your waist," he said, standing close and looking down into her face.

She could not step back because the wagon was behind her. He stood very close and pressed her against its wooden frame. "Move," she said firmly. "Get out of my way."

He leered at her. "And you will do what, if I don't?"

Her mouth felt dry. They were alone, and it seemed what she feared most was about to happen. He had left the guards on the road because he intended to try and couple with her.

She had no time to protest, or to even think further. He held her close and roughly kissed her, trying to force his tongue into her mouth. She dropped the basket and lifted her leg, kneeing him in the groin. He staggered backward and swore loudly; but he quickly scrambled to his feet and lunged at her again. He hit her across the face. "Little hellion! Proud little bitch! I'll teach you the lesson of a lifetime!"

His eyes were filled with anger and her face stung from his

blow. She felt dizzy as he hit her again, and then, as she staggered forward, he seized her and with one hand tore her dress, revealing her thin chemise.

She doubled her fists and fought him, but he was taller and much stronger. He forced her to the soft damp grass and with his leg forced her legs apart. "I've dreamed of this," he said, kneading her breast roughly. "I've dreamed of having you every night since this trip began."

She opened her mouth to scream, but he slapped her again and this time, the combined blows caused her to lose consciousness.

"Edana! Edana!" The voice that spoke to her was full of urgency and she opened her eyes and looked into the hooded face of the Phoenix. Was this a dream following the nightmare of John's fierce and brutal attack? She was unable to speak, aware only of his presence and the fact that her head hurt and a trickle of blood ran down her mouth.

At the sight of her open eyes, he seemed to be relieved. "We must hurry," he said, lifting her gently from the ground and onto his horse. In a moment, he, too, had mounted.

Edana looked about. Her vision was still blurry but she saw that John was lying on the ground in a pool of his own blood and the strongbox which had contained the rents was empty on the ground. The Phoenix spurred on his horse as he held her fast around the waist.

"I'm so dizzy," she whispered.

"It's all right. I won't let you fall."

Edana closed her eyes and let semi-consciousness flow over her, no longer fighting to retain clarity of vision. Against her back, she could feel the warmth of his body and his strong arms encircling her. She felt safe and secure—secure enough to relax and to let darkness envelop her. She did not know how long they rode, but it seemed a long while. She moaned and felt herself being lifted down and carried, then she was aware of being laid down on a thick bedroll and covered with a soft sheepskin. Her head still ached and she did not care where she was, only that she was with this man, and that John was not there.

* * *

Again the rambling house presented itself, and again she saw her other self wandering in the tall grass, then walking toward the house. The ''other'' was worried—she was apprehensive. Edana's dream faded, and she opened her eyes to an unfamiliar reality.

Beside her a fire flickered and over it, a large black pot hung. A mouthwatering aroma steamed up from the pot. Behind her, all was in darkness; in front of her she saw a circle of light. She forced herself up and into a sitting position. ''Hello?'' she said tentatively.

In a moment the Phoenix appeared, looming over her and cutting off the light.

''Where are we?'' she asked.

''In a cave. We're quite safe. How are you feeling? Do you remember anything?''

''My head still aches a little. . . . Yes. I remember. I remember John trying—trying to force himself on me. I remember him hitting me several times.''

''And then?''

''I saw both of you. He was lying on the grass bleeding . . . Oh, heavens! Is he dead?'' Panic swept through her. In spite of the beating he had given her, and in spite of what he had tried to do, she hoped the Phoenix had not killed John.

''Would you grieve if he were?''

''I would grieve for you. I wouldn't want you to have killed him. Then there would be an even larger price on your head.''

He grinned. ''And I agree—the price is quite high enough already. No, he's not dead, though the little coward deserves to die, but never fear, his headache will be far worse than yours.''

Relief flooded over her. ''Tell me what happened.''

He shrugged. ''I was following you. My intention was to steal the rent monies—which, by the way, I have done. I circled round the clearing and found you fighting for your honor with your own brother.''

''He's my adopted brother. He's made advances to me before, but I never thought he would try to—''

"He almost succeeded," the Phoenix replied. He had moved closer to her and he ran his hand through her tangled red hair.

"You're very beautiful," he said in a softer tone. "In spite of your black eye."

She reached up and touched her face. It was sore and she could feel the swelling. "I can't go home this way."

"Perhaps I should not let you go home at all."

"I must go to my father. I don't know what's happening on Mull. I am terribly afraid for him."

"You're a good and faithful daughter. But you must believe me when I tell you your brother is dangerous. You must never allow yourself to be alone with him again. And I'll not send you home right away; you will stay until you're stronger."

"Here in this cave? Are we staying here?"

"No. I can't risk that. I'll take you to friends, and when you're better, they will take you home. They will say they found you wandering about, unable to remember what happened."

"How do you know you can trust me?"

"I know you will not betray me—your own lips have shown me that."

She looked into the eyes of this man who had saved her and who seemed so concerned with her condition. "I asked before and you refused. Grant me my wish now. I want to see you. I want to know who you really are."

"My answer is the same as before," the Phoenix whispered. "You must promise me you will stay away from your brother. I want no one taking liberties with you."

With those words he bent and kissed her on the lips. She felt that wonderful sensation she so well remembered from their last encounter. She was limp in his arms and she could feel his hands moving across her back. But how could she feel this way in the arms of a man she did not know, who would not even show her his face? She felt strongly toward him, there was no denying it. She put her arms around him and kissed him back hungrily as he kissed her, on the throat, ears, and lips.

"You are a dream, a temptation," he whispered in her ear, even as he brushed her neck with his lips again. "One day soon we will be together."

He held her tightly and she shivered as he pressed to her. But he withdrew suddenly and looked at her. "If we begin," he said, looking into her eyes, "we will never stop."

Edana could not speak. She wanted him, and at the same time, she was afraid. "Tell me why you take such chances."

"I think you know. I think you understand these matters better than you wish to reveal."

"Perhaps I do. Most certainly I know what is said about you and your reasons for stealing. But I want to hear your reasons from your own lips. As you will not reveal yourself to me, at least tell me yourself why you rob and steal."

"I want to force the landlords to see to the needs of their tenants. I want to discourage support for the Act of Union, because it will give some of the most unscrupulous landlords more power. The British reward some and punish others. They play on old hatreds and create new ones. It pleases the British to keep us as we are, a nation divided."

"Yes," she answered, understanding fully that as long as severe divisions remained, the clans could not garner the strength to overthrow their British masters. It had been so since the twelfth century, and so it was today.

"What will you do with the rent monies you have taken from us?"

"Give it to those who need it. Your father was a just man, but he is no longer in charge of your estates, my woman."

Edana could not argue with him. Truth be known, she did not want George, John, and Katherine to have the rent monies. "But if you're caught, you'll be hanged," she said with concern.

"I'll try to see that does not happen."

"I still yearn to see your face. Do you use your own voice when you speak to me, or am I correct that you disguise it as well?"

"My disguise is complete."

"I will know you someday," she returned.

"You will, I promise." He turned to stir the pot.

"I'm hungry," she said with a smile.

He took two metal bowls from his pack, a ladle, and spoons.

He dished up two bowls of the thick stew, and, using a heavy cloth as a holder, set them down.

Edana watched as steam rose from the stew and evaporated into the darkness of the cave. When it was cool enough, she began eating.

"When will you take me to these friends?"

"In the morning. But I warn you, I must blindfold you before we leave this place. I don't want you to know where we are."

She nodded and ate some more of the stew. His precautions were elaborate but she felt he was truly trying to protect her.

When they finished eating, he put everything away and laid out his own bedroll next to hers. Gradually, as she watched in silence, the fire grew smaller, though the embers would last through the cold night and offer warmth. He stretched out behind her and put his arm around her waist. She felt him next to her, his body heat hot on her back, his strength comforting. She longed for him to hold her tighter and she felt certain he wanted to take her, but he did not. They lay quietly like two lovers bundled together before their wedding night. He held her tenderly, to keep her from the cold, and she responded by curling up into the shape of his body. For the first time in many months, she felt truly happy, and it ceased to matter that she had seen nothing but his eyes and had never even heard his true voice.

George stood in the center of the grand hall. Behind him a splendid tapestry covered half the wall. Once, long ago, there had been a throne beneath the tapestry. It was gone now, and in its place were a large dining table and twelve high-backed chairs. The room was used for formal occasions, but in recent years, there had been no formal occasion.

George's lips were pursed together and his body stance portrayed his anger. "I don't understand how you allowed this to happen," he said, staring hard at his brother.

"It just happened. We were overpowered. The guards ran away, and Edana— I presume she was kidnapped, because when I regained consciousness, she wasn't there." John marveled at the calm in his voice. But what would he do if Edana was all right—if she returned? She would tell George everything. He trembled slightly but felt confident his fears were not evident.

"How could one man overcome three?" George pressed.

John hardly could admit that he and the guards had been separated at the time of the robbery. The truth was, he had paid off the guards and told them not to return to Mull. "I told you, they ran away and left me to fight alone. Good Lord, look at me! I'm injured. I could have been killed. This Phoenix is a giant—he hardly seemed human!"

It certainly appeared that he had put up a struggle even if the truth was that he had been in an awkward position at the time. He was severely beaten, nonetheless. The Phoenix had strength and fighting skills that were simply overwhelming.

"It's not as if I didn't fight back," John stammered on defensively. "And it wasn't one man—there were five. Yes, there were at least five."

George raised his brow skeptically. "I thought you were attacked by that hooded highwayman, the so-called Phoenix?"

"Yes, I was. He was their leader."

"The Phoenix usually works alone."

"Well, he was not alone this time," John insisted. Then, in a moment of bravado, he looked into his brother's eyes. "You should have sent Moira's father to collect the rents. He would have taken a troop of clansmen. And who are you to be making all the decisions, anyway?"

"Katherine has asked me to look after things." George smiled. He wanted to see the look on John's face when he learned what had transpired in the weeks he had been gone. Still, his enjoyment was badly curtailed by the loss of so much money.

"Katherine? Our father's nurse and, I presume, your mistress? What has she to do with anything?"

George smirked. "Our father's nurse no longer. Our father married her several days ago. She is now his wife."

"Wife!" John stepped backward and nearly fell over a stool. "How could this be? How could you allow such a thing to happen?"

George smiled. "Let it happen? How was I to prevent it?

Should our father not have some pleasure? I am shocked to see that you would deny him anything," George said sarcastically.

"Our father is incompetent. He's demented, and Katherine is a fortune hunter."

George kept his facial expression impassive. John would soon learn the master plan. In the meantime George rather relished Edana's disappearance. Perhaps this rogue had stolen her away to be his mistress. She was certainly beautiful enough to inspire such an act. He and Katherine had discussed various ways of ridding themselves of her; now, it seemed, fate had intervened. "Katherine wants to leave Mull and move to the mainland estate. I agree with her decision. Our father can receive better care there."

John scowled at his brother even though this was one decision with which he did not disagree. "When will this move be made?"

"As soon as possible."

George smiled and attempted to look as pious as possible. "We can only hope Edana is safe."

In her room, Katherine sat before her mirror and brushed her long, dark hair. "So—Edana has disappeared."

"Along with the rent monies," George added sullenly.

"This man will be found. We'll recover the money eventually."

"What makes you so confident? He's been on the loose for some time."

"I hear things. I've heard they are close to an arrest."

"And what about Edana? We must at least appear to be concerned."

"I rather imagine she will turn up, though no doubt she will have been forced into a relationship with this criminal. Unhappily, that will make it harder to marry her off."

"My father promised she could choose her own husband."

"Your father will change his mind. She will marry a man of our choosing. It gets rid of her, and a good marriage will be beneficial."

"And if she does not return?"

Katherine shrugged. "Then good riddance to her. It is one less problem to attend."

"And what about John?"

"We'll deal with him later."

George looked at her image in the mirror. He was enraptured with her. He walked up behind her and ran his hands over her silky shoulders. She directed his hand down her chemise and smiled at her own image. "Pleasure me," she said.

He did not ask if she would reciprocate. Sometimes she did not, but usually she did, and in a most novel and delightful way.

Edana sat in the parlor, trying to conceive of all that had happened in her absence. Katherine and her father, married! She could not imagine how such a thing had come to pass, but as awful as it was, she had no choice but to accept it. She well understood her father's condition, and she now understood that he had been in some way coerced or drugged.

John sat across from her. He had told her about the marriage, and it was clear that he was not at all pleased.

"I'm so glad I'm the first to talk with you." He leaned over, a sense of urgency in his voice. "In the name of heaven, Edana, you mustn't tell them anything about what happened."

Edana stared at him hard and noted the trembling in his hand. She had absolutely no intention of allowing him to wiggle off the hook.

"You mean that I am to keep secret the fact that you were overcome by a highwayman while trying to force yourself on me?"

"Yes. George is furious. God knows what he might do if he knew how it happened."

"Just what did you tell him?" Edana asked.

"That there was more than one man. Well, there might have been."

"There was only one, the Phoenix. And had you not been forcing yourself on me, you might have been able to prevent the robbery."

"You must not tell."

"I will not tell, if you stay away from me. If you ever touch me again I shall tell them everything, do you understand? They will know just how much you, and you alone, are to blame for the loss of the rents. Furthermore, I shall see you prosecuted." She narrowed her eyes. "Trust me, John, I'll see you in jail if you don't leave me alone."

John was stunned by her strength. "I'll stay away," he promised. Then John leaned forward. "Something is going on between George and Katherine." If she hadn't noticed, he felt he should point it out.

"No doubt," Edana replied. "But you don't have our father's best interests at heart. You're concerned only about what will happen to you."

"Are you telling me you think this marriage is a good thing?"

Edana shook her head. "I am not telling you anything. I have to talk to Father; I have to talk to Katherine." She did not say she would have to speak to Moira, too, but she turned away from her brother. "Just remember—stay away from me," she warned again.

He was silent as she left the room. Silent and afraid, she thought. Good. John was one person she wanted afraid of her.

The dining table was set in a way that reflected the changes that had taken place. George now sat at the head of the table and Katherine at the foot. Edana sat across from John.

"I do apologize," Katherine said in a concerned voice. "Your return home ought to be a grand celebration. But as you can see, everything is being packed for the move to the mainland."

"I did not expect a grand celebration."

"Nonetheless, my dear, we're all glad to have you back safe and sound. I've told your father, and though he is unable to speak, I feel certain he understood."

"I want to see him," Edana pressed.

"Tomorrow morning, my dear. He is much better during the morning hours."

Katherine appeared nothing if not solicitous, Edana thought.

"We know you've had a terrible ordeal. It was so fortunate

that these kind people found you wandering about. We shall see they are rewarded."

"Yes, an ordeal indeed," Edana repeated. Though in fact she was thinking of John rather than the time she had spent with the Phoenix.

"Do you remember much? Did you ever see his face? The authorities do so want a description."

"I hardly remember anything. I was unconscious. I only remember . . . Well, I can't talk about it—it's too personal, too overwhelming." She spoke in a low voice and turned away so Katherine could not see her face. They had all made the assumption that she had been raped, and she did not correct them. They wanted to marry her off, and if she were not a virgin, a husband would be much harder to find. It was difficult not to smile—if the Phoenix had taken her, it certainly would not have been rape. There had been more than one moment when she knew she would give herself to him if he continued caressing and kissing her.

"Of course you can't talk about it. Poor, dear girl."

Edana wanted to tell Katherine not to pretend to care. But she realized that the situation called for her to be careful. Apart from Moira, she had no allies. But she had not yet seen Moira.

"Where is your wife?" Edana asked, turning to George. Then she added sweetly, "Your wife and my best friend."

"She is with her parents. She went for a visit just after you left."

Edana's heart sank. Moira had been gone and would not know the details of how this unseemly marriage between Katherine and her father had taken place.

"Of course, she will rejoin us as soon as the move is made."

Edana looked from face to face. All her senses warned that she stood alone in this dangerous situation. John was jealous and unstable. George was ambitious and, she suspected, had some arrangement with Katherine. Her father was demented and deathly ill, and Katherine was the person on whom he had to depend. Her greatest concern was for the man who had been her father and who had loved her, but she knew that there was far more to it than her personal concerns. At stake was clan leadership, and that included the wealth of the clan chieftain as well as the direction the clan would take politically. Katherine would most assuredly see that her British friends appointed George to the Scottish Parliament. Once appointed, Edana was certain George would do whatever Katherine suggested.

"I know you've had a very difficult time, my dear," Katherine said slowly, as the food was being passed around the table. "But I should like you to consider marriage sometime soon. Not now, naturally, but after we move to the mainland. I know that having you married would make your father very happy indeed. Of course, it will be more difficult now to find a husband, but I'm sure we will succeed if we set our minds to the task."

Edana did not bother to point out that her father probably would not know it if she were married. She was glad they believed she was no longer a virgin; it would slow down their plans. She was tempted to burst out and scream all the thoughts that filled her mind, but at this moment she dared not. She would have to keep her own counsel while being excessively careful.

"I shall consider it," she replied, as she began eating. She wanted nothing but to get away from them. They were greedy and dangerous—they were plotting—and again she shivered with fear for her father. George, John, and Katherine all deserved each other, but her father did not deserve any of them.

Edana stole a glance at Katherine. George was nasty and selfish; John was no better. Katherine was calculating, and she would direct George, whom she no doubt had chosen as the weaker of the two. On the way to see his friends, Edana had told the Phoenix all about her suspicions. He had promised to give her fears some thought. He also had promised to return to her and try to help. But he did not know about the marriage. Surely he would agree with her—Katherine's marriage to her father was a new and dangerous development. Sadly, it was no doubt part of a larger plot. She hoped he would come soon.

Chapter Five

February 1708

The MacLean house on the mainland was not a simple tower house, but rather a rambling stone edifice, with four square turrets and some twenty-two rooms. Long ago Donald MacLean had chosen to live on Mull because it was quieter, and indeed because his ancestral home on Mull was smaller. The cavernous hallways and high ceilings gave the mainland house a colder feel, even though its setting among the hills and between two meandering streams was more picturesque.

"At least we're together again," Edana said, as she and Moira walked about the well-kept grounds.

"I could do nothing to prevent the marriage between Katherine and your father," Moira said dejectedly. "I was sent away as soon as you and John left."

Edana felt like she would cry at any moment, and yet she knew full well that tears would not save her father. "My father is a prisoner of his mind. He has no idea what is happening. He grows weaker by the day. Moira, I think it's possible that he's being poisoned."

"Is there no one to whom you can turn?"

Edana shook her head. "Katherine is protected by the author-ities. They will do nothing. After all, if my father dies, they will just have one less clan chieftain to worry about."

"There must be someone," Moira said.

Edana shook her head in despair. As always she thought of the Phoenix, but she could not discuss her feelings for him with Moira. She ached for her mysterious love, and in the dark of the night he came to her in dreams. But he had not returned, and she was perplexed by his absence. She had been certain he cared for her, and was just as certain he would help her find a way to fight Katherine.

Edana kicked at the hard ground. It was a miracle there wasn't any snow. There had been snow in December and early January, but it had melted during an unusual thaw late in Janu-ary. Then it had grown bitterly cold again, and now the barren ground was once again frozen.

She was nearing her eighteenth birthday but she knew it would not be a happy event. She was filled with frustration, anger, and fear. Evil surrounded her father and she felt as helpless as she knew him to be. To make matters worse, Kather-ine was speaking more often of the need for Edana to make a good marriage. Edana did not openly object, but secretly she vowed she would run away if a marriage she did not approve of was arranged. Still, the haunting question remained—run to where? She was trapped by circumstances; she could not leave her father even though she could not help him.

"Katherine is actively seeking a marriage for me," Edana confided. "Hopefully everyone will want an unsullied wife."

Edana did not like lying to Moira about what happened— or, more to the point, had *not* happened—when she had been abducted. But she judged it unwise to tell anyone the truth. It was not that she did not trust her friend; it was that Moira was afraid of George, and Edana feared George might somehow get the truth out of Moira. As she thought about it, she realized that that was why the Phoenix didn't reveal himself to her. He did not trust those who surrounded her.

Edana glanced again at Moira. "You don't seem yourself at all," Edana commented.

In fact, Moira's condition was alarming. During the months they had been separated, she had grown thinner and paler. She lacked her former zest for life, as if her spirit were broken.

"Something terrible has happened," Moira confided, in a near whisper, though in fact they were quite alone.

Edana stopped walking and turned to face her friend. "What is it?"

"I am with child. As little as he comes to my bed, George has impregnated me."

Moira's eyes filled with tears and she trembled. "I fear for my child just as you are afraid for your father," she said, looking into Edana's face. "George loves Katherine. I know it. I know they sleep together. She will be furious because I am pregnant. If I have a son—"

Edana reached out and took Moira's hand. Naturally she feared for her child. If she had a son, he would be heir to the estate.

"I believe Katherine will do anything to gain power. You think your father is being poisoned—I, too, believe he is being slowly poisoned. I believe Katherine and George have planned this together. Do you think she would do these things and let a male heir live to challenge her? She's a monster."

Edana gripped Moira's hand harder.

"I cannot bear to lose you, to be alone," Edana murmured. "But you must ask George to send you home. Tell him anything, but leave this place, Moira. I believe you are right—Katherine will stop at nothing to protect her position."

"What about George?" Moira asked.

"He is her accomplice, but when the time is right, when she has dealt with all of us, then I think she will rid herself of George, too. I don't know exactly how she will accomplish all this, I only know she has powerful allies."

Moira bit her lip. "I hate leaving you, my sister."

"You must."

Moira nodded. "I shall speak to George tonight. I'll tell him I want to live at home. He'll be glad to let me go."

Edana embraced Moira. "Go back to Mull. Save your child. Be safe but know I will miss you."

* * *

Edana lay staring at the ceiling of the room to which Katherine had ordered her things brought. It was a small room on the top floor. It was as far from her father and Katherine's room as one could possibly get and still be within the same walls.

George's room was next to the one occupied by Katherine. Her father's room was on the other side of Katherine's room and it was always locked. John's room, like her own, was as far from Katherine and George as possible, but in the other wing. Not that John was there. He had taken to staying away for long periods of time, returning only now and again.

"Not that I miss him," Edana whispered to herself.

The night was bright and outside her window, across the courtyard, the flag that bore the family crest fluttered in the night breeze. The shadow of it danced on her wall, sometimes blocking the light from the rising moon. In her mind, she could see the crest—it was a tower house, an artistic rendition of the MacLean tower house on Mull. It looked much like the rook on a chessboard. Around the edges of the crest the family motto, Virtue Mine Honor, was printed neatly in Latin.

"I wonder what my real family crest looks like?" she asked the moon. Of late, perhaps because of her situation, she found herself thinking more about the woman who had given birth to her and the man who had sired her. *I will never know,* she thought, pushing her questions from her mind and returning to her dilemma.

She considered it a wonder that Katherine had not turned her out. She was no blood relation, she was adopted, and now that Donald was incompetent, and George and Katherine were in charge of everything, it amazed her that she had not been sent away. The only reason must have been that in spite of everything, Katherine felt a good marriage might yet be made. Perhaps a marriage Katherine could benefit from.

I am a pawn, Edana thought, and again she tried to find strategy to fight Katherine. "I can't let her get away with this," she said to the mottled ceiling.

At long last, when the full moon had disappeared behind a

cloud and the shadow of the flag had ceased dancing on her wall, Edana fell into a deep sleep.

She was by a clear, blue meandering stream. It had a pebble bottom, and flowed rapidly over jagged rocks. On either side of the stream, the green grass lay like a velvet carpet and flowers gave off a sweet aroma. Winter was gone; it was warm and the sun shone brightly.

At this point, her "other" appeared. She was identical to Edana, with flowing red-gold hair, green eyes, and a slender body. She took both of Edana's hands and helped her up. There were no words spoken, but Edana understood that she must follow. They walked by the stream in silence and then her "other" disappeared and Edana was alone. She searched the forest with her eyes and turned about suddenly to see the Phoenix. He was, as always, dressed in a flowing black cape and a hood covered his head and face. He did not speak in her dream but pulled her gently into his arms and began kissing her. First her lips, then her neck. As if by magic, her clothes fell away and he was kissing her bare breasts, nursing her nipples, tenderly touching her inner thighs. There was a touch of magic as his fingers played on her flesh. Her skin was cool to the touch, but just beneath the surface her blood was hot, and her breath came in short pants as he touched that special place.

She moaned slightly and then felt the gentle sensation of a mild, dream-induced throbbing. She opened her eyes and found she was damp with perspiration and her heart was beating more rapidly than usual. Her room was totally dark, and she lay in the black silence, still basking in the sheer pleasure of her dream. Never had her "other" been present in the same dream as the Phoenix, though she dreamt of both often.

She turned again on her side and curled into a ball. This would all end—she had to do something. Silently she vowed she would try to see her father in the morning.

* * *

Edana dressed quickly and left her room, determined to see her father. She wondered what excuse Katherine would give her this time. Of course, she might just simply refuse. Katherine needed no excuses, although until now she always had had one.

Edana hurried down the hall in the west wing, only to see George, John, and Katherine all standing outside the bedroom door. The stance of their bodies betrayed the fact that something was wrong. George and John were slightly slumped; Katherine stood straight, but she was still in her robe and her usually well-coifed hair was loose and tangled. Edana knew before she reached them that something terrible had happened. She knew before they could say anything.

"Father—" The word was on her lips.

"He died last night in his sleep," Katherine said. She did not lift her eyes to look into Edana's. Edana stared hard at her, but Katherine was a superb actress; she didn't even flinch under Edana's accusative look.

"It was to be expected," George muttered. "His condition had grown worse."

John's face was impassive but clearly he believed them.

"I shall make the funeral arrangements right away," Katherine said calmly.

"There are many who should be invited," George added. "I'll help you draw up a list."

Edana turned away from them and entered the room. There, in the center of the bed, Donald MacLean lay, his eyes closed, his body still.

She went to his side and took his hand in hers. It was cold and lifeless but she held it tightly. She turned his wrinkled hand over in her own and frowned at his yellowed nails. She dropped his hand and went to the window and opened the drapes. Then, she returned to the bed. Donald MacLean's whole body was jaundiced and his skin had many lesions. Surely, this was poison! She was no medicine woman, but had read that arsenic poisoning caused the nails and skin to yellow. A cold chill ran through her as her worst suspicions were confirmed. Had Katherine done this on her own, or had George helped her? The crime of patricide was monstrous! George was weak, stupid, and greedy, but could he have helped plan and carry out the murder of his own father? Edana's head filled with questions and again she cautioned herself to be careful. If George and Katherine would kill Donald MacLean, they would surely not hesitate to kill her.

She leaned over and kissed her father's cold cheek. "There will be justice," she whispered. At this moment she did not know exactly how the justice she promised would be achieved, only that she would do everything she could.

Edana stood up and left the room. Anger filled her—anger that she had not been able to stop this; anger because she feared being the next victim; anger that such a thing could happen. Yet Carolyn's voice and the wisdom she had been taught came back to her. She would not act till the time was right; she would not reveal her thoughts or her long-held suspicions.

I must wait, she thought to herself.

Bram Chisholm paced his den, drink in hand. "You're so close, and yet so far," he said aloud, thinking of Edana. Never in his whole life had he felt so confined, but at the moment he could not go to her as the Phoenix.

He looked down at his leg. It was nearly healed, but even when it was, he could not risk an appearance as the Phoenix. His compatriot had been hanged and he had been wounded. There were search parties everywhere and there was nothing to do but lie low and wait. In fact he had left the area entirely for some time, choosing to recover in London. His main task was to get information from the British. They believed him to be a staunch supporter.

Bram stopped pacing and looked up as his manservant paused in the doorway.

"Superintendent Crane is here to see you, sir."

Think of the devil and he appears, Bram thought. "Show him in."

In a moment Superintendent Crane was shown in.

"I hope I'm not intruding."

"Not at all, old man. Come in, have a chair. Let me fix you a scotch."

"Sometimes I think your estate is the only bit of civilization in this part of Scotland."

Bram forced a smile, though he was well aware of Crane's dislike for the land he himself loved so much.

"I rather thought you found solace in Katherine MacLean. Now that she's moved to the mainland you should be able to see her more often."

"Quite so. But just because I find her intriguing does not mean I'm fond of that place she's moved to—it's a veritable barn."

"Well, I wouldn't expect you to pursue her there; after all her husband might take offense." It was a prodding comment and he hoped to learn something, anything, that would tell him how Edana was faring.

"Her husband has died. In fact, that's what I came about. I want you to go to the funeral with me. It's past time you met Katherine. After all, you two are the only supporters of the union in the district."

Bram fought to keep his expression the same. Inside, he wanted to run to Edana. She was alone in a house full of vipers. But he knew he could not—at least he could not appear as the Phoenix. He could appear as Bram Chisholm, and he decided he would. He had to see her. It had been a long while, far too long, and worse yet, she had been right. Her father had been in mortal danger. Guilt flooded over him. Through no fault of his own, he had broken his promise to her. "I'd be glad to attend with you," he said, pouring another drink.

Crane sipped his own drink and looked satisfied. "Good, I hate going to these things alone."

"Well, someone must stop you dancing with the merry widow, Crane. It would be unseemly."

Crane made a guffaw. "You don't know Katherine," he returned.

The Great Hall was festooned with tartans and with garlands made of fir branches, and there were tables laden with food. Clan leaders came from far and wide, but the atmosphere was heavy with tension and Edana could feel it as she walked among the invited guests. Many of Donald MacLean's oldest friends and allies had come or sent representatives, but there were also newcomers—landowners and merchants who supported the Act of Union, and there were British government representatives as well. Those who did not support the British eyed Katherine and George suspiciously and avoided those few clan chieftains who had given their allegiance to the union.

Yes, she thought miserably, her father's funeral was a mockery, a mixing of oil and water, a party for Katherine and George to let their pro-British allegiances be known.

As was the custom at a Highland wake, her father lay in state. The belief, passed on from generation to generation, was that if the noise from the wake did not cause the corpse to awaken, then he was truly dead and could be safely buried. Hence the pipes played loudly and people spoke in natural voices rather than hushed tones.

Edana was dressed in black, as was Katherine. Edanas's long red hair was pulled back and tied neatly behind her head. Unlike everyone else, she stood near the coffin, her hands folded in front of her.

"You must be Edana," a male voice said from behind her.

Edana turned about to face a tall, good-looking man with dark hair and piercing brown eyes. His build was muscular and he looked down at her with a knowing smile.

"I am," she answered. "And who might you be?"

"Bram Chisholm, a friend of Superintendent Crane."

That he immediately identified himself as a British supporter surprised her. "Then I suppose you know my stepmother, as well."

"Yes, I know her."

Edana simply looked at him. Vaguely she wondered if he knew Katherine in the biblical sense, or was simply a friend. "She hasn't been my stepmother long," Edana said coldly. She saw no need to be nice to this man, whoever he was. He was certainly not one of her father's old friends. He was dressed in the dark blue tartan of Clan Chisholm. He wore a heavy gold pin with his crest and its motto, I Am Fierce with the Fierce.

"I've come here from Inverness-shire," he said, stepping a little closer to her.

"Many people have come—not all were known to my father," she answered.

"Frankly, I came to be with my old friend Crane, and because I heard that Edana MacLean was the most beautiful woman in the district, perhaps in all of the Highlands."

He could hardly contain himself. Being this close to her and not revealing himself was a new kind of torture. He wanted to pull her into his arms and tell her why he had not come to her as the Phoenix. He wanted to tell her how terrible he felt about her father's death.

"I don't trust those who exaggerate," Edana returned. Did he think her an idiot child, subject to flattery? What exactly did this stranger want?

"I'm not exaggerating. I have heard of your beauty from several people."

"I have heard no such idle talk," she said crisply. "I am in mourning for a man of great principle and virtue. I should appreciate it if you would leave me alone."

He raised his brow and lifted his glass of wine. Then he turned and walked away so as to hide his admiration for this young woman who would truly express herself to a man she perceived as the enemy.

Edana watched as this Bram Chisholm walked across the room. Katherine was standing next to Superintendent Holden Crane, the British representative, and George stood to one side. John was nowhere to be seen, but she supposed he had found some young woman with whom to occupy himself. Sadly, only new conquests seemed to jar him out of the mood he had been in since their return. Afraid she would tell George and Katherine the exact circumstances of how the rents had been lost, he avoided her as promised. But he was also upset by their father's marriage to Katherine and he sulked about, his anger and jealousy quite evident.

Katherine held out both her hands to greet Bram Chisholm and she stood very close to him. Chisholm touched Katherine's arm and Edana watched, fascinated. George was like a pussycat. He was so smitten with Katherine that he did her bidding without so much as a second thought. It seemed he did not have the sense to notice that he was not the only man in Katherine's circle. *I wonder how many lovers you have?* Edana asked herself, as she watched Katherine openly flirt with one man after another. And who was this Bram Chisholm? He, too, seemed to be close to Katherine. He was dressed well and appeared to be rich. She could not help wondering what he wanted, and why he had come to her father's wake. Edana watched as Chisholm gave Katherine a little hug. He shook hands with Superintendent Crane, and then he left.

Katherine caught Edana's eye and motioned her to join her and Superintendent Crane. Reluctantly Edana walked over to them.

"Superintendent Crane has some very important news for you, Edana."

Superintendent Crane smiled at her knowingly. "I have good news, my dear. I want you to know that the man who raped you and stole the rent money has been captured and hanged. Justice has been done."

Edana's mouth opened in shock but her voice was lost. The room seemed to be spinning about. He had been captured? That was why he had not come to her. . . . And hanged! She wanted to throw herself on the floor and wail, but she was frozen in horror.

"Poor girl. This must be terrible for you," Crane was saying as he grasped her arm.

"I have to lie down," Edana managed. She whirled about and fled the room. Dead? The Phoenix was dead? She ran up the stairs and through the long corridors. She ran into her room and bolted the door. She threw herself on the bed, and only then did she let her tears flow.

Murray Lachlan felt a fury deep within his soul. He had come to the mainland to see John MacLean, to tell him, without betraying his own daughter, what he thought. He wanted John to explode and in some way punish George, as he himself could not.

I'll not let them get away with it! he vowed over and over, as he waited in the village tavern for young John MacLean to meet him.

He stared into his warm ale and tried to understand what had happened, though he knew full well it was all the doing of that woman—the one who had come from Edinburgh and married old MacQuarrie.

He had arranged for Moira to marry George MacLean for the best of reasons. She would live comfortably, and his own position would be bettered. But that had certainly not been the result. Moira had returned pregnant, frightened, and with tales of the evil and immoral behavior that had taken place in the house of Donald MacLean before he died. Was young John so stupid that he did not realize that Katherine MacQuarrie and his own brother could jeopardize his future?

John MacLean, hands in his pockets, swaggered into the tavern. He saw Lachlan and walked briskly to where he was seated. "You're a long way from home," he said as he sat down.

"I was afraid you might not get my message."

"What brings you here?"

"Concern," Lachlan replied, as he lifted his beer and sipped it. "I've been close to your family all my life. You're father was more than a relative and employer. He was my friend."

John nodded begrudgingly. The tavern maid brought him some ale and he flipped a coin down the front of her low-cut dress, lodging it between her ample breasts. She smiled engagingly at him and whirled away.

"Sorry about Moira. My brother didn't treat her well." Moira was not really of interest to him, but he liked Lachlan, who had taught him to shoot. He'd spent many an early morning in the duck blind with the man.

Lachlan narrowed his eyes. John MacLean was a master of understatement. "He didn't treat her well because he is your stepmother's lover."

John made a face. Did everyone know that George and Katherine were lovers? "I know about Katherine and George," he admitted.

"And how do you sleep at night? I've got it on good authority that your father was probably murdered. I've heard you're next."

Lachlan congratulated himself on his tactless stating of the possibilities. John would think his information came from Moira. The young man was only concerned with women. If John was a body of water, he'd be a placid lake; this boy was anything but swift. Apparently the only thing he did quickly was lift his kilt.

"I suppose you might be right," John stuttered. "If I die, Katherine and George will share all the wealth."

"I imagine that's the idea," Lachlan said in disgust. Moira was quite right. It was better that no one know about the child. He wondered how a woman like Carolyn MacLean could have had two such sons. One was concerned only with sex and hadn't a brain in his head, and the other was ambitious, conniving, thieving, and possibly a murderer. Unfortunately, he had hooked himself up with an intelligent and ruthless woman who would stop at nothing to gain power. At the moment she seemed to be selling out Scotland. Donald MacLean—had he not been stricken—never would have supported the Act of Union. Not that John MacLean would care about that aspect of Katherine's power. He would only care about the money and any possible danger to himself.

John gulped down his ale. "Thanks," he said under his breath. "You've made me realize I have to do something. I'll take care of this."

Lachlan smiled as he watched John MacLean leave. The wolf was among the hens and though he wasn't quite sure what would happen, he felt certain John would cause trouble.

For days, Edana had kept to her room. She had been unable to eat and her sleep was disturbed and filled with nightmares.

At last she emerged from hiding. She could cry no more, but she could not enjoy life, either. Each day she followed the same routine: she worked in her sewing room, she read, and she walked. But nothing erased her dark thoughts. She mourned her parents and now she mourned the hooded stranger she had loved.

Edana walked down to the stream and then made her way home by a circuitous route. As she approached the front of the house, she saw a fine carriage out front and stopped to puzzle over it. She circled the carriage and when she reached the far side, she saw the Chisholm crest. What could have brought Bram Chisholm back to the MacLeans'? Her father had been buried nearly a month. It was now late March and the brisk winds had come to dry the moisture left by the melting snow.

She glanced up at the sky and saw the rapidly moving dark clouds. George was away in Inveraray and John was not about. How convenient that Katherine was alone when this handsome British supporter should come to call—and how very odd that he was still in the district.

She headed round the side of the castle, and though it was a fair walk, she entered through a door on the end of the far west wing. Then she made her way down the long corridors and headed for the study. That was where Katherine would receive her guest, and with a little luck, Edana thought, she would probably be able to hear their conversation from the room next door. Many of the partitions between rooms were artificial and not made of stone, as one might have imagined when looking at the building from outside.

Inside, where on dull days light did not penetrate, candles dimly lit the corridors. She walked softly and, with equal stealth, let herself into the library, the room beside the study.

She put her ear to the wall and listened. At first, she heard only the tinkle of crystal. No doubt they were having a glass of wine, or perhaps something stronger. It was the custom when a visitor arrived on a cold day. Surely this late in the day, and with a storm coming in, he would spend the night. Again she thought how convenient that was for Katherine, and she wondered if Katherine had expected this Bram Chisholm, or whether, in fact, it was only a coincidence that neither George nor John was home.

"I hope the brandy is to your liking," Edana heard Katherine purr. Katherine used a special voice when she spoke to men

with whom she was flirting. It was a soupy, thick voice, a voice
that was quite unnatural.

"Let me assure you that everything hereabouts is to my
liking," Bram Chisholm replied.

"I'm delighted that you decided to remain in the district for
a time. It gives us the opportunity to get to know one another
better."

Katherine was most certainly attempting to seduce this man.
Clearly George was not enough to satisfy her lustfulness; nor
was Donald MacLean's wealth enough to satisfy her greed.

If Bram Chisholm was not a British supporter and apparently
a friend of Katherine's, Edana might have felt some duty to
warn him. But as he was both, she felt no such need.

She did admit to being curious, however. She told herself
that anything and everything she learned about Katherine might
prove useful. Her father was dead and her only love had been
hanged by those Katherine supported. Her sole reason for exis-
tence, as she now saw it, was to bring Katherine to justice. It was
that desire that had given Edana the strength to stop weeping and
rejoin the world.

For the moment, no matter how difficult, she had decided
to give George the benefit of the doubt and to believe he did
not know that Katherine had poisoned their father.

She leaned against the wall again and cursed under her breath.
They must have moved away, because although she could hear
voices, she could not make out what they were saying. After
a time, she heard the door to the study open and, to her surprise,
Bram Chisholm left. He did not spend the night as she had
thought he might.

Bram Chisholm settled down in the apartment provided for
him in Fort William. Holden Crane, the superintendent, was
wonderfully accommodating to those he perceived as supporters.

Fort William was near Inverlochy. It looked as if a drunkard
had designed it. It was built in the form of a somewhat lopsided
star, on a spit of land at the mouth of the River Nevis, looking
across Loch Linnhe toward the rolling hills of Ardgour. This

was a place that already had a history—a history both wildly romantic and horrendously tragic.

Bram thought of Katherine MacQuarrie, a woman who had appeared virtually out of nowhere to deliver not one, but two important clans into the hands of British. He was uncertain as to whether her motives were political or simply a result of personal greed. Crane had hinted they were both. It hardly mattered; the result was the same.

He shook his head in disgust. He had spent some time considering exactly what strategy to employ when dealing with Katherine. It was not just Katherine with whom he was concerned. He thought endlessly about the beautiful and headstrong Edana, adopted daughter of Donald MacLean. She was in severe danger; Katherine would either marry her off or plot her demise. This was a matter he had to see to immediately, but as surely as he knew he must take Edana beyond Katherine's reach, he also knew he must continue to hide his identity from her. She was young, adventurous, and idealistic. It was still unsafe for her to know the truth.

The knock on the door startled him and he called out, "Yes, what is it?"

"You have a guest, sir," the young private returned from the other side of the door.

Bram glanced around the room. It was a quite proper office, with the bedroom being down a hall and around the corner. There were chairs and a desk. The window looked out on the mist-shrouded hills in the distance. He supposed he could entertain here as well as in any of the public rooms in the fort. "Send my guest in," he called out.

"Yes, sir."

He listened as the steps disappeared down the corridor. Clearly the visitor had been kept waiting elsewhere. He smiled; even for civilian guests this place was very much a military installation.

He heard more steps in the hallway, and in a minute the door opened and he saw Katherine. She had opened the door but did not step inside. Instead, she stood framed in the doorway looking expectant as well as stunning.

Her dark cloak was trimmed in white fur while her dark hair

framed her angular face. She was an unusually beautiful woman but he thought her personality shone through and gave her a coldness, a calculated beauty of which he personally felt wary. Immediately he thought of Edana. She, too, was a beauty, and she was made even lovelier by her kindness and concern for others, by the fact that her face glowed with her inner beauty as well as her natural endowments.

"What a surprise," he said, stepping forward to kiss Katherine's hand.

In actual fact it was not a surprise at all. She had flirted with him openly and boldly at her husband's funeral, and when he had visited. He had fully expected her to appear and follow up on what she perceived as a new conquest.

She had MacLean's power and money, since in addition to her own inheritance she controlled everything until George, John, and Edana were twenty-five, though George, as the eldest son, had the right to make certain decisions such as whom his sister would marry. But there was no doubt in Bram's mind that since Katherine ruled George with an iron hand, she would control his money even after he was twenty-five. As she was unable to control the other two, they might well not live to their twenty-fifth birthdays. Moreover, Katherine was clearly sleeping with Crane, and heaven knew who else. Did she really want him now, as well? Even if she left him somewhat cold, her appetites fascinated him.

"I hope you don't regard this visit as too forward of me."

Her voice was like thick syrup, and her eyes penetrating. He smiled back at her as warmly as possible. "Not at all, dear lady. One always hopes a beautiful woman will be at least a bit forward. It is the content of our dreams."

"You flatter me," she said softly.

"I'm sure you have many flatterers," he replied obliquely. He wondered if she would ever get to the point of this visit.

"I've come because I think our mutual interests in furthering the cause of the government necessitate that we become better friends."

The emphasis of her words dripped with innuendo.

"I think we shall become very good friends," he said, looking into her eyes. "But you will realize that while my guests are exceedingly hospitable, this is not the place to explore new friendships. There is no privacy.'' Two, he thought with humor, could play this game of suggestive seduction.

She did not blush, as most women would have. She smiled, and whispered, ''I quite understand. I should like you to come and visit with me again before you leave the district. As you may know, our rent monies were stolen by a rogue Highlander, a common highwayman, the man who was recently hanged. My stepson, George MacLean, will be leaving tomorrow to see if he can collect a little more from the tenants. It will be quite lonely without him, so I should be pleased to have a visitor.''

''I should be pleased to visit,'' he answered, looking into her eyes but thinking of Edana.

''When shall I expect you?'' Katherine persisted.

''I have business to complete here at Fort William. I will come to you in a week's time.''

''Very good,'' Katherine said, with another devastating smile. ''I shall be looking forward to hunting with you.''

''I shall look forward to hunting as well.'' He kissed her hand again and she turned to leave. In moments she was gone, and he breathed a sigh of relief. His plan, such as it was, was going quite well.

Edana sat bolt upright in bed at the sound of the loud shouting. She shook her head to dispel the sleep and listened. It was John and George. They were shouting at each other loudly, and not just shouting, but exchanging curses.

Edana climbed from her bed and quickly put on her robe. She put on her slippers and ran down the long corridor. They were in the hall and it seemed clear that both had been drinking.

''You're sleeping together! You're both murderers!'' John raged. ''You're plotting to take my inheritance! The two of you are scheming against me!''

Edana stopped short in the doorway; her hand flew to her mouth as she saw George step forward in a fury.

''You're a disgrace!'' he shouted. ''A stupid, dull, womanizing bastard! You accuse me of murder!''

"Yes!" came John's retort. "Yes, I accuse you of murder and of sleeping with our father's wife!"

"I love Katherine and she loves me!"

"And did you love her before you brought her here?"

"Yes! But that doesn't mean I murdered our father!"

"You did! You two conniving devils!"

George slapped his brother hard across the face.

John's eyes narrowed and he faced George stiffly. "That's a challenge," he said bitterly. "It's a challenge I accept. Tomorrow morning at dawn! We'll settle this then!"

"No!" Edana said imploringly. They had been arguing so intently, they had not even seen her.

It wasn't that she deeply loved them; it was more that she knew how displeased her mother would have been. Moreover, no matter who won, there would be one less of them. That played into Katherine's hands.

"This is none of your concern!" George said, turning toward her.

"Mind your own business," John added meanly.

"You must not fight a duel," Edana begged. "It's wrong for brother to turn on brother."

"He should have thought of that before accusing me of murder!" George shouted.

"And he should have thought about it before he committed the murder," John returned.

They both cursed and then stomped off, leaving Edana in the hall, shaking and with tears in her eyes. As surely as she stood in the hall, she knew one of them would be dead in the morning. It was Katherine. Somehow she had engineered this; she could only benefit if John were dead.

Edana clutched the corners of her robe and headed back to her room. Perhaps they would both forget it in the morning. Perhaps they had only been blustering. But deep in her heart, she knew they would not. They were going to fight a duel. One of them was going to die.

Edana opened her eyes in the semi-darkness of her room. It was a cold morning and she stared out the window, trying to ascertain the time. The ground outside was a patchwork quilt of dead grass and squares of dirt. She turned away and swiftly dressed. If only they decided not to go through with this!

She hurried outside, using the side entrance so that no one would see her if they were assembled out back. She cut through the woods and stopped on the far side of the clearing.

A huddle of men was assembled just outside the castle. George and John were there, dressed to duel, as were their seconds. Katherine stood to one side.

Edana felt like a heavy stone. She watched, unable to move, unable to affect the action in any way. Those witnesses present were all men Katherine had brought with her from Mull. They were her men, her witnesses to this grisly event between brothers.

Katherine moved away, but not so far that Edana could not see her. But what did it matter what she saw? She could not stop this, she could only observe, and it hardly mattered what she saw because the authorities would not listen. Whatever Katherine had decided would happen, would happen.

If only John were not so cocky, Edana thought, he might survive. But he thought himself the better shot and clearly believed he would win.

George and John stood back-to-back. They paced off the required distance, then waited. The referee raised his pistol and fired it. The shots rang out—not two, but three. John staggered forward and fell. George staggered too. He was wounded. But John was dead. Edana watched as Katherine put her pistol away. It was her bullet that had killed John. She had shot him in the back of the head the instant he had fired toward George.

Edana covered her mouth with her hand. This woman would stop at nothing! Edana turned and ran deeper into the woods. Dear God! What was she to do? How was she to fight this terrible, evil woman?

Chapter Six

Dread over came Bram Chisholm as he read the message delivered to him. It was from Katherine MacLean and it begged his indulgence in the matter of the invitation issued so recently.

> *I would still very much like to have you visit, but one tragedy seems to follow another for our little family. Please do not think that my brief explanation of events means that I am unconcerned with the horrible event which has taken place.*
>
> *John, always volatile, was drinking heavily. He accused his brother of terrible crimes and then challenged him to a duel. George tried in every way not to fight this awful duel, but John persisted and so the duel was fought. George was shot in the leg and John was killed. It was not meant for brother to turn against brother, but I have been told there was always bad blood between them. These, my dear Mr. Chisholm, are the essential facts of the case, and the reason I must beg you to postpone your visit at least for a short time.*
>
> > *Yours with affection,*
> > *Katherine MacLean.*

How swiftly she had acted! He imagined that a part of the story was true—Katherine doubtless had not intended to move so quickly against John. When the opportunity arose she seized it. But what would happen if the opportunity arose to rid herself of Edana? The answer was frighteningly obvious. Such a moment could come anytime. He vowed to take immediate action. No matter what the obstacles, even if Edana did not understand or agree, he had to get her out of Katherine's clutches. He reread the note and again shook his head. Unspoken was the fact that since George was wounded, he would not be leaving on his planned trip. That meant that when he visited, he would not be alone with Katherine and she would not have the opportunity to try and seduce him. There was no limit to her nerve, he thought sullenly. She might just as well have written, *Don't come—we can't sleep together.* He shook his head. Katherine had succeeded in ridding herself of John; George was temporarily unable to harass the tenants for more rent; and Bram was able to continue a risky game of cat-and-mouse with Katherine.

Yes, he had to act immediately; Edana was in grave danger.

Bram sat down at his writing desk and began to compose a note to Katherine.

My dear Katherine,

I have received your letter with sadness. How dreadful that such a tragic event should come on the heels of your husband's death. Naturally, I fully understand that a prolonged visit at this time would be impossible, but I should very much like to stop by and pay my respects.

Sincerely, Bram Chisholm

* * *

The heavy drapes had been pulled back to let in the maximum amount of light. Katherine stood on the wooden bench, turning slowly, while Edana sat at her feet.

Edana pushed the pin into place and looked up at Katherine. "That's the last pin," she said. "I'm ready to start hemming now."

"Excellent. I do hope it will be ready for tomorrow. We have a guest coming."

"Who?" Edana asked.

Katherine had asked her to hem up the gown, and she had agreed only because she had no reason not to agree. As horrified as she was with all that had happened, Edana had decided it was dangerous to hint that she suspected foul play in any way, let alone allow Katherine know what she had seen. Ignorance, or at least the pretense of it, was at this moment her only protection.

"Bram Chisholm," Katherine replied.

"Who is this Bram Chisholm?" Edana asked, trying to sound naive. "I have only met him briefly."

"A very rich, very charming young man—a government supporter. He has only just returned to Scotland from London. You would do well to find someone like that. In fact, you would do well to consider marriage to such a person."

Edana was glad Katherine could not see her face. Why had she not suggested Bram Chisholm himself, instead of "someone like that"? The answer was evident. Katherine desired this rich, good-looking young man for herself. Perhaps they were already having an affair. Perhaps she intended to marry him. No, Edana thought, Katherine would not marry until she had in some way secured the MacLean money. She would marry George and get rid of Edana, either by marrying her off or killing her.

"You're such a quiet girl," Katherine observed. "You just seem to drift off into your own little world."

"I was just thinking."

"May I inquire what about?"

"I was just wondering how long I should wear black," Edana lied. Stupidity was the handmaiden of ignorance, and the duller she appeared and the less she pretended to know, the less of a threat she would be to Katherine.

"For at least a month," Katherine replied without interest. "In fact, wear black tomorrow. Be sure you are wearing it when Mr. Chisholm arrives."

Katherine most assuredly wanted no competition about when Mr. Bram Chisholm called.

"I had thought I might go hunting tomorrow."

Katherine smiled pleasantly. "What a good idea. You really don't need to be here, and the fresh air will do you good."

And you don't want me around, Edana thought. Well, that was just fine. She'd had enough of watching Katherine go after what she wanted and getting it without half trying. If she married George, which would not surprise Edana at all, he would be a cuckolded husband almost immediately after the marriage, if not before. How she hated being nice to this murderess! But if she was to find a way to bring Katherine to justice, she had to continue with her pretense.

"I'm done," Edana announced.

Katherine picked up her skirts and stepped gracefully off the bench. She turned about slowly, so that Edana could unhook her. She held her head high and her body rigid, as if she were royalty. When the hooks were opened, she slipped from the gown and reached for her robe. "I shall be napping," Katherine announced in her usual imperious tone.

Edana simply nodded. She headed upstairs to the sewing room with Katherine's gown draped over her arm. Her thoughts were filled with bittersweet memories of the Phoenix. He was gone forever, but she still dreamed of him.

If Katherine MacLean was in mourning for her stepson, she chose an odd way of showing it, Bram thought, as he was ushered into the reception room. She was wearing a bright red dress in the current Paris fashion. It was low-cut and revealed a large portion of her natural endowments. It was the right color for her. It made her skin seem whiter and her hair darker. She smiled and lifted a well-shaped brow. "I'm so grateful that you could come, even if for a short visit. Shall I send for tea or would you prefer something stronger?"

"Something stronger," he replied, as he lifted her snow-white hand to kiss it. Her fingers were bejeweled and in the soft light, the diamonds and rubies on her fingers glistened. Yes, he knew he would need something stronger to deal with Katherine MacLean. She was a consuming female, a woman of single-minded ambition with no morals at all.

A servant appeared, and Katherine asked that he bring scotch.

"Are you joining me in having something stronger?" he asked, smiling.

"I'm joining you. I've had a trying few days."

"I can only imagine. You should think of going to London for a rest. I'm sure that Crane would see that you were well-received."

"Such a trip did cross my mind. But there is so much to do here. How could I leave poor George before he's made a full recovery? He's mentally devastated, as you can imagine. He never intended that John be killed. As I wrote you, he tried desperately to talk him out of the duel."

"Even though John insulted him?"

"Oh, yes. George was willing to forgive and forget. But John would have none of it. He insisted on going through with the whole terrible affair, even after the liquor had worn off. He always fancied himself the best shot, you know. He's won several competitions."

How cool she was! And how clever! She told her story without so much as a flutter of her dark eyelashes. She was an exceptional woman, a talented cannibal who devoured those about her. "Where is George?" he asked. "I should like to see him."

"I'm afraid he's asleep. His leg is quite painful so he's been given powders for pain. Then, too, there's the emotional strain."

"Then we're alone," he said, as the servant appeared with the decanter of scotch and two glasses on a silver tray.

She smiled a knowing, satisfied smile that made him feel uncomfortable. Had he made a move to embrace her, likely she would not have discouraged him even though George was upstairs. He thought of her note. She had asked him not to come because George was at home and not away as planned. But now that he was here, it seemed as if Katherine was willing to chance a liaison—it was another example of how she could alter her course to seize an opportunity. There was no doubt in his mind she intended to marry George, but apparently that did not mean she wouldn't take lovers. He studied Katherine and concluded that her smile was as unnerving as her eyes, which were huge and seemed to draw you in. He was put to mind of the poisonous spider he had been warned about when traveling in southern Europe, the one that mated and then ate its mate.

"It is nice to have someone here, if only for a short time," Katherine told him as she leaned close. "I would so like to have you come for a much longer visit. Then we could ride together. I could show you all there is to see in the district."

"If my wish is granted, we should be able to see one another often," he replied as he took a long sip of scotch.

Again she smiled her devastating, all-knowing smile.

"And what might your wish be?" she asked.

"I should like to ask for Edana's hand in marriage."

Katherine's eyes opened wide with surprise and shock. She lifted both brows and it was as if she had momentarily lost her voice. It was a lovely moment. She was totally unprepared and taken aback.

"That is why I wanted to see her brother George. Think about it, my dear Katherine. If I were to marry Edana, we could see each other with great regularity. Think of the opportunities! You could marry George, and both your political and financial gains would be secured. At the same time, we would both have pleasurable diversions."

He held out the carrot of a future relationship between them because he deemed it unwise to make her jealous of Edana. He let her know that he understood her ambitions, and watched with satisfaction as her expression of surprise was replaced by a conspiratorial smile.

"You are a clever man, more clever than most. I intend to marry George, and if you marry Edana, it would solidify our political position." She looked at him for a long moment after speaking, then she took his hands in hers. "You are quite right—we would have every excuse to be together, my dear Chisholm."

It was time to seal his bargain, to guarantee her agreement. He pulled her roughly into his arms. He kissed her hard and looked into her flashing dark eyes. "When I want something, I need no excuse, Katherine. But there is a time and place for everything and the time and place for us has not yet come."

He felt her shiver in his arms and he knew she would agree.

"Edana is yours," she whispered. "I shall speak with George right away."

"Is it is as simple as that?"

"It is as simple as I wish to make it."

Bram nodded and kissed her again. "I shall return in a month's time to claim my bride. See that she is ready to travel."

"She'll be ready," Katherine replied. "But you do understand that there is no dowry. She isn't a real MacLean—she was adopted."

Katherine was a stunning, erotic witch, an evil temptress. No dowry indeed! MacLean had left his daughter money, but it seemed that Katherine had no intention of letting Edana have it or benefit from it. Well, it did not matter. He would take care of Edana; she would live in as grand a style as she wished. "I understand that," he replied.

"And you do know that she was kidnapped and attacked. She is not a virgin."

He had to fight not to show his surprise. Edana was a clever young woman! She had played up the story of her abduction so as to avoid an arranged marriage.

"These are not the matters that interest me," he said with a wave of his hand. "Virgins can be boring; women of experience offer far more." He made certain he did not let go of Katherine's hand when he spoke. Quite naturally, she thought he was speaking of her.

Katherine fluttered her eyelashes and smiled her satisfied smile once again. She was very experienced. "It's a bargain. I shall speak with George and I assure you that you can return with confidence in a month's time to claim Edana."

"Then I shall be off for now," he said.

"I look forward to seeing you in a month," Katherine purred.

She watched him as he left and thought to herself, *At last, a true ally.* She would talk to George, but she decided that Edana would not be told till the night before.

Edana slid away from the study window. She was well-hidden by the bushes outside, but she had scratches on her arms and ankles. What were this Bram Chisholm and Katherine up to?

They had kissed passionately and she could see that Katherine was taken with this stranger. She felt confused as she carefully stepped out of the bushes and then broke into a run, heading for the barn. She would say she'd just come home from a futile day of hunting. She began to invent a story that she could tell at dinner if asked how she had acquired her scratches. But she had not gone hunting. She cursed the thickness of the walls; she had heard nothing. To make matters worse, they had had their backs turned to the window most of the time so she could not even read their lips.

She shook her head in disbelief. Bram Chisholm had not seemed the type to be smitten with Katherine. She hadn't really gotten to talk to him much, but he did seem intelligent, and in her personal opinion, no one with any sense could seriously consider becoming involved with Katherine. Old MacQuarrie had been ill, and her father, senile. George was just stupid. She willingly acknowledged Katherine's beauty, but surely men cared for more than beauty. Was there no man who recognized Katherine's evil?

Edana reached the barn and went to the loft. She sank into the hay and decided to wait till twilight to make an appearance. The longer she was alone, the better she liked it.

George sat in his chair with his bandaged leg extended and resting on a pile of plush cushions. His head hurt, and he felt miffed that Katherine had been so distant of late. No sooner had he thought of her, than the door opened.

"I've been waiting for you," he pouted.

"I've been busy," she replied. "But you won't be at all displeased with what I've accomplished."

Katherine stood behind him and she ran her fingers through his hair. "Dear, George, have I been neglecting you?"

The very tone of her voice caused instant stimulation. He knew that thick, syrupy intonation; it held the promise of satisfaction. "You've been shameful in your neglect."

"I shall endeavor to make it all up to you."

"You look beautiful. I love that gown."

"Mr. Chisholm stopped by to offer his sympathy."

George's brow knit into a frown. Bram Chisholm was a very good-looking man. Was there something between him and Katherine? "Did he stay long?" George hedged.

"Only long enough to ask for Edana's hand in marriage."

"What?"

"He wants to marry Edana. It is quite perfect."

"Does he know about her? I mean that we will give her no dowry and that she's been deflowered?"

Katherine actually laughed. "Oh, George! Your choice of words is so archaic. Yes, he knows, and he wishes to marry her anyway. She'll be gone, George. And when we're married, you can legally disinherit her. Still, her marriage to Chisholm will bind the MacLeans and the Chisholms together with the Campbells. We all stand for union; let the other Highland clans rail against the inevitable. We'll be rewarded."

"How do you think they will choose to reward me?" George asked.

"I rather expect you will be made an earl, at least."

"Have you given Chisholm an answer—about marrying Edana?"

"Yes. He will return to claim her in May and we will not tell her till then."

George smiled. "What if I disagree?"

"You would not, would you?" She had slipped her hand under his kilt and he shuddered. "Oh, Katherine," he managed.

"Close your eyes—just let me touch you."

He made a gurgling noise, and Katherine smiled to herself. George was so pliable, and it took so little to turn him into a drooling toad.

Edana felt a wave of apprehension as she paused outside the study. In the past few months she had been more or less on her own. Neither Katherine nor George, nor John before he was killed, had bothered her much. It was almost as if she did not exist. But today she had been summoned by George and Katherine, and she felt extremely ill-at-ease. She knocked gently on the door and waited; there was no use prolonging the agony.

"Come in," she heard Katherine say.

Edana entered the room. George was sitting in a chair by the fire, his wounded leg on the stool in front of him. He looked somehow worn, older by far than his twenty-four years. Katherine, whose age was a mystery, looked vibrant and energetic, as if she had sapped George's lifeblood and taken it for herself.

"We have a surprise for you. Really, two surprises," George told her. He looked up at Katherine and took her hand. "And which one shall we tell her about first?"

Katherine smiled. "You choose," she whispered.

"All right." George turned away from Katherine and looked at Edana. "Katherine and I are marrying," he told her.

Edana wondered if she should look surprised, or say that she had expected such a move. Was she expected to congratulate them or to object? Was she to comment on the nearness of this announcement to her father's death? She struggled to keep her expression nonplussed. "I see," she said softly. "I hope you're both very happy."

"We thought you might be shocked. I mean, your father has not been dead long." Katherine ran her tongue around her full lips. "I adored him, but he was older—George is more my age."

"If you love one another, why not?" Edana asked.

"Good. You're not displeased," George said, studying her face.

"Not at all," Edana answered. She could truthfully say that the two of them deserved each other, and while they both made her want to retch, she had no concern for either of them save finding a way to have them punished.

"And our other surprise involves just you," Katherine imparted.

Edana fought her nervousness. She tried to look steadily at her adversaries.

"Mr. Bram Chisholm has asked for your hand in marriage and I have granted his request," George announced, with absolute finality.

Edana felt a lump rise in her throat and she began to tremble. Marry! She hardly knew this man! Furthermore, she had seen him kissing Katherine and she knew that something was going on between them! "I don't know him," she protested.

"He is quite taken with your beauty, my dear. Taken enough that he does not care about your unfortunate encounter with that highwayman!"

Edana suddenly felt trapped. She could hardly tell them now that it was John who had tried to attack her and that it was the Phoenix who had saved her. She had hoped that having others think she had lost her virginity would protect her against a marriage such as this. Most men would care, and if they didn't, their families would. If this Bram Chisholm did not care, it was only because he was in cahoots with Katherine; something she did not understand was afoot.

"I know Mother promised you could chose your own husband," George said, "but the situation has changed. This marriage is the right thing for you. He's wealthy and doesn't care that we won't provide a dowry."

Edana continued to glare at George. So, that was it! They were not offering her inheritance as a dowry and would no doubt steal it! "You're practically selling me! I won't marry this man. I hardly even know him!"

She stepped back. Months of pretending, months of trying to find a way to make Katherine pay for what she had done, had taken their toll. "I refuse! I won't marry this man!" she shouted. "I hope you both go to hell for what you have done! You're a murderess, Katherine! And you, George, are her accomplice!"

Katherine's expression did not change. "You're ungrateful! You've completely misunderstood everything. I most certainly did not kill your father. He was old and his heart stopped."

"He was poisoned!" Edana said bluntly.

"No, he died of a stroke," Katherine insisted.

"His nails were yellow and so was his body. He was poisoned, I know it."

"And are you now a doctor?" Katherine tossed her head back. She appeared unmoved by Edana's accusation. "Of course, if you were, you would know that the body turns yellow when the patient cannot urinate properly."

"Katherine has been wonderful to you! Why are you treating her this way?" George said defensively.

Edana looked from one of them to the other. They were such accomplished liars. "I don't believe you," she finally said. "And I won't marry this man." She did not offer the fact that she had seen Katherine kill John. Katherine could protest all she wanted. Edana knew what Katherine was, just as she knew if she mentioned John's death she would be risking her life. "I won't marry him!" she repeated.

George laughed. "I signed the marriage contract for you. It doesn't matter what you want."

Katherine bent over and rang a little bell. In less than a minute, two of her men appeared. "Lock her in her room," Katherine ordered. She then turned and smiled at Edana. "Bram Chisholm is coming in the morning to claim you. He asked that you be ready to travel so I have taken the liberty of packing your bag."

Edana felt drained inside. There was no escape. She was being given to this stranger in marriage. She thought of the Phoenix. What did it matter now who she married? He was dead. She held back her tears because she did not wish to give George and Katherine the satisfaction of seeing her cry. In fact, she was determined to give them no satisfaction at all.

May was usually a fine month, but appropriately enough, the day was drizzly and overcast.

The marriage was no marriage at all as far as Edana was concerned. It was the mere exchanging of contracts, the selling of a sister to a husband.

As angry and rebellious as she felt, she had decided not to make a scene. She would go with this man and run away when she had the resources. Somehow, some way, she would find a way to make Katherine and George pay for the lives they had ruined and those they had killed.

She watched as her case was put on the back of a wagon. She was given a horse to ride, a large, tanned mare, an apparently gentle animal.

It's a three-day ride," Bram had told her. "We'll make several stops, then sail for London."

"London?" She had said the name of the capital, and the largest city in the whole of the British Isles, as if she had never heard of it. He was taking her to London? She had thought they would return immediately to his estate. Now she discovered she was being taken to London by this stranger who was legally her husband. If she had got any satisfaction, and it was small, to say the least, it was that Katherine had seemed miffed when Bram announced that he had business and that they would consummate their marriage in England. Vaguely she wondered if Katherine was jealous.

As they rode off, Edana turned her thoughts to Moira. She had been married against her will to George, and everything about the marriage had brought her heartbreak and fear. She had not heard from Moira for many weeks, but then, communications were difficult under the best of circumstances. In her last letter, Moira had spoken of the loneliness she felt. But in letters Moira was careful to disguise her real messages. She did not speak of her pregnancy or of anything else that would make George and Katherine curious or give them clues as to her condition. She wrote of her cousin who was with child and who was having a difficult time. *I wish I could be with you on Mull,* Edana thought, as she rode along. She looked up and glanced at Bram Chisholm's back. He was a fine horseman and she could tell from his posture that he was a man who spent much time traveling. She wondered if she would be alone like Moira. Were their destinies to be the same? Was Katherine to control every facet of both their lives? No, she would not stay with this man.

Edana shook her head sadly. As much as Moira disliked and mistrusted George, she would not like what was now bound to happen. George would divorce her, if he had not done so already. She was Catholic, so there could be no divorce for Moira. George would remarry, Moira would not.

Edana again turned her thoughts to Bram Chisholm. Unlike George and Katherine, he apparently had not converted to the Church of England in spite of being a British supporter. She herself was Catholic, as her parents had been. Her marriage to

Bram had been by a priest and could not be easily dissolved. She shuddered; that meant if Bram and Katherine eventually wanted to marry, that either he would have to convert, or Edana would have to be killed. She looked at him again. She certainly could say that she knew almost nothing about him, but he did not strike her as a murderer. Time, she thought, would answer all her questions, and time would also provide her with the opportunity to run away.

The first stop they made was at the home of a tacksman to whom Bram wished to speak. He left Edana outside with the guard for a short time while he spoke with the man, then he returned and they moved on. The second stop was as short as the first. Bram again left her, went into a local tavern, and returned a short twenty minutes later. He explained neither of these stops and they continued on toward the fort. It was there that they stopped for the third time, but on this occasion, Bram did not leave her with his guard.

"I suppose you already know Superintendent Holden Crane," he said casually, as he helped her dismount.

"He appears to be a friend of Katherine's. He attended my father's funeral with you," Edana replied.

"He's an old friend of mine. We'll be here for a time. We'll have tea together," he informed her coolly.

"I think he'll find my political views disturbing," Edana said. She looked at the buildings within the walls of the fort and could only think how very much she did not want to be here. Simply standing in a British fort made her feel disloyal to her mother, father, and to the Phoenix.

Bram actually laughed at her comment. "Crane has been here for some time; I imagine he's heard the views of most Scots. He is a rather hard-nosed sort. I doubt you will either surprise or distress him."

She scowled at him. "I meant that I might embarrass you."

"Did you know that the freckles across your nose wrinkle into a most delightful line when you scowl?"

Edana pursed her lips together. Damn him! He was so cocky!

And now he was laughing at her. "I am not a stupid child," she said angrily. His grin was utterly unbearable.

"I never thought you were. If you don't wish to embarrass me, then say nothing. If you wish to speak your mind, do so. I assure you, I will not be embarrassed by your views."

He was utterly damnable. She did not bother to answer him.

Such a wonderful woman, he thought as he looked at her. She was at the gate of the lion's den and she did not flinch. But then, for many months she had lived among vipers and survived. Still, he felt immense admiration for her.

"We've been riding for several hours. Come, I will show you where you can freshen up before we join Crane."

She still did not answer. But she did follow him, carrying her small satchel.

He took her to a small room in the largest of the buildings, which surrounded a square where the soldiers drilled. The room was sparsely furnished though there was a mirror, and off that room, were two smaller rooms. One had a washstand and the other, a toilet. The toilet was a rather elaborate thing, a wooden seat over a sort of bucket. But it was clean and she welcomed the opportunity to use it and to wash her hands and face after such a long journey.

Before she rejoined Bram, she also brushed her hair and rebraided it. She stared into the metal mirror and scowled at herself, watching to see what happened to her freckles as she did so. Then, for no reason, she pinched her cheeks for color, smoothed out her skirt, and rejoined Bram.

He escorted her into Crane's panel-lined office. It smelled of leather and was richly furnished, by Highland standards.

On the table, a pot of tea and assorted cakes were laid out.

"As I told you, Crane, I've married the most beautiful woman in Scotland."

Superintendent Holden Crane smiled and took her hand. He kissed it and smiled warmly. "I'm happy for both of you, and so sorry to hear about your brother."

"Thank you," Edana said. She sat down on the edge of the chair he motioned her toward and Bram sat next to her. Crane poured the tea and offered cake.

"You look tired," Bram ventured.

"And I'm furious," Crane replied.

Edana thought he sounded less than furious.

"And what has brought you to this state?" Bram asked.

"Apparently the man we hanged some months ago was not the Phoenix."

Edana had just lifted her teacup and as he spoke, her hand began to shake.

"Oh, my dear. I'm so sorry. I forgot your terrible ordeal at the hands of that unscrupulous bandit!" Crane hopped to his feet and quickly went to fetch a cloth, as Edana had spilled some of her tea. She quickly stood up and went to the window.

It was as if the whole room was moving. Edana could not control the trembling of her hands or the emotions that surged through her. He was alive! All these months she had thought the Phoenix dead and now she knew he was alive!

Bram watched her and he silently cursed himself for bringing her here. But then, he could not have known that Crane would tell her that the Phoenix was alive. Bram wanted to hold her and tell her everything, but he could not. At the same time, she had revealed the depth of her feelings for this man she had never seen. In one sense he was elated; in another, he realized it would make matters more difficult. "I'm sorry," he ventured, as he, too, stood and touched her arm.

She looked up at him and knew for certain that he and Crane misunderstood. They both thought she was upset because the Phoenix was alive when in truth, she was overjoyed and at the same time horribly upset that she was married and being borne away by another man. There were words she could not speak—words that caught in her throat. This love for a man she had not seen was something she could not explain.

Edana sat down again and somehow managed to gain control of herself. Crane wiped up her spilled tea and she leaned back.

After a short time, the two men began talking about the fort, the supplies that were due, and even about the weather. She drank her tea and prayed for this visit to end. She absently stared out the window and wondered where the Phoenix was hiding. Her eyes settled on the distant hills and in her heart she saw him and could indeed still feel the sensation of his lips on hers.

"We must get on with our journey," Bram said, as he stood up.

"How I envy you, Chisholm. London! I should give my eyeteeth to be going home."

Bram smiled and shook his hand. "I shall tell you everything when I return."

Crane shook Bram's hand. "It's not the same as going there."

"Of course not!" Bran touched Edana's arm. "We're leaving now, darling."

Edana stood up. She felt as if she were in a trance. Bram led her away and as she left, she bid Superintendent Crane farewell. Nothing, she thought sadly, was as it should be.

Edana and Bram spent the night before they sailed for London in the local inn. She had thought he would make her his wife, but he did not. In fact, he got her a separate room. They boarded the vessel the next morning, and to her surprise, Bram had arranged for her to have her own room there, as well.

It is because he loves Katherine, she decided. But she was not unhappy; indeed, she felt grateful that he had left her alone, even though on reflection she admitted he was far more attractive than she had originally thought. *But one should have the man she chooses,* she told herself over and over. *I did not choose him.*

They had been at sea for nearly a week, during which time Edana thought about the Phoenix. He perplexed her. Why, if he was alive, had he not come to her? Perhaps he did not really love her, as she was sure she loved him.

She was so deep in thought that the knock on the door of her small cabin startled her. It was early morning, and even though she was dressed, she did not understand why anyone would knock at this hour.

"Edana, we're in the Thames. Come out on deck for your first look at London."

Edana opened the door and found Bram standing there. He smiled at her warmly. "Come, my sheltered Highland lass. Come see a city."

Edana stepped out into the foggy May morning. Bram led

her to the bow of the vessel where she stared in awe at the sight spread out before her. The Thames, on which they sailed, was filled with sailing vessels and barges of all descriptions. There were so many, and they were so close, that it almost seemed as if one could walk across the river by jumping from vessel to vessel. In the distance was a great bridge lined with buildings; apparently they were houses and shops. On either bank, as far as she could see, there were houses and the many churches of London. It was an incredible sight, all these dwellings that appeared to be built practically on top of one another.

"What do you think?" he asked, smiling.

"It's huge," she said, trying not to sound naive or as stunned as she was. "I never dreamed such a place existed. But how do people survive, living one atop the other like that?" She shook her head. "Our sheep have more room."

"Some survive better than others. God knows there are disadvantages. A great fire that burned for many days and nights destroyed this city some fifty years ago, and when plague visited, it killed thousands."

"But they rebuilt it, and plague or no plague, there seems to be plenty of people," Edana said. Then she added, "I should not like to live here, like this. I would feel caged."

He smiled at her and though he did not say so, he was glad she liked the mountains and the streams, the woods and wild outdoors of Scotland. "I didn't bring you here to live, lass. I've brought you here to consummate our marriage and to show you London. I want you to enjoy yourself."

As fascinated as she was with the city, she shook her head. "I am not here willingly, as you well know. And I am not, as you and Katherine are, British supporters. How can I enjoy myself in a city that wishes to destroy the Highland way of life?" She looked at him hard, but in return he only looked amused.

"Edana, this city has no desire to destroy the Highland way of life, though I admit that the British government does. I should think that very few of London's inhabitants even know about the Highlands—where they are, who lives there, or what is going on. As for one's political views, I don't see that they should have anything to do with enjoying one's self."

"On a honeymoon with a man I had no choice in selecting?"

"Let us not forget that a honeymoon is nothing more than the first month of marriage so that the new relationship between husband and wife can be established. Most marriages are arranged."

"I believe most women have the opportunity to at least know their husbands-to-be first. I saw you only once before the marriage."

"We've been together for nine days now. Have I approached you yet? Have I forced myself upon you?" He looked into her eyes and left unspoken how hard it had been for him not to reach out to her, not to touch her hair, run his hands over her tempting curves, feel the softness of her skin or explore the depths of her emotions. The truth was, he thought she might come to him. As unrealistic as it was, he actually hoped she would recognize him as her true love.

"Doubtless you have left me alone because you are so enchanted with my stepmother, Katherine, who will be your sister-in-law by the time we return."

"Is that what you think?"

"Well, I have no idea why you married me, but I'm sure it had something to do with Katherine." She was careful not to say that she had seen them kissing.

He laughed. "I am not enchanted with your stepmother. I am enchanted with you, my beauty. And who wouldn't be? I can see the flickering fire in your eyes; I can well imagine what you look and feel like when those embers grow into a roaring fire. I can picture you unclothed in my arms, writhing with pleasure."

Edana felt her face flush and she fought for control. "I love another," she said, narrowing her eyes. "You can take me, but I will never be yours."

"Do you love another?" He raised a brow and looked at her quizzically.

"I don't expect you to understand. I was kidnapped."

"And attacked, I was led to believe."

She blinked at him. "I gave myself to the Phoenix," she lied. "I love him and I shall never love another."

Bram forced a neutral expression to his face. "But you were beaten," he said, waiting to hear all of what she had to say.

"By my brother, John. Certainly not by the Phoenix, who rescued me and looked after me. I don't care now if you know the truth because I shall probably never see him again. But I want you to know that we may be married, but I shall always love him."

She was delightful! How he wanted to take her in his arms and confess everything to her. Still, her story was wonderful! He burst out laughing. "I'll make you forget the highwayman," he said, touching her shoulder. "I'll show you this wonderful city and then I'll bed you. You won't love this thief for long."

Edana closed her eyes and turned her head to the side. "Do what you want with me! But you cannot have my heart!"

"Perhaps I would have been better off with Katherine. At least she is not in love with anyone but herself."

Edana looked at him hard. His comment about Katherine surprised her, but it did not soften her. Yet she was beginning to feel a curiosity about this man. It was not the curiosity she had felt before, but something quite different. Initially she had been curious about his politics and about his relationship with Katherine. But now she found she was wondering about him— what he liked, what he did not like. He was well-educated and apparently well-traveled. He was, she admitted reluctantly, interesting as well as attractive.

"Tonight," he said looking deep into her green eyes. "Tonight I'll have you."

She looked back at him defiantly. But at the same time, as she looked into his eyes she felt a little weak-kneed, a bit under his spell. He was a large man; she did not even come to his shoulder. His smile was slightly crooked, his eyes deep and, she thought fleetingly, the same color as those of the Phoenix. And, she decided, with total objectivity, he had a lovely nose. It was straight and strong, a good Celtic nose.

For an instant, she wondered if Bram Chisholm was anything like the Phoenix. No—no, they were not at all alike. One was brave, generous, and caring about people; the other was rich, selfish, and cared only about his own wealth and position.

"We're about to dock."

She nodded silently.

"First," he said, "we'll go shopping."

Edana did not tell him that in all her adult life she had never had a dress she hadn't made herself. "Shopping?" she queried. Katherine had gowns that were imported from Paris.

"You need some proper garments," he answered. "You need gowns that will make you look even more lovely than you look at this moment."

She ignored his compliments, though she did not find the idea of having some new gowns entirely unpleasant. Unspoken was her longing—if she was going to look special in some new gown, she wished the man she truly loved could see her.

Edana sat stiffly on the very edge of her chair in the salon of Madame Bouchet, a woman whose advertisement said she was from Paris, and one of London's most widely respected couturieres.

Edana vaguely wondered if in London *respected* meant the same thing as *expensive,* for most assuredly this was an expensive venture.

In fact, all the merchants whose shops lined this street in London's western section were exclusive-looking and finely decorated. None of them even vaguely resembled the merchants' shops in Inverness where she had gone once with Carolyn. In Inverness, most merchants brought their goods to the town square on market day. It was in the market, rather than in a shop, that goods were bought and sold. Indeed, she could only think of two or three shops in all of Inverness. They were plain and cluttered.

Madame Bouchet's place of business was a tall, thin, two-story stone building. As soon as they stepped in the front door, she could see an ornate winding staircase from the entry hall to the second floor. The entry hall opened onto a spacious room with a skylight. It was dotted with sofas and straight-backed chairs. Madame's maid had directed them to a sofa and in moments, refreshments were brought in on silver trays. Tea, little pastries, scones, and clotted cream were served.

Shortly after the arrival of the refreshments, Madame

appeared in a sweeping blue-velvet day gown. She sat down near them and snapped her elegant, well-manicured fingers. Immediately a woman appeared at the top of the staircase. She came down slowly and then turned around and around in front of them while Madame described her gown in great detail. It was only then that Edana realized the woman was wearing a gown Bram might purchase for her.

In all, there were three models who paraded one by one in front of them. When Madame had finished each explanation, Bram either approved or disapproved of the gown. Edana sat spellbound and said nothing.

"Feel free to express yourself," he said after a time, patting her on the knee.

Edana turned her head slightly. It was a huge lie, but she said, "I'm really not at all interested. Pick out what you like. Perhaps I will wear it, perhaps I won't."

He ignored her and then winked at Madame. "We shall also need to see some undergarments."

"But of course," Madame replied.

"Begin with nightgowns," Bram said, a smile crossing his lips. He glanced at her and was amused at her obvious embarrassment.

In moments, a young model returned, wearing a white nightdress made of sheer material and held together with light-green ribbons. It was trimmed in white lace. Bram inhaled deeply and wondered if Edana noticed his expression. But it was not lust for the model. The gown was suggestive and would hide little of Edana's natural beauty. As soon as he saw it, he was able to envision her in it, to imagine himself delving into its lacy folds to stroke her smooth skin and excite her sensitive body.

"That one, definitely," he said, touching her lightly.

Edana felt her skin tingle. But she forced herself to sit primly and to deny him the pleasure of knowing just how uncomfortable she felt. Another model appeared in an equally immodest gown. Edana closed her eyes. Oh, heavens! Were they going to model corsets and chemises, too? Bram was buying it all, and Madame Bouchet was cooing and murmuring, "I'll have to measure her, but she has such a lovely figure I'm sure few alterations will be necessary.''

"What fits, we'll take immediately," he told Madame. "The rest we'll have sent."

Sent? Sent where? Edana wondered. He had said nothing of where they were to stay in this huge, strange city—nothing at all.

Crane quaffed his scotch as he stood in front of the table that held the decanter. Then, without a word, he refilled his glass.

"I do believe you've become addicted to our national drink," Katherine said from across the study.

"It's May and it's still cold! In England it's summer already," Crane said, an obvious touch of longing in his voice.

"If you're cold, go and stand by the fire," Katherine suggested.

"I'm not cold, just homesick."

"For crocuses in St. James's Park? For hunting on the King's reserve?" she asked.

"For all those things," he answered in a faraway voice.

"It's only brought to mind because Bram took Edana to London."

"Perhaps that's it. How do you feel about that?"

Katherine sipped her own drink and shrugged. "I was surprised." She was cautious with her words, expression, and tone. She did not want Crane to suspect how she really felt about Edana. Edana knew too much. Katherine was proud of her own calm denials, but Edana might prove dangerous.

Moreover, Katherine felt nothing less than jealousy and hatred. Bram Chisholm actually was taken with Edana, but he had led Katherine to believe it was she in whom he was interested. Over and over she told herself that Edana was at least out of the way—though she knew it would have made her happier to marry Edana to a man who was not as good-looking, wealthy, and desirable as Bram Chisholm. In fact, Katherine now wished for Edana's death. She had certainly not wished for Edana's elevation to wealth and status. Yet Bram Chisholm was an ally and she was certain that, given time, she could turn him against Edana. In any case, she comforted herself with that plan and relished the challenge. There was almost nothing as pleasurable in life as taking a man away from another woman.

"Edana's a beautiful young girl, and she's his wife, my dear Katherine. I'm sure he is also enamored of you. A man can desire many women."

"I fully understand that," Katherine replied. "And there are women who are quite the same."

He forced a smile. "I am, thank heaven, in the company of one of them."

Katherine did not answer. There was something strange about Crane tonight, but she could not quite fathom his mood. He seemed nervous, or perplexed, or perhaps just preoccupied.

"How long will George be gone?" he asked.

"Several weeks. He's a bit slow; his leg still troubles him."

Crane studied her expression. It was quite clear that she didn't care one wit about George. "Are you sure they went to London?" he asked, frowning.

"Bram and Edana? Of course I'm sure. In any case, you saw them the day before they sailed. My guard said they were taken from the inn, right to the vessel that took them. It sailed on the morning tide. Why on earth do you ask?"

He shook his head. "I think I'm getting old. Or perhaps my eyesight is failing."

"You're puzzling me," Katherine confessed. "Ever since you arrived and all through dinner I've thought there was something on your mind, my dear man. I thought we were friends; there is nothing you can't share with me. You know that."

"Friends and sometimes lovers," Crane reminded her. Then, after a short pause, he rubbed his chin. "It's a bit silly but also a bit troubling."

"Please tell me," Katherine pressed.

"Well, as you know, I just returned from a journey deep into the Highlands. I was traveling from Fort Augustus to Inverness, and in a small village, I saw this girl. I thought it was Edana."

"Edana? That's quite impossible. Did you speak to her?"

"No. In fact, I didn't really get a good look at her. It's just that I— Well, she really looked like Edana."

"As if one of her was not enough," Katherine muttered. But she quickly realized she had betrayed her jealousy and she smiled. "It simply could not have been her. I know they left. I know they took a vessel to London because the guard watched them from the dock as they sailed."

The girl he had seen did look exactly like Edana—not a mere resemblance, but an exact replica. But Crane felt ill at ease discussing this with Katherine. She always made so much of everything. Perhaps, he acknowledged, he had made a mistake.

He slumped into a chair and watched as Katherine put down her drink and walked toward him. "George is gone. I should not like to waste this night." She stood behind him and began to rub his shoulders.

"That feels good," he said, closing his eyes and giving in to the sensations that surged through him when she touched him. He was foolish. Of course he had not seen Edana.

"Let me make you feel good all over," Katherine said, circling his ear with her long finger.

"Please," he replied, as he pushed the enigma out of his mind. Katherine walked around the chair and stood in front of him. She bent over, and slowly she began to undress him. After a few moments, he stood up. The fire was warm on his back as he reached out for her. There was no question about it. His eyes had been playing tricks on him; he could not have seen Edana. She was in London.

"You smell delicious," he said, touching Katherine's neck.

Her arms encircled him and he forgot his puzzle.

Chapter Seven

It was twilight as they journeyed through London's narrow, cobbled streets. The carriage left one neighborhood and entered another until finally they appeared to be almost out of the city.

Again the carriage turned and they were on a dirt road. Tall trees lined either side of the road, but now and again, behind the trees, Edana caught a glimpse of a stately home, hidden at the end of a lane way. They all looked like miniature palaces on acres of green land.

"Surely only royalty lives in these elegant houses," she said, straining to see out the window.

"No, just wealthy merchants and a few diplomats."

In a moment, the carriage pulled off the road and onto a long, winding drive. It came to a halt in front of a rambling two-story stone house.

Bram said nothing to her as he lifted her from the carriage. The driver and his assistant began carrying their bags and purchases to the house. A servant opened the door. "Welcome, Mr. Chisholm."

Edana followed as they were ushered inside. It was without question the most elaborate home she had ever been in. Like Madame Bouchet's, it had a winding staircase. Many of the windows were made of stained glass, and each room had fine furnishings. Tables, desks, and chairs were made from dark wood and were highly polished. Chairs and lounges were covered in delicate fabrics and many were covered in designs done in painstaking needlepoint. Paintings and tapestries hung from the walls and miniature marble statues graced inlaid tables, while rich, thick carpets covered the floors in many rooms. Most of the houses in Scotland, as well as most of the castles, were built entirely for utilitarian purposes. This house was far different; it was a feast for the senses.

"Is this your home?" she asked, after a few minutes.

Bram shook his head. "It belongs to a friend. He's on the Continent just now, so we'll have it all to ourselves."

She looked away. His words were heavy with innuendo. He might just as well have said, *Fight, scream, and cry out. We're alone, and no one will hear you.* But she had already decided she would do none of those things. He was her husband and nothing was going to change that fact. Struggling would probably give him more pleasure than he deserved, and it might result in her being hurt. So she had decided to give in to him without a struggle and, like Moira, accept the inevitable.

"First we'll have a fine meal. I believe the cook is probably waiting to serve us now."

Edana felt her mouth water. She was hungry. In the days before they left Scotland, they had eaten quite ordinary meals and the food on board the ship had been totally unappetizing.

"Come along," he said, smiling. He faced her and undid her bonnet. "Make yourself at home."

She felt stiff as he led her down a corridor and up the winding staircase. He led her into a spacious bedroom with a huge bed, a divan, and a window seat. In the middle of the room was a small table with flickering candles. It was set with fine silver, and in a silver bucket, a decanter chilled in cold water. The bed was turned down, ready for them.

"This is not a night to eat alone in a formal dining room," he said, as he opened the decanter. "Come, my dear Edana. Indulge me. The nightdress I bought you is in that package. Go into the other room and put it on, then come and join me for our supper."

Edana pressed her lips together. "Am I dessert?" she asked sarcastically.

He smiled again and touched her hair. "As you love another, I understand your reluctance. But I am your husband and I have waited to claim you, waited until this time and this place."

She turned away from him and picked up the package. There was no reason not to dress as he wished her to dress. If she refused, he would just rip her clothes off anyway. She silently left the room to find herself in a small dressing room. She trembled, hoping she would not do so later. Heavens, why had she lied? If only she knew what to expect. But she did not—she only knew what Moira had told her about coupling; and now, faced with the prospect of the act, she realized how little she knew. If only she had pressed Moira for more details.

She disrobed and put on the nightgown. She looked in the mirror and felt her skin glow hot with embarrassment. It hardly covered her breasts, and it clung to her, leaving nothing to the imagination. Furthermore, it was diaphanous. If she stood in front of the fire, he could probably see right through it! Her heart sank. What did it matter? He was going to take it off anyway, he was going to touch her in ways she had never been touched before, and he was going to do the things she had dreamed only of her masked love doing. "Heavens," she said again, closing her eyes. "I must be brave."

She stood for a long while in the dressing room. Then she heard him call out to her, "Dinner is here."

She took the thick robe she had brought from home and covered herself with it. Perhaps she could make him blow out the candles and do what he had to do in the dark. Perhaps he didn't have to see her face at all; perhaps he wouldn't have to know how disconcerted she was at the thought of the intimacy about to take place.

Edana opened the door and stepped out into the larger room with hesitation. She felt as if she were standing on the edge of a cliff.

Bram grinned at her. In fact, he almost laughed. He had bought her the most divine, seductive nightgown he had ever seen, and though she was no doubt wearing it, she had wrapped herself up in a heavy Highland robe, a great, voluminous wool robe in which her well-shaped but slender body was left a complete mystery.

"Are you cold?" he asked, trying to suppress his smile.

"A little," she replied, fighting for her dignity.

He filled her glass with cold white wine and lifted the silver cover off her food. "Quail, my darling bride. It's a real delicacy."

Edana inhaled the aroma of the well-prepared dish. She ate slowly, taking small bites, and sipped the wine, drinking more than she knew she should, praying she would go to sleep and wake up to find it all over with.

But there was no putting it off forever. Their dinner was finished and Bram summoned the servant to take away the dishes. When the last dish was cleared, Bram locked the door and turned to look at her.

Edana stood stock-still in the center of the room. He walked to her and undid her robe, letting it fall to the floor in a heap around her feet. She shivered.

She was more beautiful than he had imagined! He reached back and loosened her hair. It fell in ringlets over her white shoulders. Her green eyes were huge with expectation. But she did not cry out or fight him.

He ran his finger round her ear and kissed her neck. She shivered slightly, but he knew it was fright, not passion. This was, after all, a woman he had kissed before.

He moved his hands lightly over her body, feeling its delicious contours and warm glow. Then he bent and kissed the top of her breast as he cupped it in his hand.

He felt her quiver and suddenly she turned away and covered her face with her hands. "Please don't hurt me," she pleaded, as all attempts at dignity failed. "Please. I lied to you. I've never known a man before."

He looked at her and felt terrible. Of course, he had known already that was the case. He reached out for her soft, trembling hands and took them in his. "Edana," he said softly, "I have no desire to hurt you. You are my wife and our marriage must be consummated. Come, lie with me on the bed and I shall try to be gentle."

She was looking at the floor. "I do love another," she insisted.

He ignored her declaration. Her eyes were on the floor, and he knew she was both frightened and embarrassed because of his intimate caress. "Come," he said, leading her to the bed.

"Can we put out the candle?" she asked timidly.

He leaned over and blew it out; the room was in darkness save for the light of the half-moon as it shone through the window.

He lay down on the edge of the bed and pulled her down beside him, making room for her as she crawled in beside him and lay stiffly next to him. He was certain she had asked him to blow out the candle because she was crying, but was too proud to let him see her.

He leaned over her and kissed her again. This time he kissed her on the lips, then on the neck, then again on the lips. "You're a virgin," he said softly into her ear. "I must prepare you, my wife."

Edana said nothing. She closed her eyes but she could not shut herself away from him. He was warm by her side, and she felt him discarding his clothes.

She moved slightly as she felt him lying unclothed against her. He began touching her lightly; his hand slid across her breasts, down her stomach, over her legs. Again he kissed the tops of her breasts and his lips were warm. It was not, she acknowledged, an unpleasant sensation. In a moment, she felt him undo the ribbons and push her nightdress aside. She involuntarily moaned ever so slightly when he began kissing her breasts again. Her nipples grew hard as he flicked his tongue over them and this, she thought, was in fact a most pleasant sensation. She tried to think of the Phoenix—she felt disloyal to him. But he had not come for her! He had not saved her from this marriage! She drew in her breath as she felt Bram suck her nipple full into his mouth. Heavens! What was happening to her? She felt hot and cold simultaneously.

He teased one breast with his tongue and toyed with the other in his fingers. She began to move in his arms in spite of herself. These sensations were something she was not prepared for; indeed, the pleasure she felt shocked her. She felt him against her leg. He was large and strong. It was as Moira had described it and she felt a chill pass through her as he ran his hand between her legs.

"Be calm, my wife," he whispered in her ear. "Don't be frightened."

She shivered again as he touched her in that secret place she had felt only in her dreams. But the combination of his dancing fingers and moist lips created a much different and far stronger sensation than she had had in her dreams.

"It's a magic place," he whispered. "Let yourself feel, let yourself know pleasure."

Edana moaned again and moved more wantonly. She felt moist between her legs. She felt a terrible yet agreeable tension in her whole body; a desire—a kind of hunger. For what? She had felt it before, but not like this. This was something else; this was not as she had imagined it would be, or as she had feared it would be.

"Oh," she murmured again. He had moved his hand and she had lifted her hips seeking it! Her whole body felt hot and she wiggled beneath him as he again began to suck on her breasts while running his hands over her. He paused momentarily now and again on that spot, then she felt him slide over her in the darkness. His fingers still held her nipples and slowly played with them, even as she felt the caresses of his lips there, in the magic place. She felt she would scream with the all-consuming tension that filled her. She only feared he would stop before she could know release.

The pressure built inside her—it built until her hips were undulating and she was writhing about. Suddenly the throbbing began—it was a plunge into pure paradise. It went on and on and he held her tightly, letting her move against him. He moved up the length of her body again and held her, looking down into her face. She put her arms around him and held him tightly as her pleasure gradually subsided.

"Now, I suspect, you are ready," he whispered.

She moaned as he began his movements again, as he slowly revisited her body, exploring, touching, and arousing her to new and delirious heights.

"It will hurt a little at first," he whispered. "But I shall try to be gentle."

She said nothing, but continued to move against him, unable to stop her hips from undulating when he touched her. Instead of fearing or rejecting him, she held him tightly. Then she felt him part her legs and push into her. She let out a little cry, but it did not hurt so much as she had thought it would. He paused for an instant and then resumed. His mouth enclosed her breast while his other hand caressed her. His manhood filled her and she moved against him, feeling again the incredible, wonderful tension, the undeniable pleasure of it. She shamelessly wrapped her legs around his midsection as they were joined. She groaned as the tension built and built until her body was wet and her hair clung to her forehead as if she had been working outside on a hot summer's day. He filled her and rubbed against her magic place again and again. Her arms held him tightly; she felt it come! It was an incredible feeling, an indescribable feeling!

She throbbed against him and as it subsided, she lay in his arms breathless, her whole body damp. As she began to regain herself, all she could think was that Moira had done a very bad job of explaining coupling.

Bram smiled to himself in the darkness. She could say whatever she wanted, but she was his and he knew it. She was as fiery as he had imagined, as much a woman as any man could want. She was a dream come true and now, he thought, he only had to protect her from the reality that was his life.

Edana opened her eyes as soon as the sun began to filter through the windows. She rolled over carefully and for a long moment looked at the man sleeping next to her in the bed. The covers were pulled up around him; his eyes were closed. A lock of his dark hair fell over his forehead. He was handsome. More important, he hadn't hurt her at all; in fact—she shook her head, trying to dispel her conflicting feelings—she had liked it!

Heavens! She ought to be angry. She ought never to want to see this man who had forced this marriage and taken her even though she had declared her love for another. But she could not bring herself to hate him, or to be upset about last night. Again, she murmured to herself, "I enjoyed it!" But no sooner had she admitted that than she reminded herself that she must not let him know she had enjoyed it, if for no other reason than that she could not trust him. He was Katherine's friend; he was a British supporter. He was a wealthy landowner, and no doubt no better than other clan leaders who received favors from the British in return for their support.

Edana crept from the bed and silently tiptoed into the dressing room. She dressed quickly and then looked at herself in the long mirror. She looked so shabby! She turned and eyed the boxes of clothes that Bram had bought her yesterday. She remembered a day gown. It was green and trimmed in lace. Quietly she began looking for it. She found it in the third box and shook it out. Then she slipped off her brown woolen dress and put on the new one. She smiled now at her image in the mirror. She did look ever so much better—and what harm could it do to wear the dress? Waste was a crime, so she must not waste these clothes, even if Bram Chisholm had bought them.

She brushed out her long red hair and tied it back. Then, after one last, long look in the mirror, she decided she looked much improved.

Bram was still asleep when she stepped behind the drape and opened the balcony door. She went out into the warm May air. Below her there was an expanse of green lawn, and in beds, bright yellow crocus were blooming everywhere. It would never be this warm in the Highlands in May! But here it was like summer, and there were birds singing in the trees of this enemy city, or, as Bram had corrected her, a city of enemies.

"Turbulent years," her remarkable mother, Carolyn MacLean, had told her. She had explained the revolution and how it came to pass that the Scottish Stuarts no longer were the royal family of England. "They have still not solved their problems, and we have not begun to solve ours," her mother had concluded. Political loyalties were tied to what people could benefit from personally, Edana thought.

"You're up early," Bram said from behind her.

Edana jumped at the sound of his voice. He was barefoot and had moved silently across the floor to join her on the balcony.

"It's a beautiful morning," she answered, without turning to look at him.

"Are you thinking about the flowers?"

She turned to face him. "No. I was thinking about politics— about England's Protestant rulers."

He smiled. "There is more to it than that."

"I'm sure it's all very complicated," she said.

"Not as complicated as it will become," he said, touching her shoulder lightly. "You see, England has for many years been torn between two fears—one is fear of the Pope and the control of the Catholic Church, and the other is fear of Protestant fanaticism, of Puritanism."

"The Stuarts are the rightful heirs to the throne," she reminded him.

"Their line was not overlooked completely. Need I remind you that Mary, who shares the throne of England with William, is the Protestant daughter of James."

"His son should rule."

"Such a proper little Scots Tory," he teased.

Her face flushed. "I don't believe in the patronage that has brought such misery to Scotland."

She was magnificent. The green gown looked wonderful on her. It made her penetrating green eyes seem even larger, and they flashed at him now, warning him of the intensity of her views. How fortunate he was to have her! To have a woman of both beauty and brains, a woman who understood injustice, and who would stand by him when she knew who he was.

"I should be careful what I say while here in London," he warned, looking into her eyes.

"You must have known before you married me that I was not a supporter of this imported regime."

"I did indeed. But I'll reform you," he joked, just because he wanted to see the righteous anger in her eyes.

"I shall not change my views," she said, tossing her head back and staring at him defiantly.

"It's too early in the morning for political talk and for a

marital revolution. Come, let us eat some breakfast and then I'm going to take you riding on the private reserve of the King himself.''

"You're making fun of me! And he is not my King!''

"Well, it's the same reserve that once belonged to James, you can think of yourself as riding on his reserve if it pleases you. Now let's eat.''

Why did this man never seem to take anything seriously? "I'm not hungry,'' she replied testily.

With that he pulled her into his arms and kissed her. She struggled for a moment, but the memory of last night's pleasure overcame her. Then she pulled away from him and stepped back. "I still love another,'' she told him. "Nothing has changed.''

Bram stared at her but said nothing. She had responded to him and enjoyed herself. It did not matter to him that she could not yet admit it. Time, he thought, was very much on his side. She did not have to admit it; he knew full well she was his woman and always would be.

Clouds filled the sky over Mull. They moved on high winds from west to east, scattering showers as they passed overhead.

Moira held her infant son and rocked him gently in her arms as he suckled at her breast. He was a fine lad, strong and happy, and with relief she saw that he looked nothing like his father or any of the MacLeans.

Her father sat nearby now, and again he looked at his grandson. "This new religion is convenient,'' he said sarcastically. He picked up the letter, which had come from the magistrate yesterday, waved it for a moment, and then dropped it onto the table.

"It doesn't matter to me. I didn't want to be married to George MacLean anyway. I never did want to be married to him.''

"But you were, and in the eyes of God you are still married to him.''

The paper notified them that with permission of the authorities, George had divorced her. "I wonder if it would have been so easy had they known about the baby?" Moira said.

"Probably not. But they'll never know. I don't trust any of those people," her father said bitterly.

"Except Edana."

"Except Edana," he agreed. He rubbed his chin thoughtfully and then walked closer to her. "I want you to go to your grandmother's family," he told her slowly. "I'll miss you and the little one, but I know it's far safer for you both."

"Even now that we're divorced?" Moira asked.

"Your child, your son, is the only rightful male heir to the MacLean estates and title. Divorce or no divorce, Katherine MacLean intends to have everything. She would kill you and the child without so much as a second thought, Moira. No, I'll not chance it. I'm sending you to your grandmother's people on Skye."

Moira nodded silently though she felt like crying. It was desolate and lonely on Skye. She would have no one; she would have nothing save her child, the wind, and the sea. She looked into his little face and she shuddered. It was for the best—her father was right. Secrets were badly kept here; sooner or later, word would reach Katherine on the mainland. Katherine would learn that she had given birth to a male heir. The child would not be safe. Silently she cursed George and Katherine. He had divorced her, though no one in her family would accept divorce; he had left her with a child she had to protect. Her father had told her about Edana. They did that too! Together they had given her into a loveless marriage, and worst of all, they had murdered Donald MacLean and his son John. No doubt, George and Katherine would now be married.

Moira pursed her lips together. "But one day I'll get even," she whispered. "One day Katherine MacLean, when you are too old to fight, my son will usurp you and turn you out— you'll have to go back into the streets of Edinburgh." The mental picture pleased her, and it made the thought of going to Skye somewhat easier.

* * *

Edana and Bram breakfasted on poached fish, hot breads, and coffee. Then they went riding, and when they returned, at midafternoon, they had tea in the garden.

The sober-faced servant brought their tea and set it down on the little iron table. Edana felt sleepy, but she did not want to suggest an afternoon nap to Bram. All thoughts of returning to the bedroom with him conjured up last night, and all day she had cursed her own weakness and vowed to remain pristine in the future. So she did not mention a nap; rather, she sipped her tea and stared off into the garden. But it didn't matter that she didn't talk with him. He seemed quite content to sit silently. Finally she said, "You have not yet told me to whom this house belongs."

"Does it matter?"

"Yes. I should like to know who lives in such a fine house and how it is we're able to use it so freely."

"To a relative," he said offhandedly.

"You have a relative who lives in England?"

He frowned ever so slightly. He might have known she would ask questions about this house, about his own affluent circumstances. He did not wish to tell her that the house belonged to another one of the Seven—a blood brother, a co-conspirator in the secret war for justice. She would learn everything when the time was right.

"Have you traveled on the Continent?" she asked after a while.

"Yes. I was schooled in France and I've spent time in Italy."

"In Rome?"

"No," he lied. "In the north." He did not want her to know he had gone to Rome to the Court of King James, that he had seen the Stuart heir to the throne, or that in reality he was a supporter of the Catholic cause. The Stuarts had pledged themselves to tolerance and the supporters of the current monarchs, William and Mary, had not.

Edana finished her tea and stood up. She walked to the rose trellis and gazed out across the lawns. What was she to make of this mysterious man who answered her questions while at the same time telling her nothing?

She was suddenly aware of him behind her, and then his

arms were around her as he pressed himself to her back. She tried to stand stiffly; she tried not to respond to the heat of his body or the outline of him hard against her.

He did not move, he simply held her fast from behind. Then he put his hands on her breasts and she shuddered. At first, he simply cupped them, but then he plunged one hand inside her dress and toyed with her already hard nipples. Heavens! Was there no way for her to control her responses? His fingers worked magic on her and she felt that all-too-pleasant weakness filling her while at the same time the dampness came and she felt a terrible longing. She had already taken that first step on the staircase to satisfaction. "People will see us," she protested. But he said nothing. He simply held her and played with her breasts while she squirmed against him, trying to turn around, but unable to break free of his grasp.

He continued to hold her fast with one arm, all the while fondling her with his other hand. She felt him fumble beneath her skirts and reach under her slips to touch her in that place.

"Please," she moaned, as with one hand he fondled her breast and with the other he toyed with her place of pleasure. She shuddered against him, half mortified at the thought that the servant might return for the tea tray while he was doing this thing, and half afraid he might stop before she felt the throbbing release that so pleased her.

He was unrelenting and in a moment she was overcome, shaking in his arms, crying out and breathing heavily.

She knew her face was bright red and her mouth was dry. She couldn't speak, she was so afraid someone would come even while she was still consumed with pleasure. She heard him laughing and then he kissed her ear.

"Beast!" she hissed, as soon as she could say anything at all, and she broke free of him and, lifting her skirts, ran across the grass toward the tall trees at the end of the garden.

No sooner had she reached the trees than she felt him tackle her, tumbling her to the soft ground. He was still laughing and she doubled her fists even as he kissed her mouth and neck.

"Stop fighting!" he said, devouring her protests with his hot, urgent kisses. "I'll have my pleasure now. And stop pretending you don't like this. I can feel you—I know you like it.''

Edana turned her head to the side. He was right! He didn't have to hold her down, she was too desirous again to even want to move. He loosened his grip and began again to kiss her intimately, pulling away her low-cut dress and sucking her breasts. Each time he drew her nipple into his mouth, she moved in his arms, unable not to want more, incapable of denying him anything.

His fingers played on her flesh, tickling, taunting, and readying her. She felt him lift her skirts again and fumble with her undergarments. Once again, she felt him against her thigh, strong and ready. This time when he entered her it did not hurt at all, and she found herself wrapping her arms and legs around him, willingly accepting him, wanting him to continue his movements which so pleasured her. She was lost, lost in sensations, lost in her own divine pleasure and she fought for it, clinging to him, moving against him until she felt that pleasure again. She clawed at his back and cried out even as he shook above her—clearly he was as pleasured as she with their coupling.

He rolled off her, but still held her hand. He fumbled in his pocket and withdrew a ring. It was a beautiful gold ring with a large emerald. ''It's the color of your eyes,'' he said softly, as he slipped it on her finger. ''You are truly my wife,'' he said.

Edana said nothing, but neither did she deny his statement.

Katherine combed her long dark hair and stared at her image in the mirror. Behind her George was sprawled across their bed; his mouth was open as he snored loudly. She reminded herself not to allow him to sleep in this room any longer. He was simply far too annoying.

She scowled—not that George was the only reason she was annoyed. First, he had returned with almost no money. He had spent the entire evening moaning about the fact that he could not squeeze more out of the tenants. Frankly, she did not care about his reasons for returning without additional rent monies.

She only cared about the money. No sooner had he stopped complaining than he had desired her, muttering about how deprived he had been over the weeks he was away traveling. Did he think she was there for his pleasure? George was an idiot. She had always thought so, but now she began to consider how to rid herself of him as soon as they were married. She shook her head and tried to clear it. She had a headache and she was sure George had given it to her; or, more precisely, the thought of having to put up with him for at least six more months had made her head throb.

It really wouldn't do if he met a bad end too soon after their forthcoming marriage. People could not be expected to believe that she had such bad luck! First old MacQuarrie, then old MacLean, and then George. No doubt, if he died too soon, people would be suspicious, and unlike the others, George was a government supporter. The authorities might look more closely at the circumstances of his demise. Not that she had decided exactly how to dispose of him, though she realized that working out a plan to rid herself of him would give her a certain release from the mind-numbing days she had to spend with him.

The light knock on the door startled her, but rather than call out and awaken George, she went to the door and opened it a crack.

"There's a message for you, madam," the servant girl informed her.

"Is there indeed?" Katherine snapped. "Why didn't you just bring it here?"

The girl blinked at her and looked as if she might burst into tears. "The messenger said it could only be delivered to you," she hurriedly explained.

"Dunce," Katherine murmured under her breath. The girl turned and fled. Katherine, donning her robe, closed the door and went downstairs. With luck, George would sleep until noon and thus be out of her hair.

The rider who bore the message shifted uneasily from one foot to the other.

Katherine reached the bottom of the stairs and held out her

hand. "Well?" she said. "Am I surrounded by fools? I am Katherine MacLean, give me my letter."

He handed her the letter and backed away. "Will there be a response?" he asked timidly.

"How should I know? I haven't read it yet!" Fools, fools! Why were there so many fools in the world? "Go to the kitchen and come back when I summon you."

"Yes, madam, yes." He virtually flew down the corridor toward the kitchen.

Katherine took the letter into the reception room where morning light came in through the windows. She opened it up and read it slowly.

> My dear Katherine,
>   Edana and I have had a splendid few weeks in London and have just returned to Scotland. I will be taking Edana home with me for the present and will not return to you for some time. Circumstances prevent me from coming at this time, but I hope all is well. I'm looking forward to our next meeting.
>
> Sincerely, Bram Chisholm

Katherine stomped her foot in anger. Damn that Edana! He must have enjoyed their honeymoon very much for him to decide not come back and claim her!

"Little bitch," Katherine mumbled. "I should have strangled her when I had the chance."

They disembarked at Inverness and were met by twelve of Bram Chisholm's clansmen. The men had brought horses and a wagon to carry their luggage.

Edana thought Inverness, with its winding little streets that all led to the town square and its houses row on row, looked like a miniature village compared to London. She had accepted Bram's argument that just because one did not like British policy did not mean one could not enjoy London. She had enjoyed it. She had relished the theater and she adored the parks, the fine houses, and the shops. She did not tell him so, but she also enjoyed his stories about the Continent. Whatever else she thought of him, she had to admit that he was intelligent and entertaining. He was not boring nor was he loutish. He was strong and sure of himself. He was totally unlike any man she had ever known, and even though she knew they were at political odds, she respected him in a way she had not thought possible only a month ago.

"I'm taking you home to Inverness-shire," he told her, as the horses they would ride were saddled.

"And not to my home?" she said, lifting her brow. She had been certain that he was involved with Katherine and that now that he had made her his wife, he was going to continue his affair with Katherine just as George had done after marrying Moira.

He laughed. "Why would I take my bride back to her home?"

"So you could be with Katherine," she answered.

"I have no desire to be with Katherine," he replied. Bram looked into her eyes. Suspicions died hard. Great heaven, didn't she realize she was a thousand times more desirable than Katherine? Didn't she realize that he adored her and was so enamored of her that he had nearly told her everything! She was the most divine creature he had ever known—beautiful, intelligent, a wild, fiery little devil in bed, and loyal to a fault. She still had a girlish crush on her Phoenix, and he supposed he might have been jealous, were he not in reality the man she worshiped in her daydreams. But he wanted her to love him for himself, not for the ideals for which he fought.

Edana turned away to mount her horse. She felt unnerved and now confused. How would the Phoenix find her? And what would she say if and when he did? She inhaled deeply. Their love could never be. She was another man's wife and though she had fought it, she had responded to Bram and found herself totally unable to turn him away when he desired her. *I must be a terrible woman—he made me feel as the Phoenix did!* For a moment she wondered if she might respond to just any man, but she knew she would not. She had hated it when John had touched her. They might be worlds apart, yet Bram aroused her just as the Phoenix had.

Still, she did not yet completely trust Bram Chisholm. He was Katherine's friend, her cohort, and Katherine was a murderess.

I must learn more about you, she thought. *I must find out all about your connections with the British and with Katherine.*

"Will we live in your castle?" she asked.

"I have no castle. I have a large house on the shores of Loch Ness."

She smiled. "I shall like a house. Old castles are too large and too cold. Even with interior rooms they are always cold and damp."

"Yes, that's why I built this house." He did not tell her it was a rambling house with twenty-four rooms. He did not tell her that there was a tower house, though it was atop a hill behind the house and used only to house servants.

"Edana, please make a point of getting to know the men who travel with us. When I'm gone, they will remain to protect you."

She turned to him in surprise. "Are you gone much?"

He nodded. "By necessity; certainly not by desire."

So, that was it. He would take her to his home and leave her there under guard. Then he could go wherever he wanted. He could even go to Katherine. She stared into the distance, and fought back tears. She did not want him to leave her alone. She did not want him to leave her at all.

The pipes heralded George's arrival, as for the second time he strode through the doors of a chapel in his dress kilt, sword at his side, prepared to take eternal vows.

"That's a sword that has ne'er seen a drop of blood," Crane whispered to his friend, Major Kincaid.

"Why are we here?" Kincaid asked.

"To see the most-married woman in the Highlands become her own daughter-in-law," Crane replied, with a twisted smile. Katherine's relationships fascinated him.

"Is that what she is? How is that?" Kincaid asked, looking totally puzzled.

Crane smiled. Kincaid was not all that lucid before he had

his pre-dinner drinks. In fact, his lucidity was pretty well limited to the two hours between his first drink and his fifth.

"It's a little confusing. Katherine first married MacQuarrie, who died. Then she wed old MacLean and that made her George MacLean's stepmother. MacLean died, and she's marrying George, so I guess she must be her own daughter-in-law."

"I don't understand these people," Kincaid muttered. "Next month my time is up in this godforsaken place and I'll be home in Surrey."

"It's easier to understand them if you don't try," Crane returned. He wished he was going to Surrey. He wished he was going almost anywhere.

George was standing in front of the minister of the Church of England, and Katherine was at his side. They were quietly exchanging their vows, though almost no one was there, save four or five tenants who had been ordered to attend. Crane supposed that all crimes needed witnesses.

"Will we have drink after this is over?" Kincaid asked, a trace of anxiety in his voice.

"I imagine."

The ceremony ended and George and Katherine left the chapel together. Crane nudged Kincaid onward and they followed the bride and groom back to the MacLean castle on horseback.

In the main dining room, servants brought a seven-course meal to Crane, Kincaid, and James Fraser, a strapping hulk of a Highlander whom Katherine had just hired to collect rents. Crane thought him an unpleasant man at best, but he supposed the hulk had other attributes that might please Katherine.

After dinner, they adjourned to the study where, much to Kincaid's relief, a never-ending supply of drink was served.

"George seems quite happy," Crane said, taking Katherine aside.

"Of course he's happy. All my husbands are happy."

Crane restrained a laugh. "I shall miss you tonight," he said, squeezing her arm and wishing it were something else.

She smiled coyly. "There is no need for you to miss me.

George will not be conscious much after ten, and he will remember very little in the morning.''

Crane raised his brow. "You intend to drug poor George on his wedding night."

Katherine nodded, a strange expression crossing her face. "George has had far too many things his own way already."

"And you intend to change that."

"I intend to change everything," she replied.

Chapter Eight

June 1708

Edana looked at her new home in awe. Regardless of the interior improvements made by her adopted father, Donald MacLean, the tower castle on Mull had never lost its original character—that of a structure created for defensive purposes. Neither was the castle to which Katherine had moved them on the mainland particularly warm and comfortable, in spite of interior facades that created rooms from vast, open areas. Edana felt all castles retained a feeling of dampness.

Bram Chisholm's home was quite a different matter. It was truly magnificent, and built with considerable taste and thoughtfulness.

Like nearly all the houses and castles of Scotland, it was built primarily from local materials. Its outer walls were stone, its roof shale. In the front, there were dormered windows on the second floor, and on one end of the essentially oblong-shaped house, a rounded two-story tower provided a good view of the road. At the peak of the roof, several chimneys reached toward the sky.

Behind the house was a more traditional tower house, which

no doubt was the original family home. To either side of the old tower house there were many outbuildings that Bram explained as they circled on horseback. All the buildings, even the sprawling house, were enclosed by a stone wall.

"The old tower house is used as a lookout tower," he explained. "It was built hundreds of years ago. I use it no more, though some of the servants now live on the upper floor. That's the bakehouse," he said, pointing to a low, oblong building with three chimneys. "All the bread is made there each morning—not just our bread, but bread for many of the families who live on or around the estate. Over there is the brewhouse for the making of ale. That's the *girnal* for storing meal; the limehouse is that building over there." He pointed off toward a small low building. Piles of limestone stood on either side of the entrance.

"That large building is the dairy."

"Where is the womanhouse?" Edana inquired. The so-called womanhouse was, in fact, usually a large room where the unmarried female members of the staff had their quarters.

"Behind the tower," Bram answered. "You can just see the edge of it from here. And in the wall there are recessed bee-skeps to assure us of a regular supply of honey."

"It all seems very self-sufficient."

He smiled his slightly crooked smile. "It was intended to be so when it was built. Come along, let me show you the house."

He slipped from the saddle with the ease of a tall man and lifted her down, hugging her gently and pausing for a second to look deeply into her eyes. Again she flushed, as she always did whenever he touched her. But this time he did not kiss her; instead, as was the custom, he swept her into his strong arms and carried her into the house. He set her down in a large entranceway. To the right of the entranceway was a cozy study, which, because it was built in the corner of the house with the tower, was round. On the other side of the entranceway was a huge reception room filled with all manner of art and interesting pieces of furniture from all over Europe. Scotland traded with all the countries on the Continent, but seldom with England, which lay to its immediate south. It was an irony that Scots crossed the sea more readily than the Tweed, which was considered the border between the two peoples.

Farther down the corridor was a large dining room, and beyond that, a large kitchen. Up the winding staircase, on the second floor, there were numerous rooms: a sewing room, five bedrooms, and a small, round room in the tower, which was above the study.

"This is where I shall lock you up if you're not good," Bram joked. She glanced at him uneasily. Sometimes it was hard to tell when he was joking and when he was serious. What mixed emotions filled her head? Attraction and desire warred with mistrust and her memories of the Phoenix: She thought of stolen kisses, and of broken promises—had she really loved him? Did she really love him? How could she know? It was a love unconsummated. At this moment her encounters with the hooded stranger seemed far away. The memory of his lips was all but forgotten; it seemed that in her thoughts his kisses and Bram's mingled.

But I must see you again, she thought. *I have to tell you in person that I'm a married woman, and that while my husband is not a man of my choosing, he is—oh, heavens!—able to satisfy me.* Her imaginary conversation came to a hesitant conclusion as she thought, *Yes, without question he more than satisfies me. I long for his touch, I want him now.* Did this longing mean she was truly in love with him?

"You are now the mistress of Glen Haven. Do you like it?"

His words cut into her ruminations and brought her back to the present. "I do, yes. I like it very much."

"Regrettably, I will have to leave you here alone tomorrow. Tonight Taggert Ross will come over and share a drink with us. He is my tacksman, and while I'm gone, he'll see to your protection. He and his wife live nearby, and he's as loyal and trustworthy as they come."

Edana looked up at him. She did not want to confess that she wished he would stay. Nor did she want to ask where he was going. Perhaps, she thought miserably, he was going to see Katherine.

* * *

Heather Ross took a sip of tea and smiled shyly.

"You're not at all what I expected," Edana acknowledged. They had met only two days ago when Taggert Ross had brought his wife and come to meet her.

When Bram had told her that Taggert was his tacksman, she had expected someone older. But Taggert Ross was young, probably the same age as Bram himself, and Heather was even younger than her husband.

"I imagine you expected an old lady," Heather said cheerfully.

"I did," Edana said. "It's been awhile since I had a friend my own age. I grew up with a girl named Moira who married my brother. But my brother divorced her and she went away. I haven't heard from her for a while—I often wonder how she is.

"Divorce? Is your brother a Protestant?"

"He has become one, but not because he is religious."

"Ah," Heather said, as she grasped Edana's meaning. "For political reasons."

"I presume so. In any case, I lost contact with my friend. I hope she writes me soon."

"It's the same with me. I married Taggert last year and moved here from the mountains."

Edana knew she meant the Grampian Mountains that rose in the southeast. It was rugged country; some said, the most rugged in all of the Highlands.

"How did you meet Taggert?" Edana asked.

"Bram introduced us," she replied.

Edana did not comment. The relationship between Bram and his tacksman seemed most unusual. Usually a man as wealthy and influential as Bram Chisholm would have a more distant relationship with his tacksman, and most certainly the tacksman's wife would not be on a first-name basis with her husband's employer. True enough, Moira, the daughter of her father's tacksman, had been her friend, her only friend. But Moira's father and mother had always addressed her parents formally even though they had known each other for more than thirty years.

Edana felt doubly puzzled. "The Grampian Mountains are so far away—does Bram know many people there?"

For a moment Heather looked confused, then she quickly replied, "I think his mother's people come from there."

Edana nodded. As curious as she was, she did not want to make Heather uncomfortable by asking too many questions. She knew nothing of Bram Chisholm. She did not know about his father or his mother; she only knew he supported the British, and was wealthy. He was, she assumed, the antithesis of the Phoenix, who robbed from the rich to help the poor.

"Are the tacks high?" Edana asked. She wanted to confirm her theory.

Heather shook her head. "There's no trouble collecting them," she answered.

"That certainly is unusual," Edana said, somewhat sarcastically. "What about the poor?"

Heather shrugged. "Arrangements are made for them."

If they were like the arrangements made by George, it meant those who could not pay were expelled from the land.

"Has there been difficulty with the Phoenix in this district?"

Heather smiled broadly. "I've not heard of any."

"But you have heard of him," Edana pressed.

"All the Highlands have heard of him," she replied, draining her teacup.

"Do you read?" Edana questioned.

"Yes, I do."

"I have some books. I thought we could take turns reading to one another and then discuss what we've read."

Heather clapped her hands, "I should like that very much. Bram said I would like you, and I do."

Edana beamed. If only she didn't feel as if things were being kept from her. Bram answered her questions, but very often his answers were vague. It appeared that the same was true of Heather. There was some mystery here; she simply couldn't understand what it was, or why it existed. She was now Bram's wife and she wanted to know everything.

* * *

Bram Chisholm guided his horse along the narrow, rocky path, into the glens below the cliffs. In England, it was summer, but when they returned, spring had just been coming to the Highlands. The trees were alive with buds, and the ground cover was beginning to turn green. But here in the mountains, it was still cold in spite of it being mid-June. There was a thin covering of snow on the ground, and ice patches persisted here and there. Not that these mountains were ever lush. They were craggy and studded with huge rocks. There were trees at the lower elevations, but at the upper elevations, the ground was barren. It could be dangerous here this time of year, especially after dark, so he rode slowly and cautiously and was grateful that the night was clear and reasonably bright.

Bram reined in his horse when he reached the rock tower. It was a natural formation, but it was the place from which he had to signal. He climbed down and, using his body to block the wind, lit the lantern he carried. He swung it several times and searched the distant cliffs till he saw a light flash back, returning his signal. It was the signal that told him it was safe to continue onward up the mountain to the secret cave they called Corriedhoga. The cave was unusual. A crack had appeared between three great rocks and created an access to it. Inside, it was found to have several caverns and in one, water from an underground stream made a path on the gravel bottom.

Water had also given birth to variety of strange formations. Bram heard the noise of hooves and again stopped; in a moment a hulking Highlander galloped up beside him. Bram stared at the rider in the darkness. "Grant," he said cheerfully. "I wondered who would come to greet me."

"Even with the signal it pays to be careful."

"Are the others here?" Bram asked.

"All assembled. We've plenty of ale to celebrate your wedding, lad. We've heard you married a real beauty."

"A fiery, red-haired beauty," Bram corrected.

Grant laughed. "The best kind, lad. The best kind." Grant always called him "lad" because he was in fact the youngest of the seven. Not much younger, however. Alex MacDonald was his senior by only one year. But the others, Jack Mac-Gregor, and Bram's own three cousins, Hugh, Alister, and Ronald, were all some four years older. Alex was the newcomer to their group. He had replaced his brother, Christopher Mac-Donald who had been captured and hanged some months ago.

At the time, they had all met to decide on future strategy, to assess what had gone wrong, and to mourn their compatriot. They had left Scotland to avoid the possibility of further losses. He had wanted to see Edana then, but could not; to do so would have been too dangerous for them.

"Christopher MacDonald is gone but not forgotten. Tonight we'll make plans to avenge Christopher's death and celebrate your marriage to Edana."

They reached the cave and entered its well-hidden entrance. It was huge inside, and they tethered their horses near the entrance in the first cavern. Then they followed the stream, using the lantern for light, till they entered a second cavern. The others were all there, sitting by a campfire and drinking ale.

"The newlywed!" MacDonald shouted. "Welcome back to the nest of the Phoenix."

They all laughed, and not without good cause. Collectively they were known as the Phoenix, the legendary bird that rose from its own ashes to fly again. Their disguises were identical so they could be everywhere at once, or nowhere, if they so chose. They all fought for the same causes.

"As beautiful as your bride may be," his cousin Hugh said, slowly, "her family is our enemy."

Bram agreed, then added, "But my beauty is as much their victim as any tenant. Katherine MacLean is a monstrous woman. I believe her to be a murderess."

"Then she must pay for her crimes."

Bram nodded. "At the moment, we have bigger fish to catch." A slightly mischievous smile crossed his lips. "That's not to say Katherine could not have a small taste of retribution now, some loss which will make her angry."

"They say her fingers are heavy with rings."

"Why not?" MacDonald laughed. "She's gotten a new gold ring and diamond from each of her husbands."

"I say we relieve Katherine MacLean of her jewels," MacGregor suggested.

"A good idea, but I should like it done when I am with her."

"Is she suspicious of you?"

"Not that I know of, but I should like to ensure she won't be."

"And should your new wife, whom we hear is enamored of us, be there, too?"

Bram grinned and quaffed down some of his ale. "She is enamored of me."

They all laughed and lifted their glasses. There was much to talk about—important matters concerning the distribution of funds, and meetings with those clan chieftains who did not support the British and who were willing to make certain pledges regarding the welfare of their tenants. But for now, Bram drank with his compatriots and thought about Katherine being forced to give up her jewels for a good cause. She would be furious, and he relished the very thought of it—not that he would sell the jewels; he would keep them for Edana and give his own money to the cause.

Edana walked in the garden and circled the old tower house. Below it, down the rolling hillside, lay Loch Ness; its deep, mountain-fed waters were blue under the sky of this summerlike June day. She felt empty and, in spite of Heather's company, lonely. Bram had been gone for three weeks now, and though she was loath to admit it even to herself, she missed him. Indeed, she longed for him.

She reached inside her pocket and withdrew the letter she had received this morning. It had taken many weeks to reach her, and its contents both pleased and distressed her.

She unfolded it to read once again:

Dear Edana,

    Even though spring is coming to you, here it is cold and wretched. The wind blows incessantly. I am very alone, yet I am not alone. You will understand that I must be I careful, in case this letter falls into the wrong hands.

    To know where I am, you must think of our Princess. To know how I am, you must think of your mother. But he is beautiful, and healthy and strong. I am confused and afraid.

    Edana, please help me think of what to do.

                        Love, your friend Moira.

It would have been a mysterious letter for most, but Edana understood it. Moira still wrote the same sort of code. "Our Princess" referred to a lovely little dog Moira once had. It had been black-and-white with bits of brown on its paws and face. It was an intelligent and affectionate dog, who had helped herd the sheep. This sheepdog had been both worker and loving pet. Her father had brought it home to her from the Isle of Skye. The reference could only mean that Moira had gone to the Isle of Skye, where, as Edana recalled, Moira's grandmother's relatives lived.

The reference to her own mother was more troubling. It meant that Moira was ill, perhaps very ill. The rest was easy. She had given birth to a son. All Moira's fears were justified. Daniel was the rightful heir to all the MacLean lands, and if Katherine knew about him, she would not allow him to live.

It was all so complicated. Her father's will was clear; so was the law of the land, though its enforcement depended on the British who seemed to pick and choose exactly which laws should be enforced. The way things were set out, now that John was dead and Edana was married, George would inherit when he turned twenty-five.

In the meantime, Katherine had control over the affairs of the estate. But now that she was married to George, Katherine would inherit everything if something happened to George— if there was no male heir. Any male relative could challenge for the chieftainship, which could not be inherited by a woman under any circumstances, but the money would be hers. Now there was a way to stop Katherine, Edana thought. Unbeknownst to all but a few, a male heir did exist.

Tears filled Edana's eyes. Poor Moira! She was so afraid and so alone. Again she wondered what she could do to help her.

Edana thought, sadly, that she could not trust Bram with this information. Even though they were married and she felt love for him, the memory of his meeting with Katherine and their kiss lingered to fire her suspicions. No, the only person she could trust, the only person who could possibly help her, was the Phoenix. But where was he? Apparently he had deserted her. His promise to return was unkept.

"Edana!" Bram stood in the middle of the entrance hall and shouted out her name. "Edana! I'm back!"

In her bedroom, Edana heard his voice. Outside, it was barely light and dark clouds moved rapidly across the sky, heralding a storm.

Edana quickly climbed down from her bed and pulled her robe about her. Her red hair was braided into a single long braid that fell down her back to her waist. She put on her slippers and ran down the stairs.

He was standing in the hall, his slightly crooked smile on his face and, she realized instantly, a lustful look in his twinkling eyes. He was so handsome, so tall, strong, and muscular. She stood for an instant, looking at him.

"I rode all night," he said, as he slung his cloak over the hook.

"The servants aren't even up yet," Edana replied. Did she dare ask him where he had ridden from? He volunteered so little information. "Was your trip successful?"

He had told her little more than that he was going away on business. If only he would tell her more. She realized she did not want to believe he had been with Katherine.

"Yes, plans were made for the future." He walked to her and looked down at her. His eyes were piercing. "And did your Phoenix visit?"

"No," she answered, looking back at him.

"And do you still love him?"

Her face flushed. "I don't know," she answered honestly. What could she say? She had never known the Phoenix as she knew this man. And yet she trusted the Phoenix more.

He lightly touched her face with his hand, then ran his hand over her neck. She felt chills pass through her. His touch was light, taunting.

"Such a lovely, long white neck," he whispered.

His finger circled her ear and then he swept her into his arms and carried her up the stairs.

Edana felt her breath quicken as he set her down. He said not a word to her, but continued to look deeply into her eyes. He reached behind her and she felt him loosening her braid.

"I like your hair loose," he said, kissing her neck again. "I like to see it cascading over your bare shoulders, falling over your breasts."

She shivered with anticipation as he finished unbraiding her hair, and combed through it with his fingers. "Fire," he whispered in her ear. "Hot like your temper and your lovemaking."

She drew in her breath. The promise was unbearable. Just the tone of his voice excited her. Worse, he knew it!

He pushed her robe back and then her chemise, baring her to the waist. He again ran his hands through her hair, arranging it to suit him. He smiled and turned her toward the mirror so that she could see herself. She was naked to the waist and her hair curved around her breasts, partially covering them, even though the curve of them was quite visible.

She stared into the mirror as his hands moved down her hips and pushed her chemise off entirely. She stood naked, able to see him as his hands slid over her, setting her flesh on fire. Her mouth opened slightly and she fairly gasped for air. The sight of his hands on her body was too much—it aroused in her a heat of desire that caused her to tremble all over.

"You are a delicious creature," he whispered, as his cool hands caressed her rounded buttocks. He was still behind her; she was still in front of her mirror, watching him with burning fascination.

"Look at yourself being pleasured," he whispered in her ear.

His hands covered both her breasts and his face was buried in her neck even as he held her tightly to him.

"Look at yourself," he said teasingly. "See how lovely your breasts are when you're excited and ready."

All of her seemed to glow; her whole body blushed with the shame of her own thoughts, of feeling that she would burst if he did not soon relieve her of the tension that gripped her. His deliberate taunting was sweet torture, his words enflamed her.

He slid his hand downward and she moved involuntarily in expectation.

He spun her around, and in one swift movement had raised his kilt and lifted her to him. She faced him and she gasped when he entered her, holding her buttocks firmly. Her legs wrapped around him and she groaned with deep pleasure. She caught a glimpse of them as he carried her to the bed, whispering, "The better to pleasure you." She smiled, his naked buttocks were hard and muscular like the rest of his body.

He let her down easily on the bed and withdrew from her. She cried out and he laughed. "It shall be far too soon, if I stay," he said breathlessly, as he began to devour her breasts with kisses and light taunting movements that caused her to thrash about with expectation and pure wantonness.

"Flames crackling in the fire of your desire," he whispered, as she clung to him and murmured, "Please, please—"

He entered her again, this time slowly and deliberately. The pressure of his stem against her was true magic. She grasped his buttocks as her descent into ecstasy began. She groaned with pleasure as she felt him take his pleasure even as she enjoyed her own.

For a long time, neither of them said anything. "I missed you," he said, kissing her tenderly.

She curled herself into the curve of his body and did not move as he tenderly cupped her breast. She said nothing, sure that her movements spoke for her. He seemed too anxious for her! How could he have been with another woman? But then, she remembered her brother. He had been with Moira and with Katherine. And John could bed multiple women and apparently delight in all of them. Was Bram Chisholm like her brothers? She felt his hand fall away from her breast and heard his

breathing as it changed. She knew he had fallen asleep, tired
from riding all night, and now spent from their lovemaking.

"I missed you, too," she said softly, even though she knew
he could not hear her.

Two weeks passed and the weather grew warm with the coming
of the July sun. Bram helped work the land and was gone for
long hours, supervising all that had to be done during the short
months of productivity. With rare exception he returned nightly,
and they made love. She marveled that it did not change. It
was always the same for her and, apparently, for him. Surely
she must have been wrong about Katherine. And yet, she told
herself, she still could not trust him completely, precisely
because of his politics.

During the days, Edana kept busy sewing, making preserves,
and preparing for winter. It was no different than the activity
she had known all her life. Survival depended on preparation,
but that was so for all who lived off the land.

She was in the kitchen straining rose hips in order to make
jam, when Bram appeared unexpectedly.

"I think we should go to visit your home before the harvest,"
he said offhandedly.

She turned away from her work and looked at him in surprise.
Did he really believe she thought of it as home? Her home was
on Mull; it was now nothing more than a deserted tower house.
Home was the place where she remembered her mother and
father, the place she and Moira had once played. No, home
was not Katherine Maclean's castle—a castle shared with her
brother who had been complicit in the murder of his own father
and brother. Home? She felt more at home here in Glen Haven.

"I'd rather stay here," she replied.

He touched her shoulder lightly. "I promised we'd come,"
he told her. "I want to be here for the harvest, so we will go
this weekend."

Edana did not speak of the one thousand and one reasons
why she did not want to go to her so-called home.

"Very well," she agreed. There were simply no excuses she
could give him. One day, she hoped, she could confide her

suspicions and make him understand why she wanted to stay away from Katherine and George.

Edana watched as Katherine descended the staircase like a queen. All she lacked was a jewel-studded tiara. Katherine's expensive gown was bloodred and trimmed in black lace. It was low-cut and her hair was piled on her head.

Edana wore the green gown that Bram had bought her in London. He had asked that she wear it, and she knew he liked it because it was the same color as her eyes.

George was also formally dressed, though Edana could not help but notice how tired he looked. His eyes had a hollow appearance and lines beneath them that gave him the appearance of being much older than he actually was. He seemed strangely lethargic, too, quite unlike the George she had once known.

"The carriage is outside waiting for us," Katherine announced. "Superintendent Crane will be so glad to see you." She ignored Edana and took Bram's arm. "I'm sure he'll lay on quite a feast. You know how he likes to entertain," Katherine went on.

Edana walked stiffly beside George as they all went to the carriage that would take them to Fort William for dinner, and what the invitation had described as "an intimate party."

"Crane says he's missed your repartee," George put in, slurring his words slightly.

Edana frowned. Even George's speech was slow. "Are you all right?" she asked with concern.

"I've never been better," he muttered. He touched Katherine's arm. "She exhausts me."

Edana ignored his comment. She was sure Katherine exhausted all the men with whom she slept. And had George no sense? Had he no fear of this woman? She had killed before, and she would no doubt kill again. She would probably kill him. But then, Edana thought, she might not kill him, as long as she could control him.

"It's a fair ride to the fort," Bram reminded them.

George stood by, looking like an oaf, while Bram lifted Katherine into the carriage. Then he lifted Edana and she found

herself sitting next to Katherine, feeling miserably uncomfortable just to be so near this woman. Bram and George sat
opposite, so that they were riding backward as the carriage was
driven away.

The carriage clattered down the drive, and they were soon
out on the rutted road that led to the fort.

The meal had been excellent. There had been imported wine
and a concert by some visiting musicians. After that, there had
been dancing, and finally the evening came to an end.

Bram had put his arm around George's shoulder. "I have
business here so I'll stay the night. You escort our ladies home."

"But of course," George had said, with a flourish. His words
were still slurred, although this time, Edana could blame the
liquor. He had consumed a fair amount. She had glanced at
Bram almost imploringly. He had not mentioned he would be
staying at the fort, and the idea of going home alone with
George and Katherine caused her once again to feel suspicious
of his motives.

Bram had bent and kissed her cheek. "Just one night," he had
whispered, and this partial acknowledgment of her discomfort
made her feel better. She had just nodded and gone with Katherine and George, neither of whom had once mentioned her
previous accusations, though both had been treating her as if
she were nonexistent.

As they drove through the moonlight, Edana found that
seeing George again reminded her of Moira, and soon she was
lost in thoughts of her friend. She had not been able to write
back since Moira had not said exactly where on Skye she was
living. Nor, Edana thought sadly, had she heard from her again.
Vaguely she wondered if Moira's father knew exactly where
she was—and if Edana wrote to him, would he trust her enough
to send the message on to Moira?

"Hell!" she heard George shout.

It all happened suddenly. The carriage came to a jolting stop
and the horses reared. Katherine and she were thrown forward
and Katherine lost her balance and fell off the seat, but Edana
grabbed the velvet strap in time.

"Damn," Katherine muttered, as she pulled herself up and onto the seat.

Shots were fired, and before George could draw his pistol, there was a face at the carriage window and the door had been opened.

Edana felt her mouth grow dry, but she stifled any reaction to the hooded figure that stood by the door. His black cloak blew in the wind; his head was obscured beneath his hood, which covered everything save his brown eyes.

The hooded man held his pistol on them, then grabbed her hand. "Take off your rings," he ordered. Edana was completely taken aback. Would he return them later, as he had returned her gold chains?

"Do as he says," George urged.

Edana took off her rings and handed them to the hooded man. She fought to see his eyes—did he still want her?

"And now yours, my lovely lady."

Katherine took off her rings and handed them to him. She spit at him as if she were a snake.

What happened next so stunned Edana she could not even move.

The Phoenix motioned them all out of the carriage. A few feet away, the driver lay unconscious. Then the Phoenix pulled Katherine into his arms and kissed her, hard and long. Katherine fought, but soon fell quiet in his grasp. She appeared to be returning his kiss.

George stared blankly at them. Edana felt shocked and stunned. This man whom she had virtually worshiped, this man whom she had wished to return again and again, this man who had saved her life and so tenderly tended her wounds, paid virtually no attention to her. In fact, he did not even seem to remember her. Instead, he was kissing Katherine with passion!

"Let her go!" George protested, as somehow he found his tongue.

The masked man let Katherine go and flicked George across the nose with his finger as if he were a loathsome insect of some sort. Then he kissed Katherine again, this time for even longer. He let her go, after a long moment, then turned and mounted his horse. He rode off, disappearing into the darkness.

The three of them stood in silence for what seemed like an eternity. Finally Katherine said, "Lift the driver up to the seat, George. You drive. We'll return to the fort. I think we need an escort."

Edana sank miserably into her seat. Damn him! In the darkness, tears filled her eyes. He had forgotten her! He was certainly not the man she had dreamed of for so long.

Katherine's dark eyes smoldered with anger as she spoke to Superintendent Crane. "I should think your men could control highwaymen at least so close the fort," she fumed. "He took all of my rings. They were extremely valuable."

George was incapable of saying anything. It seemed to Edana that he had shriveled up before her very eyes.

Bram, on the other hand, appeared angry. "He really must be caught," he muttered, grim-faced.

Crane nodded. "I've sent out two patrols. If he's still in the district, he'll be found."

"I want that man hanged!" Katherine demanded.

Bram took Edana's arm. "Did he touch you?" he asked.

Edana shook her head and felt grateful for his concern. At least he didn't seem overly concerned with Katherine.

"It's Katherine's honor he besmirched," George said, attempting to sound put-out.

Katherine turned on him wildly. Her eyes flashed with anger. "Thanks to you, you spineless little weasel."

George's face flushed and once again he sank into silence.

"Exactly how did he besmirch your honor?" Bram asked.

"He kissed me—not that it matters. I'm concerned with my property."

Edana wanted to cry out that the rings were not Katherine's property; they had in fact belonged to Carolyn, Edana's mother. As upset as she was that the Phoenix had ignored her and even kissed Katherine, she did not care that he had taken Carolyn's rings. Edana felt certain that Carolyn would rather they be used by the Phoenix than worn by Katherine. As for Bram, she felt a growing warmth and appreciation of him. He did not seem at all concerned with his property. Indeed, he seemed concerned only with her well-being.

"I assume he took the ring I gave you, as well," he asked her.

Edana nodded. "Yes. I'm sorry."

"I shall give you another," he promised.

Katherine shot them both a venomous look.

Crane watched Katherine. No doubt she would be happy to draw and quarter the Phoenix herself. As much as he had enjoyed her body, Crane decided at that moment that it would be a mistake to go on sleeping with her. She was a dangerous woman, an acquisitive woman who was filled with evil. He had encouraged her because he needed her political support, but there were limits. As he looked at George, he decided he wanted to take no chances on being turned into one of Katherine's obedient pets.

"We'll stay here for the night," Bram told Edana, as he slipped his arm protectively around her.

Crane thought that the look on Katherine's face was truly revealing. Clearly she did not like Bram's doting on Edana any more than she had liked being robbed of her ill-gotten possessions.

"I'll provide an armed escort for you and George," Crane informed Katherine.

Katherine glowered at him. "We've already been robbed. There's nothing left to steal."

"They might come back and kill us," George whined.

" 'They'? There was no 'they'—it was one man, and you couldn't do a thing to stop him," Katherine said bitterly.

"He surprised me."

"A toad could surprise you," she snapped. George's face reddened and he fell yet again into chastened silence.

"Now, now, Katherine. The Phoenix has a formidable reputation. It's far more important that the three of you are safe than it is that a few trinkets were stolen," Crane said.

"They were more than trinkets," she snapped irritably. "But I suppose we do need a guard. Who knows? Next time he might steal the carriage."

"I shall summon some soldiers right away."

"Are you sure you and Edana won't come home with us?" Katherine asked, turning to Bram, with a sudden change of mood and tone.

"I have business here, and under the circumstances, I want Edana with me."

Katherine appeared mystified by his concern, Edana observed. Bram's actions all but convinced her that she had been wrong and that he did not care for Katherine. Perhaps she could trust him, after all.

Bram stretched out on the narrow bed and watched her as she undressed. His eyes made her feel warm, but she no longer felt uncomfortable in the least.

"So you saw the Phoenix tonight. Tell me, do you still love him?"

That he had said nothing sooner had surprised her, but she was not surprised now. She looked at Bram and shook her head. "I was childish," she admitted. "I don't think I ever loved him. I loved the idea of him. And he was kind to me."

"Is it because he kissed Katherine?"

That question did surprise her. "I don't think so," she answered.

"You're an honest woman," he said, reaching out to her. She took his hand and sat down on the side of the bed. "Perhaps," he suggested, "you were unhappy that he wanted to kiss a woman like Katherine."

"I can't lie—that might be part of it."

"Is there another part?"

His eyes seemed to dance with humor, and even though she realized he was taunting her, she knew she deserved it. "There is another part. I think I love you. I think I've changed since our marriage."

He touched her hair. "Not to remember you, not to cherish you, makes your Phoenix a dunderhead. Perhaps he has changed, too, perhaps he is a whole other person."

"I never know when you are teasing me and when you're serious. I must tell you, that while I feel deeply for you, I still cannot accept your politics. Superintendent Crane is a nice

man, but he is my enemy. He is the enemy of all Scotland.
The rings the Phoenix took from Katherine belonged to Carolyn,
my mother. I know she would rather the Phoenix have them
than Katherine.''

He put his hand on the back of her neck and drew her head
down, kissing her on the lips. ''Rest assured that I am quite
serious when I tell you that I accept your reservations, and that
I could never forget you.''

His lips were soft and she lay down beside him. She ran her
hands across his body and was rewarded when she felt him,
strong and ready.

''You grow bold,'' he whispered.

Edana enfolded his manhood in her hand, and at the same
time kissed his chest. ''Fires can sometimes start spontane-
ously,'' she whispered. ''You have pleasured me, my husband.
Let me show you how much I have learned.''

He lay still and let her remove his clothes and touch him
tentatively where he had always hoped she would.

''You are a wonder,'' he said, lifting her atop him. ''A
wonder and a sublime pleasure.''

Chapter Nine

September 1708

Bram guided his horse along the valley floor. In spite of the full moon and the reasonably warm summer night, Glencoe still brought a rush of memories that filled him with melancholy and aroused the deep anger that drove him to continue fighting British rule.

"Here you died," he said aloud, speaking not just to the spirit of his father, but to the spirits of his mother and two younger brothers as well. They had all been killed here, on a bitter-cold February night, in the year 1692—more than sixteen years ago. Their crime had been their hospitality.

Clan MacDonald had inhabited Glencoe for many centuries. They were entertaining the Campbells that night in February when they were turned on and massacred. Men, women, and children died. They had died to satisfy old hatreds but their deaths only gave birth to new ones.

Bram Chisholm had lived in the south of Scotland, and in England; so, better than many of his countrymen, he saw and understood the pulls and throws of his own people. He knew what had passed before, and was committed to a free Scotland ruled by the people.

He was, in spite of what many thought, a Highlander to the core. He wanted no part of union with Britain and he well understood that the Lowlanders hated the Highlands and wanted desperately to be a part of England. He likewise understood that Clan Campbell were the enforcers for the British Crown in Scotland. The feud between those clans that sided with the MacDonalds and those who sided with the Campbells reached back hundreds of years into Scots history. In Gaelic, the phrase was, *Mi-run mor nan Gall,* which meant, "The Lowlanders' great hatred." They despised the Highlanders: they railed against their language, the Gaelic tongue; against their clothes, the plaid; against their customs; and most of all, against their independence of spirit.

Sadly Bram looked about him. No one would think of ordering the massacre of a community in England. What had happened here, had happened because the Highlanders would not submit to the authority of the central government. At the same time, the massacre made it impossible for him and for the others to submit.

He looked about him and tried to picture the whole of this place, a place he knew as well as any man did. It ran east to west along the northern border of Argyll. Glencoe was both a fortress and a trap with an entrance at either end of its expanse. The east entrance to the glen was across Rannoch Moor. But Rannoch Moor was often impassable, as it was closed not only by winter blizzards but also by summer storms. It was an unstable stretch of land covered with heather and the bleached bones of a long-dead forest. Few men knew the rutted paths across Rannoch Moor.

Loch Levenside stretched along the whole of the west side of the glen. There were apparent high passes over the mountains at both the northern and southern ends of the glen, but these most often led nowhere. A climber might well find himself on a mist-shrouded cliff, or facing a great wall of granite.

An uncountable number of streams created the River Coe, the true entrance to the glen. Wide and then narrow, and suddenly wide again, the river accumulated in great pools, then bubbled over wide shallows, passing over a rainbow of blue, pink, and white stones.

Some called Glencoe "the Glen of Weeping," but Clan MacDonald, and most Highlanders, called it "the Glen of Dogs." The name reached fifteen hundred years back into Celtic mythology, when ferocious long-haired Fingalian giants were said to have made their home in Glencoe. It was told that they sailed their ships to Ireland and the Outer Hebrides. Many believed that their spirits still lived on the mountaintops and that the howling wind was their breathing.

Legend had it that the Fingalian had fought with the Vikings, that their leader had cleverly bought time until his swordsmen returned from hunting. The Fingalian had defeated the Viking warriors, but were never again as ferocious.

Bram shook his head. It was a tale that inspired Scots Highlanders. No victory had been won, yet independence had been maintained. It was that independence of spirit he now fought for; it was that for which the other Seven in Glenmoristan also fought.

He was again headed for the mountains. This trip to the Glen was an annual trip, one he had made for many years, to silently remember the murder of his family, and to rededicate himself to freedom.

He turned his thoughts toward Edana, not that his thoughts were ever far from her. He had fallen in love with her the first time he saw her, and he loved her more each day. But he knew she did not trust him. "And rightly so," he said aloud, to the spirits of the wind. She mistrusted him because he could not tell her his secrets.

He rode toward the moor and when he reached the Rock of Weeping, he saw his cousins.

"You've come from the arms of the enemy," Hugh said, lifting his hand in greeting. "Have you learned anything of value?"

"I have information concerning a shipment of funds to pay the garrison at Fort William."

"Ah," Hugh said, smiling. "Now, there's a worthwhile target."

Bram nodded. "But first there's a family that needs our help.

Have you sold the jewelry you stole from Katherine's castle while she was being robbed by Grant on her way home from the fort?''

"Yes, it brought a pretty penny. But I did as you asked, and did not sell the rings taken from her on the road.'' He grinned. "Naturally I didn't sell your wife's ring, either. Here, take them back.''

Bram took the rings. "Katherine's rings came from Carolyn MacLean and I want Edana to have them eventually. I'll keep them all and give them back to her when she can know the truth.''

He turned to Hugh. "Then, let's be off. Let Katherine's tenants pay their rents with her own money.''

Hugh laughed. "A fine idea.''

Edana stood atop the tower behind the house. It offered a fine view of the countryside and enabled her to see the loch as well as the road to the house.

"Ten days,'' she said aloud, as she searched the horizon. Where had Bram gone? Where did he disappear to when he left her? This was the longest he had been absent, and she found herself quite worried that he might have encountered some type of trouble.

She grasped her skirt and nervously crumpled its material between her fingers. It was wrong of her to suspect him—but she could not help it. He never told her where he was going or where he had been. He came and went like the wind, and sometimes when he returned he seemed distant and removed.

Was there another woman? Her thoughts again turned to Katherine. Perhaps, in spite of everything, he did go to Katherine. Heaven knew, she had wiles about her; men doted on her, and she had a way of controlling their minds.

"I must know where you go,'' Edana said. And at that moment, she promised herself that the next time he left her, she would secretly follow him. "I cannot rest till I know you truly love me,'' she said, looking at the sky. "Forgive me my lack of trust.''

Hardly had she made her vow than she saw a rider

approaching, and in a few minutes she knew it was Bram, returned once again. She ran to the stairs and then down the tower steps.

"I missed you so," she whispered.

The fire flickered in the hearth. It was the fourteenth of October, the harvest was complete, and the cold winter waited in the wings anxiously, as it always did in the Highlands. Some years it was more patient than others, Edana thought, as she stared into the flames. But the early chill in the air made her believe this would be an impatient year. Winter would come early.

"You're far away tonight," Bram observed.

"I was thinking," she said abstractedly.

"May I ask what about?"

She sought his eyes. "Should I share my thoughts with a man who disappears with hardly a word and returns days later as if he has never been gone?"

"It is not my desire to be away from you. I have business."

"What kind of business, Bram? Where?"

"Just business," he answered vaguely.

She looked down. "That is not an answer. How can I trust you if I don't know where you go? If I don't understand what this mysterious 'business' is?"

It was the confrontation he had dreaded and yet had known would come. That she had restrained herself so far was owing entirely to her nature. He looked into her clear green eyes and wanted as always to tell her the truth about himself, but he could not. And yet, as he confronted her question, he found it equally hard either to be evasive or to lie. "I cannot tell you," he said finally. "It is not my choice to have this secret from you. But it is a necessary secret, and this you must believe."

"I want to believe it," she said, looking back into his eyes. He was keeping much to himself. There was no other way out. She would have to follow him; she would have to discover for herself this secret that he told her he must keep.

He sat down beside her in front of the hearth and the nearness of him was distracting. He touched her hand, then ran his hand

up her arm, over the curve of her shoulder, and onto her neck.
He bent toward her and nibbled on her ear.

Her reaction to him was instant. A chill went through her
whole body and she turned toward him, her full lips ready for
his.

He kissed her neck and face and then he touched her lips.
At first his touch was light, then firmer as his own passion
mounted with the memory of past kisses, of past couplings,
and of the unbridled passion she brought to their lovemaking.
How he hated deceiving her!

His persistent kiss forced her mouth open and her breath
came now in short gasps as she clung to him wanting more,
and forgetting everything for the moment except the feel of
him, the maleness of him close to her, the heat of his body
against hers, the feel of the fire on her back when he moved
his hand over her.

He covered her face, neck, and ears with kisses, and returned
to kiss her lips again and again before he lifted her into his
arms and carried her to their bed.

He pulled the laces that held her dress and pushed it away,
falling on her, ravishing her with the same hungry kisses he
had visited upon her lips.

She moved beneath him as his hand slipped beneath her
undergarments, exciting her and prodding gently into her until
she thought she would scream with excitement at the ecstasy
he caused her to feel. Heat filled her whole body and her skin
glowed as he moved his fingers within her and gently caressed
her place of greatest pleasure. She moaned and tossed and was
suddenly sent reeling down, the release of her passion inflaming
her. She panted wildly and lay against him. He waited for her
to once again lie calmly, and then he returned to her, this time
to pleasure her again and to seek his own release.

"I love watching you," he whispered.

After a long while, still lying in his arms, she opened her
eyes and looked at his sleeping face.

I must know, she thought. *I must truly know this man I love.*

* * *

At morning light, Bram was out and about. Fall was short, so the days were filled with work.

Edana washed herself with water heated over the fire, then she dressed in her workclothes. There were servants aplenty, but she enjoyed doing some of her own work, and she certainly enjoyed making the preserves they would cherish during the long winter.

She looked about the bedroom and shook her head. Bram's clothes were strewn across the floor, as were her own. He had just left them there, putting on his own workclothes to go and see to the chores.

Edana picked up her own articles of clothing one by one, folded them, and put them away. Then she began to pick up Bram's clothes. He had worn his kilt and it was spread out untidily. She carefully folded it according to the ritual fold so that the next time he wanted to wear it, the creases would be in the right place. She picked up his sporran and from it a clatter of treasure fell on the stone floor. Edana covered her mouth in surprise.

"Heavens," she whispered, as she gathered up the rings. She turned her own ring over in her fingers. Where had they come from? How had Bram obtained them? Had they been recovered by the soldiers at the fort?

Edana sat on the floor, holding the rings, and leaning against the side of her bed. Had Bram been with Katherine, as Edana had originally suspected, and had Katherine gotten back her rings as well as this one from the Phoenix? He had, after all, given Edana back her gold chain. She shook her head. This was very strange. It deepened the mystery of him. She had been plagued by questions and now she added another. Why had he not told her the ring had been recovered? Then, carefully, so he wouldn't know she'd seen them, she replaced the rings in the secret pocket of his sporran. Perhaps he would give her ring back to her and tell her how he had gotten it back. But deep down inside, she knew he would not.

The moon was but a sliver but the stars were bright, as Edana led her horse along. She followed Bram at some distance; she was mystified because he headed for the house of his tacksman rather than toward the fort, which was in the same direction as Katherine's. But what mystery could there be in visiting his tacksman? Odd questions filled her head, but she plodded on, silently, hoping he would not hear her.

It was half an hour later when she came upon the Ross home. Through the windows, she could see the glow of the fire and the lamps. But she dared not venture close enough to hear what might be discussed. Still, there was no question that Bram was inside. His horse was tethered out front, while hers was hidden.

She waited just behind the low wall that surrounded the front garden where Heather Ross grew the household vegetables. Its produce had been harvested, and now it consisted of barren rows mulched with dried grasses.

Edana wrapped her cloak more tightly about her. It was cold, colder than it had been before, and she cursed herself for not dressing more warmly. After all, she had no way of knowing where he was headed.

In a moment, the door of the Ross house opened. Edana heard Heather call out, "Good luck!" and then her husband called out, "Happy hunting!"

Was Bram going hunting? She peered at the door and when she saw who stepped through it, she nearly fell backward. It was the Phoenix! He was dressed in his dark cloak and hood. He wore his hood and he paused only a moment before he mounted Bram's stallion, a horse that only Bram could ride.

Bram was the Phoenix! The reality of it almost caused her to cry out. How could this be? How could he not have told her?

Then she thought of his most recent attack and how he had ignored her and passionately kissed Katherine. Of course he had ignored her! He could have her whenever he wanted to—she was his wife! Vaguely she wondered how he had got out of the fort and then back in time to be there when they had returned, but it seemed possible.

Tears of anger and surprise filled her eyes. "Damn you!" she muttered. He had deceived her, and considering what she had told him of her own encounter with the Phoenix, no doubt laughed his head off at her. She felt hurt as well as angry.

And where was he off to now? He had turned his horse in the direction of Fort William, in the direction of Katherine's.

On wobbly legs Edana lifted herself from her hiding place and bolted for her own horse. She mounted and turned toward home, riding blindly into the darkness, tears streaking down her face, her whole body shaking with shock, frustration, and anger.

"How could you deceive me so?" she sobbed.

But no answer was forthcoming, because she was quite alone.

The early-morning sun was hidden behind a shroud of low mist, and a light fog rose from the sodden ground, giving the rocky barren landscape an otherworldly look, as if it simply appeared and disappeared like the legendary enchanted village which materialized only every hundred years. Bram thought of the story; as a child, it had been one of his favorites.

His mother's people had come from Clan MacDonald and she had taken her husband and other sons to visit her family in Glencoe at the time of the massacre. He remembered being there himself as a boy.

Life among his mother's family was unique. Summer began with the Feast of Beltane on the first day of May. Each village built a fire, and from the fire, embers were taken into each individual home. The women made bannock. It was left out for the wild animals of the glen so that they would not harm the cattle that grazed on the slopes of the mountain called the Herdsman. They also left bannock on the braes of Black Mountain and on the shores of the Loch of Cows that lay on the west side of Rannoch Moor. In all those places their live-stock grazed, and had to be protected. At the end of fall, both the people and the cattle returned on the day of the Feast of Samhain, which marked the beginning of winter.

Summer was a happy time. The women spent their days making butter and cheese. They spun wool, and sang as they worked. The boys, like he had been, attended informal classes in military training, where they learned to wield the broadsword and the ax, as well as learning to use the musket and properly protect themselves with the hide shield. In the evenings there was dancing, singing, and tale-telling. He smiled to himself; they commonly drank ale, but there was whiskey too, and there was one special whiskey which Southerners were warned against. Like all whiskey, it was made from corn, but it was distilled five times, and all those who drank it said that more than two teaspoonsful could take a man's breath away.

Again he thought of the storytelling, of the superstitions with which he had grown up, of the tales that filled a boy's head. But no oracle had foretold the massacre; there had been no sign of it coming, no hint of the horrific killings that had taken his family and so many who had lived in Glencoe.

He thought of Clan Campbell and how they had aided the British and massacred those who lived in Glencoe. Land was taken away from others and given to the Campbells. Their empire was expanded; their appetites seemed insatiable. Their motto was Do Not Forget, but it might just as well have been Gain at the Expense of Others, Bram thought bitterly.

He listened, and his thoughts of the past fled. The time was at hand, and he could not allow himself to think of other matters.

He looked down and saw the King's men riding on the road. They were five in all, and their saddlebags bulged with the payroll for the fort. They were relaxed and unsuspecting.

The Phoenix would strike this morning, and though he was not alone, those attacked would not realize that there was more than one because one man was all they would see.

The riders came to an abrupt halt as their horses nearly stumbled on the mist-shrouded felled trees that blocked the road. They turned in disarray, guns drawn, but it was too late. A series of small, bright explosions startled both horses and riders and drove them off the road and into the trees. They were close together, as intended, and even as the explosions continued, a great net was dropped from above.

They were entangled, frightened and struggling, when Bram called out to them from his hiding place. He ordered them to discard their pistols or be killed. They discarded their guns even as they looked about, craning their necks to see from where the disembodied voice came.

They were told to dismount and to lie on the ground with their eyes covered. When this was done, he gathered in the net while his compatriots, still in hiding, watched with their guns drawn. If any of the prisoners were to make a false move, they would be fired upon.

One by one, the prisoners were taken, bound, and blindfolded. Each one saw a Phoenix, but no one saw them together. In the meantime, Bram emptied the saddlebags of their treasure. It would be taken to the shores of the loch where a boatsman waited to carry it far away to safety.

When he returned, each of the prisoners was made to drink from a flask. He smiled to himself. It was the five-times-distilled whiskey, and gulping it down caused his prisoners to cough and complain. But their complaints were short-lived. The legend of the whiskey's effect was not far from the truth. It made them uncoordinated, and left them in a drunken stupor.

When he was satisfied they had drunk sufficient whiskey, he scattered their horses, collected their pistols, and ordered them to strip. His compatriots left silently and Bram himself left as well, headed back to his home via a circuitous route. The victims were separated, drunk, naked, and without horses. It would be some time before they reached the fort, and a long while before search parties were sent out. As always, they would tell tales of being netted and robbed by one man who had been everywhere at once. Such tales naturally made others more afraid, so that each time they attacked government troops, there was less resistance. Legends, he concluded, could be most helpful.

Edana, her hair loose and falling over her slim shoulders, sat at the spinning wheel. Working with her hands helped her to think clearly. *That is what I must do,* she told herself repeatedly.

It was so hard to sort through it all! From the first moment she had encountered the Phoenix, she had felt a deep attraction to him, even though she had not known what he looked like. He had rescued her from John's cruel advances and seen to it that she was nursed back to health and returned home. It was during that time that she had come to believe she loved him. Later, she had been given in marriage to Bram and between them had grown a stormy, passionate lovemaking that had made her forget the kisses of the Phoenix. Then the Phoenix had appeared again, and seemed only interested in stealing kisses from Katherine.

Now she knew the truth—Bram was the Phoenix! And yet the timing still puzzled her. At first she had thought it possible that he could have left and returned to the fort in time, but then she doubted it after reflection on the distances. How had Bram gotten back to the fort by the time they had arrived? And if he had been gone, why hadn't Superintendent Crane realized it and wondered if Bram and the Phoenix were the same man? But these questions, which filled her head, were secondary to the fact that he had seemed interested in Katherine, and that his interest persisted even though, since he was the Phoenix, he had to know what Katherine stood for and how dangerous she was.

Through her muddled thoughts Edana heard the footsteps on the stairs and she looked up, just as the door opened. There, framed in the doorway was Bram. He grinned at her expectantly, waiting for her to fly into his arms as she always did when he returned.

Her spindle fell to the floor and she stared at him. He had come home sooner than she expected; she felt caught off guard. She had not yet had time to plan what she would say. She had not had time to ponder what his response might be.

"Did you tire of Katherine?" she asked. She could hear the bitterness in her own voice.

The smile faded from his handsome, boyish face and was replaced by an expression of puzzlement. "Katherine?" he repeated. "I have not been with Katherine."

"I am sure you have," she answered. She was looking directly at him, her green eyes steady and unflinching.

"I really have no idea why you think I might have been with Katherine," he returned.

"Perhaps because you find her so attractive."

"She's a beautiful woman, but you are the only woman I desire."

She got up and walked closer to him. Her lower lip quivered slightly and he could feel her emotions rising to the surface as she stood looking into his eyes, studying his face. "I could

believe you if I not seen you kiss her so passionately—I could
believe you if you had ever told me the truth."

"Edana—" He reached out to draw her into his arms, but
she stepped away.

"I know you are the Phoenix," she said steadily.

He looked at her in surprise. But then it was clear to him
that she did know. "How?" he managed.

Edana drew in her breath. "I confess, I followed you the
night you left. I saw you come out of the Ross house dressed
as the Phoenix."

He let out his breath. Denials would be useless. "Yes, I am
the Phoenix. I didn't tell you in order to protect you."

"You did not tell me so that you could carry on an affair
with Katherine. How could you?" Her eyes filled with tears
and her voice quivered slightly. "You must know what she is
like. I don't know what happened to old MacQuarrie, but I
know my father was poisoned, I know that George did not kill
John in an honorable duel. Katherine shot him. I saw her do
it with my own eyes. And whatever George's crimes, I believe
she gives him something—poison, drugs, I don't know what.
She drove my friend Moira to Skye, and I'm sure she wants
me dead!"

His face knit into a frown. "I know much about Katherine,
but I did not know she had poisoned your father and shot
John."

"I wanted to tell you, but I was afraid you loved her. I know
now that at the very least you must be enamored of her."

Bram leaned closer to her and this time she did not move
away. "How do you know this?"

"Because when you robbed us, you kissed her. It was no
ordinary kiss. It was a very passionate kiss."

He moved quickly, pulled her into his arms, and kissed her
full on the lips, hard and strong. She struggled against him,
but all the memories of their time together prevented her from
struggling long. She went limp in his arms and when he let
her go, she was still crying.

"Did I kiss her like that?" he asked.

She looked back at him. Her eyes were still defiant. "It is
you who gave the kiss."

He shook his head. "No, it was not."

"I saw you with my own eyes."

"You thought you saw me. Edana, I cannot tell you everything. Not all secrets are mine to tell. But there is more than one Phoenix, and if you don't believe me, you have only to ask Crane. He will tell you I never left the fort."

Edana felt her own surprise. Was this possible?

"It was I who came to you on Mull. It was I who saved you from John. Edana, I love you and I have loved you since the first moment I laid eyes on you."

"More than one Phoenix? This story is too fantastic."

"This story is true."

"Who might the others be?"

"I told you, not all secrets are mine to reveal."

"I don't know what to believe," she admitted. She decided not to tell him she had discovered the rings.

"Believe there is more than one Phoenix. One was hanged; another robbed you and the others that night after you left the fort. Edana, you are my only love." Again he pulled her into his arms and began to kiss the tears from her cheeks.

At first, she felt stiff and reluctant. But she could not fight him or deny him. His touch was fire on her flesh, and she responded to him, unable to control herself, unable to break away, unable even to mutter the slightest protest.

"You must believe me," he whispered again and again. She yielded to him, but she was still not certain she believed him. Over and over again, she asked herself if it was possible that there was more than one Phoenix. There was only one way to find out. She would indeed have to ask Crane if Bram had remained at the fort. But how could she ask him without casting suspicion on Bram?

Bram stood by their bed and looked down at Edana. She lay curled on her side like a child, her gorgeous, fiery-red hair in disarray, her plump, lovely breasts one atop the other, their nipples erect in the cool air. She was the most beautiful of women, he thought as he bent and tenderly covered her so she would sleep. He bent and gently kissed her on the cheek.

"In time you will believe me," he said to her sleeping form. He turned and walked to his writing desk. He would leave her a note. As much as he did not want to leave, the Phoenix had business that had to be seen to. He scribbled a note and left it for her. Then he hurried to the tower behind the house, where Hugh, his cousin, waited.

Edana chose to wear a hunter's-green traveling suit trimmed with fur. She braided her thick red hair and wound the braids around her head. Her cloak was dark green, too, and she knew that in appearance she looked prim and proper.

"This way, ma'am." The young soldier seemed somehow awestruck as he ushered her into Crane's office. It was a large office, with walls that were half dark green and half wainscoting of a dark wood. A large desk took up most of one side of the room, though there were several straight-backed chairs.

Edana sat in one and waited. She was glad that she had to wait, because in truth, she did not have the foggiest idea what she was going to say, or how she would elicit the desired information from Crane.

"My dear Mrs. Chisholm, what a surprise." Crane entered the office from a door behind the desk, rather than the door through which she had been ushered into the office. She assumed his private quarters lay beyond his office. She had been to the fort only twice before. Once with Bram and then again on the night of Superintendent Crane's little party, the night of the robbery. When she had come with Bram, they had met in another room, and the night they were robbed, they had dined in a private dining room in another building. That night, after the robbery, she had spent the night here with Bram, but it had been spent in a small apartment in yet another building that housed the fort's officers. This was the first time she had seen his office, and she realized he had decorated it to look like an English drawing room.

"I was on my way home," she lied, "and I thought I would stop and ask if there is anything new to report concerning the robbery."

Crane smiled at her. Chisholm certainly had made the right

choice marrying this one rather than becoming entangled with Katherine MacLean. Edana MacLean was far more beautiful, and she was neither conniving nor evil. "Robbery?"

"Yes, the robbery, the attack of the so-called Phoenix. You recall, my husband remained here with you and we were all set upon on our way home. You were going to investigate."

"Ah, yes, I remember. Please forgive me. Only recently the Phoenix attacked and robbed some soldiers on their way here. I'm afraid that incident temporarily eclipsed all others from my mind. But of course, I do remember! Bram and I spent the evening discussing the sale of some uniforms—and you and George and Katherine headed toward your castle and were set upon."

Edana nodded, and forced herself to remain impassive though in fact she wanted to jump for joy. Bram had told her the truth! There was more than one Phoenix! "I'm shocked to hear he attacked again," she managed.

Crane cleared his throat. "I'm sorry to say I have no information on any of the goods you reported stolen. But I may have some soon. To tell you the truth, and I know I can trust you, we've enlisted the help of the Campbells. There's been a trap set, and I hope that soon, very soon, we may have this criminal under arrest."

Edana struggled to maintain her composure. "A trap?" she murmured, hoping her expression did not reveal the fear that suddenly gripped her.

"A trap—yes, indeed. A well-laid trap. And I've made Campbell promise that if he succeeds in capturing this man, he will wait till I come to unmask him. I can't tell you what pleasure that will give me. He's caused a great deal of trouble."

"He certainly has," Edana said. Her only desire at this moment was to escape this office, to somehow find Bram, to warn him. But where was he? Where was the trap being set?

"You have so many important things to do," she said, in a near whisper. "I really must be going."

"It's been a pleasure to see you. I'll let you know how things turn out."

"Thank you." She stood up as if to leave. Then she turned back and looked at him, her green eyes wide with innocence.

"When might I hear something? I am ever so anxious about my rings."

Crane smiled. "Within two days, I imagine. Campbell is supposed to be returning to Argyll from London with some especially valuable possessions. He will appear to be traveling alone along the Argyll road tomorrow night. But we'll have soldiers from Clan Campbell nearby and if the Phoenix attacks, it is he who will be captured." Crane looked completely satisfied. "We've spread the story of Campbell's return far and wide. I'm quite certain the Phoenix will take the bait."

Edana wanted to ask where on the Argyll road, but she deemed it best to be satisfied with what information she had. Too much curiosity might make him suspicious. "My husband will be most pleased if you catch this man," she said, as she turned and all but fled out the door. *Heavens,* she thought to herself. *I hope he did not notice how agitated I was. How will I ever find Bram on the Argyll road?*

Bram headed into Argyll with a certain trepidation. Perhaps, he thought, he should have contacted the others, but there was no time, and this was a large and desirable prize, a prize well worth a risk. But he was cautious.

This was the part of the Highlands where support for the central government ran high, he thought, as he headed south. Support for government had most certainly paid off, for no clan knew the wealth the Campbells knew.

In 1607, Archibald Campbell, Seventh Earl of Argyll, was granted all the former MacDonald lands in Kintyre. In 1613, Campbell of Cawdor was allowed to purchase Islay and most of Duart and Jura that had belonged to the MacLeans of Duart. For a time, during the restoration of the monarchy, the Campbells had done badly but then, once again their fortunes rose. Only a few months ago, King William, the Dutch usurper of the throne—which to Bram's way of thinking should have belonged to the Stuarts—made Campbell the Tenth Earl of Argyll and the Marquess of Lorne and Kintyre. Beneath that, quite-long-enough title, King William had bestowed a dozen or more lesser titles on Campbell. He was also made a high-ranking officer, and Crane had confided that he expected Campbell would eventually become commander in chief of the British Army.

Bram had heard that Colin Campbell, one of the richest of his clan, would be headed home with a large amount of gold. He was alleged to be traveling alone so as not to attract attention. It was far too tempting to pass up, although, he admitted, he would have to be careful with Crane in the future. He would, when this robbery was successfully completed, have to lie low for a while, as the saying went.

But the joy of it! To take from Campbell was his greatest pleasure. He thought for a moment of Edana, and corrected himself: she was his greatest pleasure, and robbing Campbell would be his second-greatest pleasure.

Chapter Ten

October 1708

Moira sat propped up in bed, writing. Now and again she put down her pen and glanced across the room at her son, Daniel MacLean, who slept peacefully.

Dear Edana,

How I would have liked to see Daniel grow up. A few weeks ago I would have begun crying, but I am now beyond tears and have come to accept the fact that I am dying. The pain that has wracked my body for so many months has worn me down, and I want relief from its torments almost as much as I want to be with my young son.

Since the day I came to stay with my grandmother's relatives, I've felt myself in exile. Although the Isle of Skye is close to the mainland, it seems to have an aura of remoteness. At home the neighbors were closer. Here, even the landscape is, to my eyes, somewhat boring.

Mull had a greater variety of scenery. Its rugged coast, mountains, hills, and fields made it feel larger than it actu-

ally was—while here on Skye it is all mountains and moors and the winds seem to sweep across it with a vengeance.

During my first months on Skye I was pregnant, and after Daniel was born, I fell ill. My son had to be taken care of by my aunt and a village woman who had sufficient milk to nurse her own child as well as mine.

As the days and weeks went by, I suffered more and more pain and my body began to waste away just like your mother's. You would not recognize me. I am a skeleton. This is an illness that does not care about the age of its victims but strikes at random. I have not received an answer to a message I recently sent you. I will give this letter to my aunt Corrie MacLeod to keep for you. Love Daniel for me.

Love Moira

Moira put down her pen and looked up as she heard the door to her room open. In the half-light, she saw the nurse.

"Has the messenger returned?" she asked, in a voice so weak that the sound of it surprised her.

"Not yet," the woman replied.

It was an all-too-familiar answer. She had written to Edana a second and most important letter weeks ago. Each day she hoped that the messenger would return with an answer, but each day she was disappointed.

"I've brought some medicine for you," the nurse said.

She propped up Moira's head and held the cup to her lips. The white powder had been dissolved in the liquid and it tasted vile. Moira closed her eyes and forced it down. However horrible it tasted, it numbed her pains and made her sleep. The sleep brought her strange dreams, dreams filled with color, dreams of fantastic beings clothed in all shades of the rainbow.

"I'm sure the messenger will come soon and bring the letter for which you are waiting."

The nurse's voice was already growing more distant. Moira turned her head, and though she could not move her lips, she silently spoke to her sleeping son. *You are the heir to all the MacLean estates. Divorce or no divorce, you are a legitimate child, born of a legal marriage. Live to claim what is yours.*

She thought again of Edana. Edana would help her son; she would see to it that he inherited, that Katherine and George were punished. It was completely true that Moira had not wanted to marry George MacLean, but neither had she wanted to be forced into a divorce. *"I never wanted to leave my friends and family to keep my son safe from the unscrupulous woman who took control of George. Katherine bends George to her will as if her will were the wind and he were a bit of heather,"* Moira had written Edana.

"You will live to take it all back," Moira said to Daniel. Then the fog of drug-induced sleep began to surround her and she let herself go. Yes, Edana would help her. Edana was her best friend and she knew she could trust Edana to look after her Daniel.

Katherine peered into the pot as it bubbled over the fire. She licked her lips and inhaled the aroma. She stirred the mixture slightly so that the white tentacles of the plant's roots rose to the surface and, for a moment, floated like the boiling worms in a witches' brew. The berries also rose to the top, popping like cranberries as the brew bubbled.

She removed the ladle and wiped it off. Katherine was alone in the small roundhouse she had insisted be constructed at the end of the garden. It was a quite simple structure, with a hole in the middle of the ceiling so that the smoke from the fire could escape. This was her special place and it was filled with herbs, spices, and the drying remnants of local plants.

In front of the structure, laid out in neat rows, was her garden. It was bordered with lilies, roses, pepperwort, rue, rosemary, mint, Greek hay, and climbing bean. In each of two rows, she grew sage, costmary, iris, pennyroyal, watercress, cumin, lovage, and fennel.

What boiled in her pot today was not something that had been grown in her herb garden. Rather it was an assortment of dried leaves and roots, which she had purchased from a French importer. It was a wondrous concoction from a plant of many purposes.

Used in the eyes, it made her pupils huge and luminous, though the disadvantage was that she could not see well until it wore off. Boiled and combined with other ingredients to disguise its somewhat bitter taste, the same brew taken internally acted as a slow poison and resulted in a prolonged illness and an apparently natural death.

Most often, she gave it to George in mulled wine. He loved the wine and could taste nothing of the poison that was gradually killing him. George was a terrible bore. Worse yet, he was given to fits of melancholy and guilt over his father's demise. He had recently extended his fits of guilt-induced depression to include his brother's death as well. He never blamed her directly, but it was clear he knew she was responsible and, when combined with his ever growing guilt, Katherine deemed such knowledge to be a threat.

"And so, my dear," she said meanly, to her boiling pot of poisonous nectar, "you must go, and the sooner the better."

But it was not just a necessity, she decided. It would be a pleasure, and it would free her for other endeavors. Bram Chisholm seemed an endeavor worthy of her time. Not only was she certain he could satisfy her, but she was certain he was wealthier than both of her husbands combined. He could offer her great luxury and considerable pleasure for as long as she chose to remain with him. Then, if he became a bore, there was always her delightful nectar.

Katherine stirred her pot again. The only thing standing in her way was Edana. Katherine cursed under her breath. She would have to think of some way to rid herself of Edana. She had put up with her for far too long, and besides, Edana was suspicious—not just about her adopted father's death, but about John's as well. She knew too much and she was far too pretty.

"Bram Chisholm is enchanted with Edana," Katherine said in a low voice. "I did not expect him to be so enamored of you." She narrowed her eyes and recalled how she had believed Bram was excited by her and would not see Edana with lustful eyes. *Well, it did not work out that way, but soon it will work out as I desire,* Katherine promised herself. *When Edana's dead, he'll mourn her, and I will be so comforting. . . .* A smile crossed her face.

She returned her thoughts to George. "Tonight we'll have a feast and after dinner, poor George, you will most likely drink too much of your favorite beverage, my mulled wine. To greater things,'' Katherine toasted, as once again she stirred her pot.

The sun was already beginning to set when Edana crossed over into Argyll, all of which was now Campbell territory. The Campbells were disliked by many, hated by most, and feared by all.

Her mind was filled with thoughts of the past and future as well as self-recriminations for not having trusted Bram, for being so stupid that she did not realize sooner that he was the Phoenix, or one of them. In spite of her guilt, she was filled with a certain awe. No wonder the authorities could not catch the Phoenix—as they were more than one, they could be in more than one place at a time. But now—now a trap had been set and the Phoenix they would catch would be Bram.

"I'll never find him," she thought miserably. After a time, she reined in her horse, dismounted, and let the horse drink from a nearby stream.

"I must think as these men might," she said aloud. And in her mind, she tried to visualize the Argyll road, which led to the castle of Colin Campbell.

Bram would not attack Campbell close to his castle where the road was no doubt watched by Campbell guards. Surely he would choose a spot past where the main road from Edinburgh joined the Argyll road; there was too much wagon traffic on the main road to Edinburgh for him to risk making his move there.

It was then that Edana remembered the area of the road near the Arogartan Forest. She had ridden there once on a trip with her father. It was a lonely stretch of road with heavy woods on one side and rocky land on the other. There were neither towns nor villages. It would be the kind of place Bram would choose; he would lie in wait for Campbell—but he would not be the only one lying in wait.

Edana remounted her horse and rode off into the night.

* * *

She reached the area of the road she felt likely to be the place where Bram might attack, around midnight. She continued to ride, keeping to the wooded side and praying that if Bram were waiting, he might waylay her and then she could tell him about the trap before it was sprung. They could escape the area together and Superintendent Crane would be none the wiser.

But just as she turned a bend in the road, she heard a sound that caused her heart to sink. Shots filled the still night! And they came from just ahead of her.

As quickly as she could, Edana guided her horse into the deep woods. She slipped from the saddle and tethered the animal to a tree. Then she set off on foot, moving with as much stealth as possible, following the sound of the shots and the shouts and curses of men. Her heart beat wildly. She silently prayed that Bram had not been shot, that somehow he had escaped this ambush.

She circled around through the woods and approached the road, keeping to the heavy bush, hiding in the thick shrubs. She peered out onto the road in horror. Bram was there, still hooded. Colin Campbell led the soldiers who surrounded Bram. They had formed a circle around him, and were laughing and making threats.

"Take him to Inveraray and lock him in our dungeon," Campbell ordered. "When Crane arrives, we'll unhood our prize and then see to his hanging!"

Edana shook uncontrollably as she watched Bram being securely tied in a wagon. As they tied him, they took turns hitting and kicking him, until he fell onto his side.

It took all of Edana's self-control not to cry out or run forward and try to help him. But of what help could she be now? Force would not free him from his situation; only guile might stand a chance.

As silently as possible, Edana stole back through the woods to where she had left her horse tethered. She could not stop the tears from running down her cheeks but at the same time, she knew she must act decisively. She had watched helplessly as Katherine murdered her father. She had been unable to do anything when Katherine had shot John. But this time she vowed to act whether she succeeded or not. Bram was everything to her—she loved him with all her heart, and if she had failed to trust him, she would not fail to help him now. "I'll go to Inveraray myself," she whispered, although she had no idea of what she would say or do when she got there.

A light mist rose from the valley floor and caressed the low areas of the moor, obscuring them, then revealing them again as the wind lifted the vapors and moved them on to another spot.

Bram looked out across the moor to the loch beyond. Its blue water was also kissed by the low fog, giving it an ethereal appearance, as if ghosts had emerged from the loch's depths and were now playing in the hazy morning sunlight.

He saw Edana. She seemed to rise up out of the water; her long, wild fiery hair was damp. It circled round her breasts, just covering her roseate nipples. Her skin was like fine ivory, her eyes clear and large, only slightly softer than emeralds.

She extended her long, graceful arms to him, and the hair fell away from her alabaster breasts, revealing them waiting for his touch.

Bram felt a deep longing, a hunger to be with her, a desire that transcended all other sensations. He reached for her and she seemed to step away. But still she held out her arms, inviting him to embrace her, begging him to hold her close, wanting to feel him against her, to quiver in his arms. The mist descended. Edana disappeared for a moment.

Confused images surged through his mind. He saw his beloved fully dressed and riding her fine horse. She had the complete innocence of a young girl. That was how he had first seen her, that was when he first knew the hunger that would drive him to follow her, to watch after her from afar, and finally, to make her his wife.

He relived the first time he took her, and the memory of the fire within her seemed to warm him in spite of the cold. How could all this be? He was entangled with her in passionate lovemaking, and yet she rose naked from the mist-shrouded blue water, holding out her hands to him, her sensuous lips mouthing his name.

He tried to struggle toward her but with each step he took, she seemed to float farther away. He tried to call out her name, but his lips would not move—it was as if his lips were sewn shut. His voice was filled with silent cries. He forced himself to the water's edge, then plunged in, trying to swim toward her hovering form, wanting to reach her, trying to call out her name. But it was cold! It was so cold! It was as cold as being waist-deep in the snow of the Grampian Mountains, as cold as the icy waters of the Irish Sea in January.

Bram blinked open his eyes and realized that the cold he felt was not the blue water of the Loch, the snow, or the frozen sea, but rather the cold of a damp stone floor.

The vision of his beloved disappeared and was replaced by the blurred image of booted feet. He was aware of feeling incredible pain, in his ribs, in his left leg, and on his face.

He could feel the swelling around his right eye and he gradually became aware of the fact that his nose was bleeding and that he was in fact lying facedown in a pool of his own blood. At almost the same moment, he realized, with an absurd sense of relief, that he was still hooded.

"You don't seem so formidable now," one of the men who surrounded him said.

He did not lift his head, for fear of being kicked again. There was little joy in beating an unconscious man; so as long as they believed him to be unconscious, they would probably leave him alone, he reasoned.

"You must be curious," one of them said.

Bram heard a sneering laugh and he knew the voice belonged to old Colin Campbell.

"I'm curious, all right, but I promised Crane he could do the unmasking, and the bounty on this man is a pretty penny— pretty enough for me to keep my promise!"

"I admire your self-control," the first voice said.

Bram suddenly felt his head being lifted by the back of his shirt. He felt a short choking sensation, and he gasped for air as his head was held up, and he peered, blurry-eyed, into the face of Colin Campbell.

"I can't tell if the bastard is awake or if he can't close his eyes because of the swelling."

Campbell's face reeled before him. It was an oblong face, with a scruffy one-inch growth of hair the color of salt-and-pepper. His skin was deeply pockmarked, his dark eyes narrow and rodentlike. His shoulder-length hair was greasy and somewhat matted, and his body gave off the odor of urine. His long nose, true to the origin of his family name, was crooked.

At the worst possible moments, bizarre thoughts cross the human mind. Through his pain, all Bram could think about was how much Campbell could benefit from a bath. A smile must have crossed his lips because Campbell swore an oath and Bram's head was released and fell to the hard stone floor. That was followed by yet another hard kick in the ribs. He groaned involuntarily.

"Chain him to the wall in the dungeon!" he heard Colin Campbell order. "Leave him so the rats can lick his wounds till Crane arrives."

He felt strong arms lifting him and then dragging him. As they approached the doorway, he heard another voice, someone behind him.

"There's a woman here to see you," the voice said. "She's a real beauty, with long red hair and eyes like jewels. She's got a fine figure, too."

"Where is she?" Campbell snapped.

"Waiting in the reception room. She says her name is Edana."

Edana—how could that be?

They dragged him away. He could not say her name; he dared not think about her being here, about what might happen to her. Why was she here? Had she somehow followed him? He was consumed with concern for her. Somehow, for some reason, Edana had been drawn into the bosom of the enemy. Did she even have an inkling of the danger she was in? Crane would come and Bram's identity would become known—she would be arrested, too. They showed no mercy toward women. After they had killed the men of Clan MacGregor, they had branded their women and exiled them. When his identity was known, that was what they would do to Edana. They would brand her and exile her into bonded servitude in one of the colonies. The thought inflamed him, and he began to struggle against his captors. But once again he was held down and savagely kicked and beaten. In moments, the sweetness of the dark again enveloped him.

Colin Campbell strode toward the reception room. It was late at night; Crane would not come till tomorrow. But what could bring a beautiful young woman at this hour? Campbell felt vaguely intrigued. He smiled happily. His doctor, Kenzie Scott, had just left after giving him a clean bill of health, a beauty was waiting for him, and the Phoenix was in his dungeon.

When he opened the door of the reception room, he found the woman standing in front of the fire, and his initial intrigue turned to pure lust. She was a ravishing creature, and surely one of his own—she had the hair of Clan Diarmid, the family name before it had become Campbell. Not that all of them had that flaming, fiery hair. It was unusual coloring, the red-gold hair and the deep-green eyes. Such hair spoke of a fire beneath the surface; it was a silent promise of unstirred passions and of lustiness. It was especially prized among women, for it was said their lovemaking knew no bounds, and that they left their men drained.

Campbell ran his tongue around his lips and stared at her. She was young and not just beautiful, but stunning. She had proud, high breasts, which pressed against the material of her conservative dress. Her waist was tiny and her hips rounded.

Edana shifted uneasily from one foot to the other. Colin Campbell was unpleasant in his appearance and he was leering at her. He was a discomforting man with a horrendous reputation. Nonetheless, she commanded herself to remain calm.

He stepped closer to her. "What brings such a young beauty into my lair so late at night?"

Edana smoothed her skirt with her hand and then looked up. "I've come from Fort William, from the office of Superintendent Crane."

The mention of Crane's name caused Campbell to frown at her. Clearly this was no ordinary woman.

"Crane sent you?" he asked, attempting to clarify the reason for her presence.

"I was visiting with him and he told me you were part of a scheme to capture this highwayman who calls himself the Phoenix."

Campbell felt immediately annoyed that Crane had told anyone of the plan; secrecy was imperative to its success. Still, it had been successful. He peered at her. "And?"

"A short time ago I was traveling with my sister-in-law, Katherine MacLean, and my brother George MacLean. We were set upon by this Phoenix person and he took our jewelry. Among the items he stole from me was my wedding ring. I should like to have it returned, so I have come here to confront the Phoenix myself."

He did not bother to disguise his annoyance at the fact that she was married. He took great delight in deflowering virgins and bragging about it. Still, a woman of experience could be interesting, too. The more distressing thought was that she was related to Katherine MacLean—if even by marriage. Katherine MacLean was known far and wide as beautiful, and deadly. Worse yet, Crane knew her well. He felt doubly annoyed; he could not treat this woman as he might have treated another.

"And how do you know I have him?"

"I don't. But I was told by Superintendent Crane that this plan was to be carried out almost immediately."

She seemed to know a great deal, and he could not decide if that made her seem more or less suspicious.

"As it happens, the plan was carried out this very night and the man in question is in our hands. I have promised not to unmask him till Crane arrives, so he is in my dungeon, although I'm afraid he's not in very good condition—not that it matters."

Not in good condition? Edana's heart raced. What had they done to Bram? She shook slightly, but again forced herself to remain impassive. "Was he wounded?"

"No, just given the sound beating he well deserves. Of course, he'll be hanged, so it matters little if he is battered and bruised."

How easy it must have been for them to hold him down and beat him! What cowards these men were! How she wanted to fly at Colin Campbell now and scratch his eyes out! But that would not free Bram or save his life. She had to remain cool; she had to keep her wits about her. "If Crane is coming tomorrow, he'll vouch for me and tell you that everything I've said is true."

Colin Campbell walked slowly to a small cabinet. He withdrew a decanter of scotch and without asking, poured two glasses. He handed her one without a word even though he was trying to assess her, trying to see what her reactions would be. And yet, he reminded himself, he had to be careful. If she was who she said she was, if she was a friend of Crane's, it would be best to treat her with respect. After all, he had nothing to lose. What could a mere slip of a girl do?

"I offer you my hospitality for the night," he said graciously, as he handed her the scotch. Edana took it. She seldom drank liquor, but tonight she felt the need for it. Her plan was still vague, still fraught with danger. She would try to free Bram tonight. She would creep down to the dungeon and try to free him.

"That's very kind of you," she said, sipping the scotch and feeling its warmth as it trickled down her throat.

Colin Campbell forced a half-smile. He decided he would post a guard outside her door, just in case she proved to be a new and attractive version of a Trojan horse. He would instruct the guard to follow her and to notify him if she tried anything; if she did, he would enjoy himself with her and not give Crane a second thought. A woman could be a delightful distraction, and he had had few distractions of late.

Ian MacDonald of Clanranald was a huge man of six feet, seven inches, a veritable giant from a race of giants. Legend had it that he and all the MacDonalds were descendants of John of Islay, Lord of the Isles. On the island of Texa, which lay off Islay, there stood a carving of the likeness of the first MacDonald, a fourteenth-century Celtic prince wearing a quilted coat with chain mail, and a conical helmet. This carving

was known as the Cross of Ranald. Ranald had been the son
of John of Islay and Amy Macari, who had been the heiress
to the great Lordship of Garmoran, a huge inheritance of land
that extended from the Great Glen to the Outer Hebrides. From
these two, sprang the MacDonalds of Clanranald, the MacDonalds of Glengarry, the MacDonalds of Sleat, the MacDonalds
of MacDonald, and the McDonalds of Glencoe. It was a proud
line, a line loyal to the Stuarts, and now, the sworn enemies
of Clan Campbell.

Behind Ian MacDonald rode over fifty MacDonalds, all
armed and ready to fight. They had come to a halt on the crest
of a knoll overlooking Colin Campbell's castle on the shores
of Loch Fyne.

It was a fine stone castle with a square tower on one side,
and four tall turrets. It might have been an impregnable bastion,
had not Colin Campbell felt so secure in Argyll. As it was, the
great castle gates were open, and only a minimal number of
guards were posted about.

"It's ours for the taking," Ian MacDonald muttered—not
that they intended occupying it. Anything so reckless would
bring the British army down on them. By necessity, hit-and-
run raids were their trademark. They would kill whoever was
about, free the prisoners in the dungeons, if any, and capture
any comely maidens and carry them off to the outer isles; there
they would either be held for ransom, or be married off if no
one was willing to pay for their return.

This, Ian contemplated, would be one of their most daring
raids yet. They were entirely in enemy territory, and though
vessels waited to bear them back to the islands when they were
done, their foray was extremely dangerous.

"Forward!" Ian shouted. "Move with stealth!"

George came into the study and looked at the small table in
front of the fire. It was set for intimate dining and the aromas
rising from the covered plates made his mouth water.

"I do hope you're hungry," Katherine said, in a sweet, thick
voice.

It was the tone she used to speak to him, George thought,

as he looked up to see her in the doorway. But it wasn't just her tone that held out a promise of delights to come; it was her clothes that excited him. She was dressed as she had once dressed for him, in a skintight, low-cut, slinky gown. He suddenly felt filled with unnatural energy. She was so magnificent! She was a wild creature, a seductress of many and varied wiles.

Tonight she was dressed in a tight, soft velvet gown that was bloodred in color. Her thick, lustrous hair was loose, her lips were the color of her gown, and her eyes were huge and hypnotic. Her quite wonderful gown was partly open, revealing her cleavage and the whiteness of her skin. *She would not dress this way if she were not desirous of me,* George thought.

"I'm very hungry," he said, not allowing his eyes to stray from her form. She was a vision.

"I'm so glad. I spent all day preparing this meal with my own hands. I've selected special herbs for seasoning and for your pleasure."

How well he knew what she meant! Her herb garden was famous, and when she set about seeing to the food, which was not near often enough, she could prepare dishes of great elegance and incredible flavor. Sometimes her food seemed to have other effects as well. It seemed the aromatic herbs made him even more desirous of her than he ordinarily would be. Then, too, she always rubbed her whole body with lavender, and when he inhaled the scent of her skin, it made him as deliriously drunk as her superb mulled wine.

She came and stood very close to him and he inhaled the potent lavender. She touched him and caressed him intimately until he felt positively fevered. Then she moved away and poured him some mulled wine.

He took the goblet and drank it. He felt dizzy, yet still wanton.

She was putting bits of chicken on his plate and covering it with a thick golden sauce. He was certain it was honey from their hives, and mustard from her garden.

She gently bade him sit down and then, as if he were a baby, she began feeding him small bites of the succulent meat.

"It's delicious," he mumbled.

She smiled and lifted some more meat to his mouth. When

he took it, she ran her finger around his lips. "Tonight, I predict you'll sleep more soundly than you've ever slept before."

He tried to smile at her. She knew he suffered from night terrors because he often woke up tossing in his bed and wet with perspiration. Then he would scream and sob until he realized that his persistent dream of killing his father and brother had indeed been a dream.

He ate as she slowly fed him. He slid his hand inside her gown and surprisingly, she didn't object or even try to pull away.

"I can't take my eyes off your eyes," he slurred slightly, and felt hot all over, yet curiously unable to ready himself for having her.

"Have more wine," she urged, once again lifting the silver goblet to his mouth. "Drink it all."

"It tastes more potent tonight."

"It's your imagination," she purred, as she stroked his ear. It sent a chill through him in spite of the yearning that swelled within him.

He felt himself beginning to fall, albeit slowly. His hand slipped away from her breast and he crumpled to the floor as the world went completely black. The flavor of the wine seemed to linger in his mouth and he was sure he was still caressing her.

Katherine laughed lightly, and remembered Shakespeare's words: "It provokes and it unprovokes. It provokes the desire, but takes away the performance."

You, dear George, you have performed for the last time.

Edana looked about the room where she had been taken. It was small, and though it had all the necessities, it lacked any kind of warmth. The walls were unadorned and made of cold, damp stone. The floor was strewn with grasses, but not with the sweeter flowers that might have given it a nicer aroma. The bed was narrow and small, and the only covers offered were rough sheepskin.

Not that I care, Edana thought. The important thing was somehow to get to the dungeon and help Bram escape. She

bolted the door behind her and sat down on the edge of the
narrow bed. She leaned over and blew out the lamp, plunging
the room into darkness. Then she waited, all her senses alert.

Edana waited until it was after two in the morning. She marveled
that she felt no weariness. She was, in fact, wide-awake, her
nerves on end, her senses heightened. She took off her shoes
and walked silently to the door. Carefully she unbolted the lock
and eased open the great wooden door, praying that it would
not squeak on its iron hinges.

Then she crept out into the pitch-dark hall and moved along
the wall, feeling the stone as she went. The stairs were some
distance down the corridor and she walked with great care,
knowing for the first time what it must be like to be blind.

After what seemed an eternity, she felt the wall come to an
end. She bent down and felt with her hand. Yes! It was the
staircase that wound its way down to the first floor and then
down yet another floor to the dungeon that lay beneath the
castle.

She sat down to descend the stairs, for fear of falling in the
darkness. She went down one step at a time in a sitting position
till she reached the main floor. She stood up and shook herself
off. She rounded the corner and came to the second flight,
which led to the dungeon. Again she sat down and went down
the stairs from a sitting position.

When at last she reached the bottom, she stood up again and
waited. Then she began to move forward. Heavens! Was there
no light anywhere? Surely she would come to a room where
the guards were. Surely there would be a torch.

Then Edana heard a noise in the darkness. Was it a rat? She
stood stock-still and listened. Then she gasped. Huge, hairy
arms grabbed her from behind and she let out a scream.

"Light the torch!"

The angry voice of Colin Campbell was unmistakable even
in the pitch-darkness. There was the scuffle of footsteps on
stone, the glow of embers, and then the torch was lit and it
illuminated the walls of the outer dungeon. The shadows of
the men danced on the walls like monsters of yore. Edana was

being held fast by one of them and Colin Campbell was again leering at her, a mean, nasty sneer on his face.

"I thought you were suspicious, my little pretty. So, you came to try to rescue the Phoenix. What is he to you? A lover, perhaps?"

Edana struggled for control of her voice and her body. "I only want my jewelry," she insisted.

Colin Campbell laughed. "I think you want something more valuable."

He stepped closer to her and she smelled the odor that rose from his body. He reached out and roughly grabbed her breast. "Take her to my room, and tie her to the bed!" he ordered. "First I'll have her and then I'll beat the truth out of her."

Edana felt her knees go weak. Tears would not even come to her eyes. She had failed Bram! Now he would die! At the moment, she could not think of what would happen to her. She was consumed with fear for the man she loved and all she could do was stare into the distorted face of Colin Campbell.

Colin Campbell watched for a moment, then he turned and walked toward the cells of his dungeon. His men were still kicking at the Phoenix. "Enough," Colin shouted. They fell back instantly, and with a wave of his hand, they all left the cell.

Colin stood and stared at the hooded man. The Phoenix was a strong, muscular man and there was something familiar about him.

"The hell with Crane," he muttered. He bent over and pulled off the hood that covered the face of the Phoenix.

"Bram Chisholm!" he whispered. His eyes narrowed; small wonder the Phoenix had known just where and when to attack. He was a bloody traitor! He pretended to be a British supporter when in fact he was their greatest nemesis.

"And you married Edana MacLean—I remember now! The pretty little bitch upstairs is your wife! Ah, I will have my amusement! Had I known, I would not have let them beat you unconscious. I'd have made you watch!"

With that, he turned and stomped away, still cursing under his breath.

* * *

Edana's hands were tied behind her, and her ankles were bound as well. She was lifted off the ground by one of Colin Campbell's servants. He slung her over his shoulder, and with little concern for her, began the long climb from the dungeon to the rooms on the upper floor.

At last he reached a large wooden door, and as he was compelled to hold on to her struggling body, he kicked the door open, strode inside, and slung her on the bed.

Edana fought him as hard as she could, but he struck her hard across the face. Then he first untied her arms and ankles, and then retied her arms and feet to the four bedposts. Cursing, he left her there, spread-eagled, unable to move, and entirely vulnerable to Colin Campbell's desires.

Edana waited in extreme discomfort, yet her mind and heart were so filled with thoughts of Bram that she could not think of herself.

She heard the door open and Colin Campbell came in. He walked to the edge of the bed and looked down on her. A hideous smile crossed his face and he removed a long, sharp knife from his belt.

"Such a pretty little thing," he whispered, as he leaned close to her. "Let's see what you look like without your clothes." He began to cut her clothing away, and Edana cringed as he cut away her dress and then stared at her chemise, touching it with his hands, then running his hand over her neck and shoulders.

Edana closed her eyes against the sight of him, though she could do nothing to shut out his odor. She forced her thoughts away from him. *I will not give him the pleasure of hearing me scream,* she vowed.

Chapter Eleven

This was a nightmare beyond all nightmares. Her wrists and ankles hurt, the ropes that bound her were tied so tightly. The man who loomed above her was a foul monster.

In her mind, Edana tried to travel somewhere else; she tried to force all thoughts of what was about to happen away. She clung to thoughts of her childhood, then she let her mind run through her dreams—dreams of the "other." But it was all to no avail. She could not blot out reality, or numb herself against the reality of Colin Campbell. She closed her eyes tightly.

Edana could feel him above her; he was so close she could feel his breath on her neck and it sent more shivers of revulsion through her. His hand covered her breast.

She heard a strange noise, a muffled groan, and that was followed by an indescribable sound, a deep gasp. Then Colin Campbell fell on her, but he no longer fondled her or caressed her. He did not move at all. He did not even twitch. And suddenly there were other voices.

Edana opened her eyes and looked beyond Colin, whose heavy body was still atop her. She saw a giant of a man looking down at her and Colin. A deadly garrote dangled from his hand; a huge grin covered his elongated face.

"If I'd dreamed of a time of death for this bastard, I could think of no more fitting way for him to die than unfulfilled."

"Get him off me!" Edana cried. She could hear the hysteria in her voice—and yet she had been spared. She fought to regain control. "Untie me at once!"

The giant put his hands on his hips and laughed. "Clearly he held you against your will, lass, but just as clearly you must be one of them. You've got the hair of Clan Diarmid, from whom the Campbells claim to spring."

"Get him off me! I am not one of them," she protested. "I'm a MacLean." And the moment she had said it, she regretted it. Katherine and George had seen to it that the MacLeans were now allied with the Campbells in support of the government. At the moment, she did not know who these people were except that they were enemies of the Campbells.

As if he read her mind, he roared, "Being a MacLean is not much better these days!" He spit on the floor.

"Please get him off of me and please untie me," Edana implored. She shivered again at the feel of the deadweight that lay across her.

The giant nodded. "I like a well-mannered woman." He seized Colin Campbell's lifeless form by the neck and threw it with some force on the floor. "Aye, if I could kill the bastard twice, I would."

Then with his long knife, he slashed the ropes that held her wrists and ankles.

Edana struggled up and quickly pulled her tattered clothing together. She rubbed her wrists. Her hands felt full of pins and needles. "Thank you," she said.

He strode across the room to a large wardrobe and opened it. Then he pulled out a long, warm cloak. "Cover yourself with this," he ordered. "You'll need it, against the cold night air."

"Where are we going?"

"I'll not be freeing you, lass. You might have some value to us. You'll be coming with us."

"Coming where?" she asked again.

"No more questions!" he shouted at her, and his expression was fearsome. She fell silent, deciding that for the moment she

would not fight. It did not seem that he intended to harm her
and, she reasoned, her situation would be much worse had he
not come along. But what of Bram? He was still in the dungeon
and she had to see him freed.

But before Edana could speak, another giant of a man came
in the room. He wore the distinctive black-and-red tartan of
Clan MacDonald. Though she did not completely understand
the situation, she realized that this no doubt was a raid, another
blow in the ongoing war between the two clans. Just as quickly
she realized it was better not to give her married name or to
tell them her husband was in the dungeon. After all, Bram was
ostensibly an ally of the MacLeans and the Campbells in support
of the British government. These people did not know he was
the legendary Phoenix, a supporter of Scots freedom.

"She's a beauty," the second giant said, as he rubbed his
chin and looked at her. "What do you propose doing with
her?"

"We'll hold her for ransom and if no one wants her, we'll
give her to Ranald as a bride. He needs a wife to care for the
children, and he's always been partial to women with fiery
hair."

Edana started to protest again, but instead she decided to
hold her tongue. Bram was a wealthy man and she did not
want him to have to ransom her. Truth be known, she had no
idea what his relationship with the MacDonalds might be.

"We're near done loading the valuables," the second giant
said. "And we've unlocked the cells in the dungeon."

Edana's heart leapt. Bram had been freed!

"Did you speak to any of the prisoners?" MacDonald asked.

"No, most of them were asleep, but one of them had been
beaten to pulp. He's dead, but the rest will awaken free men.
I didn't talk to them. It's better if no one is able to identify
us."

It was Bram who had been beaten! They had killed him!
She began to shake uncontrollably. Was he really dead?

The first giant turned to her. "Come along peacefully and I
won't have to tie you up."

Edana was lost in grief. She followed him out of the bedchamber where Colin Campbell lay sprawled on the floor, his neck

horribly twisted. Tears flooded her eyes and she trembled. Bram was dead! She didn't care what happened to her. Nothing mattered anymore. She knew how much she loved him—this was so much worse than when she thought the Phoenix was dead. Even though she now knew them to be the same person, her love for the Phoenix had been the love of a girl ... *But my love for Bram is a mature love. It is so much deeper, so much stronger.*

"Did you know the dead one, lass?"

Edana nodded.

He said no more, though he motioned her to follow.

Bram opened one eye only to discover that the other was swollen closed. His head throbbed and it seemed no part of him was without pain.

He looked around the dank cell and focused on the door to his cell. Was he seeing things? The door was wide open.

He pulled himself forward on all fours, and when he reached the cell door, he used it to pull himself up. For a few minutes he could only stand there, leaning against the door, breathing heavily. He felt dizzy; his head throbbed. After a time, he took a few steps out into the semi-dark corridor. He looked down the corridor. It was illuminated only by a torch that hung on the wall some thirty feet away. But he could clearly see that all the cells were open, and as he heard no sound, he assumed that all were empty and their inhabitants had fled.

He staggered forward and, dragging his foot and holding the wall for balance, he made his way into the central part of the dungeon even though he had to fight to remain conscious.

The guard was sprawled on the floor, lying in a pool of dried blood. Bram drew in his breath. The Campbells had been attacked, that was clear enough. It was also obvious that, as was the custom, all those held prisoner had been freed. He looked about and saw his own sword. It was lying behind the guard's table. He picked it up.

He painfully dragged himself up the stairs and into the main hall. The Campbell castle was as silent as a tomb; indeed, it was a tomb.

"Edana!" He called out her name with all his strength but there was no answer.

One by one, he searched through the rooms. There were fourteen bodies in all. Locked chests had been pried open and objects of value had been taken—probably all the valuable items that could be easily carried, he reasoned.

He went upstairs and found Colin Campbell—the mark left by the garrote was still visible. He stared at the bed; a sick feeling flooded over him. Someone had been tied to it: the cut ropes still hung limply from the four posts. *Edana!* His mind raced. He looked at the inanimate body of Colin Campbell and he cursed and kicked him hard, though all reason told him Colin was quite dead already. "And a good thing, too," he cursed. "You'd have had nothing so merciful as strangulation from me!"

But where was Edana? Clearly those who had killed Colin had set her free and perhaps taken her with them. He felt a sudden pain in his head, a sharper pain; then the constant aching began.

He had turned and started to leave the bedroom when he heard noise downstairs. There were shouts in English and he realized the shouts came from British soldiers. Then, through the pain of his pounding head, he heard Crane's all-too-familiar voice shouting orders.

Bram quickly pulled off the rest of his disguise. Fighting the darkness that threatened to overcome him, he rolled his disguise into a tight bundle and hurriedly shoved it under the bed. He threw his sword on the floor and lay down, not far from Campbell, and closed his eyes. It would be easy to pretend he was hurt, because he was. In any case, there was no time to run away. He would have to bluff it out, if only he could remain lucid.

He was in place not a moment too soon. The soldiers stormed through the partially open door with Crane in their wake.

The soldiers muttered and one swore an oath. Crane looked at the room and under his breath swore, too. "Damn, what's happened here?"

It was a rhetorical question and he circled the two men on the floor and then touched Campbell with his tip of his boot.

"He's been garroted, sir," one of the officers said authoritatively.

It seemed a propitious moment for Bram to groan loudly, so he did. *I have to make Crane think I was hurt defending Colin.* It was his only course of action.

Crane bent over him. "Quick! Get some water—Chisholm's alive!"

Bram looked into Crane's face and said nothing. After a few moments, the water was brought and he gulped down a little and groaned once again, but this time because of the sharp pain in his side.

"Bloody hell, man, you've taken a terrible beating," Crane muttered. "You must have put up a terrible fight."

Bram nodded. "I did what I could. Do you have anything stronger?" he asked, as he pushed the water away.

Crane nodded and withdrew a small silver flask from his pocket. It was quite elegant and Bram took note of it, thinking that if the opportunity ever arose to separate Crane from his belongings, he must remember to take the silver flask. He gulped down the whiskey. It warmed his insides and, for a moment at least, gave him the ability to focus on his story.

But neither Crane nor his wounds took his mind off Edana. Those who killed Campbell had taken her. Perhaps, he prayed, they had come before Campbell had hurt her. At the moment he strongly felt that she was safe—or, more to the point, not in immediate danger. Had those who killed Campbell intended to harm her, they would have done so and left her body.

"Who did this?" Crane asked. "All the guards are dead and Campbell's been garroted."

Silently Bram breathed a sigh of relief. There was no one to identify him. Campbell may have seen him, and perhaps one of the guards had seen him, too. He was unsure. "I don't know who they were," Bram said, trying to grasp his thoughts. "They wore no tartans."

At least in this matter, he thought, he was telling the truth. He had awakened to find his cell door open and the other prisoners gone. He could not say who had done this, but if he had to guess, he would have said it was the MacDonalds and that their vengeful attack had come at just the right moment.

Not that the Campbells didn't have other enemies; they had enemies aplenty, but few of their enemies had the resources to carry out a raid on Inveraray.

"What brought you here?" Crane asked.

Bram looked Crane in the eye. "Campbell had asked me to come and discuss a campaign to convince the other chieftains to accept the union. I could ask you the same question—though I admit, I'm glad you came."

"Campbell captured the Phoenix. We were to unmask him together."

"If that's the case, perhaps he was attacked by friends of the Phoenix." He was aware that he was beginning to slur his words, but he thought his answers sounded all right for a man on the verge of passing out.

Crane scratched his head and then shook it doubtfully. "I don't think so; I think the Phoenix works alone."

"Is the captive still in Campbell's dungeon?"

Crane shook his head. "Apparently all the prisoners were freed."

Bram felt increasingly nervous, having Crane leaning over him on the floor. One glance under the bed could reveal his hidden disguise. "Help me up, will you? I'd like to sit in a comfortable chair for a few minutes and have a little more whiskey."

"Of course, old man," Crane said obligingly. He scrambled to his feet and then held out his arm for Bram to lean on.

Bram staggered upright and then collapsed into the chair. "I just need a few hours to recover."

"I think it will take more than a few hours. We'll appropriate a carriage and take you back to the fort in comfort. Then we'll send you home with an escort. You know, I saw your wife the other day. In fact, I told her about our plan to catch the Phoenix. She was on her way home. A beautiful woman, your wife. I wouldn't leave her alone for too long, were I you."

Bram felt great pride for Edana. She had talked to Crane and probably had learned Crane and Bram had indeed been together the night her rings were taken. She knew he was telling the truth. Clearly, when she had learned of the plan from Crane she had risked everything to come to Inveraray to help him.

Bram forced a smile. He had to find Edana as soon as possible, but he could not appear to know anything about what had happened here, and he certainly could not admit that Edana had been here.

"You know, now that I think about it, I suppose Campbell might have been attacked by friends of the Phoenix. I mean, we have no proof that he works alone."

"I'm sure he does," Bram said, not wanting Crane to dwell on any ideas that might cause even more trouble.

Crane pursed his lips together. "I'm so angry. We were so close. We had him and now he's slipped through our fingers again."

Bram nodded. "It's very frustrating, old friend. Very frustrating indeed." He motioned toward the flask and waited while Crane obligingly poured him another drink. He quaffed it and stood up unsteadily. At that moment, everything went gray, and then black.

Holden Crane paced his panel-lined office, pausing periodically to take a gulp of whiskey and to curse loudly. His office was, in fact, the only place he could curse loudly. Officers were supposed to be well-bred gentlemen, and well-bred gentlemen did not curse in public.

Andrew Martin, his young secretary, sat in a blue velvet chair, listening to him and watching him. Crane did not think that Martin was much of a secretary, but he was an excellent listener, and once in a while he even offered some sensible comment. More important, he didn't mind foul language.

"This place is ungovernable," Crane ranted, as he paused for yet another drink. "We ought to just draw a line where the Highlands begin and leave them all alone to kill each other off as they've been doing for centuries."

"Campbell was loyal to the Crown, sir."

"Of course he was, and don't you see, that's the problem. I'll be expected to produce his killer."

"Somehow the MacDonalds seem the most likely."

"Likely? Yes, I suppose they are. But as usual no one heard or saw anything. My only witness said they wore no identifying tartan. Besides that, he was beaten senseless and is still in and out of consciousness. So the question remains—who are these faceless men? On the present evidence I can promise you none of them will ever be arrested.''

''There's another possibility,'' Martin offered.

''And what might that be?'' Crane asked, feeling more than a little testy. He had already received four messages on the matter of Campbell's murder from Edinburgh, and two from London.

''The evidence indicates that Campbell was about to rape a woman at the time he was murdered. Perhaps her relatives killed him.''

''How do we know he was about to rape someone?''

''There were ropes on the bedposts, sir. They'd been cut.''

Crane frowned. Martin was young and somewhat inexperienced. He obviously didn't know how popular bondage was, or how common it was for a man to tie a woman up in order to take her without being clawed to death. On the other hand, Martin's theory offered him a way out. If this were simply a common ''rape and revenge'' crime, as opposed to another strike in the never-ending battle between the Campbells and the MacDonalds, he would be off the hook, militarily speaking, anyway. God, they wanted him to go off on some foray to the islands to find the MacDonald culprits! Such an adventure would be suicide! As if these people would give up their own even if the reward were a million pounds! As if a trek to the islands was some sort of picnic instead of a deadly trip into the world's bleakest area. Frankly, he didn't understand government policies. Visitors went to the islands and swore the scenery was wonderful. They returned awestruck with descriptions of wind and sea. But he could see none of it. He found the Hebrides to be rocky and barren, overcast and generally miserable. Why the government wanted it to be unified with the rest of the country was quite beyond him. He would go if he had to go, but he would know the outcome at the onset. He would return with nothing, if he returned at all, because he would be unable to prove anything. It would just be a long, wretched journey fraught with danger. And that, he thought, would make his superiors all the more angry.

"Ropes on the bedposts, you say?" He wondered why he had not noticed them—and if someone were about to be raped, why hadn't Chisholm mentioned it? He looked toward Martin. "Is there more evidence in this lurid tale?" A lurid tale he now considered turning into an official report.

"Well, sir, Campbell had his boots off."

"Suspicious," Crane muttered. He still wondered if his superiors would accept this story even though he had already decided to try it out; how much worse could such a report make his position? Yes—why not? Campbell kidnapped a comely maiden and her kin attacked and murdered him and his guard while rescuing her. It all sounded rather plausible. And if Chisholm could not testify to any of this, he reasoned it was possible that Campbell had freed her earlier when he was finished with her. Or maybe Chisholm, who had rushed into the room after the melee began, might not remember anything. He had been severely injured.

He sat down in his chair and began to feel a little better. "Have a go at writing that up, will you?" he said to Martin. And, he thought, when Martin finished, he would have a go at a little literary embellishment.

Martin nodded. "Sir, there's one other matter."

Of course there was. There was always one other matter. "What is it now?" he asked wearily.

"Mr. George MacLean, sir. While you were away, he succumbed."

"Succumbed"? What a lovely word. Crane felt a cold chill grip him. Why hadn't Martin told him this right away? MacLean was also a government supporter. Not that Campbell and MacLean had been killed by the same person, or people. Nonetheless, his death would also demand a report, and in this case, it was going to be touchy. It was Katherine. She had murdered George just as she had probably murdered old MacQuarrie and old Donald MacLean. And again, there would be no evidence because Katherine was a brilliant and sinister woman. *My God, she frightens me!* Well, she had what she wanted. Perhaps that would end it. "I'll make arrangements to interview his wife later," he said.

"Sir, there's a lot of talk about her. They say she poisoned him the way she poisoned her other husbands."

"*They*," "*they*" . . . He shook his head. "They" were all faceless, nameless people who could offer him not one shred of evidence.

And yet he knew they were right.

Katherine turned this way and that, assessing her image in the mirror. Mourning was such a bore! She much preferred red to black, but of course she could not wear red—or any other color, for that matter—while she was in mourning. Not that she felt like mourning. Not at all. George was dead, and as there were no male heirs, the entire estate would be hers!

It seemed to Katherine as if George had taken an eternity to die. She had devoted months and months to his demise, but his constitution was as strong as his mind was weak, and in the end, she had had to prepare a potion three times stronger than normal. But now it was over, George was buried, and she was free!

She spun around, and, leaving her bedroom, went downstairs. She would have to remain here for a decent period, and then, she thought with great happiness, she could go to London. There was no need for her to remain in the Highlands, no need at all. After a time, she might even return and see about Bram Chisholm. A broad smile crossed her face at the possibilities.

Katherine was in the dining room when the servant appeared. He was such a nervous man, she thought as she looked at him expectantly.

"There's a Mary MacAdam here to see you," he said quickly.

Katherine scowled and wondered what woman would come to see her. Why was it no interesting men came? She did not like the company of women, and presumed she had made that clear to everyone in the vicinity. That, quite naturally, was why she was surprised to hear a woman had come to see her.

"Did she say what she wanted?" Katherine asked sharply.

"No, madam. She simply said she had information that would be of interest to you."

"Show her into the reception room. I'll come in a few minutes."

If someone had information, Katherine knew full well it was good not to appear too anxious to have it. Information was almost never given freely, especially here, where it seemed to her that everyone wanted money for doing absolutely nothing at all.

Katherine ate her breakfast with deliberate slowness and then sauntered to the reception room.

"I'm sorry I was so long. I hadn't finished my breakfast," she said curtly, as she sized up her guest.

Mary MacAdam was not someone she knew. She was hard-looking, short, but heavyset with short dark hair and broad, manly shoulders. Her bosom was heavy and droopy and her stomach and hips were huge. Her legs however, appeared like spindles, giving her the appearance of an inverted clock pendulum. She had piercing blue eyes.

"I see you're in mourning," Mary said, without bothering to introduce herself.

"My husband just died," Katherine said impatiently.

"How unfortunate," Mary replied. She did not sound concerned in the least.

At least, she was not disingenuous, Katherine thought. "Have we met?"

"No. I am from Mull, a neighbor of the Lachlans'."

Katherine scowled at her. "The Lachlans are no concern of mine."

"Perhaps they ought to be," Mary said, sitting down and making herself comfortable without invitation.

Mary's apparent confidence made Katherine feel uncomfortable. "I don't understand," Katherine said. "Why are you here?"

"I have information you should have. But nothing is free in this world. We're poor folk and even the Lachlans are rich by comparison."

"So you want me to pay for this information when I do not even know what it is?" Katherine laughed, although as soon as she did so she regretted it. There was something about this woman, something cocky in her manner, as if she must have truly important information.

"You go ahead and laugh at me. You think you're so high and mighty. Well, you'll see that you're not. Soon you'll be as poor as a mouse, too."

"That, I doubt," Katherine replied with bravado. "Tell me what it is you know."

"When you've written a letter appointing my husband your tacksman on Mull, then I'll tell you."

"I doubt any information is worth that much," Katherine mused. "A tacksman is able to skim off money from the rents. They all cheat." Katherine punctuated her accusation by raising her brow.

Mary narrowed her eyes. "I promise you my information is worth a great deal to you. Unless, of course, you don't want to inherit everything."

Katherine's intuition told her something was wrong, horribly wrong, and that this woman did indeed know something. Well, what was given one day could be taken back the next. The trouble with these people was that they were so occupied with feuds over some skewed definition of honor, they didn't know how to deal with someone who could give their word one day and break their word the next.

"I need a new tacksman on Mull in any case," Katherine said. "I suppose having one with an ambitious wife is not the worse thing." With that, Katherine sat down at her writing desk and began to write the necessary document appointing the man in question her tacksman. "And what is your husband's name?" she asked.

"Bruce MacAdam," Mary answered.

Katherine finished writing and handed the paper to Mary who actually read it.

"Now, you will tell me."

"There's a male heir to the MacLean estates," Mary said calmly, without preamble. "Moira Lachlan was pregnant when your late husband divorced her. She had a male child."

Katherine fought for control, though she felt her blood turn cold. "Where are they?" she snapped.

"On one of the islands with her grandmother's relatives. That's all I know."

Katherine stared intently at Mary and then nodded. Her head was filled with thoughts of what all this could mean. There was no choice concerning her next move. She had to kill the child and, just to make certain, the child's mother. And she vowed to do it as quickly as possible.

"I'll be going now," Mary said, as she folded the paper and stuffed it down her dress.

Katherine could not speak, she was so angry. She left the woman in the reception room and hurried upstairs.

Edana lay on the bedroll and stared up at the stars. Beneath her, the ground was hard and around her, the MacDonalds snored loudly. Gradually over the last week she had regained some of her strength. But she was still in deep grief, unable to sleep soundly, unable to accept the fact that Bram was dead.

She thought briefly of those who had taken her captive. At first she had thought them simply a band of warriors out to avenge their kin. The vengeance was accurate enough, but the warriors were not alone. After looting the castle of all that could be easily carried, they headed south rather than north. They traveled a full day and then joined up with their women, who had come with them from the islands. In order to appear less suspicious, they split into small groups and went off in different directions.

The group she traveled with included Ian MacDonald and his brother Thomas. There were two other MacDonald men as well, Robby and young James. Both of them had their wives with them, and one of the women was nursing a small child.

For days now she had thought of trying to run away. The MacDonalds didn't tie her up, and generally they treated her not as a prisoner, but as one of them. She cooked with the other women, and a hundred times during the day she knew she could have escaped. But there was really no place to which she could escape. She had no horse, and she was a very long way from home, in hostile territory. She had no money, she knew no one in this area, and so, she reasoned, running away was pointless. In any case, she didn't care where they took her or what happened to her. Bram was dead. No matter where she was, she had no future.

"You're restless," said Isabel MacDonald, who was lying next to her. "Can't you sleep?"

"No. I was thinking of someone I've lost."

"We'll be returning to Skye tomorrow night. There's a ship waiting for us at Loch Arkaig. It'll be easier on you once we're back. Then Ian will try to ransom you. You'll be home eventually."

"Skye," she said, and suddenly she felt her heart pounding. Moira was on Skye! Moira, yes—Moira was her friend and wanted to see her. The only person she had ever loved was dead. But Moira had a child. She could use Bram's resources to destroy Katherine and see to it that Moira's son would become chieftain.

Edana turned over and closed her eyes against the brightness of the stars. Bram filled her thoughts, and she imagined herself curled next to him on the bed. *What a fool I was!* Again she chastised herself for not believing him, for thinking he was having an affair with Katherine, for not trusting him.

Sleep came over her slowly, numbing her limbs and then her mind. At first there were no dreams, only the silent, velvet blackness of untroubled sleep.

Edana tossed slightly as the familiar wall came into view. It was a stone wall, built with the strength of men's backs. Like so many in Scotland, this low wall was constructed of flat slate stones that extended for many miles. Such walls were built from stones that were taken out of the ground in order to grow crops, and provided a partial blockade for the lazy sheep that grazed on the green grasses.

The house was as familiar to her as the wall. And the girl was there on the grass in front of the house—the girl who was her but was not her. The girl who was her "other."

The girl was in distress and Edana could see that she was crying. In her sleep, Edana called out and ran across the field to try to reach the "other." The faster she ran, the more distant

the girl became. Yet nothing moved—not the house, or the
wall, or the lazy sheep.

I'm not close enough to know she's crying, Edana thought.
And yet she knew "the other" was crying and she felt her pain.
What was this cursed dream! She opened her eyes suddenly to
see the stars above her, to realize there was no wall, no house,
no "other." And yet this dream came again and again. It came
when she was alone, when she slept with Bram, and it came
to her now as she slept near the shores of Loch Arkaig. Why
did it keep coming?

At length, she closed her eyes again and this time she concentrated only on Bram. She could feel his hands on her body,
remember the sweet seduction of his kisses, relish in the memory of how he touched her, aroused her, and how she felt in
his arms. She shivered in the night air and curled herself tighter.
If only he were here to warm her.

Bram lay in bed and turned restlessly on his side. Then he
opened his eyes, aware that for the first time in days he was
able to focus his eyes properly and that his head did not hurt.
He had broken ribs and the doctor had bound several bones.
His worst injury had been to the head. Apparently he had been
lucid for only a short time before the swelling had caused him
to black out completely. He vaguely remembered not being
able to see for a time, and he could not recall all that had taken
place.

"You're awake!" Heather Ross said cheerfully.

He nodded. "Is Ross here?"

"Downstairs. Should I call him?"

"Please."

Bram watched as she left the room. When she returned, Ross
was with her.

"You're a lucky bastard! They had you, and you got away,"
Ross said, winking.

"I owe that to luck and to the MacDonalds, though I don't
know which MacDonalds, or where they've taken my wife."

"She probably won't tell them she is your wife, Bram. She
doesn't know who is who."

''She knows who I am. She went to Inveraray to save me. I have to find her.''

''You won't be leaving that bed till the doctor says you can,'' Heather said firmly.

Ross smiled. ''You're a lucky man. Edana's as brave as she is beautiful. You know they won't harm her.''

Bram nodded. ''I'm only concerned because they might think she's a Campbell.''

''With that hair, it's possible. But if that's the case, they'll hold her for ransom,'' Ross laughed.

''Another reason why she won't tell them I'm her husband. The woman is beautiful, brave, and stubborn,'' Bram concluded.

''It's not as if you have no alternatives. Go to the mountains. Your compatriot Alex MacDonald will be able to find her,'' Ross suggested.

Bram nodded. It would be yet another long trip and more time spent. But Ross was right. Alex MacDonald would be able to find Edana.

Edana leaned over the rail of the vessel as it bobbed in the calm waters of an inlet off Loch Arkaig. It was a larger sailing ship than she had expected, and that, she hoped, would make the trip to Skye both safer and swifter. Of course, the whole trip was a ruse to lead off track any who followed. Skye was extremely close to the mainland. One need not go this absurd route by sea; there was a ferry that traveled the short distance between the island and mainland at the closest point. But no, the MacDonalds did not choose to take this easy route which involved crossing only a few hundred yards of water. They had chosen to travel southward and take a vessel out onto the sea, approaching Skye from its far eastern side.

All her life Edana had heard stories about the crossings between islands and between the mainland and the islands. The water beyond this sheltered inlet had a reputation for testing men's spirits; it was rough, choppy, cold, and subject to sudden storms, which churned the sea and swamped smaller vessels.

She had been told that they would sail at high tide and so

she waited apprehensively, wondering if the calm of this inlet belied rough seas that might lie beyond. In spite of dark clouds in the distance, it was hard to think of the possibility of rough seas while anchored here. It was a truly picturesque inlet, quiet and peaceful. The beach was wide and covered with pebbles. Beyond the beach, giant, jagged rocks gave way to woods.

Tears filled Edana's eyes as she once again thought of Bram. It had been nearly two weeks now, and she ached for him. She forced her thoughts momentarily away from him and tried to think of Moira. She had never been to Skye and she had no idea how large an island it was, or what the terrain was like. But she was certain she could find Moira and help her with her infant son. Yes, her life would have some purpose.

"You're deep in thought," Isabel MacDonald said, as she came up to the rail and stood next to Edana. "I've good news. News that will make you smile."

Edana looked at her and managed to force a half-smile for Isabel's benefit. Isabel could not understand her mourning, because she did not know about Bram. "And what might this good news be?" Edana asked.

"Ian told me he has written your kin and asked for ransom. He wanted to wait till we got home to Skye, but he sent it today instead. The message will reach them within a day or two."

Under ordinary circumstances, Edana might have rejoiced, but Ian MacDonald's demand for ransom would go to Katherine and George and neither of them could be expected to give even a cockleshell for her return. It was almost funny.

"Aren't you happy?" Isabel asked.

No doubt Isabel had asked Ian to do this. She was a good-hearted woman and Edana did not want to hurt her feelings. "Yes, thank you," she said, reaching out and patting Isabel's arm. She hoped she sounded sincere. She thought of Katherine and George receiving this demand for ransom. It was such an irony! No doubt they would write back offering to pay the MacDonalds to keep her forever.

Chapter Twelve

Crane stared out his window at the rolling hills. They were not like the smooth hills of England, but were rock-studded and uneven. He drew in his breath and expelled it slowly. Everything was so incredibly complicated.

Outside his office, Martin was holding Katherine at bay. But she could not be kept waiting forever, he thought glumly. There was no way he could avoid her, and so he rang the bell on the corner of his desk with resignation. Perhaps she wouldn't stay too long; perhaps she would not test his vow to give her up; and perhaps she would not want anything important, after all. He shook his head; perhaps the world really was flat.

"It's been so long," Katherine said, as she paused in the doorway.

She really did look breathtaking. Her black gown was daring in the extreme and her white breasts were revealed almost to the point of indecency. Her tiny waist was held even farther in by a wide black leather belt and her skirt fell over her rounded hips. Her dark hair was pulled back except for two curled strands, which hung down, loose, on either side. Her eyes, as always, were huge black pools into which he felt drawn in spite of all his knowledge of her.

"If you don't come to see me more often, I shall think you don't like me anymore." Her full lips pouted ever so slightly.

He cursed silently as he felt himself growing stiff. Her voice was incredibly suggestive, her appearance even more so. He felt utterly and completely weak as she came closer to him. He inhaled and smelled the musk perfume she always wore.

"Really, you must make some time for me."

When their relationship had begun, he had known he was in charge. Now he knew he was just like all the others. Katherine was in charge, and regrettably, she sensed her power. She was like a tracking dog: she had the scent of blood, and she was relentless in her pursuit.

She walked still closer until her breasts were touching his chest, until he was looking directly into her dark eyes.

She actually took him in her hand and he felt dizzy as she caressed him. She was bold. She did things no other woman did, and the memory of her flooded over him. In a moment he had encircled her waist and buried his face in her cleavage. She continued to move her hand and he felt he would burst. It had been too long!

"Do take off your breeches," she whispered.

He could feel his face grow hot, and he dropped them immediately.

Katherine had lifted her skirts and revealed her long white legs. She wore no other undergarment save her petticoats and he shivered, desiring her while at the same time knowing what she was and what terrible crimes she had committed.

He pushed her backward onto his desk, and all his reports scattered on the floor. Her arms were around his neck, and her legs wrapped around him in a snakelike fashion. She was simply too tempting. He closed his eyes and even as he buried his face in her bosom, he felt her close around him. He panted wildly and then felt release. It was over! It was over too soon! But now that his desire had been satisfied perhaps he could speak with her rationally.

He withdrew slowly and then stopped to pull up his breeches. Katherine smoothed out her skirt and smiled at him. "I really came to say good-bye."

He looked into her unnaturally large pupils and repeated her words as if she had spoken in a foreign tongue. " 'Good-bye?' "

"Yes, I'm going to Edinburgh for a few weeks."

"I see." He could not imagine why she was telling him this, but he somehow felt relieved that she was leaving. Now that George was dead, she was no doubt bored, and though he admitted that when she was with him he could not resist her, he also knew his resolve was solid as long as he did not encounter her in person.

"I would appreciate it if you could look after things for me while I'm gone."

"Of course," he mumbled.

"Bram lives too far away," she said calmly.

Crane kept silent. She clearly did not know that Bram had been hurt; just as she clearly had not yet heard of the attack on Inveraray.

"Are you just going on vacation?"

She smiled sweetly. "I'm going to the doctor. I believe I may be pregnant."

An absolutely cold chill went right through him. Katherine, pregnant? He wanted to scream, *By whom?* but he was afraid to hear the answer. George, after all, had not been well for some time. And yet it would explain why she had killed George when she did. If she were pregnant with a male child, the child would inherit everything. That made her position strong indeed. Until that child reached the age of twenty-five, Katherine would make all the decisions for the future chieftain. It gave her absolute control of both the money and the clan. It was true that she had the money now, but a new chieftain would try to put restrictions on how it was spent. No, the power she had now could not last. She would eventually be challenged by a male relative, even if the relationship were somewhat distant. A son would make all the difference. What terrified Crane was that he might well be the father of this child.

"You seem surprised," Katherine said calmly.

"I suppose I am."

Katherine smiled sweetly. "Things turn out strangely, don't they?"

He nodded.

Again her eyes locked on his. "I'll be back," she said, and he knew she would be, though it seemed more of a threat than a promise.

Katherine returned home to begin readying herself for the journey ahead. She was satisfied that Crane thought she was leaving for Edinburgh. Naturally, she was not going to Edinburgh, but to search for Moira and her child—though she did intend to go to Edinburgh after she finished her business. She did not really think herself pregnant, but had decided to say she was. She intended to steal a baby and tell everyone it was hers and that George was the father. No one could challenge her then. But Moira's child was the firstborn and Katherine must rid herself of him. Yes, it would be better if no one knew she was looking for Moira at all, and much better if those who mattered thought her to be elsewhere.

"Not a pleasant journey," she said to herself, as she began to pack. "The islands are so dreary."

"Madam?"

Katherine looked up to see a young man dressed in the Campbell tartan and dressed to ride.

"Your manservant let me in and told me I'd find you here."

"And you have. May I ask your name?"

"Ronald Campbell, cousin to the late Colin Campbell."

A frown covered Katherine's face. " 'Late'? I don't understand."

"Inveraray was attacked well over a week ago. Colin and fourteen of his men were murdered."

Katherine trembled slightly. Had they been attacked because they were Campbells, or because they were government supporters? She did not wish to ask. "Have you any idea who committed this dreadful crime?"

"MacDonalds, most likely. Thieving, illiterate bastards, they're a scourge on the land."

"I agree, and there are far too many of them. Do the British know of this crime?"

"Of course. Superintendent Crane and his soldiers were there within hours of the attack. I've heard they were on their way to Inveraray to unmask the Phoenix, who had been caught in a trap laid by Colin.''

Katherine suddenly felt filled with anger. Crane had told her nothing of this—the miserable wretch was keeping secrets from her!

''You said 'most likely' it was the MacDonalds; are there other possibilities?''

''Yes. Possibly friends of the Phoenix, or friends of the unknown woman Colin was with—apparently he tried to have his way with her.''

''I see.'' In point of fact, she did not see. Clearly it was the MacDonalds who had killed Colin, and just as clearly, Crane did not want to act against them because they were far too powerful. What a coward! He was afraid any action against them would cause a general uprising. ''It's good of you to come and tell me these things,'' Katherine said.

''I was sent by Colin's brother, Angus, to warn all government supporters, just in case it was not the MacDonalds.''

''I shall take care,'' Katherine replied. Vaguely she wondered how old this young Campbell lad was. He certainly was of age, and he was very good-looking. She smiled warmly. ''You've ridden long. Won't you stay for dinner? Let me offer my hospitality for the night. We've plenty of room.''

''That's very kind of you.''

''Not at all. I'm a widow, you know. I'll enjoy the company.''

He grinned at her and Katherine smiled back. Generally she enjoyed older, more experienced men, but youth had its compensations.

Katherine busied herself in her boudoir and thought seriously about the best method of seducing her young guest. She was in the midst of selecting a gown when her maid entered. As usual, the girl looked nervous and apprehensive.

''Well, what is it now? I don't bite, you know.''

The girl curtsied and held out a letter. *Messages and more messages, visitors and surprises. Now what?* she asked herself as she snatched the letter out of the girl's trembling hand. ''Go downstairs and make certain dinner is almost ready.''

Again the girl curtsied, and then scurried away.

Katherine opened the letter and read it slowly; and then, because its contents were so bizarre, she read it again.

> *We are holding one Edana MacLean, and demand a ransom of five hundred pounds for her person. If this ransom is not agreed to, she will not be returned. You will send the money to the following address in London. . . .*

Katherine burst into peals of laughter. It was like all ransom notes from the MacDonalds. She had seen them before. Edana was being held prisoner by the MacDonalds and this note had come to her instead of to Edana's husband, Bram Chisholm. Doubtless, for some stupid reason, Edana had not told them to whom she was married. Bram was far wealthier than she! How had this all come to pass? She sat down on the foot of her bed and studied the note.

How had Edana fallen into the hands of the MacDonalds? If it was the MacDonalds who killed Colin, could Edana be the woman he had been about to rape? The MacDonalds might have rescued her from Colin's grasp when they killed him, but not knowing her, decided to hold her for ransom. She must have told them she was a MacLean. Again Katherine began to laugh. It was too delicious! But what had Edana been doing at Colin's in the first place? Obviously, Bram did not know where Edana was.

"I'll work this out," she murmured, then carefully tore the letter into many pieces. "And now, my sweet Bram Chisholm, you will never know where Edana is."

She gathered up the remnants of the letter and threw it into the fire.

Bram wound his way up the familiar mountain path. At the appropriate place, he gave the signal, and soon he was met by his cousin Hugh, who dismounted and embraced him.

Bram winced. "Watch the ribs. I'm told three are still mending."

"By heaven, you've had a close call. We've all been lying low."

"A wise decision," Bram said, as they tethered the horses and walked through the narrow passages of the cave and into the larger cavern. Torches glowed from the walls, and the fire made the whole subterranean chamber seem warm.

"Better sit down," Hugh suggested. "You've had a long ride, and obviously you're not fully recovered." He pointed Bram toward a great pile of sheepskins. They were soft and comfortable. Gratefully Bram sank down, stretching out his long legs. The ride had made him all too aware of the fact that he was far from fully healed. Not only did his ribs still ache, but on occasion he suffered dizzy spells. He was also aware of having lost weight during his period of recovery.

"It's a wonder Campbell's men didn't kill you," Alex Mac-Donald said, shaking his head.

"They tried," Bram admitted, "and nearly succeeded."

"Who killed Campbell?" Hugh asked.

Bram shrugged, "I don't know. But I think it was a band of MacDonalds. Owing to the fact that they didn't know who she was, I believe they took my wife."

"Won't she tell them who she's married to? If they're told, they'd certainly return her at once," Hugh said confidently.

"I don't think she'll tell them I'm her husband. She only just discovered I was the Phoenix—or perhaps I should say *a* Phoenix. She would be afraid to tell them."

"Smart girl. You don't move till you know the lay of the land," Alex said with a grin. "But I suppose that's why you've come. You want me to take you about and discover just which of my kin have her."

"Exactly."

MacDonald laughed. "If she is a stunning woman—we'd better find her before they decide to keep her and marry her off to one of their number."

"I'd like to leave in the morning," Bram said.

"That's fine. The only question is, do we start in the outer islands and work our way back toward the mainland, or do we begin on the nearest islands and work our way farther afield?"

"I'd guess these MacDonalds didn't come from too far away. I think we should start looking on the inner islands."

"Then let's share a good meal and some ale, and we'll begin our journey in the morning."

"Where do you suggest we go first?" Bram asked.

"Rhum," Alex answered. "We'll go to Clan MacDonald at Keppoch. If they're not the ones holding her, they'll surely know who does have her."

Bram smiled and took the ale offered to him. He knew he would dream of Edana tonight; she filled his thoughts and he longed to be with her, to hold her, and to know she was really safe. Soon, he told himself, they would be together again.

Katherine instructed her guard to wait outside the Lachlan house. She stood in the center of its main room and looked about with disdain. It was homey and comfortable and the aroma of fresh bread filled the whole house.

Moira's father stood uneasily while Katherine looked about. "I've never been here before."

"Your late husband came here often."

She did not ask which late husband; she knew he meant Donald MacLean.

"I suppose you're able to live well because of all the money you skimmed off the rents you collected."

"There was no skimming," he protested.

"Well, you can't cheat me anymore. I've hired a new tacksman."

"You've made a mistake," he said, looking into her strange dark eyes.

Katherine glared at him. "I shall have you put in irons if you're not cooperative. I have that power now. I'm in charge."

He looked at her unblinkingly and wondered how long it would be before her authority was challenged. But he did not respond to her, because for the present, she indeed had that power. In fact, she had the power of life and death over all those who lived on her estates. "I'm always cooperative," he answered.

"Good. Tell me where Moira is. I must see her."

"I'll not tell you," he replied.

"Then you shall be jailed and I shall find her on my own. You'll be sorry you didn't tell me what I want to know."

She turned imperiously and called her guards. "Lock him up!" she demanded.

The guards seized him roughly and he glared at her as he was led away. He prayed this witch would not find his daughter. There was no question in his mind that she would kill his daughter and his grandson. She was a killer—he could see it in the depths of her dark eyes.

Most of the tower houses on Skye appeared to be in a ruinous state. Like those on Mull, they had been built largely for defensive purposes and had few amenities. The MacDonalds possessed such a tower house, but they lived frugally, and like their close relatives who had once occupied Glencoe, they preferred to be out-of-doors as much as possible. Soon it would be entirely too cold to be outside; then, she presumed, they would all move inside to occupy the tower house.

Edana found she did not mind this way of life. The constant presence of children to tend kept her mind occupied, and there was always work. She did weaving, spinning, and cooking with the other women. Often when she looked after the children, she told them tales. She worked hard, glad to be busy so that she could sleep at night.

For the present, Edana had given in to her circumstances. She had decided to remain with these MacDonalds for a time, at least until she had learned more about the island and had time to make discreet inquiries about where Moira might live. Running away without a plan could place her in a far worse position than she was in now, remaining with her more or less benevolent captors.

On this day, it was unseasonably warm. She and Isabel had gone together to gather the sheep that grazed nearby. Later in the day, they would begin to dye the wool that had been taken the previous spring. The dyes were made from elderberries, lichens, blue iris, and crocus.

Edana had been spinning and sewing all her life, but many

other of the MacDonalds' activities were new to her. She had never gathered sheep, or made dyes, or baked bread in large outdoor ovens. Naturally, the telling of tales was common, but from the MacDonalds she heard new tales or new versions of old stories.

As they walked to the side of the hill, she and Isabel talked. Perhaps, Edana thought, this would be the best time to find out more about her surroundings. "How large is Skye?" she inquired.

Isabel frowned. "Near fifty miles long, I'm told."

Edana did not need to ask if there were mountains. She could see them; they were called the Coolins and their snow-covered peaks were often hidden in the morning mist.

"Is it as wide as it is long?"

Isabel shook her head. "No—oh, no. I'm told you can't get more than five miles from the sea."

Edana digested the information and tried to decide how suspicious her next question might sound. Still, it was a question that might give her an idea as to where she might find Moira. "Are all those who live on Skye MacDonalds or their kin?"

Isabel laughed. "Oh, no. I don't think we are even the majority. Our kin are spread out over all the islands. Many of us who now live here on Skye came from Glencoe."

Edana felt badly for having asked. Glencoe was legendary. The massacre had taken place ten years ago, but the very mention of it brought great sadness to the hearts of those who knew about it. That these MacDonalds were survivors of Glencoe or the relatives of victims explained why Colin Campbell had been set upon so viciously.

"What other clans live here?" she asked, hoping that her questions, if phrased more directly, might elicit the response she needed.

"Mostly MacLeods. They live on the other end of the island, near Dunvegan Castle."

"I see," Edana said thoughtfully. Yes, she remembered now, Moira's grandmother was a MacLeod. It seemed reasonable that her family might live somewhere within the vicinity of the castle.

"Ian hasn't heard a word from your kin," Isabel said abruptly.

Edana shrugged. "I am not so anxious to go home."

"If they don't ransom you, you'll have to marry Ranald. He's not a bad sort, though, and he needs a wife."

Edana did not answer. She certainly didn't want to marry anyone. She never wanted another man to touch her. Bram was the only man she had ever loved, and she loved him still. She dreamed of him, and though she knew he was dead, she couldn't really believe it. "I can't marry anyone," she said, without elaboration.

Isabel looked at her oddly, then said, "It's not wise to cross Ian; he has a terrible temper."

"Then I shall have to face his temper."

Edana turned back toward the flock of sheep. Fifty miles. . . . If there was a pass through the mountains, it would take near four days to walk to Dunvegan Castle. But it was already cold in the mountains and it was growing colder by the day. Snow could be expected at the higher elevations. It would probably take twice as long to walk around the coast. *But no matter how long it takes, I must go,* she decided. *I must find Moira, for I certainly cannot marry Ranald.*

Katherine looked around the MacAdam house with the same disdain she had felt at the Lachlan house. It was tiny, but less homey than the Lachlans' had been.

Mrs. MacAdam wore a long, tentlike garment, which did not succeed in hiding her rather odd shape. "I'm surprised you'd come here," she said, ushering Katherine to her table.

"Necessity is a hard master," Katherine replied coldly.

"Can I offer you some tea?"

"Yes. I have need to talk with you. Are we quite alone?"

"My husband won't be back till the sun sets."

"I'm glad to see his new position is keeping him busy," Katherine said sharply.

Mrs. MacAdam took the steaming kettle from the hearth and

poured it over the leaves in the pot. "A real delicacy, this. I bought it from a ship's captain who docked in Oban."

"Apparently there are very few delicacies here," Katherine retorted. "Frankly, I spent nearly a year and a half on this godforsaken island and it was far too long."

"It's no better or no worse than other places."

Katherine actually laughed. "That just shows how few places you have been. But I did not come here to banter. I came for information."

"I've told you all I know."

"That may be, but you'll find out more, even if you have to talk with everyone on this island. But I warn you, I'm in a hurry."

"What is it you want to know?"

"I want to know about the Lachlans—where they come from and where their relatives live. I want to know who Moira's grandparents were and where they came from. Doubtless the girl is with relatives."

"Her father won't tell you where she is?"

"I expect he'll rot in prison first."

Mrs. MacAdam stared at Katherine. "You put him in prison?"

"Yes. And you will find out what I need to know, because what has been given can be taken away. I'm sure you would not want to be without funds to provide yourself with the few joys of life, like imported tea. Naturally, I could also arrange for your husband to share a cell with Moira's father."

"They said you were a she-devil," Mrs. MacAdam muttered.

"And you, my dear Mrs. MacAdam, have entered into an agreement with me. Think about that: you must be the devil's handmaiden, not that you are exactly a maiden. Now, find out what I need to know."

Mrs. MacAdam poured the tea and Katherine smiled as she sipped some of the hot, steaming liquid. When she had drained her cup, she stood up and smiled. "I shall be back in four days' time."

Mrs. MacAdam did not answer, but it seemed obvious to

Katherine that she understood and would find out the necessary information.

Edana lay on the floor of the roofless hut and looked up at the star-filled sky. Tomorrow night she planned to leave—making her way around the rugged coastline of the island, avoiding the colder, more dangerous mountains.

For over a week now she had stored away food and hidden it safely in a rock cairn. She planned to take a sheepskin for warmth and to tie it all into a pack.

For several nights she had lain awake trying to plan a disguise, and finally decided to dress as a young boy since she was far too slight to pass herself off as a man. She would put her red hair beneath a MacDonald clan bonnet she had hidden away. She hoped that no one would challenge her right to wear it, since a bonnet was earned, rather than bestowed on a young man.

The MacDonalds would have the advantage when they looked for her, as she was a stranger on Skye and they knew the island. She wondered if she was truly worth a prolonged search at a time of year when everyone needed to be working in order to prepare for winter. The truth of the matter was, she did not know how hard the MacDonalds would look for her. As far as they knew, she had no financial value since no one had paid the ransom they asked. It was true that they could marry her to Ranald, whose previous two wives had died and left him with a total of nine children to care for.

Perhaps, had she gone to Ian MacDonald himself and asked to be freed, he might have granted her freedom. But she was afraid to ask, afraid that he would say no and tell her she must marry Ranald.

Edana turned on her side and closed her eyes. She needed sleep tonight because tomorrow night she would have none. She closed her eyes and willed herself to sleep. As she drifted off, the familiar dream of the "other" filled her mind.

* * *

"Murdering witch," Mary MacAdam hissed, as she stood by the window of her house and watched as Katherine MacLean alighted from her carriage and walked imperiously toward the door. Still, she thought to herself, it was better to be a collaborator than a victim. It was obvious that Katherine MacLean would stop at nothing.

Mary MacAdam dried her hands on a cloth and opened the door just as Katherine reached it. Katherine stopped dead on the threshold; she was obviously no more enthusiastic about coming in than Mary was to invite her.

"Have you my information?" Katherine asked.

"Yes. Moira's grandmother was a MacLeod from Skye. As there are no close Lachlan relatives, it seems she went to stay with her grandmother's people on Skye."

"Where on Skye?" Katherine prodded.

"Near Dunvegan Castle, I'm told."

Katherine made a face. "I've not been to Skye."

"Nor I," Mary MacAdam replied. She had no desire to prolong this conversation.

Katherine turned about, and without so much as a thank-you, left. Skye was days and days away. She began to regret not telling Crane she would be in Edinburgh longer. "Dunvegan Castle," she repeated. It might as well have been the land of the Vikings, it was so remote.

Rhum was a small island and part of the Lochabar estate of the MacDonalds of Clanranald. Alan MacDonald had become the fourteenth chieftain at the age of fourteen in 1686. Now he was exiled in France, having been the staunchest of Jacobites, fighting bravely to restore James VII to the throne. But it had not mattered that he was in France. His people had remained loyal, and even in his absence, he had remained their undisputed chief.

Keppoch—indeed, all of MacDonald territory—was rich with folklore and wealthy in Gaelic literature.

The English would never understand, Bram thought bitterly. They hated Gaelic and had vowed to stamp it out in both Ireland and Scotland. Bram's mother had been a MacDonald, and he had heard the stories, songs, and poems from her. The MacDonalds owed the MacMhuirich family much, for it was they who had preserved the verse. For centuries the MacMhuiriches had been the bards of Clanranald and they had set down two volumes in Gaelic, known as *The Blackbook of Clanranald* and *The Redbook of Clanranald*. Few clans had such a rich history and Bram was proud to have MacDonald blood flowing in his veins.

It was David MacDonald who met them in the round room on the ground floor of the ancient tower house that looked out on the sea. It had a great fireplace, but it was clear that the MacDonalds did not live here when the weather was decent. It was a place where they came to fight if they were under siege; it was a place where they greeted guests.

"This is Bram Chisholm," Alex MacDonald explained. "He is my close compatriot and his mother was one of your clan. She and her husband perished at Glencoe."

David embraced Bram tightly. "Welcome to Rhum," he said sincerely.

"We've come to impose on your hospitality and to find Bram's wife. We believe she was mistakenly taken by a branch of Clan MacDonald following a raid on Inveraray."

David looked vaguely distressed. "Would she not tell them she was a Chisholm and that her husband's mother was a MacDonald?"

"No. She only recently discovered my true loyalties and she would not know whom to trust."

David nodded sympathetically. "I've heard you are trusted by our enemies and that their trust has provided much useful information."

"Without Bram we would never have been so successful," Alex said. "Do you know who carried out the raid on Inveraray?"

David laughed heartily. "Ian MacDonald. I imagine he and his men have already returned to Skye."

Bram grinned. Skye was not so far away. He and Edana might well be united within the week.

"You can leave by boat tomorrow, but tonight let's celebrate the demise of Colin Campbell."

Bram nodded. "I should enjoy that."

* * *

It was like the celebrations of his childhood. It was not carried out within the confines of the tower's oddly rounded walls, but outdoors in the middle of the field. A great fire was built, a fire that could be seen for miles.

A lamb was slaughtered and roasted. They ate fresh bread, and greens, and succulent lamb. Then the pipes were played and the girls of Clanranald danced till the ground shook beneath their feet. After that, when everyone was sleepy, tired, and drowsy, the tale-tellers gathered, and one tale after another was spun out from the lips of those who carried history in their memories. After a long while, when at last the moon hung high in the middle of the sky, the MacDonalds sought out shelter and prepared to sleep.

For the first time in a long while, Bram went to sleep feeling good. Soon he would be with his beloved; soon he would wrap her in his arms and hold her tightly.

Edana came to him in his dream, well after midnight and just before the first rays of the creeping dawn. She rose out of the cold waters of Loch Linnhe, her flesh white as snow, her breasts firm and tipped with rock-hard pink nipples. Her fiery-red hair fell all about her, a tangled magnificence that drew him closer. Her clear eyes mesmerized him and he took her in his arms and caressed her gently, running his hands over the supple skin of her back and down over her exquisite, perfectly rounded buttocks.

He kissed her sensuous lips, and felt the fire in her ignite when he touched her. Nor was she still or inanimate. Her warm hands moved over him until he felt that he would burst. And then came a gentle release, unlike what he experienced in reality but warming nonetheless.

He opened his eyes and stared at the black-velvet jewel-covered sky. He longed for her—not just to possess her in dreams, but to possess her in reality. But even as he thought of her, a feeling of ill ease came over him. It was a feeling he had not experienced since the night Colin Campbell had threatened her. This was a feeling of impending danger, a feeling that although everything seemed to be going well, something evil lurked in the future, something that would threaten his beloved Edana.

It took all of his self-control not to awaken Alex immediately and tell him they must leave. It was irrational. The boat could not leave till the tide came in. His desire to be on his way would have to wait no matter how strong his feeling.

Edana walked as fast as she possibly could, and throughout the long night she stopped only three times to rest and to refresh herself.

The moon was full, and it made her journey easier because she could see where the larger rocks were, and so she did not stumble over them.

The part of the MacDonald clan she had been with lived on a peninsula and thus she had to walk nearly ten miles to reach the main part of the oddly shaped island, with its many inlets and irregular coastline. She felt that as long as the moon was bright, and the weather remained fair, she could travel ten to twelve miles a night. She deemed it safer to travel by night and to find a hiding place to sleep through the day. That way, she did not have to fear being attacked by wild animals while she slept, nor did she have to build a fire, which might be seen.

Edana looked toward the east and saw on the horizon the first line of dawn. On the stony beach, below the path she followed, she could see the great gulls searching for their prey as they waddled along the beach. Now and again, they would take off suddenly, as if startled, and with much noise they would fly upward. They were like white, fluttering hankies against the now purple sky of early morning.

"Eight days," she said aloud. In eight days she would reach Dunvegan Castle and somehow find Moira. It would be good to once again be with an old friend, good to have someone in whom to confide. *Dear Moira,* she thought. *I have wondered about you so often, but for so long communication was impossible.*

* * *

They ate at a long table and it was Isabel who dished up the large bowls of hot gruel.

Ranald banged his ladle on the wooden table and looked into Ian's eyes. "I say we go after her. She was our prisoner and she shouldn't be allowed to run away."

Ian scowled back at Ranald. "She turned out to be worthless, and I see no point in chasing after her. We've work to do."

"It is I who was to have her," Ranald complained. "She was good with the children."

"I think you're more concerned with having her than with her motherly qualities. Frankly, you wouldn't have so many children to look after if you didn't lift your kilt so often."

Ian's blunt remark caused a flurry of laughter from the women.

But it was Isabel who touched Ranald's shoulder. "A woman who would run away would not make a good wife. Ian is right. We should just let her go. She'll probably come back anyway. Where's she going to go? How will she live?" Isabel added.

Ranald did not sit down. "It's bad for our reputation to be letting hostages escape," he finally argued.

Ian looked up. What Ranald said made sense. "Then take a few men and look for her. But I want you back here in three days' time for the gathering of the sheep in the mountains."

Ranald took his seat. A smile covered his face. "I'll go right after breakfast."

As dawn broke in the eastern sky, Edana wrapped her shawl around her more tightly. It was always coldest just before the sun rose, when the cool wind blew across the land from the nearby sea.

The ground was too hard for her to leave footprints, and she well knew that the MacDonalds possessed no tracking dogs, as the British did.

As it grew lighter, she began to look for a hiding place. The most obvious place to hide was among the large boulders, which were scattered up the hillside—and most certainly, she reasoned, that is where they would look for her first. So instead she hid herself in a culvert beneath a wooden bridge that crossed the road. The culvert was no more than five feet across and the bridge was covered with earth and hardly noticeable. Moreover, the culvert was dry and filled with brush. She clawed her way into a narrow space, one surrounded by high grass.

She curled herself up and went to sleep.

Edana was unsure how long she had slept, when she was awakened by the sound of hoofbeats. She was nearly deafened as the horsemen approached and she was terrified when she heard Ranald's voice call for them to halt.

How far away was he? He was not directly overhead but she was certain he was not more than a few feet away. She made herself as small as possible and listened as he gave his men orders to search the rocks above the road. She waited and then she heard his horse move directly above her.

She prayed she would not sneeze or cough. It seemed an eternity.

"There's no sign of anyone up here!" one of the men shouted from above.

"Then we'll not waste time, we'll move on!" Ranald shouted back. His voice was deafening; it was as if they were in a small room together.

She dared not even breathe and she could hear her own heart pounding. She closed her eyes and clenched her fists and waited. Then she heard him cry out again and the hooves of four horses crossed over her. It was like the thunder of the gods in her ears.

When they had passed, the silence was as deafening as the horses had been. Edana let out her breath and was well aware that she had been shaking like a leaf in the wind, and indeed, was still trembling.

But they were gone! She waited a long time, then she pulled herself out of the gully and stretched, surprised how stiff she had grown. She climbed the hillside and this time selected a wide bit of ground between two sun-baked dark rocks. She stretched out in the warm sun and instantly fell asleep. Her searchers were ahead of her and she would only have to be careful that they did not find her when they doubled back. But they had already searched here, and it seemed unlikely that they would return.

Chapter Thirteen

November 1708

On the eighth day of her long journey, Edana felt secure enough to travel by day. She had been perilously close to those who searched for her on the first day, then on the third, she had been hiding near the road when they rode back, clearly heading toward home. Perhaps Ranald had been given a specific period of time in which to find her, or it was possible he did not want to irritate the MacLeods by venturing into their domain.

Edana thought of Bram as she walked, and she recognized a new phase in her mourning. At first she had tried to forget; now she tried to remember, and knew beyond all doubt that though he was dead, she would carry him always in her heart. She loved him fiercely—not just because of their wild lovemaking, but because of the kind of man she knew him to be. They had both believed in family, in honor, and in keeping Scotland free. Tears still filled her eyes unexpectedly but she told herself it was important to carry on his work. The MacLean clan had adopted her and cared for her. She had loved her parents dearly. But now Katherine had taken everything and changed the clan's political stance in the process. *But I can, and will, undo that,* Edana promised herself.

Edana passed by crofters' huts and dozens of sheep grazing lazily. People noted her passing, and on two occasions she was asked who she was and where she was going. Disguised as a young boy who was unarmed, she raised little suspicion and she always answered forthrightly that she was a MacDonald on her way to Dunvegan Castle. She had to lie about her clan since she wore the MacDonald bonnet. Young men often traveled around the Highlands and as long as they were not armed and had a destination, no one bothered with them.

As she approached Dunvegan Castle, the moorland gave way to gentle hills and then to flatland strewn with rocks and low trees sculpted by the wind. When Dunvegan appeared, it was a magnificent sight. Built on the edge of a high cliff overlooking the sea, its tower was high and straight, like a sentry at attention. As she drew closer, Edana could see that Dunvegan was not a true castle in the classical Scottish design; rather, it was a large, square stone house with three full floors, many windows, and at least six chimneys. She had first seen its one tall tower. The whole edifice had an aura of strength and permanency as it stood defiant, protecting its inhabitants from seaborne invaders.

Dunvegan was a place of history. She had learned about it and many others from her tutors who saw history and myth as inseparable. Dunvegan had been built in the ninth century by the MacLeods who, it was told, were originally Norsemen. According to the history she had learned, Leod was the son of Olaf the Black, the last King of Man and the North Isles. When Olaf died, Leod inherited the islands of Lewis and Harris, and a good part of Skye. Leod then married the Norse steward of Skye and built Dunvegan, seat of Clan MacLeod.

For a long while, Edana stared at Dunvegan, even though Dunvegan was not where she must begin. It was the tacksman she sought. As the tacksman collected the rents, he would know where everyone lived, and without a doubt he would know where Moira's relatives lived. Edana knew her arrival would have been noted. In all communities, people knew a great deal about one another. Strangers were compelled to recite their family ties and explain their presence.

Edana trudged on toward the castle. After a time, she came to a small, neat cottage. She knocked on the door and in a few moments a woman answered.

"I'm Edward MacDonald," she said, using the name she had chosen to match her disguise. "I'm seeking the MacLeod tacksman," she explained, in a voice as deep as she could make it.

The woman looked her up and down somewhat suspiciously, but then nodded.

"I'm in need of information regarding a friend of mine who came here to live some time ago. I believe the tacksman may be able to help me," Edana explained further.

"We don't see many strangers here," the woman commented. "But I can tell you you'll find the tacksman's house at the end of this road, which goes across the moor. It's some two miles."

"Thank you," Edana said politely. She turned and walked away quickly. Those who loitered would seem even more suspicious to an already careful populace. Mainlanders were bad enough, she thought, but the islanders seemed doubly troubled by strangers.

It took her nearly an hour to reach the tacksman's house. It was not a grand cottage, but it was affluent enough that it stood out from the others she had passed by. It would not do to lie to the tacksman, Edana decided. In any case, she was near the end of her journey, so she paused to change into her dress and shawl and let loose her hair.

She knocked on the door, and again a woman answered. But beyond the door, Edana could see that a table was laid out with the noon meal and that a man sat at the head of the table, eating. The aroma of the food made her own mouth water and reminded her that she had not eaten since yesterday when the food she had carried for her journey had run out.

"I'm Edana MacLean, originally from the Isle of Mull," she began. "I'm a lifelong friend of Moira Lachlan, whose grandmother was a MacLeod. She wrote me to say she had come here to stay with her grandmother's relatives and I have a great need to see her." The woman stepped aside, a distressed expression on her face. At once Edana felt apprehensive.

"Did you hear, Richard?" the woman said, turning to the man, who had stopped eating to listen to Edana.

"I heard," he replied. "Tell her to come in."

Edana stepped into the warm room.

"How did you come here, lass?" the man at the table asked.

"I walked across Skye, sir. But the rest is a long tale. Do you know where my friend resides?"

"I shall have to hear your long tale. But sit down—you look hungry."

Edana did not argue. She was famished, and she sat down and gratefully took the food as it was passed to her.

The tacksman waited patiently until he could see that she had eaten as much as she wanted of the thick soup. "Now, tell me how you came to walk across Skye."

"I was being held prisoner by Colin Campbell when the MacDonalds came on a raid. They freed me and took me for ransom, but my family would not pay the ransom and so I fled on foot to find my friend Moira. My husband, Bram Chisholm, was killed by Colin Campbell."

"I'm afraid I must add to your mourning," the tacksman said. "Moira came here to Skye and lived with my sister. I'm the son of her grandmother's sister. She gave birth to a son, and some months later became very ill. She died, and now my own sister has the child."

Edana felt the pain of yet another death—Moira, poor little Moira. She had known so little happiness. It was unjust, and her misery was yet another of Katherine's crimes. Edana did not bother to hide the tears that filled her eyes. "I loved Moira like a sister. We were very close. But you must know that Moira's child is heir to all the MacLean estates. He is the legitimate son of my brother, George MacLean."

The tacksman did not look surprised. "She left a letter for you. She wanted you to care for her son till he comes of age to inherit."

Edana let her tears flow freely for Moira. She thought again about her own position. She would return to Glen Haven and take Moira's son with her. He would make her less lonely.

"I shall need help getting home since I have been held

captive,'' she told the tacksman. ''But I should be happy to fulfill Moira's wish. Please, take me to her son.''

Moira's relation, Corrie MacLeod, was as round-faced as Moira had been, and when Edana looked into her eyes, she felt as if she were talking with an older, rounder version of Moira herself.

She was a widow and her cottage was neat and clean though it was small, and had Corrie not been so diligent, it would surely have been cluttered.

''I miss her so much,'' Corrie confided, as she sat by the hearth, her hands busy with sewing. ''But the little boy's a godsend; he keeps me busy all right.''

''He's sweet,'' Edana said, as she glanced over at the sleeping child. He looked like Moira too. She smiled to herself; he did not look at all like George.

''She wanted you to rear him, but I tell you, I'll miss him.''

''Then come with me,'' Edana suggested. ''I'm a widow, too. I'll need help.''

Corrie set down her sewing and looked at Edana seriously. ''I've lived on Skye all my life. We're not a people who move about much.''

''Still, it's not so far.'' Edana wanted to say she had a lot of room, but that would have been an understatement. Bram's estate was huge. She drew in her breath and unconsciously touched her womb. Bram, her beloved, was dead. But it was possible he had left her with a great gift. She wasn't completely certain yet, but she had missed her blood and it seemed likely that she was pregnant. The prospect sent her spirits soaring. She decided that if she was pregnant, she would rear the two children together.

''Perhaps I could come with you.'' Corrie MacLeod finally relented. ''But first you stay here for a few days. Get to know the child and rest. You've had a long and hard journey.''

Edana nodded her agreement. ''I must send a message home. I must let my husband's tacksman know I am all right.'' Although she could not have said it without more tears, she also wanted to let Ross know about Bram. Somehow his body had to be retrieved and properly buried at Glen Haven.

"My brother can arrange for a messenger," Corrie said reassuringly.

"Thank you," Edana murmured.

It was nearly dark when Alex MacDonald and Bram Chisholm reached the MacDonald compound on Skye. From a distance, Bram could see the outline of the tower house and a proliferation of small huts. In the middle of the compound a great fire roared and the smell of roast pork drifted across the still night air. It was already cold outside, but the MacDonalds, a hearty lot, continued living outside as long as possible.

"Who goes?" A veritable giant of a man stepped from the bushes into the middle of the road. He held his broadsword at the ready.

"Alex MacDonald and Bram Chisholm. Don't you remember me, lad?"

Matthew MacDonald peered at the two of them in the semi-darkness. "Aye, I remember." He stepped forward and embraced Alex and then Bram. He withdrew his ram's-horn from his belt, and blew it. It signaled visitors to those gathered round the fire.

"Follow me," he said cheerfully.

In moments, they reached the fire, where the whole village was gathered to celebrate the rounding-up of the sheep and the dyeing of the spring wool. Introductions were made and Bram was immediately taken into the fold.

"We've a feast prepared," Ian thundered. "Join us!"

It was as much an order as an invitation, and Bram grinned. "We'll be honored. But first I've questions to ask. I believe you're holding my wife for ransom. She's a flame-haired girl who was at Colin Campbell's the night you raided.

"Your wife!" Ian MacDonald's voice boomed across the clearing and even the grazing sheep looked up, startled.

"Yes, she was being held captive by Campbell. I was one of the prisoners whose cell you left open."

"By God, man," Ranald muttered. "Not only did we not recognize you, but we took you for dead."

"My wife," Bram said, "was she—?"

Ian shook his head. "Campbell was killed before he did anything to her, though his intent was clear enough."

Bram drew in his breath; he was relieved beyond words. "Please take me to her; we've been apart too long."

"I'm afraid I can't do that," MacDonald answered.

Bram stared at him. "Has she been sent home?"

"I sent a ransom note—of course, I didn't know she was your wife. I sent it to her kin, but there was no answer. No, she seems to have run away."

Bram cursed Katherine under his breath. She had known all along where Edana was and she had not even sent him a message. "Katherine MacLean is your enemy and mine," Bram said.

"Why didn't your wife tell us she was married to you?"

"I presume because she didn't know for certain if we were on the same side."

Ian MacDonald nodded.

"How long has Edana been gone?" Bram asked.

"Near a fortnight. We didn't look for long; the sheep were ready to be shorn."

Bram was puzzled. Perhaps Edana was trying to get home.

Ranald rubbed his chin. "You know, she may believe you to be dead."

"What would give her that idea?"

"I remember now," Ranald said slowly. "I came to the bedchamber where she was with Ian after Campbell was killed. I told Ian the prisoners had been set free and that one—I believe I described you—was apparently dead.

Bram stood thinking. Perhaps she was on her way home, perhaps not. Where would she go? Certainly not to Katherine and George. And then he remembered Edana's friend, Moira, George's first wife. When in London Edana had talked a lot about Moira. After Edana had learned he was the Phoenix, she had told him the crimes for which she believed Katherine was responsible. Edana had included Moira's having to flee to Skye. He did not know why she had been sent here—perhaps to escape the embarrassment of having been divorced by George. Now, as surely as he stood here, Bram knew Edana would try to go to Moira. He concluded that since Moira was not a

MacDonald, she must be a MacLeod. There were only the two clans on Skye.

"I suppose we could look now," Ian MacDonald suggested. "But she's been gone for quite a while."

"I don't think that will be necessary. I think I know where she's gone," Bram said. "How far is Dunvegan?"

Ian shrugged. "Walking, eight days. By sea, much faster."

Katherine crossed over to the Isle of Skye at Kylerhe. This spot, on the southwest tip of the island, was the place where the island was separated from the mainland by only a few thousand yards. At this point a barge crossed from one side to the other, enabling the traveler to take a small wagon or horses to the other side.

Katherine did not travel alone. She traveled with two guards, men she employed, men she had known for some time, and whom she trusted to carry out her orders, regardless of what those orders were.

In spite of the nearness of Skye to the mainland, the distance between Kylerhe to Dunvegan was great and the road was difficult, as it went through a mountain pass and across miles and miles of moorland. By necessity, Katherine followed this circuitous route in order to avoid the higher mountains.

She reached Dunvegan, and with imperious self-confidence, went directly to the ancient castle to confront the chieftain, Alister MacLeod.

The twentieth chieftain of Clan MacLeod was a redoubtable man in his late fifties. His thinning blond hair and piercing blue eyes were a throwback to his Viking ancestry, as was his robust build and sharp mind.

He looked at Katherine with unsympathetic eyes. "You are not welcome here," he said coldly. "I am not a supporter of the union."

"Neither do you stand against it," she replied confidently.

"Fifty years ago more than five hundred MacLeods were killed by the British in the Battle of Worcester. We no longer fight on either side but that does not mean we welcome supporters of the union.''

Katherine smiled her sweetest and most beguiling smile, hoping to melt the heart of the old grouch. ''I did not come here about politics,'' she said softly. ''I came on a personal matter.''

Like most men she chose to charm, MacLeod's expression softened slightly, though not as much as most did. ''And what did you come about?''

''I came in search of my daughter-in-law, Moira Lachlan.'' Katherine used her former relationship to Moira, rather than her current one as second wife, and widow, to Moira's poor, late, departed husband.

''Moira Lachlan. Yes, her mother was a MacLeod, a relative of my tacksman. She was staying with his sister. But I'm afraid she fell victim to wasting disease. She is survived only by her son. I can draw you a map showing you how to reach her relative, who looks after Moira's child.''

Katherine forced an expression of horror onto her face. ''This is terrible news,'' she said, covering her mouth with her hand and forcing tears into her eyes. ''Only a month ago, her husband died. Now the poor child is orphaned.''

''I don't understand. I thought she had left her husband.''

''And that's why I am here. He had wanted to reconcile with her before he died. I came to take Moira home, back to the estate her son will inherit.''

MacLeod nodded. ''A most unhappy story.'' He tried to assess the woman who stood before him. There was something about her—something that made him uneasy.

''Please, draw me a map so I can go directly to this relative. I must take them both home with me and see to it this child is reared to be chieftain.''

MacLeod went to his writing desk. Katherine strained to keep the look of grief on her face. The truth was, she felt like smiling. The end was near for Moira's child, and when the child was dead, nothing could stand in Katherine's way.

* * *

Alister MacLeod watched as Katherine MacLean rode off with her entourage. He scowled after her, puzzled by what she had told him, and feeling an old and familiar mistrust, a mistrust that had served him well in the past.

He turned to his manservant. "I want that woman followed by guards till she leaves our domain," he instructed.

His manservant bowed ever so slightly and disappeared.

Yes, old MacLeod thought. One could not be too careful. This Katherine MacLean was beautiful, but there was something odd about her. He tried to think about what it was that bothered him. She was dressed well, and her manners were good. It was, he decided, her eyes. They seemed unnaturally large and somewhat hypnotic. She seemed too concerned with her daughter-in-law and too concerned with the child. It was a good idea to have her followed, just in case she was up to no good. One could not just trust outsiders. Outsiders were, more often than not, trouble—a lesson he had learned young, and a lesson he had learned well.

They were together, running across the moor in the bright sunshine through the heather. They were holding hands, and Bram's large hand grasped hers tightly.

When they reached the clear stream, they stopped and then fell onto the soft grass in a tight embrace. He covered her with kisses and she felt the warmth of him close to her, the strength of him next to her.

Knowing hands roamed her body until she felt hot with desire and flushed with the memory of all that was their love. Intimate kisses, tender kisses, and fulfillment in ways she had never dreamed possible. There was a noise, a loud noise, and Edana cried out, *Oh, you can't be taken from me!* It was a silent cry, and yet it woke her, brought her back to a conscious state in the dark of the night.

She opened her eyes, and in the darkness could only make out a few objects. Little Daniel, Moira's son, slept in a crib against the wall. Edana slept on a great pile of sheepskins, a comfort after her journey and the nights spent on hard ground.

There was another sound and she suddenly realized that the

first noise had been real and not a part of her dream. Her senses suddenly became alert. What had awakened her? Not her dream—it had been a dream of lovemaking, not a dream from which she would willingly withdraw. No, what woke her had been the strange noise, as if someone was walking about the outside of the cottage.

A terrible premonition suddenly swept over her and Edana fairly leapt from her bed. She pulled on her dress, slipped into her shoes, and grabbed her shawl.

She ran to the crib, and just as she was about to lift the child, she heard the front door opening. Corrie's screams filled the night, and there was shouting. Then, for a single second, Edana stood paralyzed. A shot rang out and Corrie's scream faded.

Above the shouting of men, Edana heard Katherine's voice; it was a voice she knew well, a voice that haunted her.

Edana did not hesitate another second. She grabbed the child and ran out the back door, closing it behind her. She ran some distance, then warily circled back around the house where the horses were tethered. She thanked heaven that the child did not cry, and she held him close. Well-hidden, she peered out from the brush. There were horses out front—not just those which had been there before, but three others.

She prayed the child would not cry as she cradled it close to her. Her mind raced. She took her shawl and tied the child to her tightly, nestling his head between her breasts. Then she sprang across the distance between her hiding place and the house. She untied one of the horses and led it away, sure that at any moment Katherine would come out of the house with her men. She stopped, aware that the child was slipping, and again tried to tie him to her in a way that would allow her to mount the horse.

Edana looked up, as several more riders galloped up to the house. Guns and swords drawn, they stormed in through the already open door.

Who were these men? Edana was momentarily rooted to the spot. There were more shots fired and Katherine ran from the house with a man in pursuit. She turned toward the brush and for an instant, her and Edana's eyes locked, though the distance between them was great. Curse the full moon! Edana knew that Katherine had recognized her.

But before Katherine could move in her direction, a man ran from the house and grabbed her. Katherine cursed loudly, kicking and fighting.

Edana bound the child close and quickly mounted the horse. She rode through the woods and turned on the road that led to Kyleakin. It was farther to the mainland from Kyleakin than from Kylerhe, but Kyleakin was easier to reach.

In the distance behind her, she heard more horses and more shouting. She heard gunfire, and yet she kept riding. Whatever was going on, Katherine was there and Katherine had seen her. Katherine meant to kill Moira's son and now she would have to kill Edana, too. Edana was as sure of Katherine's intentions as she was of her own name.

Katherine wrenched free of her captor just as one of her men shot him. Then, to her dismay, another shot killed her man. She looked around; all four men were shot, her two guards and the two soldiers who had come to the aid of Corrie MacLeod.

Katherine cursed. Edana had been here and Edana had escaped with Moira's son.

Katherine tripped over the thick vines and cursed again in the darkness. She reached one of the horses and mounted it, heading down the road at a gallop. At last, convinced that no one followed her, she stopped, fists clenched tightly, her anger evident in her tense body.

"Curse Edana!" she hissed. Somehow the wretched girl had gotten free of the MacDonalds and found her way to Dunvegan. And curse that horrible old woman! Katherine remembered the old woman, obviously Moira's relative. She had fought like a soldier and Katherine herself had shot her.

But most of all, curse Alister MacLeod! "He must have had soldiers follow me," she said aloud, angrily. They had burst into the house and engaged her men in fighting.

She looked around her. At first she had not been sure in which direction she traveled.

She stared at the moon and then drew in a deep breath of

the night air. "I'll have to find the road back to Kylerhe and leave Skye at once," she muttered. MacLeod would know she was responsible for killing the old woman. After all, he himself had given her the map to find the woman's house. "Damn," Katherine muttered. Edana had the child and they were both still alive somewhere. They had to be eliminated, or all her work would be for naught. "It should all be mine," she said, shaking her fist at the moon. "And it will be!"

Bram judged Alister MacLeod to be a formidable man. He was well-educated, experienced, and he had sound judgment. In fact, Alister's character made the story he told all the more alarming.

"I did not trust her," MacLeod said. "This Katherine MacLean is a stunning yet cunning woman. She is one who knows how to make herself attractive to men. She is one who kills, and from what you have told me, she has killed three husbands."

"It's her eyes," Bram said. "They're unnatural, they draw you in. They're like great pools of blackness."

"Belladonna," Alister MacLeod concluded, as he poured them all another drink. "My brother studied medicine; I remember him talking about belladonna. Apparently, it's a poison that is made from the flowers, berries, leaves, and roots of a plant that grows on the Continent."

"There's always been talk that she poisoned MacQuarrie and MacLean," Alex said, rubbing his chin.

Bram drank from his glass. Edana had suspected Katherine of killing her father. "But why would Katherine want to kill Moira?"

"Not Moira—she died some time ago of wasting disease," MacLeod said, "but her son. The child is the legal heir to the MacLean lands."

"Child?" Bram said in surprise. He had not known that Moira had a child. He had only come here to find Edana. He had now learned that Moira was dead, that Katherine had been here, and that while her men had been killed, she had escaped. Moira's relative, Corrie MacLeod, had been killed with one shot, but no one knew who had fired the shot; a fight had taken place between the men MacLeod had sent, and Katherine's men.

"Where is the child now?" Bram said, as the information came together in his mind.

"Gone—disappeared, too. I hesitate to think that this woman, Katherine, may have him."

"But where is my wife?" Bram asked.

MacLeod shrugged. "I don't know. I don't know if she was even here. Certainly she did not come to see me."

"No, she wouldn't. I think she would seek out your tacksman for information." Anxiety flooded over him. He did not yet know everything, but he knew Edana was in danger. Most certainly, Edana knew that Moira had a son.

"We'll have some lunch while we wait," MacLeod said. "I'll send for my tacksman and we'll see what he has to say."

Bram's every instinct was to mount his steed and try to find Edana at once. But he was unsure where to look, or even if she had arrived here safely. Alex must have sensed his anxiety because he reached over and touched his arm in a gentle gesture of restraint.

Richard MacLeod, second cousin to Alister MacLeod, and his tacksman, arrived within the hour. His face was lined with concern, and he was obviously filled with emotion.

"I can't believe my sister's dead," he said in a stony voice. "She was a good woman; she worked hard all her life."

"We believe she was killed when a woman came, either to kidnap or kill Moira's son," Bram explained quickly.

The tacksman looked up, clearly confused. "A young woman came a few days ago. She was very beautiful, and I knew her name because Moira had spoken of her often. It was Moira's wish that this woman raise and protect her child."

Bram's mouth opened in surprise. Edana had not just come here to seek help; she had come to provide help, probably to fulfill a promise she had made to her friend. "Did she take the child?" he asked quickly.

The tacksman shook his head. "No, she was to stay for a

time. Then Daniel and my sister were to go home with her. But how can this woman be your wife? She said she was a widow."

"She believes me to be dead."

"Ah," the tacksman said. "She was very sad and distressed."

"I think Edana must have escaped with the child when Katherine came," Bram concluded. "We must find her before Katherine finds them both."

Alex stood up. "I think we should leave immediately."

"I'll send more men out. A crime has been committed against my kin. This woman must pay," Alister MacLeod said firmly.

Bram looked at MacLeod. Alister was a righteous man. If he or his men found Katherine first, she would be hanged for murder.

Edana kept off the road, and instead traveled in the shelter of the woods. The motion of the ride seemed to keep Daniel quiet, but he would need to eat soon, and so she was forced out of the woods and into a area where she might find grazing animals. She searched for a female goat or cow that would have milk. What else could she give the child?

At long last, she saw a small cottage. She could wait no longer; Daniel was hungry and had begun to cry. She knocked on the door and in a moment a woman answered.

"I've come to ask your help," Edana said. "My son needs milk and I have none."

The woman stared at her harshly. "It is not your son," she said, looking at Edana. "I can tell that you've never had a child, and certainly never nursed one."

"You're most observant. And you're right; this is not my son. This child belongs to my friend who died. I am to care for him, and we are both in terrible danger."

The woman looked skeptical, but she also looked curious. She opened the door and let Edana in. "Take your child and sit there," she instructed. "I'll fetch some milk and then you will tell me your tale."

Milk for entertainment, Edana thought. At the moment it

seemed a fair bargain, but she could not help wondering where Katherine was, and if she was being followed. Her mind was a muddle. Katherine had come with her men to kill the baby, but who were the men who had attacked Katherine? "But for them, we'd both be dead," she said to the infant she had now cradled in her arms.

The woman returned with a skin of milk. "Now you will tell me your tale," she said as she sat down. "And I will show you how to properly carry a child while you are riding."

Edana smiled warmly. In this world, women understood one another's needs. A child in need was a bond between them, even if they were strangers in a place where strangers were suspect.

"Miserable little bitch!" Katherine mumbled, as she headed at a full gallop for Kylerhe and the ferry that would take her back to the mainland. It would be impossible to search for Edana and the baby here on Skye. First, she did not know the island. Second, there was no doubt in her mind that the old coot Alister MacLeod would have his men looking for her.

But MacLeod could not touch her once she was off Skye and back in her own territory. There, she would have the British to protect her.

Yet escaping Skye did not solve her problem. The child still had to be killed. She bit her lip. Bram was away, or at least he had been away when she left. Edana would go home; she would go back to Bram's estate. But it was too risky to try and take the baby from her there.

She thought for a moment, and vaguely remembered that Bram had written her a couple of times. The letters had been sealed with his own seal. . . . That was it! A plan began to form in her mind. She would have to lure Edana away with the child, trap her someplace where she could be sure no one would interfere with her plans, and then, eliminate them.

Alex rode by Bram's side. "It's a near hopeless task, man. This island is large—there are forty million places to hide.

Surely Edana will head for home. Shouldn't you go there and wait?''

The sun beat down on them. It seemed as though they had been looking for weeks, though in fact it had been only four days. Bram wanted to keep looking—he felt strongly that Edana was in danger, but rationally he knew his friend was right.

"She's a resourceful woman, man. I know she'll be able to get home."

"She is resourceful," Bram allowed. "By what route do you think she would travel home?"

"The obvious way is on the barge across to Kylerhe. But I think she would go the other way. I think she would cross to the mainland at Kyleakin and then by land to Loch Lochy. I suppose she could then parallel Loch Lochy by land or go by boat into Loch Linnhe.''

Bram considered the route. Once on a boat heading down Loch Linnhe, it would not take her long to reach home. If she reached home, Ross would protect her till he arrived.

Bram nodded. "I'm certain you're right. Come, we'll head for home."

Alex shook his head. "You'll head for home. I think things are too hot for us now, that we should lie low. I'll be heading home for a while myself."

"I'll see you in twelve months," Bram said, smiling, "when we all meet."

Bram turned his horse toward Kylerhe and Alex turned his the other way. "In a year!" he said, as he rode off.

"Let her be there," Bram said to no one, as he rode toward the crossing at Kylerhe.

Edana thought that she had never felt so tired as she felt now. Days of riding had left her legs sore. But home was in sight and she felt safe as she guided her horse toward the Ross house. It was necessary to see them first, to tell them everything. Taggert Ross would see to security, of that she was certain.

She reined in the weary horse, dismounted, quickly tethered it, and hurried to the door.

"Edana!" Heather said, as she opened the door and pulled

her inside. "It's so good to see you! But where is Bram? He went looking for you weeks ago! And what is this? You have a child?"

"Bram?" Edana felt her mouth go dry. "Bram is dead, killed by Colin Campbell."

"You poor girl!" Heather exclaimed. "Bram wasn't killed. He was badly beaten and it took him some time to recover, but he's very much alive!"

Edana felt her heart leap. Bram was alive! She felt light-headed and suddenly free, in spite of her weariness. "I can't believe it," she laughed. "He really is a Phoenix!"

"He went in search of you as soon as he could."

"I was on Skye with the MacDonalds. I thought he was dead. Ranald MacDonald said he was dead."

"I'm sure they took him for dead," Taggert said, from the table. "Sit down and rest. We'll take you home when you've had time to eat and tell us about that child."

Edana undid her wrap. Moira's son always slept soundly when she was riding, but he usually awoke when the motion stopped. He did so now, and emitted a loud cry. "I shall need some milk and soft gruel," she said.

Heather laughed. "And some clean cloths, too, from the smell of him."

For a few minutes, the two women occupied themselves with the baby. He was washed, changed, and fed. Then Heather set him to play with a rattle she produced from a drawer. "Now we can talk," she said with satisfaction. "Tell us whose child this is."

"It's my friend Moira's child. He is heir to my father's estates. I have promised to raise him as my own, and I will if Bram agrees."

"Bram is a man with a heart of gold. He will agree—I've no doubt of that," Taggert laughed.

"This child is in grave danger," Edana confided. "Katherine has already tried to kill him."

"She's a devil woman, that one," Heather said under her breath.

Edana sat down at the table and began to eat. Every mouthful

was delicious and she marveled how, in seconds, her world
had changed.

A part of her felt like dancing and singing because Bram
was alive. *How I want him to come home to me,* she thought.
But another part of her was still haunted by the thought of
Katherine and the danger she represented. Katherine would
stop at nothing.

"I can certainly tell you were hungry," Heather said, smiling.

Edana nodded and continued eating. She said nothing of her
own condition, but her blood still had not come, and she was
certain she herself was with child. *I want to be,* she thought
happily. *How I want to be!*

Chapter Fourteen

Superintendent Crane looked out his office window. It was one of those bleak November days, the kind of day that was a true harbinger of winter. There was a knock on his door. He looked up and remembered that his assistant was in the infirmary. "Come in," he called wearily.

The young soldier came in and saluted. Then without a word he handed Crane a letter. Crane waved him away and returned to his desk where he tore open the message and read it quickly.

Dear Crane,
    I am quite at your mercy, though if this country were free of robbers and criminals I should not require your mercy at all.

Crane read the first sentence and could not suppress a smile. The woman was without shame! She had gotten herself into more trouble, and wished not only for his help, but for him to take the blame for her difficulty. But he read on nonetheless.

    I find myself at one of your remote military outposts near Bernera. I have neither men to guard me (not that

*the ones I had proved useful) nor means to return home.
I have imposed upon the lieutenant who is in charge here,
telling him you would be most unhappy were I turned
away. Please write and tell this young man to arrange
passage for me to Loch Linnhe and from there, home. I
should appreciate your doing this immediately as I am
in a great hurry and this place has few of the amenities
to which I am accustomed.*

Sincerely, Katherine MacLean

"Bitch!" Crane muttered. But there was no crossing her, at
least not at the moment. For all he knew, she might be pregnant
with his child, though he certainly hoped she was not. The
political situation was bad enough as it was. Indeed, it had
reached a critical state. London preached at him and the Campbells raved. The remainder of the clans were either untrustwor-
thy or committed to the Jacobites. He reluctantly admitted that
he needed Katherine's support even though she was a criminal.

He sat down at his writing desk and scribbled the order to
have her escorted home. He sniffed and twitched his nose; he
frankly doubted that the Queen got such preferential treatment.
And what the hell was Katherine doing in Bernera? She had
told him she was going to Edinburgh and the two were in
completely opposite directions. Well, considering the trouble
this was causing, he vowed to ask her. After all, the British
army did not exist just to escort Katherine MacLean around
the Highlands.

Katherine disembarked from HMS *Sturdy* at Fort William on
Loch Linnhe. But she did not bother to go to Crane to thank
him. Instead she rented a carriage and went directly home. As
soon as she arrived, she hurried to her bedroom.

She rooted through her desk. The letters from Bram were
somewhere, and she knew if she kept looking, she would find
one of them.

At last she uncovered one and as she unfolded it a smile of
triumph crept across her face. It was the letter he had written
her so long ago, the one where he told her that he could not

come to see her. It was a miserable letter in which he explained
that he and Edana were to go to London to celebrate their
marriage.

"And to think I almost tore this up!"

She sat down and studied it for a long while. One of the
artisans could easily duplicate the design of Bram's wax seal.
It was a design which bore the Chisholm family crest. As for
the note itself, it was printed in a straight hand. She felt confident
that she could imitate this handwriting sufficiently well to fool
Edana.

But what if Bram had returned? She decided that she would
instruct her messenger to make inquiries. If Bram were absent,
the messenger would be instructed to deliver the message to
Edana, and if Bram was home, the messenger would not deliver
it. "Then," Katherine said, "I shall have to think of something
else."

Katherine kicked off her shoes and sank into her boudoir
chair. "I must select a meeting place, a place Edana will go,
a place far away from all habitation so that there will be no
interference. . . . The Black Cottage in Glencoe," she whispered. Yes, Glencoe was perfect. It was remote and lonely; it
was filled with the ghosts of the past, and it was a renowned
dangerous place full of bogs, roaming packs of wild dogs, and
all manner of animals. Yes, Glencoe suited her. The only real
pity, she thought, was that the moon would not be full.

Above, the November sky was filled with dark, ominous clouds,
propelled by high winds. The waves pounded on the jagged
rocks with incalcuable force while the sleet stung Bram's face.

Bram watched miserably as the barge was smashed against
the rocks, unable to make the crossing to retrieve him as he
waited on the opposite shore, stranded by the storm on Skye.

He wanted more than anything to go home to Edana, but he
knew the vile storm ruled out his getting there quickly. There
was nothing he could do but wait it out.

He shook his head. Thank heaven Taggert Ross was there.
He would see to Edana's welfare and let her know he was
alive.

"Soon, my darling," he said, as again his eyes looked upward. Then he turned away and sought the shelter of the local inn, praying that the storm would be over soon.

Edana sat in her bedroom and held little Daniel. She sang to him, rocking him in her arms as she did so. "I shall be your mother," she promised as she looked into his eyes, "and I think Bram will not mind being your father. You'll have a good home, be reared by a good man, and when you're old enough, you'll become chieftain of Clan MacLean. You'll have a brother or sister, too. You know, being adopted by loving parents is not such a terrible thing. I was adopted and I loved my adoptive parents as if they were my own.

"Still, I do have questions about my real parents and about my dreams." She smiled and hugged Daniel. "You won't have so many questions. I'll tell you all about your mother." She fell silent for a minute. "And your father, too," she added. But she thought, *I might not tell you the whole truth about George. Half-truths can sometimes be a mercy.*

Edana sang a little more, then she took Daniel and put him in his cradle. She had found it in the storeroom and concluded that it probably had belonged to Bram when he was a child.

She left the room on tiptoes, satisfied with the silence.

She had been home only one day and every hour she wished that Bram would come. *Still, there are things I must do,* she thought, as she went to the study. There, on Bram's writing desk were two letters. One was a message from British headquarters. Oddly, it was addressed to her. The other was from George.

She looked at the two letters and tore open the one from George first. She sat down to read it, noting that it was written in a shaky hand.

> *Dear Edana,*
> *Forgive my writing. I am not myself of late. I am writing to ask your forgiveness. I am haunted by my guilt and bound by an illness I cannot control. John should not have died and father was probably poisoned. It is my*

*fault. I want to give Katherine up, but I cannot. She holds
me with some power I cannot fight.*
   Please forgive me. God help me.

Edana's mouth fell open in surprise. George did have a
conscience after all! She closed her eyes and rocked back and
forth for a moment. How could she help him? Clearly he wanted
to be helped, to be relieved of Katherine. His love for her was
a sickness, a sickness he seemed unable to cure.

After a moment, she opened the second letter, the one from
the fort.

Edana read it not with surprise, but with anger and anguish.

Dear Mrs. Chisholm,
   *It is my duty to inform you that your brother, George
MacLean, died on Saturday a fortnight ago. I have reason
to believe that you may not know of this since Katherine
MacLean left on Tuesday for Edinburgh.*
   My condolences.
                Sincerely, Superintendent Holden Crane.

Edana let out her breath. George had repented and sought
help too late. Katherine must have realized that his guilt was
overwhelming him and he would soon cause her trouble. Edana
shook her head. Katherine had killed at least three times, and
perhaps more. Her father, John, George . . . She was uncertain
about old MacQuarrie, but Katherine no doubt had killed him,
too, and even if she had not pulled the trigger, she was surely
responsible for the deaths on Skye.

Edana closed her eyes. Katherine had lied to the superintendent about her destination. She had not gone to Edinburgh but
to Skye to kill Daniel.

Just how Katherine had learned of Moira's son was still a
mystery, but she had—that was a certainty.

Edana shivered. Certainly she was in as much danger as the
child. But she felt safe here and Bram would come home soon
and she would tell him everything. He would know exactly
what to do about Katherine.

* * *

Taggert Ross stood in the hallway uneasily, shifting from one foot to another. Edana came down the stairs and smiled at him. "Good morning," she said cheerfully.

"A messenger brought me a message for you this morning," Taggert told her. He withdrew the envelope and handed it to her. "It must be from Bram—it bears his seal."

Edana took the envelope and for a second looked at the seal. Then she carefully opened it and withdrew the message.

> *My darling Edana,*
>   *I have been searching for you, and I know about Moira's son. You and the child are in grave danger, but for reasons I cannot disclose, I cannot return immediately to Glen Haven. I want you to bring the child and come to the Black Cottage on the edge of Rannoch Moor. You must come alone and you must tell no one where you are going.*
>
>   *Love, Bram*

Edana read the message twice.

"Is it bad news?" Taggert inquired.

"It's puzzling," Edana replied. She touched her tongue to her lips and tried to think. Surely when Bram said to tell no one he did not mean Taggert Ross. Taggert was his close confidant; Taggert knew Bram was a Phoenix.

"Perhaps I should not do this, but I want you to read this message," she said, handing Taggert the missive.

Taggert read the message and his brow furrowed. "Rannoch Moor is a treacherous place, especially this time of year. It's odd he wants you to come alone with the child."

Edana nodded, glad that Ross agreed with her. "This is his handwriting, is it not?"

Ross studied it. "Aye, it is. But still, it seems an odd request."

"Bram would not ask me to meet him there without a reason," she said thoughtfully. "Perhaps he knows something neither of us knows—perhaps this has something to do with his activities, with the Phoenix."

Taggert rubbed his beard thoughtfully. ''That does seem possible,'' he allowed.

''Then I shall go,'' Edana said. *But I will not go unarmed and I will not take Moira's son.*

There was a woman who lived on the edge of the estate. Her name was Clara MacGregor and she was the mother of three. Edana had heard that Clara often volunteered as a wet nurse since her youngest was only a few months old and she had a bountiful supply of milk. Edana decided to leave Daniel with her and carry instead a bundle that would look as if it were a child. Bram would forgive her caution, but she knew she would never forgive her own recklessness if somehow this were a trick.

The weather was clear, though clouds on the horizon indicated that another storm might well come by nightfall. Bram rode at a gallop toward home, his thoughts on a joyful reunion with his wife, who by now most certainly must know he was alive.

He dismounted and hurried through the door. His manservant greeted him. ''Is Edana here?'' Bram asked anxiously.

The manservant shook his head. ''No, sir. She rode off this morning bright and early, shortly after Taggert Ross arrived.''

Bram felt his heart sink at yet another delay in their reunion, and at the same time, he wondered what could have taken her away.

''Do you know where she might have gone?''

The man shook his head. ''No, sir. But I'm sure Taggert Ross will.''

Bram wiped his brow. He was tired from riding so long. ''Summon him at once,'' he said, sinking into a chair.

Within the hour, Ross appeared, and as soon as Bram saw the expression on his face, he knew something was wrong.

''Why are you here?'' Taggert blurted out. ''Why aren't you in Glencoe meeting Edana?''

An uncontrollable chill ran right through Bram. ''Why would I go there?'' he asked.

Ross pulled the message from his pocket. ''Edana told me to keep this—just in case.''

Bram read it in disbelief. The handwriting most assuredly looked like his—and the seal was his. "My God," he whispered. "She didn't go, did she? Tell me she didn't go!"

Taggert nodded dumbly. "She was sure it was from you. She was so anxious to see you."

"We must leave immediately," Bram said. "Bring some men and follow me."

"Of course, but what about your seal?"

"Probably copied from a letter I once sent Katherine. We must hurry—Edana and the baby are in great danger. Katherine is a murderer."

He said no more but ran from the house. They took fresh horses and rode them toward the loch that wound its way through Glencoe. The clouds darkened, and the irony of the supposed meeting place did not escape him. He had lost all those he had loved to violence in Glencoe; he prayed he would not lose Edana there, too.

The Black Cottage on the edge of Rannoch Moor was uninhabited, but surely haunted by the spirits of the dead, Edana thought as she approached on horseback. She carried a carefully wrapped bundle that resembled a swaddled infant and she climbed down from the saddle and walked toward the darkened cottage.

The cottage was not in fact black, but white. Originally it had been built of the black slate common to the region but it had been whitewashed, though its roof was still black. The glaring white gave it an eerie appearance in the light of the half-moon.

Why would Bram want to meet her here? She was filled with excitement at the thought of seeing him and yet she also felt apprehension, as if something were not right, and she knew a part of her mind feared a trap, even though the message had been in his handwriting and had borne his seal.

This cottage stood here only because its black stones had not burned the night of February the thirteenth in the year 1692, the night of the massacre.

The massacre at Glencoe was seared into the hearts of all

true Highlanders. On that night, the order had been given to kill the MacDonalds who lived in the glen. It was told that the order had been written on a playing card, the nine of diamonds. Ever since that night, the card was said to be the curse of Scotland.

The story of the massacre was a terrible tale and one that Edana had heard often. The Campbells had been the guests of the MacDonalds. In violation of the rules of Highland hospitality, they had turned on their hosts and massacred them under orders from the British. Men, women, and children were thrown on dung heaps and shot while others were burned alive in their homes. Those who were attacked that night had nowhere to run from the soldiers—there was a blizzard and the snow was deep and the night cold.

They had fled on foot eastward, up the glen. On the west was the loch and the soldiers with their guns blazing. North, and above them, was the sheer escarpment of Aonach Eagach, which was known to be over three thousand feet high. To the south was another wall of mountains covered with deep snow and obscured by the blizzard.

And in the east the glen narrowed to a great fall of rock cased in ice.

Those who succeeded in running away had hidden in a place where once they had hidden their cattle, and some had survived to tell the tale of that night of horror. Edana had only recently heard the whole story from her captors, the MacDonalds. More than one of them had survived that night and round the campfire on Skye it had been retold in great detail.

It was not February now, she thought, as she looked across the glen. Still, it was treacherous. She had rowed down the Coe and entered Glencoe by boat. The only other way out was across the moor, which was now soggy and dangerous; parts of it were covered with thin ice and in other sections there were large areas of sinking mud, and bogs that were said to swallow people whole.

Again she asked herself, why would Bram want to meet her here? Was it a place where the Phoenix rendezvoused? And yet, in spite of her apprehension, she had come.

Edana cautiously approached the apparently deserted cottage.

Then she circled it and finally tested its heavy door. It was not locked and she pushed it open a crack. It made little sense to wait outside. The wind was beginning to come up and she had no doubt it would grow colder.

The door creaked as she pushed it wider and stepped into the cottage. It was musty-smelling and she jumped as she heard a skittering across the floor. "Only mice," she said to herself.

She fumbled in her pack for flint and candles. In a moment she found them. She went to the hearth. She could feel bits of wood and dried leaves. In a few seconds she had started a fire and lit a candle. The two weak sources of light cast weird shadows on the wall.

She looked about the room of the cottage in the flickering light. There was more dry wood and another bag of leaves. The last person here had been thoughtful enough to have left firewood and leaves to start the fire.

In the center of the room a long, crude table sat lopsided. One of its legs was broken. Several broken wooden chairs lay about, and there was one that appeared to be in one piece.

Edana dragged the one unbroken chair over to the fire and sat down. She put her bundle down nearby. This was a strange and haunting place; even more haunting than she had imagined. To the side of the fireplace she saw a great blotch on the wall. She shivered, it was a bloodstain—at least it looked like one.

This wasn't right. Edana took her pistol out of her pack and set it on her lap. She covered it with her hand, feeling slightly more secure than she had before. She sat awhile longer.

The disembodied voice came out of nowhere.

"How charming to see you again," Katherine said sarcastically.

Edana jumped to her feet, her fingers still clutching her pistol. "Katherine," she said, looking where the voice had come from.

Katherine stepped into the room from the darkness of a second room. She was dressed entirely in black and her hair was tangled and loose around her shoulders. Even in the flickering light of the fire, her skin looked ghostly pale. The light caused her shadow to look large and elongated. Edana stared at her. It had been a trap! A thousand questions filled her mind, but she fought to focus on the woman across the room.

"Thank you for bringing the child. I watched you arrive. He's a sound sleeper. That's good."

Edana watched, frozen to the spot, as Katherine walked to where the bundle lay. Edana watched as Katherine reached out to jostle it—then Katherine whirled about, her face twisted with anger.

"This is not a child!" she said, with unnerving calm.

"Of course not." Edana replied, fighting to sound as if she was not afraid.

Evil as Katherine was, Edana now sensed something more than evil. She sensed a kind of insanity, as if something had snapped, as if Katherine's inner demons had broken free of their bonds and appeared naked to the observer. Katherine did not look normal; she sounded even less so. It seemed obvious that she was having great difficulty controlling herself. In this state, she was like a drunk or a person drugged. In this state, Edana thought, Katherine was more dangerous than ever; she was no longer able to control herself or even appear normal.

Suddenly Edana saw the glint of a long blade. It shimmered in the firelight. Katherine plunged it into the inanimate bundle and screamed, "This is not the child! This is not the child!"

Then she withdrew the blade and turned toward Edana. "Tell me where Moira's son is! Tell me!" She took an advancing step toward Edana.

"I will never tell you. He is safe—that is all you need to know."

"I shall kill you." Katherine took another step.

"Then you shall never know, will you?" Edana still held the pistol beneath her shawl—her fingers gripped the trigger—and yet she knew how difficult it would be to use it, even on this evil, insane woman. To shoot a person . . . She was not certain she could do it.

Katherine stopped short and stared at her. "I should have rid myself of you long ago. You have always opposed me, you have always been in my way."

Edana said nothing.

"You will tell me where the child is—you will!" This time Katherine did not hesitate; she ran toward Edana—and Edana lifted the pistol and fired.

In one second she knew she had hesitated too long. The bullet grazed Katherine's arm, but did not stop her. It was as if her insanity had given her abnormal strength. There was no time for Edana to cock the other barrel. Katherine tackled her, and Edana fought back, aware that Katherine had dropped her dagger just as she had dropped her pistol.

Katherine's nails raked her arms. Edana fought back with all her strength, but Katherine was stronger. As she struggled to remain conscious, Edana knew she could not win. Then Katherine lunged at something, and in a minute Edana saw that she had retrieved the pistol. Edana saw the glint of its barrel and heard it being cocked.

Katherine rolled away and quickly stood up, pointing the pistol at Edana. "You're such a good girl. You couldn't fire it fast enough, could you? Well, rest assured I have no such scruples. Get up, you little bitch! Get up and walk!"

Edana staggered to her feet, gripping her stole. Katherine motioned her toward the door and in a few seconds they were outside in the cold night air.

"Walk!" Katherine shouted. "Walk, or I'll kill you where you stand."

Edana walked forward, clinging to the hope she could escape this madwoman.

Superintendent Holden Crane paced the perimeter of his room. It was nearly midnight and he still could not sleep. How could this have happened?

His mind ran over the dispatch he had received just after supper. It had been a most disturbing dispatch, one he had not understood at first, but now understood all too well.

It had come from Colonel Deevers, the ranking officer on the Isle of Skye. It informed him that Alister MacLeod, the Laird of Clan MacLeod, had filed a formal complaint against one Katherine MacLean for mayhem and murder. It went on to say that while MacLeod was not a government supporter, he was also not one of those chieftains to have involved himself or his clan in nefarious activities. Colonel Deevers therefore advised that he was treating the complaint as most serious in nature, more so because MacLeod was not without influence in London, and had also sent copies of the complaint to members of the House of Lords. It went on to explain that an investigation had proved that Katherine MacLean had shot a woman on the Isle of Skye; that the victim was related to the Laird; that she had ordered two of her men to kill two of the Laird's men; that she had endeavored to kidnap a child; and that further, she had fled the Isle.

He shook his head again. The only answer was obvious. The fault was his, all his. He had accepted Katherine's support, entered into a torrid affair with her, and ignored her criminal activities. She had killed old MacQuarrie, as her neighbors said she had. No doubt she had poisoned old MacLean, too; killed John and poisoned George, as well. Heaven only knew what other crimes she had committed, or would commit.

He realized now that Katherine had not gone to Edinburgh as she had told him, and that she had been escaping from Skye when she had asked him for an escort home! "Damn her!" he muttered under his breath.

He knew beyond a shadow of a doubt that he had become entangled in her web and that he would be most fortunate to escape with even a modicum of his career intact.

There was no escaping the inevitable; first thing in the morning, he would have to issue an arrest order for Katherine. But what if she was carrying his child? What if she decided to make their relationship public when she was arrested or during her trial?

Again the answer was obvious. He would be ruined, his career would be over. He walked to the cupboard and opened it, withdrawing a bottle of scotch. He poured himself a stiff drink and downed it in one long gulp. Then he sat down on the side of his bed. There was nothing for it. He was not going to get one wink of sleep tonight. He might just as well wake up his secretary and have the arrest order issued tonight. The whole affair was bound to be sensational. Everyone hated Katherine; her trial would attract half the Highlands; and her hanging would be widely attended. It was rare for a woman to be hanged, rarer still for a woman of great beauty to be hanged. But she was a murderess, and he knew as well as any that she had killed more than once.

The night was odd, Edana reflected. Then she marveled at the strange thoughts that crossed the mind at moments like this. The sky above was mottled with clouds. A few stars were visible and the moon was bright, yet it was only a half-moon. It was cold, and the wind had abated. There was an uncanny stillness; it seemed to Edana as if she could hear her own heart beating. She walked along rapidly, knowing that Katherine was just behind her, knowing the pistol was aimed at her back.

"Where are we going?" Edana called out.

"Just keep walking, and ask me no questions!" Katherine shouted.

It was a disingenuous question. Edana knew full well they were headed toward Rannoch Moor. The more important question was, Why? Surely Katherine did not think Edana had brought the baby here.

She wondered exactly how far behind her Katherine was. She wondered if she stood a chance of making a clean break of it if she broke into a run, or if Katherine was near enough to get off a good shot and kill her. Edana remembered Katherine's deadly aim the morning she had killed John. Edana decided not to run.

"You could at least tell me where we're going," she said again.

"Just keep walking!"

This time Edana took more note of Katherine's voice. She judged her to be not very far back. She trudged on, aware of the fact that the brush was growing denser, even more aware that the ground was soggy beneath her boots.

"This is unstable ground," she called out.

"I feel quite safe—you're in front of me," Katherine answered.

Edana shivered. But scarcely had the vision of terror entered her mind than it became a reality. She let out a shriek. "Katherine! It's a bog! I'm sinking!"

She could feel herself in the thick, sinking mud. She could

feel it now at the tops of her boots. She tried to move but could not. "Katherine!"

"You'll sink here! You'll be buried alive!"

"Katherine!" Edana could hear the panic in her own voice. She struggled and then remembered she had been told never to struggle in sinking mud, as struggling would make it worse.

"I can save you. I can throw you a branch and help you out." Katherine's voice was thick and sweet. It was a voice Edana had heard her use with men.

"Then help me!" she shouted back.

"Just tell me where the baby is. Then I'll help you."

Edana was more frightened than she had ever been in her life. This was a horrible way to die, and once more she tried to struggle free, but could not. She could feel the mud creeping up her thigh; in just these few minutes, she had sunk farther. But she could not let Katherine kill the baby. No matter what happened to her, she had to protect the child.

"Tell me!" Katherine shouted. "Tell me now!"

"Go to hell!" Edana called out.

"Then die here! Wait till the mud starts to fill your nostrils! Wait till you can taste it and you choke on it."

Edana silently prayed for strength.

"I'll find the child without you! I'm sure it's not far from the estate. It's not that easy to hide a child that age!"

Edana fought against the mud and managed to turn around. She saw Katherine in the light of the half-moon, her cloak billowing in the wind; then she was gone, out of sight.

Edana could feel the mud around her waist. While the moon was not behind a cloud, she twisted as far as she could to see if there was anything she could grab on to. The effort caused her to sink still farther and her eyes filled with tears as the moon again disappeared and she was left in the still darkness of the night.

But there had been a tree in back of her; there was a limb hanging down across the sinking mud.

She did not move and noted that her sinking slowed. She waited. It seemed like an eternity, an eternity of horror as the mud rose—she could feel it just below her breasts.

Then the cloud moved away and again there was moonlight.

She saw the tree and the branch. She reached out; it was only a few inches. She strained, aware of sinking farther, but she managed to move slightly, then another effort, and a few more inches. Her arms were still free, but the mud was rising. She strained and strained and just managed to grasp the branch.

"Please don't let it snap, please. . . ."

She pulled on it and finally was able to put both hands on it. Again the moon went behind a cloud, and Edana's world was plunged into total darkness.

But she had the branch in her grasp and she was not sinking farther. She pulled herself toward the tree, hand over hand, slowly—slowly ascending from what almost had been her tomb.

After a long while, she could feel solid ground beneath her feet and she pulled her mud-encrusted body up and next to the tree. But it was too dark to move. She could not tell where the ground was stable and where it was not. She climbed into the tree and found a place where she could sit, between the wide, gnarled trunk and a large limb. She huddled there, cold from the wretched mud and fearful of falling and landing yet again in sinking mud. She shivered violently as the wind began to come up again and the clouds gradually came together to block out all the stars. Time passed slowly and then it began to snow. Edana closed her eyes and prayed she would not go to sleep and fall from her tree. Her teeth chattered and she thought that in all her life she had never been this cold.

Bram looked up at the sky. It was completely clouded over, and pitch-darkness enveloped the land. Yet he knew the loch well, and he knew where he was as the barge containing men and horses was guided toward the shore.

"It's a hell of a night," Taggert Ross observed, as he looked around. "It's going to snow."

"I imagine it is snowing at the higher elevations," Bram said. He could only hope that Edana had dressed warmly and that she was safe. It was cold, and getting colder.

He shifted uneasily. It was hard for him to wait for the barge to be secured, for the supplies and horses to be unloaded. It was hard for him to wait for anything. He wanted to be on his way; he wanted to hold Edana in his arms, to know that she was safe.

"We'll be ashore in a few minutes," Taggert said, as if he had read Bram's mind.

Bram glanced at him and nodded. He imagined he was not hiding his agitation well. He felt twitchy all over, anxious to be on his way to Black Cottage.

"If Katherine has hurt Edana, I'll strangle her with my own hands," he said, not bothering in the slightest to try to control his anger.

"We're secured, sir," the young man at the front of the barge called out. Bram took his horse's reins and led the animal ashore and onto the sodden ground. It wasn't far to Black Cottage. He mounted swiftly and was aware only that Taggert was at his side and the others followed.

Bram galloped off across the moor toward the cottage. In a few moments it came into view and a few seconds after that, he and Taggert were dismounting in front of it.

"Looks deserted," Taggert said.

Bram felt his heart in his throat as he lit his torch and kicked open the front door, which was, in any case, slightly ajar.

He held the torch high and looked around the room. "Someone's been here recently," Taggert observed. "The embers in the fire are still hot."

Bram nodded and looked about.

"What's that?" Taggert asked.

Bram walked across the room to the bundle and looked at it. It appeared to be nothing but a bundle of soft grass; it had been stabbed repeatedly and with some force, at least enough force that the grass was spilling out onto the floor.

"My God," Bram said. "Katherine must have thought this was the baby."

"Smart girl, Edana. She didn't bring the baby and she didn't tell anyone she hadn't."

Bram sucked in his breath. "But where is she—where are they?"

The two men turned toward one another and then, as if they

had both thought of it at the same time, they mouthed the words, ''Rannoch Moor.''

''We'd better hurry,'' Taggert said, as they both ran outside and mounted their horses. Neither of them spoke of what was on his mind. It was far too horrible to contemplate.

Chapter Fifteen

Edana clung to her precarious perch, shivering as the wind picked up and blew across the moor. The branches in the tree above her chattered in the cold and the snow stuck to her mud-covered body.

She fought to stay awake, to hold on to the tree. And then she heard hoofbeats, not from one horse but from several. It was certainly not Katherine, who had been alone. Edana dared to call out in the darkness. She shouted as loudly as she could, "Help! Help! Over here!"

"Edana!" the hoofbeats stopped, but she heard Bram's voice.

"Here! I'm over here in the bog! Be careful, there's sinking mud," she called out in warning.

"Light the torches!" Bram ordered.

In a matter of minutes Edana saw the light of the torches. It was a comforting sight, and she looked about her. To one side, the side with the low branch she had used to climb to safety, she could see the area of sinking mud. On the far side of the tree, the ground appeared stable. "Here!" she called out.

It was Bram who dismounted, Bram who hurried to her and lifted her down from her perch. She shivered uncontrollably with cold and her teeth chattered even though his warm, comforting arms were finally around her.

"Bring blankets!" Bram shouted out.

In another moment Taggert was there and they were wrapping her in warm blankets. "Where's Katherine?" Bram asked.

"She went to look for the baby," Edana managed. "We must go now and get him. She's insane but determined; she might find him."

Bram could hear the resolution in her voice, and he loved her all the more for caring so much and for putting the life of another above her own. "Katherine led you to the sinking mud, didn't she?"

"She held me at gunpoint and ordered me here. She thought if I was sinking I'd tell her where the baby was hidden. But I didn't tell her. She went off to find him. Please, we must hurry."

Bram lifted her into his arms and carried her to his horse. He set her atop the horse and then mounted behind her. Then they were off, back toward the loch and the waiting barge. It was the fastest way out of the glen, and to home.

"How is Katherine traveling?" Bram asked.

"I'm not sure," Edana answered. "I think she must have come on horseback."

"She'll leave across the moor."

"She seems to know the moor well. She's certainly been here before."

Bram digested the information. He held Edana tightly against him. "Where is the child?" he asked.

"With Clara MacGregor. But we must hurry. Katherine is clever—she will ask questions and she'll find out Clara is a wet nurse. She'll figure it out."

"It's my first instinct to take you home. You're covered with wet mud and you've been through a terrible ordeal."

Edana looked up at him imploringly. Her face was streaked with mud and tearstained. "I'm strong and healthy. I'm not cold now, just uncomfortable. Please, we must go to Clara's first."

"We will," he assured her. "I know there is no arguing with you, my beloved."

She looked up into his eyes and he kissed her. "You know you are quite beautiful even when you are covered with mud."

Edana leaned against him. Once again the moon had come out and the clouds had disappeared over the mountains. Ahead, she could see the loch and the outline of the barge. Most important, Bram's arms were around her, holding her tight, pressing her close.

It was nearly dawn when they reached the estate. It was a gray dawn, and it was colder than it had been the day before. They went directly to the house of Clara MacGregor, and Edana almost collapsed in relief to discover little Daniel resting peacefully.

"Bring your children and whatever you need," Bram told Clara. "You will have to stay in the main house till Katherine is found. It is not safe for you here."

Clara gathered up what she needed and everything was put into the wagon. To Edana's relief, they headed home—home to Glen Haven.

Bram immediately ensconced Clara and her brood, including Daniel, in the west wing of the house where the old nursery was located. He placed guards around the house, and while Edana was bathing, he sent a message to Holden Crane. Crane could no longer afford Katherine or her support. She had become far more of a liability for the British than an asset.

Bram then climbed the stairs. He hoped he would find Edana sound asleep. She had been through much, though in fact he had heard only a part of her story.

He entered their bedroom and found her standing by the window. She wore the beautiful nightgown that he'd bought her in London, and as the morning light shone through the window, its diaphanous material shimmered even as her beautiful body was revealed through its folds. Her long, fiery-red hair hung loose and damp, curling at the ends. This was no vision, but a reality. He had dreamed of her this way for many weeks and now she was here and his to take.

She turned when he came into the room and he thrilled at the look of love in her emerald-green eyes. She held out her arms to him and he went to her, embracing her tightly. "You should be in bed resting," he whispered. "I know you're still ill-at-ease. You were looking for Katherine, weren't you?"

"I feel she is out there somewhere."

"You're safe here. The baby is safe, too. Katherine will be caught, Edana, and she will be hanged for killing so many people."

Edana leaned against Bram's strong chest. The scent and feel of him erased her fears and sent the thought of Katherine running from her mind. She was in the here and now, Bram was once again holding her, and for the moment nothing else in the world mattered.

He kissed her neck tenderly and then her ears. "You must be tired," he whispered, even though holding her made him want her. The heat she always caused enveloped him.

"I'm not that tired," she whispered, as she gently touched him.

He did not speak again, he did not have to say a word. He lifted her in his arms and carried her to their bed. There, he undressed her slowly and she undressed him as well.

His mouth covered her breast and his fingers toyed with the other.

"I have missed you," she breathed. She ran her fingers through the hair on his chest, over his strong shoulders, down his arms. She felt him slide down her body and set her aflame with his intimate caresses. He was everywhere at once and she writhed in his arms, begging him to touch her here and there, to kiss her again, to hold her close.

"You are my woman," he whispered, "the only one I shall ever love."

Edana wrapped her legs around him as he entered her. She was one with him as the tension within her grew, as she felt it growing within him. They moved against one another, seeking and taunting, luxuriating in their own desire for fulfillment and then, just as she felt herself about to scream with need, it came and she clutched him tightly even as his seed spilled into her.

For a long time they held one another, and then they separated and she crawled happily into his arms, there to sleep feeling warm, satisfied, and protected. Her last thought was for the baby she was sure was growing inside her. She would tell Bram soon. As soon as she herself was certain.

Katherine returned home for a short time. She packed some clothing and took a little money. She left at daybreak in a wagon.

If one wanted to know something, the place to go was the market. There, farm families came from miles around to trade goods, to sell whatever they had to sell, and to talk and gossip. How fortunate that it was market day, Katherine thought to herself. She would not have to wait to begin her investigation, and chances were, she would have the information she wanted by nightfall.

The market was held in a field on the shores of the loch. Villagers, farmers, and merchants traveled by water from miles away. They came with sheepskins, wool, preserves, clothing, blankets, and all manner of farm produce. Some, who lived closer to the sea, brought goods from the Continent, bought from vessels which had docked at Loch Arkaig or sailed down Loch Ness from Inverness.

Katherine's usual custom was to come to market and buy whatever she desired. Today she did not want goods; she wanted information. In order to obtain it more easily, she disguised herself as a common person, and she filled her wagon with sheepskins to sell.

Anyone caring for a stranger's child most certainly would be the object of talk. She would listen to the women talking, she would sell her wares, and she would decide whom she could bribe for information. Almost all the families who lived on Bram's estate came to market. She was certain to hear something, and when she knew where the baby was, she would go there and kill him.

She laughed to herself as she drove her wagon toward the loch. No doubt she would also hear about the unfortunate demise of Bram Chisholm's wife. *Poor girl,* they would say.

She died horribly in sinking mud. Why on earth do you think she went there? Perhaps, Katherine thought, she would spread the rumor that Edana had gone there to meet another man. Yes, what a fine rumor to spread! Bram would be furious, and it would most certainly ruin Edana's reputation.

When Katherine arrived, wearing the disguise of a crofter's wife, the market was already busy. She climbed down from her wagon and began to unload her skins, though it was a wretched task. Unfortunately, if she was to pass as a commoner, she had to look and act like a commoner. She crinkled her nose at the smell of the skins and cursed silently when she broke off her long nails.

Now and again Katherine glanced at the sky. Dark clouds hovered on the horizon. It was a gray day, an ominous day. Winter was coming, and soon there would be no more market days. "I have so much to do," she said to herself again and again.

As she busied herself, a group of four British soldiers rode up. She stopped working and watched them curiously as they went to the side of an old barn that bordered the field where the market was held. She frowned as she watched them nail up a large poster.

Others were also curious and in a few minutes, a crowd had gathered round. Katherine joined them.

The crowd hummed like a swarm of bees, she thought as she pushed herself forward so she could read the poster. It was written in large letters and as she read it, the words seemed to dance in front of her. How could this be!

WANTED!!
LADY KATHERINE MACLEAN,
FORMALLY KATHERINE MACQUARRIE.
THE BRITISH CROWN WILL PAY A REWARD OF ONE GOLD SOVEREIGN FOR KATHERINE MACQUARRIE MACLEAN, WHO IS WANTED FOR THE MURDERS OF CORRIE MACLEOD, ARDELL MACLEOD, AND JACK MACLEOD, ON THE ISLE OF SKYE. SHE IS ALSO WANTED FOR QUESTIONING IN THE DEATHS OF GEORGE MACLEAN, JOHN MACLEAN, AND DONALD MACLEAN.

"About time they did something about that one!" a woman standing next to Katherine said.

"A witch, I hear," another added.

"That's a hanging I'll want to see," one of the men muttered, and those about all laughed.

Katherine dared not speak a word for fear her very voice might give her away. She pulled her cloak closer and her hood down ever so slightly as she eased out of the crowd. Her head pounded. How could Crane do this to her? She was a British supporter! This was unseemly! A part of her argued that she should go directly to the fort and confront him; but through the fog of her own insane ambition another voice told her she should not. Crane would not have gone this far had he not been forced to do so. Katherine knew her choices were few. She could not now look for Moira's son. Indeed, with an arrest order for murder out against her, it made little difference who inherited the MacLean land. What did matter was that she get out of the district immediately, that she go where she would be safe. Katherine sucked in her breath; there was only one place. But, she thought miserably, she had not brought much money. She would have to sell her sheepskins and go immediately. There was no time to waste, none at all. She cursed under her breath. She would even have to break into her own home to retrieve her sellable valuables and cash.

Bram stood behind Edana as she brushed her hair. She looked rested and restored to good health.

"I know you will worry about Katherine until she's dead, but you really shouldn't. I have guards everywhere, and Clara MacGregor can stay as long as she wishes."

Edana turned around and smiled. "I was in the nursery earlier. You know, she's very good with children. I think she would make a good nursemaid, and her own children will be playmates for Daniel."

"You're suggesting she stay?"

Edana smiled mysteriously. "We will need a nursemaid."

He smiled. "I suppose Daniel will be a handful."

Edana put down her hairbrush, stood up, and walked over to him. She put her arms around him. "I don't want you to think me lazy, or that I cannot take care of one small child."

"I would never think you lazy. I would never—"

Edana put her finger on his lips. "Listen," she said, as her eyes danced mischievously, "soon there will be more than one baby. I believe I am with child, Bram—our child."

A smile broke over his face and he lifted her off the ground and twirled her about, laughing. "A child! We're going to have a child?"

Edana nodded and laughed. "It is not so surprising, you know. One thing does tend to lead to another."

He laughed with her and kissed her. "I am the happiest man in the Highlands, the happiest man you can imagine."

"And I am the happiest woman."

They were in the midst of a long kiss when the servant knocked on the door.

Edana leaned against Bram, her arms around his waist. "I suppose we must respond," she answered.

"I would let them knock forever, but you're right." He let go of her. "Come in," he called out.

Bram's manservant came in. "Superintendent Crane is here to see you," he announced. "He says it is most important."

Bram took Edana's hand. "I only sent him a message last night. He's very prompt."

Edana winked. "Well, you are one of his most faithful supporters."

He took her hand and they went downstairs together.

Holden Crane was pacing back and forth in the den, his hands clasped behind his back. He was filled with anger and frustration. He looked up at Bram and Edana and forced a smile.

"I got your message this morning, but oddly, it came after I had issued an arrest order for Katherine."

Edana glanced at Bram. "If you just got Bram's message, how is it you had already issued an arrest order?"

"Alister MacLeod made a formal complaint. I cannot ignore

the evidence. She killed a woman on Skye and was responsible for the death of two of his best men, both relatives.''

"Katherine killed John. I saw her shoot him,'' Edana said. "She has been trying to kill Moira's son, the rightful heir of all the MacLean estates; that is why she was on Skye.''

"I rather imagine you believe she killed your father as well.''

Edana nodded. "I believe he was poisoned with arsenic. But she used something else on George. He had no signs of arsenic poisoning—at least, not the last time I saw him. I have a letter from George. It was written just before he died. He confesses everything.''

"You should have come to me ...'' Crane began to say, then he shook his head. "No, I probably would not have believed you, and I might not have done anything if I had.''

Bram raised his brow. "You're being disarmingly honest.''

Crane shrugged. "I only want to go home to England. I've had enough of it here.''

Bram resisted the desire to say he wished all Crane's countrymen felt as he did. Even though Crane was obviously in an apologetic mood, Bram did not want to reveal too much.

"Do you know where Katherine might be?'' Bram asked, after a moment.

"I've had WANTED posters made and posted all around the area. I rather imagine she has left the area. It will not be easy for a woman like Katherine to hide.''

"She is filled with guile,'' Edana said. "I still worry that she will come here.''

"Keep guards posted, and I'll let you know if there are any developments in the case.''

"Good. Will you join us for breakfast?''

Again Crane tried to smile. "If I may.''

Edana felt sorry for Superintendent Crane. For a long while he had turned a blind eye to Katherine, but in the end she had deceived him, too. "Of course you may,'' she said.

Katherine guided her wagon along a narrow path that paralleled the high wall that surrounded the MacLean castle, its outbuildings, and its inner gardens. On her left was the river, on her right, the remnants of a rose garden. Ten feet or so behind the dead rosebushes was the wall. Beyond the wall were the formal gardens that led to the back of the house.

She drew the wagon to a halt and climbed down, tethering the horses to a nearby tree. She glanced up at the sky. There was neither moon nor stars. The night was dark; the only light came from the candles in the servants' quarters, and those torches left burning inside. The blackness of the night was both a blessing and a curse.

Katherine pursed her lips together. Anger still filled her whole body and she fairly shook with rage, though she fought to control herself, fought to think logically.

Crane would have sent soldiers here to look for her, and in all likelihood he would have left a guard to arrest her if she returned.

For a few minutes she simply sat there, wondering if she could find the secret entrance to the dungeon in the dark. George had showed it to her only once, but she had stored the information away, though at the time she hadn't dreamed she would need it.

She drew in her breath and walked through the rose garden, and in the darkness the thorns of the leafless bushes reached out and tore at her clothing. Katherine cursed. She fought her way through the tangle and felt blood on her hands from the sharp thorns. But at last she reached the wall, and for a moment she leaned against it, breathing hard.

She felt along the wall and cursed again. She was certain she was in the right place, or near enough that she would find it if she persisted. She moved farther, and was rewarded when she grasped the huge iron ring.

She pulled on it with all her might, and then she pulled again. It would open, she knew that. It had been opened only a few months ago when George had revealed it to her. She tugged again, and the iron door at the base of the wall slid open.

Katherine breathed a sigh of relief. She had not felt it was safe to light a candle aboveground where a guard might see the light, but once she was belowground, a light would be safe enough. She fumbled in her pocket for flint and candles and as soon as she had descended the first few steps, she lit one to guide her on the rest of her journey.

The steps down to the tunnel that opened into the dungeon were steep. She took great care as she walked down into the ever-prevailing dampness. The tunnel and its secret entrance were several hundred years old. It had once been used to escape the castle when it was under siege.

In front of her, Katherine could hear all manner of rodents scatter before her light. She walked as fast as she could and finally reached the dungeon and the stairs that led up. Silently she stole up the stairs. On the ground floor she heard the snoring of sleeping guards and she continued to climb.

Once in her bedroom, Katherine packed her valuables in a small case.

She stopped short when she heard a creaking on the stairs, and extinguished her candle, plunging the room again into total blackness. She heard footsteps and her heart raced. She flung herself down and crawled under the bed and waited. In a moment the door opened and two soldiers came in. They held up their torch and one said, ''See, it's nothing! Just rats!'' They left, closing the door behind them.

Katherine waited for a long while before lighting her candle again. She hurriedly finished packing and, blowing out her candle, she stole away, back to where she had come, in the darkness of the night.

Holden Crane cursed and threw a book from his desk against the wall. He had posted a guard and Katherine MacLean had broken into her own castle and stolen her valuables away. *She'll get away now,* he thought miserably.

Again he wondered if he really wanted her caught.

November passed into December and the days were short, the skies continually gray, and the wind howled continuously.

Katherine MacLean dismounted in front of Glenbrier, the rambling estate belonging to Dr. Kenzie Scott. It was an ornate dwelling that spoke of Kenzie's wealth and good taste.

She knocked on the door and Kenzie's manservant answered.

"I am Katherine MacLean," she announced. "I must see Dr. Scott immediately."

The manservant stepped aside and ushered her into the house. "I haven't seen you for a very long time, madam."

Katherine brushed past him. She had endured a long journey and felt less than herself traveling in disguise, as she had been doing. She looked forward to a hot bath, to once again wearing fine clothes, and to having a good meal with Kenzie. He was one man who could not turn her away. "A safe haven," she sighed. There would be no more danger from British soldiers and no more running. Kenzie would help her sell her valuables and arrange for her to go to London. There she would remain, at least for a time.

She took off her cloak and smoothed her skirt out.

The manservant returned. "You are to wait in the upstairs study, madam. Dr. Scott will meet with you there."

Katherine nodded and began to climb the steep, winding staircase. She had just reached the top of the stairs when a door in the hall opened and Edana stepped out and stood placidly looking at her.

Edana was dead! Edana had been left in the sinking mud more than a hundred miles away! This was a ghost come to haunt her—a ghost! An apparition! Edana's red hair glimmered in the candlelight; her eyes shone like emeralds.

Katherine's shock was so great that her mouth opened and she emitted a scream just as she stepped backward. She lost her balance and tumbled down the steep staircase.

The manservant came running and so did Dr. Kenzie Scott. He looked down at Katherine's crumpled, lifeless body. "By heaven," he said, "she must have lost her balance."

"She—she just screamed and fell backward," the young woman said, as she grasped the rail to steady herself.

Kenzie Scott wiped his brow and looked at his guest. "I'm so sorry this happened in front of you, Mrs. Cameron."

"I don't understand why—"

"Please—neither do I. But I do know she was unstable. She's one of my oldest patients. Please, go back to your room and I'll take care of this."

She nodded and went back to her room. She had been at the

end of the corridor when the woman had stopped, looked at her, screamed, and fallen. She had never seen this woman in her life, and yet she felt vaguely responsible. As distressing as this terrible accident was, Aileena Cameron suddenly felt a wave of relief flood over her. It was not her own personal relief, but the relief of her "other"—the woman who was her, but was not her. Never had her oft-felt experiences of "otherness" felt as strong as did this one. She shivered, and as she had done many times, she wondered why these odd feelings overtook her.

Edana was midway up the staircase on her way to kiss Daniel good night when the feeling came over her. It was a sense of relief and liberation so intense that she whispered, "Katherine is dead." In her mind she saw a steep, winding staircase. She shook her head, tried to focus her thoughts—the words were not hers, but rather the words of her "other."

Could this be true? It was madness. It was wishful thinking. She had no way of knowing where Katherine was or what she was doing. She had no intention of allowing the premonition, or whatever it was, to cause her to let down her guard. A "feeling" was not enough. She had to know for certain that Katherine had been arrested or was dead before she could relax her vigil.

Kenzie walked down the stairs and knelt by Katherine's lifeless form. She was quite dead, her neck broken. He drew in his breath. He would have helped her, but now that she was dead, he could inform the British. It would be just another feather in his cap. Katherine had been a fugitive, after all. He smiled. She would have complicated his life in any case; it was probably better this way.

Superintendent Holden Crane stood in Bram Chisholm's study. Outside the window he could see the snow falling and he thought of London and what it was like during the Christmas season. If he concentrated, he could all but hear the boys' choir singing in St. Paul's, and taste the heavy puddings and strong brandy. He couldn't get home in time this year, but he would be there next Christmas. He was finished in the Highlands, relieved of his duties, and being sent home to await a new assignment, perhaps in the colonies, most likely the Massachusetts Bay colony. What a relief! He imagined it was quite peaceful there.

Bram and Edana came into the study. "Sorry to keep you waiting," Bram said. "Sit down, we'll share a scotch."

Crane smiled. "I would enjoy that."

"I trust you'll stay for dinner," Edana said.

"I'd be delighted. It's a long ride back to the fort. I've come with news. Rather strange news, actually.

"Katherine MacLean is dead. She went to a well-known doctor, Dr. Kenzie Scott. Apparently he was someone she had worked for in Edinburgh. No sooner had she arrived, than she reportedly fell down the stairs and broke her neck. A very odd accident."

A violent shiver went down Edana's spine. She had seen the staircase; her "other" had been there when Katherine died. Edana looked hard at him. "Are you certain?"

"Quite. Her body was sent back here for burial. There is no doubt at all that it is Katherine."

Edana leaned against Bram. "I can finally relax completely," she confessed.

Bram kissed her hair. "I knew you were always on edge."

"Well, no need for concern now. Justice has been done," Crane said with finality. "Now, how about that drink?"

Bram went to the decanter and poured out three drinks. He gave one to Edana and one to Crane. "To a better year," he toasted.

Crane raised his glass. "To a better year," he repeated.

"Are you going back to London?" Bram asked.

Crane smiled. "For a time. Then I'll be reassigned to one of the colonies, likely Massachusetts."

"We're leaving, too," Bram revealed. "Edana and I are taking Daniel and going to the Continent for a time." He did not say that they were going to France to the Court of King James. Edana was excited at the prospect and together they had decided to leave since lately far too much attention had been focused on the Phoenix.

"That requires another toast," Crane suggested.

Bram laughed. "You just want another drink."

Crane grinned and nodded. "It's the one thing I'll miss."

Bram watched as Edana bathed. Her wonderful hair cascaded down her back, her breasts were rosy from the warm water, and her nipples wonderfully erect because she knew his eyes were on her.

She washed slowly, tauntingly. She knew he enjoyed watching; she knew that when she stood up, he would dry her and carry her to the bed and they would once again make love.

"You are quite yourself now," he said softly. "No more worries about Katherine."

Edana truly smiled. "No more," she repeated. "Moira's son will be chieftain, and our son, if I have a boy, will have a true and dependable friend."

She stood up and he went to her and wrapped her in a towel. She said nothing, letting him dry her. It was a sensuous experience and when he was finished, he ran his hands over her.

"Your skin is like silk."

She put her arms around his neck and he lifted her into his arms as she wrapped her legs around him. "I love you with all my heart," she said into his ear.

Bram kissed her hard and laid her down. "And I love you, my wife. We will always be together."

Edana kissed him back. She was in love and she was at peace. The only mystery in her life were her dreams of the "other." They were dreams which came more frequently now. Dreams that had a new vividness and urgency. She had told Bram about them, and he always listened, unlike the others in whom she had confided. *He listens because he loves me,* she thought, as he began his teasing ritual. She put her dreams out of her mind and gave herself over to his kisses and his furtive, gentle movements. The desire that raged in her whenever he touched her, began anew.

"I shall love you for all of my tomorrows," she whispered. "Always and forever."

ABOUT THE AUTHOR

Joyce Carlow lives in Canada for seven months and is in the U.S. for five months of every year. She is the author of seven Zebra historical romances. She is currently working on the sequel to *Highland Fire, Highland Flame* (Aileena's story), which will be published in December, 1999. She loves to hear from readers and you may write to her c/o Zebra Books. Please include a self-addressed stamped envelope if you wish a response.